THE PRINCESS AND THE STRAY

She dared to touch his arm. The touch brought his gaze snapping to hers, as if she were dangerous.

She felt danger in the air, too. It was screaming in her mind. *Mason!*

"Shouldn't be this way," she said.

"Shouldn't be what way?"

"You should be claimed," Cari said. Her heart went wild at the idea.

"You gonna claim me, Dolan?" he joked bitterly.

Her face heated, her voice got all tangled up, and she lost track of her words.

"Cari, I'm sorry." He always noticed everything.

She shook her head and looked down toward the water. Then she changed her mind and forced herself to turn toward him.

He had somehow gotten closer, though she couldn't remember him moving. Whispers of the fae rose around them. Time stopped. Sparks of magic hung in the air. And he looked at her, so seriously it made her sad. But she couldn't help it. She was about to get him in very big trouble.

She moved closer still, until she felt his breath brush her skin. She could almost sense the future moment when that breath would be inside her, his mouth on hers.

A question glinted in his eyes.

She looked down at his mouth and went tingly when she saw the slight, wondering smile that appeared there. She smiled back. It was an answer. Yes.

Published by Kensington Publishing Corporation

SOUL KISSED

The Shadow Kissed Series

ERIN KELLISON

ZEBRA BOOKS
KENSINGTON PUBLISHING CORP.
http://www.kensingtonbooks.com

ZEBRA BOOKS are published by

Kensington Publishing Corp.
119 West 40th Street
New York, NY 10018

All Kensington titles, imprints, and distributed lines are available at special quantity discounts for bulk purchases for sales
promotion, premiums, fund-raising, educational, or institu-
tional use.

Special book excerpts or customized printings can also be
created to fit specific needs. For details, write or phone the
office of the Kensington Special Sales Manager: Attn.: Special
Sales Department. Kensington Publishing Corp., 119 West
40th Street, New York, NY 10018. Phone: 1-800-221-2647.

Zebra and the Z logo Reg. U.S. Pat. & TM Off.

ISBN-13: 978-1-4201-1898-8
ISBN-10: 1-4201-1898-6
First Printing: September 2013

eISBN-13: 978-1-4201-3270-0
eISBN-10: 1-4201-3270-9
First Electronic Edition: September 2013

10 9 8 7 6 5 4 3 2 1

Printed in the United States of America

For Jessica Faust,
who has her own magic

Prologue

Mason waited for his son to climb out of the car, then slammed the back passenger door shut. "One more time, please."

"Ugh, *Dad*." Fletcher's gaze was off across the tire-matted stretch of grass that acted as parking for the fairgrounds. Families with strollers and groups of summer-ready teens slowly streamed toward the entrance and ticket booth.

"Fletcher." Mason put a little warning in his voice.

Fletcher dragged his attention over and sighed with exaggerated eight-year-old suffering. Repeated by rote, "I'll do whatever you say."

Mason didn't like this. It was one thing to go out into the open himself. Entirely another to take Fletcher. "One mistake—"

The eye roll, which was new this year. "Jeez, Dad. I know."

Mason let the point go, though anxiety still riddled his nerves. He fished out a tube of sunscreen from a plastic grocery bag. "Hand."

Fletcher held out his palm for a squirt. He smeared the lotion all over his face. When he was done, Mason had a Red Sox baseball cap waiting. And when that was settled on his son's head, Mason held out a twenty-dollar bill. "So you don't have to bug me for every little thing."

Fletcher grinned, showing front teeth too big for his mouth, empty gaps on either side. The sight did something to Mason's heart. It took so little to make his son happy. And so very much more to keep him safe. And yet, this was the time he'd been born into; better that Fletcher start learning to handle himself now, before the world grew even darker.

They started across the grass, host to lots of small, biting flies. The grass grew sparse nearer the ticket booth, where the buzz turned to bees dancing around the still-sweet trash bins.

Mason had his head down to his wallet when he felt the tell-tale sing in his blood of a mage passing by behind him. He glanced at Fletcher, who kept his attention on the booth as well, though Mason knew his son had to have sensed the passage of Shadow too. The magic would have pulled at his son's own power. Awareness of Shadow nearby was a family trait.

Keep a cool head, and Fletcher will do the same. Mason had read about modeling behavior in his parenting books. He just hoped his son didn't know what he did to make a living, or the teen years were going to be a nightmare. The cursing was already a problem.

"All right." Mason turned. "Should we stuff our faces first, or do you want to hit the rides?"

Fletcher went for long-suffering again. "Rides." The kid wisely left off the implied *duh*.

The sideways pie of the Ferris wheel loomed thataway. Other side of the fair. Mason put his wallet in his back pocket. "Come on."

The Stanton public recreation department had gone all out for the city's annual May Fair and Market. More interesting was the full-page invitation in the city's newspaper, inviting the "Shadow people" to the event—a friendly, if desperate, measure in an increasingly frightening world. The fair's committee had elected to go medieval with the theme, probably thinking magekind would like it. As if mages hadn't been around in every era.

The main path was festooned with ropes of fragrant flowers, all leading to the central park, where a many-ribboned may-pole had been erected. Vendors lined the walkways with art, dragon jewelry, face painting, and sugar-crusted deep-fried donuts, the latter of which made Mason's mouth water against his will. Might have to get one of those. The bass and drums of live music bounced down the paths, though the band was playing at the far end, on a stage erected at the closed-to-cars traffic circle. Droves of people congested the walkways, some because the May Fair was tradition, but all hoping to spot a real live mage.

The open invitation to magekind was an attempt on the part of the mayor to draw out his mage constituency and to show that he was friendly to their interests. Very clever. Risky, but clever.

In most places in the world, the idea that there were people with magic in their blood was still met with derision. And yet, it had been years now that soul-sucking wraiths skulk-ing the alleys had been caught on mobile phone cameras and uploaded online. And though mage law forbade the use of Shadow in public, it was happening more and more often. Plus, the earthquakes last year had never been fully explained.

The awful truth? Shadow now saturated the world. Mages could feel the return of power in their blood. And they were organizing various schemes to suit themselves.

The newspaper invitation had done its job, and the "Shadow people" had come, mostly for the fun of it. People with magic-black eyes were everywhere: standing in line for the twist-and-spin, winning at the ring toss, and wolfing down mustard-dipped hotdogs on a stick.

Yes, a very friendly venue.

The rides made both Mason and Fletcher nauseous, so of course they had to eat. Mason scanned the crowds as they headed toward the food alley, and spotted Fletcher's friend Bran and his father, Riordan Webb, head of Webb House, an instant before Fletcher grabbed his arm. Riordan was thinly built with long limbs, like a human daddy longlegs. He was aged closer to grandfather than father, but then he'd had to go through three wives to get an heir.

The boy, Bran, took after his mother—stocky, tow-headed, always chattering.

"Can I?" Fletcher's face had flushed with the late spring heat. He had a cloud of boy sweat around him.

Mason steeled himself inside—*here we go*—but nodded. Webb was someone he'd hoped they'd bump into. "Okay."

Connections like these were why they'd come in the first place. That, and curiosity. Would this be what the coming Dark Age would be like?

"Riordan," Mason drawled when Webb joined him to watch the boys whoop and wrestle in the dust.

"Mason," Webb returned, holding out his long, thin hand. "Was wondering if I'd see you here."

"Couldn't resist after I saw the invitation."

"First open invite to Shadow in our lifetime. No one could resist."

Mason's point exactly.

"I've been hearing things about you," Webb mused.

"Oh?" Mason had been doing work for a lot of terrible causes lately. Maybe Webb had a job for him, too.

"How did a lousy stray like you catch the Council's ear?"

Stray meaning no family, no House to claim him or Fletcher. He and his son were at the mercy of all the hellish things this world and the other worlds beyond could throw at them. The more friends Mason could make, the better Fletcher's chances at surviving.

Mason laughed and shook Webb's hand. Riordan had deigned to speak to a stray, which was a good beginning. That the master of Webb House gripped his hand was even better. It meant respect.

"I have my uses," Mason answered.

"So I've noticed."

Which was the point of all Mason's work. Not that he remotely cared what the mage Houses thought of him. In fact, he'd been prepared to walk away from magekind some nine years ago.

Then came Fletcher, and life had radically upended, like a sudden magnetic reversal of poles. The mage Houses became everything: safety and strength. Mason just had to find, connive, coerce, or thieve his way into one. Right now Fletcher might as well be exposed in the open with a hurricane bearing down on him. These people all around—debating hand-made jewelry and licking the sides of their ice cream cones for drips—they had no idea what was coming.

Fletcher came running back, babbling about a sword and begging, "Please, Dad, five more bucks," and repeatedly saying, "Epic!"—a word he must have picked up from Bran.

Mason hoped the verbal tic was temporary.

One minute later, the boys were thrusting and parrying and making asses of themselves in the middle of the path. The cost of the sword was robbery, plain and simple; the fact that Fletcher was playing with the heir to Webb House, invaluable. Webb House would be ideal.

"We should talk." Webb's eyes had gone flinty.

Mason knew the tone, knew the look. Webb had work. And if he was thinking of employing a stray, then the work had to be some degree of illegal.

Well, they had to start somewhere.

"I'm in the area for a few more days." Mason retrieved a card from his wallet.

Webb took the card. "Meeting with another House?"

Mason pulled a half smile. He wasn't going to answer that, and Webb knew it. "As far as I know, I'm not working on anything that would conflict with the interests of Webb House."

Admitting as much was generous, a show of good faith. It was up to Riordan now to follow through.

Gasps brought his attention back to the boys. A group of three or four humans had stopped to watch them.

"Shadow people," whispered one.

A mom just passing yanked her children back, as if Bran and Fletcher were dangerous.

Mason frowned, and put himself in human shoes to see what had captured the bystanders' attention. Fletcher and Bran merely looked like two almost-troublemakers, just this side of a warning. Then Fletcher thrust with his sword and Mason saw it: Bran had bullied up the shadow he cast into the shape of a man-sized, fire-breathing, scaly-tailed dragon. Fletcher's shadow had taken on the proportions of a broad-shouldered knight. This was part of Webb House's magic—shadow play.

"Been good seeing you," Riordan said over his shoulder, as he grabbed Bran by the elbow and pulled him up short. The shadows disintegrated.

It took only a look from Mason to shrink Fletcher from hero to boy.

Fletcher pointed at Bran. "*He* did it!"

Mason cocked his head. "Do I really have to tell you why that excuse won't fly?"

Webb and Bran had already moved away to blend back into the throng of fairgoers, preferring to leave suspicions behind them. Typical of mages, stirring up fear and uncertainty. To the frightened mother still gripping her children, Mason shot a look, parent to parent, and said, "Boys this age."

The band's song ended, but instead of drumming into

another, there was a short pause, and then a man cleared his throat into the mic.

Mason looked down the way toward the stage, while simultaneously bringing Fletcher close by his side. Poor kid had been outed as a mage in public. Maybe bearing the long looks and unease of the humans around them would teach him a lesson.

From the speaker on the stage: "Thank you to the Larry Trumpet Blues Band for starting us all off rocking this morning."

A smattering of applause. People were too closely packed, too hot to muster more enthusiasm than that.

Mason could make out a few figures standing on the stage. If one was the mayor who'd invited the "Shadow people," this could get interesting. He kept a hand on Fletcher's shoulder and milled forward with the crowd to be able to see better. Webb and Bran were up ahead, even closer. Mason spotted several other mages among the throng as well, black eyes fastened on the action at the stage.

"And a thank you to the organizers of our May Fair, led by our intrepid Judy Hart Langley."

More polite applause while some woman in a pink pantsuit waved to the crowd.

"And now, to welcome you all here today, Mayor Bingham!"

Bigger applause. People wanted to hear *this*.

The mayor was wearing a suit too, and probably sweating through it. Though his hairline was receding, he seemed surprisingly young. But then that made sense. It would be the younger generation who more readily accepted the existence of Shadow. They'd spent hours online poring over those wraith videos and watching the *Fact-or-Fiction?* shows on TV, modern monster hunts and the like.

"Our May Fair has been a tradition for the two hundred and seventy-three years since Stanton's founding. I'm personally thrilled to have discovered that one of our very first businesses was run by a family with ties to the Shadow people—my own."

The mayor held up his hands to quiet murmurs; he was loving being associated with this new, exclusive group. Dumb. Possibly dead.

"I don't have any magic—or *Shadow* as they call it. Wish I did. But when reports began circulating about these people who could do wonderful things, I tended to believe them. Fear does no one any good."

Anyone with common sense would know that fear is a valid reaction to a perceived threat, and with reference to magekind, a necessary reaction—*be afraid*—but it was nice that this guy was preaching tolerance. Very optimistic of him.

"Which is why, on this very sunny morning, I am more than happy to welcome Shadow people here today—or *mages,* as I've just now learned is the correct term. In fact, for the past twenty minutes I've been having an interesting conversation with a mage, and he has graciously agreed to say a few words to you himself."

Mason didn't breathe until he saw the mage in question—Ranulf Cawl, as antihuman, antitolerance as mages could come. He still kept wraiths in his employ, even after the Council had banned their use last year, which begged the very obvious question: Since wraiths fed only on human souls, how was he feeding them?

Fletcher didn't need to learn *this* lesson today.

The crowd tightened with interest, phones raised high to catch everything on video.

Mason picked Fletcher up around his middle, ignoring the horrified, "Daaad!" at being treated like a baby.

Too bad. It had been risky to come. They'd made a little

headway with Webb; that was more than enough for a day's work. A stray mage knew when to run. That, or he died young.

Mason was shouldering his way roughly through the crowd when Ranulf Cawl began to speak, feedback squealing through the mic. "Thank you, Mayor Bingham, for inviting me to say a few words."

Mason lifted Fletcher over a park bench, then vaulted over the back himself. But it didn't get them far. People had closed in all around them. The car was on the other side of the fairgrounds.

"Mayor Bingham has this idea that we're all basically the same. And in many ways we are. Family, for example, is very important to us. And loyalty is one of our most prized character traits. Power, too, is highly sought after among my kind."

Mason glanced over long enough to see the mayor's smile faltering. Yeah, buddy. Little late now.

The crowd was utterly silent.

"But it's best you know that we're fundamentally different, so much so that there can never really be peace between us." Cawl continued, "Point of fact, you humans have souls. We don't. We have dark magic within us. There was a time when you humans used to hunt us down and burn us alive. It's time for Shadow now."

That mother who'd seen what Bran Webb could do was looking at Fletcher, her features growing tighter. Mason knew what she was thinking, or would think soon enough—that no soul meant soulless, which meant evil.

Mason held his son, his reason for living, even tighter. What Cawl had left out was that each mage had an umbra deep within, a source of magic, not so very unlike a soul. Fletcher was all good, in every way. A person would be *lucky* to know him.

Cawl kept talking, ". . . what the Dark Age will bring . . ." but Mason thought he'd already made his point. No peace.

Mason looked for escape. The car was too far, the crowd too tight to make much progress. Up ahead, Webb was doing little better with Bran. Any minute now, some mage was going to use Shadow to get free of this place or to make a point. And then there would be chaos.

He squeezed Fletcher. "Everything I say."

Fletcher nodded.

"Keep your head down."

With that, Mason adjusted his hold—the kid had grown; why did he keep doing that?—and plowed toward the nearest break in the crowd. He elbowed into backs and barged through groups. The rank smell of sweat hit his nose, that and greasy food too long in the sun. Blood, no, ketchup smeared up his arm.

The crowd made a sound of astonishment, one voice that rolled through the gathering, which had become a single organism.

Mason swore, though he usually tried not to around Fletcher, and craned his head to see what kind of magic had finally been used to break away from this place.

A black snake of Shadow darted and twisted above the heads of the crowd.

Mason didn't recognize this kind of Shadow. What was it? Who controlled it?

He squinted to see better, adjusting Fletcher again, who was trying to see as well.

The sky snake of Shadow branched out, while rushing toward Cawl, who'd trailed off speaking and was gazing into the air. Guess he didn't know what kind of Shadow it was either.

The Shadow spread into a dirty blanket of haze and enveloped Cawl.

Mason was too far away to see what the effect was, but the scream of the lady in the pink pantsuit made things clear enough. When Ranulf Cawl collapsed on the stage, Mason was pretty sure the mage was dead.

More black snakes twisted through the air.

And more screams rose from within the crowd. Like birds startled by gunshot, people scattered. Mason was buffeted by the rush, but dived into a jewelry stall to avoid immediate trampling. Others got trampled though. Strollers were abandoned, children clutched in parents' arms. Humans and mages weren't so different after all. Not where it really mattered.

"It's going to be okay." Mason put Fletcher down. The booth, with a thick plastic-and-steel girder, would protect them for the moment. "Stay *right* there."

Mason's attention was caught by a mage some twenty feet away, visible only intermittently through the flock of fleeing humans. Mason could see that he'd raised his arms to hold back the darkness, when he should've known that Shadow could permeate anything.

The murk descended upon him and the mage convulsed, his skin pock-marking with burns, as if from the inside. His eyes rolled back to the whites, then grayed to viscous ash, and the mage collapsed.

Mason came to a simple conclusion: the May Fair wasn't about peace; the fair was a trap set for mages.

How many times throughout history had a hearty welcome been the early guise of a massacre?

He'd been so stupid. A stray ought to know better.

Mason looked to the sky, now polluted with thin Shadow. The death-dealing stuff was inking closer. The booth wasn't safe anymore.

Mason hauled Fletcher outside. "We run. As fast and as far as we can. We run, or we die."

Could an eight-year-old understand?

Mason would have carried him again if it would have been safer, but the humans had grown more dispersed, and frankly, Fletcher could run faster than he could. Kid had speed and power in those legs. Mason's eyes burned as he cursed again. He just hadn't anticipated Fletcher would have to run for his life so soon.

They got as far as the parking lot access road when black doom torpedoed overhead, poisoned Shadow picking out the mages from the panicked crowd.

They weren't going to make it to the car.

Mason made a grab for his son, who was still in flight. Fletcher jackknifed in the air—the muscle in Mason's shoulder shredded—but he brought his son to his chest and went down on his knees on the street.

He'd have prayed, but if there was a God, he'd long ago forsaken the Shadow born.

Mason curled his body around Fletcher. Screams of fear and pain ripped the air so close, Mason groaned. He strove to make a boy-sized hollow out of his chest and belly, kneeling on the pavement and hugging his son, hands splayed over Fletcher's face and head, his own head bowed to close the man-made cocoon. Within his grasp, Fletcher trembled, his heartbeat fast like a rabbit's. Mason's own heart had stalled. His throat had strangled shut with horror. All necessary body function was diverted into willing his son to live, at any cost, including his own life.

Black, smoky arms of terror reached among the throng, brushing by Mason like whispers of vicious gossip. He felt the Shadow singing in his blood as it drew near; ironic that his aptitude with magic would help him know when his death was near. The dull thump and burn of a body falling nearby brought bile searing onto his tongue. Another mage down, moaning, then gargling into death.

"To the Webb wards!" Riordan's voice, far away, rallying the stricken mages.

Yes, House wards would protect the mages who'd come to the May Fair. House wards were impenetrable magicks of safe harbor. And Webb's wards were the nearest, just ten miles from the fair site.

But since Mason had no House, no wards, that option wasn't open to him. To his *son*. Not yet. Though he would have begged if there'd been any chance or service he could have traded.

Stray mages were outsiders, no matter how friendly the handshake. How many times did Mason have to learn that lesson?

Humans whimpered and ran, their passage bumping Mason's shoulder, riffling his hair, as if they were the ones at risk. Stupid. This was a trap for Shadowed blood.

Inside Mason was frantic: *Not my son. Please, not Fletcher. Pass over. Pass him by.*

It wasn't supposed to be like this. Today was supposed to have been about peace, an opportunity to make friends.

Someone somewhere was laughing.

Mason ground his teeth against the burning in his eyes. He clutched Fletcher and vowed again, as he had a million times before, he'd do better for his son. Keep him safe. No matter what in blackest Shadow he had to do.

Chapter One

Cari Dolan sat on a hard straight back chair in the servants' access hallway to the study, where her stepmother and stepsisters wouldn't think to look. Her gaze was fixed on the white wall before her. Her eyes were hot and gritty, but she wasn't going to cry. If she breathed shallowly, the smell of smoke from her father's funeral pyre grew faint, almost absent. The rest of her was in a cold grip, arms folded for heat, her body painfully tense, which made moving an unthinkable effort.

Out of the corner of her eye, she saw a maid peek down the hallway, then dart back out of sight.

This chair was for Allison, the housekeeper, who was supposed to wait outside the study until called upon by a member of the grieving family. Like when Cari was four and her mom had died; her father had summoned Allison to take her from the room with the instructions to tuck her in bed and read a nice story and to stay by her side until her father could come himself.

Now the Dolan heir was hiding there instead of standing tall next to her stepmother and silently vowing reprisal. Part of her mage brain knew this was a time for heat and curses and dark plots, but . . .

Cari rocked forward, foundering in a wave of loss. She hadn't been ready to lose him. To become him. She wanted her father back to protect her from the storm of everything that was to come. His loss made her feel so unready. So scared.

For several weeks now, starting with the Stanton May Fair Massacre, unexplained attacks on magekind had taken place. Shadow, the strength of magekind, had been poisoned, and the death it brought was a catching kind, a plague.

A quiet had settled over the Houses, a hush of abject terror. Some caught the plague from direct contact, falling where they stood in a fester of hot wounds. Others carried it unknowing with them back to their Houses. A touch here. A kiss. And the poison worked more slowly, but nevertheless, claimed its victims. It had riddled families and left heartache in its wake.

And yet some Houses the death passed over, when a member of that family had clearly been touched, but had never fallen ill. Suspicions were aroused—Why *my* House and not yours?—and blood oaths taken. More lives were claimed, this time by violence.

Until each House was closed to outsiders, and the spread of the plague was halted.

Cari looked down at a welt now healing on the inside of her elbow—so ugly. The mage plague had taken her father, and it had almost taken her. She remembered too well the burn inside her. Remembered screams ripping up her throat—but she had somehow lived through it. If this smothering quiet was living, that is.

Even whispers of staff and family were banked by half breaths, so they sounded more like the sighs and hisses of the fae who watched from the other side of the veil.

The common conclusion: Some ruthless House was orchestrating a takeover, Shadow against Shadow. They meant to cripple magekind, their own people, with fear and death, and usher in the Dark Age themselves as Lords of a fallen land.

She should be striving to find out who was doing this, who had killed her father, and almost her. But somehow she was trapped in yesterday, so tired, so heartsick, and she was just now discovering that the past turned frigid as time pushed relentlessly forward.

And yet, there were so many things to take care of now that her father was in ashes. So much work. She'd always thought of him simply as her father, but to everyone else he was Caspar Dolan, and that meant something. She had no idea where to start beyond trying to remember to breathe and blink.

Her father answered voicelessly inside her: *Secure the succession.*

Right. But the acknowledgment came bitterly.

The House guards had done that by dragging her away when her father had fallen to one knee, midstride, in the courtyard of their family's business compound, his skin mottling with gray eruptions. Murdered. By then every mage House knew it was a contagious kind of attack, so she couldn't even hold her father's hand. The strain of bucking to get free of the guards still racked her body. All sound had been drawn out of the memory, but she could still see her father collapsing in front of her.

How ironic that she'd caught the mage plague anyway. And both guards had died as well.

She closed her eyes and pressed the heels of her hands to her lids.

But yes, technically she'd survived the attack, so the Dolan succession was secure. Now she had an unfathomable amount of work before her but no heart to begin. *Father?*

Protect the House.

She nodded to his memory, which had a bit of his warmth. *Yes.*

House meant family, and she had a lot of it. Her stepmother

Scarlet, and her stepsisters Stacia and Zel. And her uncle on her birth mother's side, and cousins, their spouses, children, indentured mages, assorted dependents, who'd taken shelter within the wards. Dolan House was full to bursting, and she had to provide for them all.

Cari felt lightheaded with the load of work ahead.

She'd have to look into the Dolan finances immediately. Get a grip on the money.

Pitch, Cari swore to herself, thinking of Zella's betrothal and the political dancing that it required.

And then there was DolanCo, the family business, which she must now run. The special project that her father had thought would sustain the House through the advent of the Dark Age could not be ignored. The fact hadn't changed—it had actually grown more imperative—that they would need a highly valuable source of revenue or trade when the human markets collapsed, and DolanCo's more mundane products wouldn't provide for the House. Now that was up to her, too.

She broke in a half laugh-half cry at the absurdity of it all, took a shuddering breath, got a nose full of her father's smoke, and wheezed into a sob, tears spilling over swollen banks.

No, no, no. She wiped at her face. Tears accomplished nothing. She was the Head of the House now.

Maybe she ought to start with a list. Yes, that's what she'd do.

Her father would have paper and a pen in his desk.

She was wiping her nose when she pushed into the study. She expected to find Stacia or Zel, who'd shadowed her every step since yesterday afternoon, watching and worrying and trying to feed her.

But seated in front of the desk was a strange woman. Her deep red hair was impeccably coiffed. She'd dressed in sleek black slacks and a vibrant blue silk blouse. Her ankles were crossed, legs angled to the side. The room positively simmered with her presence. She had to be greatmage Kaye Brand, High Seat of the Council, the one who'd started this civil war in the first place.

Cari's heartbeat tripped.

How had Brand gotten through the Dolan wards? Was she infected? Had she brought more death here?

Brand slanted her gaze Cari's way. "Are you done feeling sorry for yourself?"

Cari's attention narrowed, yesterday and today colliding in a silent cataclysm, and with an inner burst of heat, she finally felt her sluggish blood rush.

Kaye Brand was going to die. If not for her, none of this would have happened. Cari's father would still be alive.

"Please, sit." Kaye gestured to the chair at Cari's hip. She didn't seem the least bit worried for her safety, even here within the House of an enemy. "We have a lot to talk about."

"How did you get inside?" Cari demanded. Then, to the closed study door she barked, "Zella!"

"I have a vassal, Marcell Lakatos," she said, "who has an aptitude for crossing boundaries. He assisted me."

Very handy person to have on hand. And too dangerous to live. Lakatos should be killed.

But Brand seemed healthy enough, in spite of her transport. How dare she come here at a time like this? Anger felt good. Felt strong.

The door opened and Cari's eldest stepsister leaned partway inside, her white-blond hair sliding over her shoulder. She held a plate with a sandwich. The hopeful look in her eyes turned to alarm when she spotted Brand.

"I need a weapon," Cari said. When Zel didn't move, she added, "Now, please."

Mages killed their enemies.

Kaye Brand examined her manicure. "I've done nothing to harm you or your House."

Zel had left the door open and was summoning the guards,

what few they had left. Rapid footsteps sounded down the hallway.

Cari sputtered. Nothing to harm her? If not for *Brand* . . . "You divided magekind, set House against House." She'd *started* the conflict that had just taken the life of her father.

Which would be enough to kill Kaye here and now, and yet there was more. Kaye had also betrayed magekind to the Order of angels. The Order, who'd again and again throughout history struck Shadow down, trying to wipe the soulless mages from the world. The Order would not allow magic to rise. But Kaye had taken an angel for a lover—his prick a key in the lock of their Council, opening their ranks to intrusion.

The bloodshed had started soon after, Houses turning on each other, each climbing over another to topple Brand from the High Seat. And now this latest assassin, slowly working his way through magekind with his plague . . . Everyone would know the killer when he claimed the High Seat for himself.

Guards burst into the room, guns drawn and aimed at Brand. A commotion sounded in the great hall as other family gathered for this new crisis. Her uncle's voice rose. One of the kids started crying again. Staff murmuring. Her stepmother demanded to know what was going on.

Cari stepped back out of the guards' line of fire, satisfied. Kaye might've gotten inside Dolan House, but she was not leaving it alive. Her father had wanted the High Seat of the Council for Dolan; well, this was Cari's chance.

Kaye glanced impassively over her shoulder at the guards, then back to Cari. "I could have killed you when you were crying in the hallway."

Cari saw Zel's gaze flick to the service entrance. No more hiding there. No more hiding anywhere.

Cari shrugged at Kaye. "Too bad for you."

"And"—Kaye opened her hands—"I am unarmed."

"You're never unarmed." Brand was a fire mage.

"I came to help," Kaye said. "I don't want to hurt anyone."

"You should've thought of that before you spread your legs." Dolan had never been allied with Brand, but still Cari's father had respected the House, at least until it was clear how Kaye had risen so quickly in power and who her protectors were. Vicious angels.

Dolan House did not support the Council, would not, with Brand in the seat. Lines had been drawn.

"You don't know what you're talking about," Kaye said. "Point is, you've been targeted."

"We know who our enemies are."

Protect the House. Her father's voice again.

Cari looked to Zel, who was peeking back in the office. "Get out, get everyone away from here, but stay inside the Dolan wards."

Zel shook her head. "I'm not leaving you."

"It wasn't a request," Cari shot back. She had a duty to her family. "Get everyone out." Brand might not be contagious, but she was deadly.

With a long, desperate look, Zel fled the study. The guards stood their ground. Dolan only employed the loyal. The voices in the great hall rose for a moment, then broke into disparate pieces of quiet as her family fled to the sub-houses or shelters on the property.

Now it was just Dolan against Brand, and by the pitch of Shadow, Dolan would prevail. Cari would not disappoint the memory of her father. She would be enough for this. She'd make his memory proud.

Kaye shook her head. "No one knows which House is responsible for the recent deaths. There is no faction among us that has been left untouched."

"Then whoever is doing this is simply covering their tracks." Didn't take a seat on the Council to be able to figure that out. "Kill someone from their own side to avoid reprisal."

Kaye looked thoughtful. "Excellent point. And what if your

father was murdered, your House challenged, not because of his own power and clout, but as a decoy in a larger plot?"

Took a second for the word "decoy" to attach to "father" in her mind.

No.

Couldn't be. Her father was too great a man to die as a mere decoy.

Brand smiled. "And the killer left an inexperienced young woman in possession of Dolan House."

"I'm only a year younger than you." She could handle herself. She could be her father's daughter. A gale of emotion was battering her like a cruel wind, but she turned her face into it. She wouldn't fail him.

"I was not inexperienced when it came time for me to act."

"I don't want your kind of experience."

The insult seemed to sail right past Kaye. "Nevertheless, it is still time for you to act."

"I'll do what I have to." Cari was done crying at least. She could thank Brand for that much.

"I know," Kaye said, "which is why I've come to help you."

Cari shook her head no. Brand help Dolan? What a crock. Brand would take advantage of the turmoil in Dolan House to get Cari to do what she wanted.

Cari would fight her instead. Dolan Shadow was old and powerful. Brand fire against Dolan's umbra.

"How about some incontrovertible facts?" Kaye winked. "Jack Bastian, my . . . significant other . . . works very hard to see that I am safe."

Cari snorted. Significant other. Maybe it was her angel lover that was picking off mages one by one.

"But eventually whoever killed your father will attempt to kill me. Perhaps he or she already has tried, and Bastian's angel light has kept the killer at bay."

Cari smiled. "Or maybe the killer thinks you'll be the instrument of your own destruction."

"I admit, I am my own worst enemy." Kaye smiled back. "But I don't want to die. And I want this killer found before he can get to me. There is one House, and only one House, I know of that can identify the person responsible."

Cari's belly twisted. Something had been nagging at the back of her mind, something she'd refused to think about.

Kaye continued, "I was wondering if you got a sense of the killer when he attacked your father."

"The sickness came out of nowhere."

"But surely you searched for the antumbra before it dissipated into Shadow?" Kaye was direct, all business now. "You'd be able to recognize the mage from whom the tainted Shadow originated if you were to meet him or her again."

By the time her father had fallen, Cari had already been feeling the effects of the poisoned Shadow. She hadn't thought to search for the antumbra, the unique trail of magic a mage leaves behind. The ability was a Dolan property of magic—to see into the shadow souls of mages, past and present. To name them, to know them. The guards had dragged her away. And even if they hadn't, she'd been too overcome to think . . . to act. She'd been caught in one extended, silent scream. *Father!*

She could've named his killer.

Kaye dropped her gaze to her hands, obviously waiting for Cari's horrible realization to pass. "I've made some very painful mistakes myself."

Cari burned; Kaye was right. She should've fought harder, *thought* harder. Her father would've still died, but she would have his murderer.

"But *your* mistake," Kaye continued, "can be undone. You have only to investigate the scene, perhaps the next death, to discover the information you missed the first time. And in so doing, you could show magekind that Dolan House is still strong, still able, and is out for blood."

That's right.

She could try again.

She had to try again.

"And as you survived the plague, it stands to reason that you are immune. Very few have survived this."

Cari put a hand to a welt on her neck, still so sore. She'd survived, was stronger than the plague. It suddenly occurred to her that the scars she would bear would show everyone that Dolan Shadow had been stronger.

"I propose a temporary alliance."

Cari frowned at Brand. Fire wanting to ally with umbra?

"For the sole purpose of combining our talents and information to destroy the House responsible for the plague ripping through our people. We can't afford to be weakened now; there are too many threats, from too many directions, to suffer this plague from one of our own kind."

Kaye was talking like Cari's father had, making sense. Yes, there was too much to worry about to let a mage destroy them from the inside.

Kaye cocked her head, surprise flexing her expression. "I'm glad you agree."

"This mage needs to be stopped, his House broken."

"We agree again."

Cari couldn't believe she was about to cooperate with Kaye Brand of all people. "I presume you have a plan as to how I would go about finding the next victim before the killer's trail is lost."

"Not a plan. More like a partner, another survivor," Kaye answered. "He's loyal to the Council, so that should appease those who won't trust Dolan alone with this task. The pairing will keep everyone, or most everyone, cooperative."

Kaye was deluding herself on that point, but Cari pressed on. "Who is it?"

"Mason Stray will be assisting you"—Kaye delicately cleared her throat—"once he agrees."

Cari's anger surged. That lowlife? For her *father?* "You've got to be kidding."

Mason stood in the open doorway of his refuge cabin. He lifted his shotgun the moment he caught the sun glinting off the black of a Lexus LX SUV through the spare desert trees on the windy drive up his mountain.

He knew who it had to be. And he didn't care.

Didn't matter that the High Seat herself had traveled cross country and had hauled herself up his mountain. She wasn't getting anywhere near him or his son. No mage was until this scourge had passed. The May Fair Massacre had claimed seventeen lives, and many more had fallen in the weeks since. He and Fletcher were lucky to have survived, but Mason wouldn't count on luck again. He never counted on anything. Not where Fletcher was concerned.

A lizard skittered up the weather-bowed trunk of a mesquite tree. The high desert of New Mexico smelled dust dead, heat-stricken, a scorched bone of the world. It was why he'd chosen this place over his other refuge in the east.

The car slowed to a stop, dust hovering in a cloud around its wheels. The driver's side door opened and Jack Bastian, Kaye Brand's angel consort, got out. Tall, well built, the man had a backbone like an arrow—and his mind was just as sharp, just as deadly.

Mason cocked his rifle, hating the blare of the sun overhead. "Don't come any closer!"

How many times did he have to hang up his phone on Brand to make her understand?

Jack Bastian looked over at him as he rounded the front of the car, a wry expression on his face, but his eyes hard. He didn't stop to open the front passenger door, as Mason expected, but approached the house directly.

"I'll allow no mages here, Jack," Mason called out. He'd shoot; they knew he'd shoot. "Not even her."

Jack stalked right up to the barrel of the gun. The angel had balls of steel. "You've made your point. It's just me today."

Mason glared back at the car, but no matter how hard he tried, he could not sense any Shadow within it. He swallowed to ease the fist of his heart, then lifted the shotgun so the barrel pointed to the sky.

Jack inclined his head in thanks as he bumped by Mason's shoulder on his way into the cabin.

Mason slammed the door shut behind him, forcing himself not to look at the false wall behind which Fletcher hid. Mason was glad he'd long ago sound-proofed the hidden room, a precaution taken when his son was a baby.

"How'd you find me anyhow?" He'd chosen this remote spot on this scrub and scorpion-infested hill for a reason.

Jack looked at him over his shoulder. "I'm an angel."

"Angels track souls, not Shadow." It was how mages had hidden from the Order throughout the centuries. If angels could track mages, the war between them would have been long over, in favor of Order. "I ask again, how did you find me?"

Because if Jack Bastian could locate him, then others might as well. Which meant this place wasn't safe. Mason adjusted his grip on the shotgun, his mind racing through alternatives.

"No one else knows." Jack took a seat in the center of the old plaid couch that had come with the cabin. He winged his arms out to the side to rest on the back cushions, making himself very much at home. "Not even Kaye knows."

Mason felt his sarcasm rising. "You don't share everything? No pillow talk?"

The angel still hadn't answered his question. How in Shadow's pitch had he found him?

"Have a seat, Mason." Now Jack sounded tired. "It's about to get worse, so save your anger for where it counts."

Mason cursed. "What has our High Seat done now?"

Kaye Brand lived on the wick of danger. One scratch, and she and everything in her path would go up in flames.

Jack closed his eyes for a moment. When he opened them, his gaze was even harder. "She's done you a favor."

"She does nothing for free."

"No, she doesn't," Jack agreed without humor, "but this time I think you'll thank her just the same."

"Surprise me then."

Jack went very still, too still for Mason's liking. This had to be bad if she'd sent her angel all this way to tell him, leaving herself vulnerable. "She's arranged a place for Fletcher."

"I'm sorry, what?" Mason had heard his son's name, but hearing it in this context made his brain flash cold. If Brand dared to meddle with Fletcher, she was effectively ending their uneasy friendship. She shouldn't even speak Fletcher's name. Not her business. Not her pawn.

"Fletcher needs wards, does he not?"

Since the May Fair all the Houses were hiding behind their wards. And those that dared to leave their safety did so at their peril. Jack had to be referring to Kaye's newly built castle, Brand House, protected by the Brand ward stones lodged into its foundation.

"No, thank you." Mason waved away the offer. "Kaye has more enemies than I can count. No matter what protection she employs, Brand House is still the single most treacherous place on this planet. My son and I will not be sheltered there. Might as well put targets on our foreheads."

Jack opened his mouth, probably to argue, but Mason beat him to it.

"And I'm not going to the Segue Institute either. No matter

how much I like Adam and his people, they are at war with Martin and have no wards at all. We're better off here."

"You finished?"

The ideal place, of course, would be Walker House, where Fletcher's mother Liv was. Mason had tried to contact her many times over the years, but each silence was like Liv abandoning them again.

Mason looked the angel squarely in the eyes to be absolutely clear. "No one makes arrangements on our behalf."

"She has negotiated the fosterage of your son to Riordan Webb."

Mason blinked with irritation. He seemed to be having trouble keeping up.

Fosterage?

His mind churned through the idea. "You mean until this mage plague blows over?" The possibility lifted his spirits. He was suddenly heady and high. This could be the answer. Yes. Fletcher could be safe, much safer than here.

But Jack shook his head. "Webb is not volunteering to babysit. He requires the traditional fosterage agreement: A formal contract through Fletcher's adolescence to strengthen the ties to Brand, and therefore the mage Council."

Political in nature and common among aristocratic families in ages past, fosterage was alive and well within modern-day magekind. It meant Webb would raise Fletcher in return for favors from the High Seat of the Council, Kaye Brand. It meant power.

Stunned, Mason's arguments hovered in the air around him, but he found the right one. "She can't take my son away from me."

The words came out like a threat, just as he intended.

"She's not," Jack said. "You'd have to agree to the contracts."

"Then no." Jack had been right. This was much worse than

he'd thought. "She has wasted her time, and you are wasting mine. Get out of my house."

"I thought you liked Webb."

Not the point. Mason had hoped to do work for Webb, earn a place for them both, perhaps become one of Webb's vassals. Safety for Fletcher, a home, in return for work. But fosterage was tantamount to giving up his son, giving him away to be raised by someone else. It was a formal arrangement, bound by contract, enforceable by mage law.

They could continue to hide out just fine.

Mason pointed to the door. Brand had no business, no right, to screw with him and his family. He felt sick, angry, and betrayed at the same time.

"Fosterage will protect Fletcher behind Webb's wards."

The angel was missing the point: Mason was not letting his son go. He would not abandon Fletcher, as his own father had abandoned him. Brand had overstepped.

When Jack didn't move, Mason lifted the shotgun and aimed it at Jack's head. Angels could heal superhumanly fast, but they could also die. Decapitation would do the job nicely.

"And he'll have the company of Bran, as well as the luxuries of a strong mage House."

Mason felt his concentration narrowing as he aimed down the barrel. He knew soldier Jack had seen a lot of action in his thousand years of toil on earth, so he should be able to recognize an impasse when he saw one.

The hard gaze didn't waver. "You cannot protect Fletcher. Webb can."

I've protected him thus far.

The mere thought of life without Fletcher hollowed Mason, a sharp pain whistling around his empty ribcage.

They'd managed eight years. Through all sorts of upheaval and danger. And a mage toddler is just about the most fearsome kind of mage ever. They might be strays, but they were getting by just fine.

But you *are not a stray, Mason. You are human.*

The angel's voice in Mason's head sent him staggering back.

Jack looked sad and tired. *And I was able to find your hide-out on this hellish mountain because you have a soul. Any angel could find you.*

Mason laughed and refocused his aim. Jack Bastian was full of surprises. "Wicked trick. You have three seconds to leave, and then I'll fire."

And the reason why you and Fletcher survived the May Fair Massacre is because the plague doesn't kill humans, and your soul shielded him.

They'd survived because they were lucky.

Webb and Bran were lucky. You had a soul.

"Stop that! Get out of my head!"

Jack leaned forward. "You are a parent, and to be a parent is to bear all sorts of excruciating pain and fear. If magekind discovers you have a soul, that you are human, Fletcher, who *is* a full mage via his mother, will never be accepted. He will be a pariah at best during this, the advent of the Dark Age."

Mason's aim faltered; the room went hazy. "I'm not *human*. I use Shadow every day."

"All humans use Shadow—in dreams, nightmares, inspiration, art."

"No, but I *use* Shadow." All the things he'd done . . .

"You craft with Shadow. You animate with Shadow. It's not so different from how other humans use Shadow. Your mage mother increased your ability. But your human father gave you a soul. And anyone with a soul is human. You can't tell me that you didn't suspect—you're too canny about such things."

"I'm a mage, a stray."

"Your son is a mage, a stray. Nature is unpredictable that way. He wasn't born like you; he favored magic. And he has a chance to be fostered within his kind, safe behind the wards of a strong House."

"You're insane if you think I'll give him up." Never.

"I know you will. You'll fight me, you'll fight Kaye, and you'll scream at the sky. But you will give him up to save him from the mage plague and to save him from magekind itself."

A queer feeling overcame Mason's nerves. "We'll stick together; we'll be *fine*."

Jack's gaze finally dropped to the floor. "Fine? You have barricaded yourself in a cabin on this desolate mountain plateau, shotgun at the ready, to keep him safe. This fight is just beginning. It may very well ravage the world." The gaze found him again. "Tell me you can do better than Webb House. That 'fine' will be *enough*. Even if you were simply a stray and not human."

"I'd die for my son."

Jack nodded. "I know. But would you let him go?"

The angel slid that sword into Mason's belly with surpassing skill, but then he'd had millennia of practice. Mason was bleeding, guts shredded.

"I'm sorry, friend."

Mason's insides hurt too much, like a vital organ was being cut away with the angel's invisible blade. He couldn't speak, though his mind raced: He could agree to this for now, while the threat was pressing. Then later, when it was safe, find a way to dissolve the contract. Or if that didn't work, kidnap Fletcher and . . .

"And Brand would bear the repercussions," Jack finished for him.

"Stop reading my mind."

"Fine," Jack allowed. "I know you'll think through this proposition over and over and come to the same conclusions that I have: This world is not safe. There will be some new dire threat after the plague has passed. A storm is most definitely coming. Do you really want to go into negotiations on behalf of your son with the intent of not honoring the contract? And how would you feel if Brand and Webb were to do the same?"

Mason pulled the trigger, blasting a hole in the back of the house. He knew the gun had fired, but hadn't felt the report or heard the boom. Dust motes wavered in the new rays of sunlight.

He was going to vomit.

Jack leaned back again, as he had at the beginning of their conversation. "Once again: Brand has done you the favor of negotiating this safe place for Fletcher."

Oh, they were back to that. What had come next? Right. Mason numbly lowered the shotgun. "And Brand doesn't ever do anything for free."

Mason felt strangely bodiless, as if he were no longer in sync with his flesh. He'd sworn to keep Fletcher safe.

Jack nodded once, shallow. "She does not. In return, you will hunt the source of this plague and end it."

"Because you think it can't kill me." He still didn't believe he had a soul. He'd have known if he did have one. Surely humans could sense their own souls. The angel was lying.

Jack raised a brow, as if he wasn't going to dignify that last thought with a comment. "Your soul, combined with your knowledge of Shadow makes you ideal. Magekind thinks that you have contracted and survived the plague. We'll have to scar your body to make it look as if you have. I suggest you immediately bend your skill with Shadow to shrouding your soul. I know it can be done, and with your facility with magic, you should be able to do it."

Mason heard the words scar and shroud, but they passed by him. He stared at the false wall, behind which Fletcher was hiding. He'd wanted to earn a place for them *together*.

"You'll have a partner—one who is not aligned with the Council—so that all mage Houses will cooperate with your investigation," Jack went on. "Cari Dolan's father was recently murdered by this thing, but she survived the illness. And she has agreed to use her House's ability to see the antumbra of a mage's Shadow to identify and locate the perpetrator."

Mason's mind fractured into the abstract. Cari Dolan. He'd known her when they were dumb teenagers. Livia, Fletcher's mother, had been one of her friends.

Jack continued, "You'll have to be careful though. And clever. If she or anyone else discovers that you're human, Webb will have grounds to renege on the fosterage contract. He won't have reason to protect Fletcher."

"He's a father, too," Mason argued.

"A father who would appear to all magekind as having been duped by Kaye Brand into sheltering not only a Stray, but the offspring of a human."

No mage liked to look like a fool. Few could afford it. Not after the "cleansing" the last High Seat had inflicted on the Houses—any mage with a soul, any mage weak in Shadow, had been killed to purify their race.

Fletcher.

That Jack could come here with this message revealed the angel for the unflinching bastard he was. The angel was heartless. But then, the Order was well known for its cruelty.

Jack stood, his business obviously concluded. "The Order is not the architect of your suffering. This situation is wholly mage-made; they are all agents of chaos, including, God help me, my Kaye."

The angels of the Order were killers, Jack here among the best of them. Just look at the carnage he'd wrought today.

Jack stalked to the front door, opened it, then paused on the threshold. "When next you receive a call from Kaye Brand, you will take it, and you will hear her out."

Mason didn't know what he'd do. Couldn't even remember how to breathe. Give up his son?

"And if it comforts you at all, consider that Fletcher is one of the very few in this war who is protected by both Order and Shadow. I give you my word."

A wheeze of disbelief escaped Mason. Order and Shadow were at *war*; his son now in the middle.

The only person who really acted on Fletcher's behalf was him. And now he had an impossible decision to make.

Fletcher stepped back from the wall, wiping his face dry. Tears were for girls.

The Shadow that had let Fletcher extend his senses across the barrier faded away. His dad didn't know he could do that—see through walls; Fletcher hadn't said because his dad would be mad that he had been overlistening to stuff for a while. And his dad did some pretty cool shit. The wall became hard and real again. The poster of Batman glaring through his mask jumped back into sharp contrast.

Fletcher swallowed to get the choke out of his throat. He didn't understand a lot of what he'd heard. Only that his dad wasn't a real mage. Wasn't like him. And that he'd have to go live with Mr. Webb.

Didn't matter. His dad was still his dad.

I'd die for my son.

The echo made him toughen up. Of course his dad would put him in the safest place. He always put him in the safest place. Fletcher could still feel the tight hold that had saved him from getting sick and burning from the inside out like those other mages at the fair. Eyeballs going sloppy and gross.

And now his dad had to track the one who had killed all those people? The mage Council had chosen *his dad* out of everybody. And that was because his dad could do *anything*. The poster of Batman went blurry. His dad just had a secret identity is all—human.

Being human was bad to some, like being a stray, but Fletcher didn't care. What it meant was that his dad might need a little help for once on his secret missions. Finally.

And Fletcher was just the man for the job.

Chapter Two

A knock at Cari's bathroom door, and Stacia peeked in, a wing of her red and black hair falling around her face. "Mom had Erom wait in the office."

Cari's belly fluttered with nerves.

She'd been seeing Erom Vauclain for the past six months. Vauclain was a good House, strong family; their business interests aligned perfectly with Dolan's. She no longer had the luxury of waiting; it was time to make this official. He had to have guessed why she'd finally allowed him to come after his repeated requests, when before she hadn't wanted him to risk the plague. His agreement was therefore assured. All she had to do was . . . ask.

In times of upheaval, joining forces made sense. It was a good strategy, supported by her stepmother, who was a little self-satisfied because she'd gotten them together in the first place. And Cari could explain in person that she was working on behalf of the Council to find the source of the mage plague. These were smart steps.

"Thanks, sis." Cari smoothed the skirt of her little gray dress, made sure the three-quarter sleeves covered the worst of the bandages from her plague welts, and centered the buckle of the slim belt on her waist. She checked herself in

the mirror. No signs of sleeplessness, though she'd closed her
eyes for less than six hours since it had happened. No signs
of the hysteria she'd locked in her ribcage. She was, in fact,
on the verge of screaming. She'd blown her hair into submis-
sion, working the round brush until her triceps burned. A
person might think she was composed and ready for business.

Stacia gave her a long, silent look of appraisal. The disap-
proving kind.

"What?" Cari had been at this too long already this morning. He was waiting; she'd let him through the House wards
over twenty minutes ago.

Stacia shrugged. "You look pale. Your dress washes you
out."

"Well, I'm not going to wear pink."

"You never wear pink."

"I was making a point." The House was in mourning.

Stacia smiled. "I was making a point, too. You look like
you're going to a board meeting, not a romantic rendezvous."

Cari made a face—she *had* worn this dress only to
DolanCo functions. But she wasn't going to change now. No
time. Instead, she handed her stepsister the blush brush. A
compromise.

Stacia sat up on the sink counter, blocking the mirror. She
dug through the make-up drawer and found a compact. "FYI,
oh mighty head of our household."

Cari made a face at the exaggerated title. "What now, oh
brat who steals my shoes?" She really didn't want to be the
one that her stepsisters had to come to for permission, but authority went with the territory. They'd overcome the "step"
thing years ago and were now "sisters," but her new status as
the head of the household separated them again. Felt lonely.

"Since you and Zella are planning to get hitched, Mom
wants me to start thinking about it, too." She dabbed the compact for color, blew off the excess, and dusted Cari's cheeks.

Stacia was twenty, old enough for an arrangement. And

with everything going on, yes . . . Scarlet would think along those lines. Stability. Connections. Although technically, as head of the House, Cari was now the one who should take care of such matters. Scarlet might need reminding. Her meddling would look bad for them all, as if Cari couldn't handle her own House business.

"Please don't make me get married."

Cari groaned. "I'll talk to her." Though it wasn't going to be fun. In fact, she'd rather impale herself with a Martin House dagger.

Stacia held up a "wait" finger while she hunted for the eyeliner. "And I don't want to go back to school either. I want to find a job when this is all over."

"A job?" Cari scowled at the make-up. "Take it easy."

Stacia ignored her, re-lined her eyes, and then flipped the eyeliner pencil to the smudge side. "And I already know Father would've told me to stay in school until I figure it out, so you don't have to."

Seemed like he'd been talking in Stacia's head, too.

"Well, I'm not Father." Cari felt hollow. "Don't worry about this now. We'll work it out. A lot of things are changing." The admission brought a rise of fresh panic.

Stacia must have heard it in her voice and gave a quick squeeze of support. Then she made a flourish toward Cari's face. "Voilà. You may now get engaged."

Cari checked herself in the mirror and found she actually looked alive. Her stepsister had skills, but then Stacia had glamour in her Shadowed blood.

"Do we like him?" Cari's knotted stomach was getting the best of her.

Erom Vauclain. Was he the one?

Stacia's brows went up. "He's hot."

"He is that." So their chemistry problem had to be her.

Never mind. House first. The other things would come with time.

"Love you." Stacia looked relieved. Then she winced. "A good sister would make you change into that plunging red dress, but then I'd have to fetch it from my closet."

Cari laughed—it felt rusty, surreal. "You do need a job, so you can buy your own stuff."

"Exactly my point." Stacia flashed her big grin again. "Go snag that fine specimen of a man. Put that desk to good use." She made a rude gesture to illustrate.

Cari snorted. "Stay out of my closet."

The hallway outside still had that hush, which quieted the odd lift in Cari's mood. For a second there, it had seemed like some things could go back to the way they were. But she knew they couldn't. Not really. She was now responsible for their lives. The knowledge made Cari want to do right by her family.

Put the desk to good use. She'd never.

"Cari." Erom stood at her approach and came around from the seat of her father's desk to greet her. Dark blond hair. Golden tan. Keen black eyes.

She crossed the office to walk into his embrace.

Why had he been sitting there? That was her father's desk.

His hands went to her waist, mouth lowered for a kiss, leading with the woodsy-snap of his aftershave. But that bursting panic within her surged—*no air*—and she gave him her cheek.

His expression was a little tight when she pulled back. "We will find the monster who did this to your House."

She'd wanted a close hug, to be enveloped in warmth. To go to bed with him and forget for a while. Or that's what she'd thought she'd wanted.

Cari nodded to answer. Yes, she would find the killer. Mason Stray was arriving later that afternoon—so much to do before then. She'd assess what the stray had to offer—he used to show off with Shadow when they were younger; maybe he'd learned some control since then—and then determine the capacity in which he'd best be used. And then she'd get started.

"Timing is critical." Erom gestured toward a leather bench by a window in her father's office. He wanted her to sit. She could guess where he wanted the conversation to go. It's why he'd wanted to come, and why she'd finally let him. He'd never been one for foreplay.

But every muscle in her body was restless. She couldn't sit, couldn't be still, couldn't sleep. This feeling was driving her crazy, and she didn't know how to explain it without seeming . . . compromised.

"Cari?"

She nodded again, but paced to the desk and touched her fingertips to the surface. She'd lived right here day-in, day-out since it had happened.

Maybe she was just nervous.

"You're the head of your House now," he said behind her.

She didn't need the reminder. She'd been present every moment for the change-over, from the funeral pyre to signing papers until her hand ached.

"The new me." If she closed her eyes she could still see the white-bright of her laptop's screen, burned into her retinas from being up all last night reviewing company accounting. She officially loathed spreadsheets.

"We need to think our next steps through." Erom's voice was stern. "The Houses are watching."

Cari traced a grain of the wood with her fingernail. The Houses were all grieving their dead. Except, of course, the one who had done this.

But it was good that Erom wanted to take careful steps, to protect what was theirs. She knew he would. He would make a good partner.

She didn't know why she felt suddenly so distant, when she'd been looking forward to seeing him. She'd thought it through . . . had decided it was time . . .

Then Stacia. . . . *Please don't make me get married.*

Erom approached to stand by her side, an arm coming around to comfort, a strong hand on her shoulder to show he was there. Solidarity. "The sooner we marry, the better. I wish it were under other circumstances."

They had talked about marriage before, and she had spoken with her father about the match as well. Erom's father and brother also approved. It made sense on all levels. She'd been reviewing the decision for days; her stepmother had patiently gone through the pros and cons with her. Erom's House was strong, a longtime ally, and though he was a second son of Salem Vauclain, he'd acquitted himself well in a series of international negotiations between the Houses and clans abroad.

Cari glanced over to give him a smile. As ever, he was impeccable. His dress shirt, a gray on gray pinstripe, was open at the collar. He had a clean shave. She touched the slight pucker of a scar on his lip from a fight some years back. It was her favorite thing about him.

Her father had asked her to wait a year before making irrevocable decisions, as mage couples never divorced.

Erom was right. Marrying under other circumstances would've been better. And yet, a sixth sense, just waking, told her that, for Erom, these circumstances were probably . . . fine. She had the feeling that things weren't good for him at home.

Plus, he liked her father's office. Hadn't he been just getting comfortable on the action side of Father's desk? Add a thriving company to Erom's international network, and they both could rise among magekind. His objective was natural— he was a mage after all—and she'd shared it with him. His ambition was one of the reasons he appealed to her.

Wait a year, her father had said.

She just didn't know how much she, as a *person*, figured into Erom's plans.

Wait, her father had said, but she heard him better this time, maybe because she realized it herself. Her father had been saying, *Erom Vauclain is not the one.*

For the first time today, her belly settled.

She didn't need a year to think anymore. She owed Stacia a shopping spree. Big one. Maybe for that new job when all this was over.

"About marrying." Cari let her tone give her away.

The air in the office was absolutely still, but it seemed as if she was turning into that harsh wind again and it was going to blast through her. She'd face it anyway.

His arm around her tightened. "I spoke too soon." A gentle, but steady response. "You're grieving."

He had no idea. Grief was just the beginning of what she was feeling.

A flush of magic rolled through her, a little power, which she needed. She couldn't believe what she was about to say. "We're not going to work out after all."

She wanted her father's office. She'd gotten quite comfortable here these past four days. And in time she could make contacts overseas herself. The product was almost ready.

"I should've waited to mention marriage." His voice had roughened. "I just don't want you to bear this alone if you don't have to."

A perfect response. "You always know what to say." Except when he didn't.

Why hadn't she picked up on it before?

She couldn't afford a mistake on this scale now.

"You need time. I tried to give you as much time as I could, but I just had to see you."

Her father must have noticed something. Everything too well played. Her father had been waiting for her to notice, too.

Well, now she had.

"I've got time." Years and years of it. "I respect you too much to continue this way." He'd be within his rights to be angry;

she'd allowed him to risk the plague to come out to Belmont Hill for nothing.

His handsome brow furrowed. Really, he was wonderful. But.

"You need a break while you regroup," he said, "while you see to your House. I wish you'd let me help you."

Apparently, she had to be clearer. "Erom, this is a break. A breakup."

He stepped back, his expression going circumspect. "You're not yourself. This is too sudden a shift for you to mean it."

He was still being careful. Hopeful? Or desperate. Dolan was a great House, and he was a second son who wanted out from under his brother's thumb.

"Things happen suddenly all the time." Her father's death, for example. It had knocked her off balance, knocked her down. But this decision, made so fast, felt solid. The wind could blow and blow at her, and she could take it.

Erom put his hands on his hips, a gesture that flexed his very nice chest. "I have to think about this. I wish you would too. We have other matters to consider—our project at DolanCo, for example."

An uncomfortable problem she'd have to solve. He'd been working on building their network. But she had the prize.

"I've made my decision." The words were an echo.

Erom noticed, too, and said harshly, "You sound like your father."

He'd slipped, not so perfect this time, because there was only one response to that.

She lifted her chin to say it. "Thank you."

The preternaturally tall trees surrounding the Webb estate were sentry-still, like great spears thrown by angels, now staked into the earth, left over from an epic battle that humanity didn't remember, but magekind never forgot. Likewise, the house beyond was a fortress, which was the only reason why Mason had consented.

Webb House was indisputably . . . safe.

Mason turned onto the drive that led to the gate.

"I hope Bran is here!" Fletcher said for the third time in the last half hour. The excitement had long eroded from his son's tone, leaving him a live wire of anxiety. Mason was past anxiety; some kind of constrictor snake now lived in his chest, and with growing frequency, without warning, squeezed blood and breath from him.

The kid had taken it well. Had even said, "It'll be okay," as if he were eighty instead of eight.

"I hope Bran is here, too."

Because then this change might seem like going away to camp or some boarding school. Not that Fletcher had ever gone to either.

Mason swallowed a curse. He'd tried everything.

That Livia Walker and her House would not take Fletcher in, her own child, Walker's own blood, when all this was happening made Mason crazy with rage.

He gripped the wheel. *Her own child. Even temporarily* . . .

The massive iron gates to Webb House opened for Mason's car to pass, but he didn't advance; the real barrier was still in place. There: a dark shimmer in the gray air, and the Webb House wards lifted for their entry. *Wards.*

Brand must have assured Riordan that they weren't plague carriers.

The wards slid across Mason's mind, licking cold and sharp at his consciousness. The sensation steadied him. Wards were what he'd come for. Wards were what gave him the will to put his foot back on the gas. Wards would shield Fletcher while all Mason had was tricks and muscle and maybe the unthinkable—soul—none of which could keep his son whole for long.

Mason pulled on Shadow to conceal that damning part of himself in darkness. The magic came more readily now—he'd been practicing since he'd made the decision to give his son to Webb. He filled himself with Shadow until he steamed with magic. He didn't want to ruin Fletcher's new life by revealing that his son had a human father. No one could know about the soul.

Mason slowly accelerated up the drive to stop at the wide terraced steps that led to the deep porch and further to the imposing stone edifice that would now and henceforth be his son's home. Servants waited to take Fletcher's bags.

And, sweet Shadow forever, down the steps ran Bran, oblivious to the fact that a plague was raging in his world. ". . . been setting up your rooms all morning . . . right next to mine . . ."

Fletcher looked up at Mason, his mage-black eyes smiling, actually smiling in the midst of all this. Kid needed a haircut. "Can I?"

Mason worked his emotion-locked throat. "Yeah. Go check it out. I'm not leaving for a while." The contract. And then he'd damn well see those rooms himself.

Cari closed the accounting files and put pen to paper to write herself a note. Erom needed to be taken off DolanCo's Special Projects Committee. Keycodes had to be changed as well. This, in the midst of everything else, was bad timing. But the decision was feeling better and better.

Her stepmother had looked at her as if she were out of her mind—*Erom Vauclain!*—but had accepted her decision with a passive-aggressive, "This is your House."

Cari wouldn't let herself be manipulated into backtracking to say, 'But this is *your* House, too,' and invite (endure) further discussion on the matter.

Because, yep. This *was* her House. Her life. Scarlet could mutter all she wanted. On paper, it had been a decent match. In reality, not so much. And just wait until they spoke seriously about Zella and Stacia. No one would get married if they didn't want to.

Word of the breakup filtered through the household—Cari could almost feel it reaching everyone's ears. Unlike Scarlet, the rest of the clan had gentle questions.

No, she and Erom had not quarreled, but after the first ineffective explanation—"just not right"—she shut herself in the office to work. Let them think what they wanted.

She had a job to do, and she'd concentrate on that. The stray was on his way right now to help her.

Mason, she corrected herself.

There was no reason she couldn't use his name, even if she didn't trust him. Their moment of past history meant nothing. Less than nothing. She'd had a crush, that's all, intensified by the fact that she'd been painfully shy as a teenager.

She'd been seventeen, had just reached her majority, and was celebrating with a late-night picnic with her friends. She'd bravely—audaciously—invited Mason to come along as well, even though he'd dated and broken up with Liv, who was there, too. The potential for warfare had hummed in the air all night.

They'd gone up to Walden Pond. The moon had been bright in the night sky. The other boys had already been in the water, skinny dipping. Liv had sauntered down to the edge to watch, but Cari lingered behind, taking the opportunity to talk to Mason away from the others. Which had been the whole point of the birthday picnic in the first place.

Every time he'd looked at her, she'd had to try not to smile.

"No swimming for you?" Cari had managed without a quaver in her voice. Mason, naked. Sweet Shadow. He'd been lean then, his muscle perhaps too well cut. Maybe hungry.

"Too easy for someone to drown," Mason answered. "I like my feet on the ground." The stray thing. And yeah, thinking about it, Erom and the other guys might've easily messed

with him. Mason already moved stiffly. But there were few
choices open to him, and fighting back wasn't one of them.
They'd kill him.

She dared to touch his arm. The touch brought his gaze
snapping to hers, as if she were dangerous.

She felt danger in the air, too. It was screaming in her
mind. *Mason!*

"Shouldn't be this way," she said.

"Shouldn't be what way?" His voice lowered. He flicked a
worried glance at the boys in the water. They'd had enough of
him with Liv.

"You should be claimed," Cari said. Not shut out of his
mother's House. It was cruel, his life. How he was treated.
Someone as strong as he was should belong to a great family.

Her heart went wild at the idea.

"You gonna claim me, Dolan?" he joked bitterly.

Her face heated, her voice got all tangled up, and she lost
track of her words.

"Cari, I'm sorry." He always noticed everything.

She shook her head and looked down toward the water.
Then she changed her mind and forced herself to turn
toward him.

He had somehow gotten closer, though she couldn't remember him moving. Whispers of the fae rose around them.
Time stopped. Sparks of magic hung in the air. And he looked
at her, so seriously it made her sad. But she couldn't help it.
She was about to get him in very big trouble.

She moved closer still, until she felt his breath brush her
skin. She could almost sense the future moment when that
breath would be inside her, his mouth on hers.

A question glinted in his eyes.

She looked down at his mouth and went tingly when she
saw the slight, wondering smile that appeared there. She
smiled back. It was an answer. Yes. Permission. What she'd
really wanted for her big birthday.

But the kiss never happened.

"Cari!" Liv had shouted.

And the moment between her and Mason had exploded. Never happened.

A moment. That's all it had been. And then, soon after, all magekind had found out just how dangerous a stray could be.

A two-and-a-half-hour drive, and Mason arrived at the deserted campground that was his rendezvous location between the Taconic Mountains of Webb House and the suburban Boston estate of Dolan. Drought had made kindling out of the underbrush, and so the park had been closed rather than risk a forest fire. That's what all the notices said on the narrow drive to the park's interior, though the thickets of birch and maple trees looked lush enough to him. A cluster of cabins ringed a central lodge.

He'd just signed away his son.

Fletcher was eight, almost nine. And he would not reach his majority in magekind until he was seventeen. The time until then was almost exactly double Fletcher's life. The early years had gone by so fast, but Mason knew that from now until then each moment would creep by, snickering at his agony.

Fletcher was safe; that's all that mattered. Mason held on to that fact with everything he had left.

Three angels, in all their eerie perfection, exited the main lodge as his car slowed to a stop. Jack Bastian was not among them, and Mason was glad for that reprieve. He didn't want to hear one more platitude about how the Order was looking out for Fletcher, too. Light was just as opportunistic as Shadow.

Mason got out of his car and slammed the door shut.

A white-haired angel came forward. Though his body had the ease of youth, the man had the weight of ages in his eyes.

If Mason had any feeling left, he might have been frightened. Not today.

"I'm Laurence." The angel didn't try to shake his hand, which Mason knew would've broken him. He was not in the mood to shake hands. "These are my companions Jorge and Frederick."

Mason barely glanced at them. He grimaced what he could of an acknowledgment.

"This way." Laurence gestured toward the lodge door.

Mason followed them inside. The place smelled of fresh wood; logs and beams made it rustic. Benches and cafeteria-style tables were stacked over by one wall. A gurney waited in the middle of the room. One table had been opened to hold a metal suitcase with tools couched in some kind of foam.

The plague scars. To make him look like a mage.

With his shroud of Shadow in place, Cari would not know him for what he was.

"If you will disrobe," Laurence said. Polite words uttered by power.

Mason got the feeling that the angel could look right into him. That he could see the scraping filth that had been his early childhood. The tough living as a boy, like a stray dog begging for scraps. The hours he'd spent squatting in the dark, attempting to master his Shadow craft, trying to make something of himself as he labored with clumsy fingers at this or that invention. Then the teenager, showing off for pretty mage girls. The wild hope that was Livia. So reckless, loving danger. Then being shut out of her House, a dog again. And finally Fletcher, who'd made the world and this life finally make sense.

But Laurence didn't speak of any of that, though Mason knew for sure that the angel had seen it all in one glance. "Your clothes, please."

Mason nodded. He stripped until he was naked—in front

of them he was naked regardless—and then climbed up on the table to lie on his back.

One of the angels brought up a tool. "An anesthetic."

But Laurence stayed his hand. "He's numb already."

And it was true. Mason felt the burns as if from a distance, an abstract kind of pain. One on his chest, and another at the lymph node near his groin. Sizzle, snap.

The wounds had to be able to be hidden by clothes, or Webb would have noticed their absence.

His thigh burned. Then some scattered pocks like blisters. And another tool to accelerate the healing process. Each welt itched and crackled as his flesh reknit. And he didn't really care.

The worst of them were covered with cotton bandages and tape—drug store stuff. And then he dressed to leave again. He didn't like being here; didn't like the knowing gaze of one angel in particular.

But as Mason made to leave, Laurence touched him on the arm. "You wondered once how you might perceive your soul."

Laurence had seen too much.

Mason shuddered. He didn't want to know. Didn't need proof to distance him even more from his son. Not anymore. Please not today.

But Laurence didn't pity him this time. "Mason Stray."

Every atom of Mason's body reverberated, as if struck with a tuning fork. The welts finally ached, pain blooming everywhere, especially his heart. He staggered.

"You *are* your soul."

Mid-scrawl on a notepad, an inset window popped up on Cari's laptop screen over her flooded e-mail inbox. The window showed streaming video of an old blue car, what an optimist might call vintage, awaiting entry to the Dolan

grounds. A dialogue box below the video read, *Mason Stray,
here on business for Ms. Dolan.*

Here we go.

She looked at the time. 2:35 p.m. He was running late.

Lifting wards now, she typed to notify the guardhouse.

A deep thought and Cari reached for the ward stones
buried deep within the foundation of the house. The resonant response in her umbra grounded her. Stones meant
strength, an echo that rippled through the diffuse magic in
the room.

In the window on her computer screen, Mason's car
crossed the wardline and drove out of sight, toward the main
house.

She had to remind herself that he was like her—he'd already contracted and survived the mage plague, and was not
a carrier. Mason was safe for her House and her family. But
his arrival still made her uneasy—she did not like people
going in and out. Cari moved to meet him herself; she didn't
want the ceremony of staff leading him to her. It felt awkward
with a stray, with *Mason*, as if he were beneath her. She would
meet Mason head on.

She found her stepmother in the hall looking out one of the
slender windows that flanked the sides of the massive front
door. Scarlet managed to be elegant, even in mourning—
black slacks, black silk. Pearls. Her silver hair styled away
from her face, highlighting her high cheekbones. The look of
censure was gone from her eyes though. Progress.

Blue streaked past the window, which had to be Mason,
winding around the driveway to park.

"I don't like him. What he did to poor Livia Walker." Scarlet put a hand to her mouth and shook her head, as if the
scandal were happening right now.

Or maybe not progress. Mason was just juicier gossip.

Cari felt a tired smile coming on. At least her stepmother
was distracted from both her grief and the upset of losing Erom

Vauclain. The story of Livia Walker made a very effective cautionary tale about what happened when a mage girl forgot her House.

Once upon a time, it could've been Cari. Easily. Burned a little, remembering. The Mysterious Mason Stray, so tempting, so dangerous.

But Cari refused to think about what had almost happened at Walden Pond. It was ancient history, anyway.

Shortly thereafter word had gotten out that Liv was pregnant, probably from fooling around with him before they'd broken up. As Mason was stray, he couldn't marry Liv, a House-born mage woman. So he'd convinced her to run away with him, to have the baby—a baby that because of Mason would be accepted nowhere, just like him. And as the child constituted Liv's firstborn, no other mage would marry her and risk the bastard child making succession or inheritance claims.

Two lives ruined: Stupid Liv, who'd soon grown tired of living on nothing and had returned alone, to be outcast in her own House, and the child, wherever the poor, unwanted thing was. All because Mason Stray liked to screw dangerously.

"I don't like him much either." He was a means to an end, that's all. And—shock of the century—he actually had the Council's respect.

A man-shaped shadow loomed outside the front door.

Scarlet's voice went raspy. "Please be careful."

"I will." The search for the killer would be fast, the resolution final.

Scarlet flicked her gaze toward the door to direct her meaning. "Mason Stray should've been neutered. Now, if you were *already* engaged . . ."

Cari smiled. Kissed Scarlet's cheek. She was, after all, only trying to be a good mage mama.

"I can take care of myself."

Scarlet lifted her brows, as if to question the Erom decision again and then retired up the stairs.

Cari turned and opened the door.

Nine years and the man only had gotten more . . . Mason. Older, yes, with fine lines around those haunted eyes, and he hadn't bothered to shave, so he looked like a bandit from the old West about to rob a train. His hair was a reckless shock of dark brown, begging for scissors. And he was taller than she remembered, his shoulders wider, taking up the doorway. Smelled the same though, Shadow take him.

Poor, stupid Livia.

"Mason," Cari said, haughty, in defense of her old friend.

"Cari," he returned, just as hard.

Mason couldn't shake the excruciating feeling that he was missing a vital part of himself, that he'd left his arm or lungs or heart somewhere, and he didn't know how to function without that missing piece.

He was surly and restless. He wanted to fight something big and mean with his fists until he was too bloody for consciousness. But he could only grip the doorframe to Dolan House and hope the carved wood didn't crumble in his hands.

Cari had opened the door, the princess herself.

She'd grown up, or rather, *into* herself. Her wide, smart eyes used to inspire stunts to impress, but now something in their depths made him wary. Grief, that's what it was. Her cheekbones were set for classic beauty, with creamy skin that glowed in contrast to glossy dark brown hair, which broke in natural waves on her shoulders. Her black eyes betrayed her Shadowed heritage and she had a full, expressive mouth, which had always said more without words than with. Like now for example.

Didn't matter if she hated him. At the moment, he was beyond caring.

She stepped out of the way for him to enter. "Welcome to Dolan House."

He stayed put, but remembered his manners. A stray mage without a House, or worse, a *human*, always had to remember his manners. "I'm very sorry for your loss. Your father was a great man and a brilliant mage."

Every word was true. The Dolans were well-known for their facility with umbras, which was probably why they had always been able to make discerning decisions regarding staff and allies. But Caspar Dolan's power had gone beyond that. Mason had tried many times to understand the source of his strength, but had gotten nowhere. Caspar was an enigma.

"Thank you," she said. His courtesy had bounced right off her armor. "Are you coming in?"

"No." Like her, he didn't have it in him to make small talk. What was Fletcher doing now? "Have you been back to the site of your father's attack?"

Cari frowned. Her stance shifted to one hip, arms crossed. Less formal, even more tense. "I was waiting for you. I thought we'd discuss how we were going to proceed, as well as what you and Kaye Brand think you can contribute while I'm searching for my father's killer."

This was going to go just swell.

"I'd rather do this on my own, too." Mason looked beyond her into the house. The foyer was bigger than the total square footage of any of his places. And if he let his eyes lose focus, just for a second, he could sense movement in the Shadow. He'd been inside a mage House two times in his life: when he'd pled his case to Livia Walker's father, and just now, when he'd left Fletcher with Webb. Both Houses had ripped him apart.

Cari made a self-satisfied line out of her lips. "But you can't track umbras."

He gave her a failed smile of his own. "You don't have the Council's information."

"With a call, I could get it. Your services aren't necessary."

The head of her House. Good for her. She did the job charmingly.

"Why don't you do that then?" He turned to go back down the walkway toward his car. He had to keep moving or he was going to go insane. Why had he bothered parking in the first place?

He had no patience for playing power games with Cari. The girl he remembered hadn't been interested in games; seemed like she was all grown up now. He was here for one purpose only—to make good on his side of the bargain for Fletcher. He would find the perpetrator, and after that . . . ? He had no idea. The course of his life was now plunged into darkness. *Human?*

One thing at a time.

The engine had been idling ten minutes when Cari deigned to open the passenger side door. Instead of getting in, she leaned down to make eye contact. The shift revealed the scorch of a plague wound at her neck. "My car has an integrated computer with wireless and is stocked with provisions for just about anything we might need."

Cari had obviously made her call, but the Council belonged to Brand and Brand was siding with him.

"My car doesn't need gas." It ran on Shadow. What *human* could do that? "Have a seat."

"I require my guards"—she looked back to the rear bucket seats—"and you don't have enough room."

He ground his teeth into a smile. "No guards necessary. I'll protect you." Him and his Shadow-tricked Glock.

She stood her ground, which he respected, so he made a concession so he could let his engine have its way with the road. "Okay, how about I meet you there and I'll fill you in on everything the Council has learned about your father's killer . . . later."

She straightened. All he could see was her body and her

uptight clothes—gray dress to her knees, fitted but plain, shiny slender black belt. Her figure more than compensated for the serious packaging. Cari had never realized her own impact. He'd liked that about her. Simple. Direct.

A century passed while she was making up her mind. House pride was a bitch sometimes. But there was no way he was taking her car and becoming either her driver or her passenger on this escapade. He could not allow himself to be put into a secondary position, where he could be bossed or worse, overlooked. Both situations were a short step to an inconvenient witness. And witnesses were often disposed of after dealing with sensitive mage matters. Pride had nothing on basic survival among magekind.

Cari finally settled herself in the passenger seat. She didn't seem impressed that he'd restored the interior to its original chrome, leather and walnut, but then she was used to nice things.

He waited for her to put her seatbelt on. Leaned over to make absolutely sure she didn't require anything else. "If you're ready?"

Cari smiled, her eyes narrowing dangerously.

It was the kind of smile a wise man might do well to avoid, but he wasn't feeling wise. A strange and warm sensation had settled into his bad mood. Provoking Cari Dolan was just the thing to help him get through the next five minutes, maybe hour, without turning his car in the opposite direction and spying to see how Riordan and Fletcher fared. Riordan didn't know what brilliantly idiotic schemes Fletcher could come up with when left to his own devices. And with Bran as an accomplice . . .

"What does the Council know?" Cari's voice was business direct. She'd learned at Caspar Dolan's knee. More bothersome was the concentration of Shadow he could sense humming within her. He'd felt something like it around Kaye

Brand, when she worked with fire. But never before with
Cari. Late bloomer?

Mason settled uneasily back into his seat, shoved the stick
in gear, and took the turn of the drive fast enough that the surrounding trees suddenly went luminous, not unlike the forest
of Twilight. "In a nutshell: they think it's one of theirs."

"You don't say." Unimpressed again. "Who do they suspect?"

So sure of herself. Well, why shouldn't she be? Dolan had
stayed strong throughout magekind's history. Considering the
gathered night he sensed inside Cari—when *had* she come
into such power?—he was starting to understand the House's
longevity. Dolan had thus far sidestepped violence and
reprisals; knowing whom to trust made a big difference.

And now once again, Dolan was in a position to know.
How did they manage that when Mason had to trade blood
and favors for his puzzle pieces?

"When Kaye took over the Council from Ferrol Grey, most
of the original Seats supported her because she is so adept—
spectacular, really—at fire. Made her seem like one of the
Old Ones in the mage story books." Maybe Cari was like that,
too. Maybe this new Dark Age bred old power. Mason continued, "Plus Brand is an old House, and she seemed to have
contacts everywhere."

"And then the Council found out about the angel," Cari
supplied.

"Yeah," Mason said, turning onto I-95. He spat out the
name: "Jack Bastian."

Cari looked over, eyebrow raised. "And?"

Mason shrugged. "He's a son of a bitch. Older than the
hills. I don't know how much he qualifies as an angel anymore, except that technically he is one."

Cari snorted. "I'm surprised the Order keeps him, a soul
crazy enough to sleep with Shadow."

Mason found it ironic that he'd unknowingly done the same

with Liv, all those years ago. And yes, it had been crazy. Brand and Bastian should take note.

"Most Houses are disgusted, including the ones that still back her. And some feel outright betrayed. But since Brand and Bastian seemed to forestall a strike by the Order against magekind, the Houses have tolerated his presence with her in the Seat."

"Until lately," Cari said. "Brand mentioned that she was concerned someone might target her."

Mason chuckled bitterly. "Kaye Brand isn't scared of anything. If she seemed vulnerable, she was manipulating you." He still believed that Kaye was the only thing standing between magekind and open hostilities with the Order. But without Ferrol Grey and his iron ring, there was no House holding the Council together.

"So who do they think it is behind the plague?"

"A Council insider, possibly a member, since some of the deaths could only have occurred if the perpetrator had privileged information. Whoever it is has killed children in this ugly enterprise as well."

Silence from Cari. Then, soberly, "The contagion has ripped through many Houses. Which children?"

Mason listed the names and the Houses to which they belonged. The House responsible for this plague would be crushed until all that was left was its broken foundation.

"Parents must be worried out of their minds." Cari looked out the side of her window, but Mason caught the sheen of tears.

Was Fletcher homesick? Would Webb do right by him?

"Yes," Mason said in an undertone. "We are."

Chapter Three

"And your child?" Cari couldn't have felt more awkward. She didn't even know if he'd had a boy or a girl. She'd heard nothing about the baby after Liv had gone back home so long ago. The subject was taboo among the Walkers.

Plus, she'd been a little devastated herself.

"Safe." His low, clipped tone permitted no further discussion.

Since Liv had run off with him, Cari hadn't wanted to know anything about Mason Stray and his exploits. But now she was older, wiser, and immune. She wanted to add *informed* to that list.

Mason turned into the DolanCo Business Center, the place where her father had died.

The center had always reminded her of a blocky cruise ship in a sea of grass that ran unbroken to the horizon. The main building was multi-storied, but at the tenth floor, the structure drew in to accommodate a large patio with a wide lip. The grounds had an outer courtyard and several smaller buildings, all white concrete, so that as one approached, the structures looked like the frothy wake of the ship's passage.

Mason parked in the general lot—she hadn't thought to direct him to the Dolan garage on the other side. Maybe it was better this way—she remembered how he'd frowned at her house and refused the better car. Maybe he was sensitive to *things*, having them or not having them. Made sense, considering he was a stray, but it was short-sighted of him. Things didn't matter; family did.

They walked in silence down the path that led to the courtyard and the spot where her father had fallen. The buildings seemed to close around her. Someone, recognizing her, started to approach, but Mason held up his hand to keep them back.

Cari appreciated the gesture. She was having a hard time coordinating the in and out of her breathing as she was once again confronted with that terrible moment. The Center employed hundreds of humans, but she had no idea what they'd been told about her father's death. By now everyone would connect what had happened at the Stanton Massacre to what had happened to her father, and they would know that they were employed by mages.

"Over there." Cari motioned toward the fountain where some people took their lunches, now empty in the late afternoon.

This was where her father had fallen. The desperate panic that had been her companion since his death tightened her chest. Felt as if she'd just been here. Just seen it. As if it was still happening and wouldn't stop. She was going to burst.

"What do you see?" Mason's voice was almost gentle. He respected her loss. She remembered how he could be kind when he wanted to be. It'd surprised her years ago, so it shouldn't have now.

He would know about her House's ability to see the umbra trails of mages. Every mage did. But right now, she could perceive nothing. Just the cold, gray day. A dank heaviness to the air.

"Cari?" His low tone plucked a bass string within her that resonated on a primal level. She remembered that too. The lingering vibration helped her find her voice.

"Okay." Time to do this. She should have come as soon as she'd recovered. Fact was, she'd been scared to do it alone.

She called upon her umbra, and Shadow sprang readily from the concrete and saturated Cari's senses with a rough wave of awareness that rushed her blood, mind, and vision. A week ago she'd had to pull and coax the stuff to do her bidding. But now . . . so very much breathless Shadow exploding from within her. A cold sweat broke out on her skin, but she could see the dark paths of what had to be herself and Mason trailing to and from the parking lot. She wasn't interested in them, so she pulled harder, felt herself grow somehow bigger, grow vast as she fought time, forcing it to reveal the Shadow trails that had passed *before.*

Her attempt to look back in time should've been laborious, but today turning back the clock was easy.

You are the Dolan now, said a strong voice in her head. Her father's?

I am the Dolan, she repeated, understanding that this ease of power was part of her inheritance, and how she would keep her House strong in his absence. There were so many things that she would have to work for now that her father was gone—every day seemed more difficult—but it seemed that Shadow wasn't one of them. She hoped that it would give her the edge to survive, to honor her House and his memory.

Starting now . . .

No mages had walked these paths since her father's death, so the very first silhouette to form out of magic was his own. And next to him, what had to be hers. Yes, that was her, though it was difficult to recognize herself. She seemed like a stranger.

And there were the guards as well, who'd been following them everywhere since the May Fair Massacre. The two imprints they made were full-bodied Shadow, filled with constellations of dark light.

She remembered a few humans, the executives, who had joined them as they crossed the courtyard to enter the big ship, but no sign of their ephemeral passage remained.

Cari could see no one else, no killer, in their group, no mage lurking nearby, but had to witness once again the moment her father staggered. She sobbed openly as it all played out again.

Cari-from-before lunged forward to help him up.

Her father swiped a command at the guards to get her away. She'd missed the gesture before—that her father's last act was to protect her.

The guards pulled her away as she fought them. Her arms had clawed the air for purchase. Back into a car, where she'd started to shiver herself. One guard sped her away, while the other returned to kneel by her father.

The Cari of today filled with desperation. Who had killed him? Where was the assassin?

She demanded more Shadow, more magic.

And it came to her. Easily.

The Earth was thrown into darkness; a black wind scoured the ground. The ship became a wrecked vessel, foundering on the plain, as ancient trees populated its passage.

But no killer was revealed, no tell-tale sense of person, whom she could later identify.

Too many days had passed. She should've come earlier, no matter how sick or afraid she'd been.

A sudden prickling in her mind warned her that someone was near. Now. The assassin?

Who's there? She whipped around, but saw only the smoking Shadow of Mason's tall, broad-shouldered form, waiting for her nearby.

A breath on her neck. She whipped the other way. Someone was definitely here. And not as a thumbprint left behind at the scene of the crime. Someone was here now.

Mason shouted Cari's name from far, far away. He sounded urgent.

So she released her pull on Shadow. Gladly, to get away from this feeling of being watched. Stalked.

The humid gray of the present settled back upon Cari and her vision dulled. Magic washed away from the plain before her, the ship and its wake coming back into the ordinary.

"What happened?" Mason demanded.

A girl! Maeve's joy sent birds leaping upward from the branches of old trees, bowed with magic, and into the Twilight sky. All the creatures of faerie sang a lament of delight.

And she was just now trying her power. Which meant Caspar was gone to dust and his heir was female. Maeve loved surprises, how they burst within the breast. The stubborn old man hadn't told her anything!

The Dolan males didn't fit Maeve well enough for her *to see* or *to feel* or *to thrill* to the pleasures of the mortal world. Neither did males offer the chance *to cross* into that realm and partake of the pleasures in person. Only *a girl* afforded that chance.

And Maeve was going to snatch it up. A hunger lengthened her nails to claw for purchase in that realm.

The last female Dolan heir had been such a disappointment—she'd been too obstinate and hard, like the age into which she'd been born. Her death had come before a solemn and gray tribunal of humans. Their faces had been as pinched and cold as the lives they lived. They'd spurned color in their apparel for piety, and had bent the exquisite passions of the body toward the ecstasies of suspicion and hysteria—the witch hunt.

Maeve enjoyed these, too—anything that quickened the blood was good. But not if they killed the Dolan! Her

House had spurned her for madness, and the girl wouldn't
do anything to save herself. She'd wanted oblivion, if only
to shut Maeve up.

So unkind. So ungrateful.

A loop of rope had gone round the Dolan's neck.

Maeve promised her power and riches and sex, one last
time.

The girl did not reach for Shadow. She hummed to herself,
urgently, as if that would block the voice in her head.

A nod from an ugly man in black.

A brief blur of motion. Then a *crack*, bringing darkness.

Centuries of darkness.

Now Maeve peered through the new Dolan's eyes at a
smoky stack of man nearby.

Much better view. A Dolan girl after Maeve's own heart.

The man's features were cast in Shadow, though his soul
burned bright blue and sharp like a star in the void. A half-
breed. Best of both worlds. His shoulders were wide, legs
braced. She giggled, imagining what hung between them.
The angles of his form, the cut of muscled youth. She wanted
to stroke his naked body with her mouth. Take a bite somewhere juicy.

If the new Dolan heir saw him this way, then yes, Maeve
had finally found her match.

She hadn't had a girl in *so* long. The Dolans bore too many
sons. They didn't know that desiring sons was a human con-
ceit, not worthy of magic.

But a girl . . . !

The lesser fae that followed in Maeve's wake made a quail-
ing sound—fear, joy—it didn't matter as long as the noise
lifted to the sky. Twilight's trees shuddered, the craggy old
beasts. They didn't know fun. Or pleasure.

"Cari," the man said.

Maeve leaned in to taste his voice. *Cari* seemed to be made for his throat, his tongue.

Maeve's heart fluttered. She wanted to be pierced by the star of his soul. *Pierce me!* She laughed. Human men, young ones, were glorious. She could eat him alive.

Maybe she would.

The new Dolan, Cari, turned at the man's call. Maeve did too; they'd live in tandem like this. One to another. Flesh to faery.

The new Dolan was a gift.

Caspar had kept his child secret from her. But he'd loved Maeve all the same to have sired a female for his heir. After the years they'd shared, the Shadow she'd delivered into his keeping, just see how he'd blessed her back.

Cari Dolan. Maeve would see to it that she had *everything*.

Mason grasped Cari by the shoulders, and shook the Shadow from her clouded eyes. He'd seen many mages work Shadow, but this was the first time he'd seen Shadow work a mage.

The Cari he remembered had had control. She'd been a credit to her House, everyone said so. She was the example held up to others—accomplished, graceful, smart. Heir to the old and mighty Dolan House. Liv had been friends to her face, but had hated her behind her back. "Perfect Cari."

Shy Cari. Sweet Cari. Sly Cari. If you knew what to watch for.

The umbra thing. That had to be it. The Shadow within. Mason had always thought it was a passive ability, an almost intellectual one, considering how present and mindful Caspar had always seemed. Cari, too, for that matter. The Dolans were rarely given to the drama so frequently found in other mage households.

But the way Cari had been overcome just now—her skin

taking on that anti-luminescence. The crawl and grasp of
Shadow around her body had made him think that she was
receding from the world instead of calling on the magic
within it.

He was sure that the Dolans knew their business, but this
seemed . . . off. Not wrong, necessarily. But inside-out.

Cari didn't fight his grasp, but when awareness came back
into her gaze, she turned her head to the side—still shy,
then—and shivered.

"Are you all right?"

She squirmed a little, as if to stretch. He could feel the
darkness within her flex.

Mason tried not to curse. He didn't want to be . . . *rough*
in front of her.

"I'm fine," she answered.

"You don't seem fine."

She lifted her black gaze. "I'm excellent, in fact."

Somehow her skin, even through that tidy dress, was too
hot. Or too electric. Dangerous, anyway. It had always seemed
dangerous to get too close to princess Cari. Mason let go of
her. Strays weren't fools. "Did you get what we needed?"

Her expression gathered. The sadness he recognized. And
frustration. Whatever had gripped her was passing. Good.

She shook her head. "It's been too long. I should've come
back immediately."

"You sensed nothing?" He couldn't quite believe her, after
all that.

Her mouth tightened.

"There's more," he guessed. That mouth never lied. Someone should let her know before the wrong person discovered
her tell. She had a House to protect.

"Maybe the fae," she suggested. It sounded like the truth.

He had to make sure. "The fae?" Creatures of Twilight

were drawing closer. And with all the Shadow she'd just used,
the fae would be attracted.

She shrugged. "I don't know."

Mason looked away to take a deep breath. This was going
to take time. They'd just started. And finding a killer was
nothing Cari had been prepared for. They'd put it together.
Eventually.

It'd be easier if he hadn't liked her so much back then,
when they were kids. It made him worry for her now.

His vision focused on a group of people—humans—who
were watching him and Cari from across the courtyard.

What had they seen? Not much from over there. Cari might
have appeared ill, which was warranted considering her father
had just died. Her eyes had been the most frightening during
her episode, clouding with Shadow, but the humans were too
far away to see, and only he could have sensed the storm
inside her.

They'd witnessed nothing really.

But Mason recognized the character of their heavy stares.
It was an us-and-them kind of expression. He'd felt it many
times as a stray. These humans knew Cari was a mage and
probably thought he was as well.

Just a few months ago only human elites were really aware
of magekind—the politicians and wealthy trying to get the
edge on the new age of Shadow. But these were everyday
people, just like at the May Fair.

Now they knew and they believed.

This was her chance.

Leah watched her boss Ms. Dolan and the hot guy in
jeans and a black tee—had to be a new bodyguard minus the
suit jacket.

Ms. Dolan must have come to pay her respects to her

father. That spot was where he'd died, after all. It was so sad.
No one ate lunch out there anymore. Felt weird and creepy.
Only the gamer guy from IT did it, but he'd been nasty to
start with.

As soon as Ms. Dolan seemed finished, Leah would ask.
Five more minutes wouldn't make any difference. It'd been
years already.

"Burn 'em," Thomas from accounting muttered beside her.

Leah didn't respond. The witches debate had gotten old
quickly, but the consensus was that while some innocent
people might have been hanged as witches way-back-when,
obviously some real witches had been as well. Everyone had
seen the footage from the Stanton May Fair. Magic was real.
In fact, the word *mage* was now synonymous with anything
bad, scary or unexplainable.

Hear a wraith scream? Magey.

Almost get in a car wreck? Magey.

Lose a sock in the dryer? Okay, that was magey, too.

The guard was shaking Ms. Dolan. Maybe he was a family
friend instead. Not a boyfriend. Ms. Dolan had been dating
that other guy for a while. Everyone in accounting called him
Mr. Slick Shit. This new guy wasn't her type at all.

Ms. Dolan turned, as if to continue on and enter the main
building.

Now.

Leah walk-jogged after her, ignoring the "wha?" from
Thomas behind her. Took a sec, but she finally caught up.
"Excuse me?"

Ms. Dolan kept walking, but the guy in jeans looked over
his shoulder. "Not now."

Leah wasn't about to stop. Her family needed to know.
"Please?"

Ms. Dolan had slowed. Now she turned around. "It's fine,"
she said to the man. To her, "Yes?"

Look at those black, black eyes. Witch, definitely.

Leah gulped. She'd never told anyone this before. "My sister . . ."

Ms. Dolan got two little lines between her eyebrows, as if she didn't get what this had to do with her.

Yeah, well it did. "My sister became one of those wraiths."

And damn it, she was going to cry. Especially because Ms. Dolan and her friend seemed to immediately understand. They'd shared an uh-oh look. People like Ms. Dolan had known all along. It burned that these Shadow people had known, while everyone else was so scared.

Five years of her mom's sad eyes. Leah had to know, even if it cost her job. "Is there a cure?"

Neither one answered. The muggy air clung. Leah could feel it oppressively holding them all together in the moment.

"Because you have to be one of those mages, right?" Leah asked Ms. Dolan. "The magic stuff. Shadow or whatever."

The man put his shoulder in front of Ms. Dolan. He had black eyes, too. Crap.

"I'm very sorry," he said, "but there is no cure after someone becomes a wraith."

He sounded so straight, like a doctor giving bad news.

Leah ignored him and kept at Ms. Dolan. "But if she was infected by Shadow or bitten by something, and changed"—the possibilities raced through Leah's mind—"then maybe . . . ?"

"Shadow has nothing to do with wraiths," the man said.

Leah wasn't talking to him. She was talking to Ms. Dolan. Just asking a simple question, that's all. And they seemed to have the answer, but weren't telling.

This was her *sister* she was talking about.

But he seemed to think Ms. Dolan, a *mage*, needed protection.

"Has to be Shadow." Leah tried to step around him to get

to her. "Couldn't be anything else because wraiths are *monsters*. What they do . . . How nothing hurts them . . ."

"I'm sorry. The sister you knew is gone." The man was trying to sound nice, but it felt patronizing when obviously he was lying. "She's just not there anymore. Only her body remains."

Leah flashed angry. They would tell her the truth. She'd make them. Her mom hadn't been the same after what happened. "Well what happened to her? If she's 'not there,' then where is she?"

Ms. Dolan finally reached out a hand, but Leah flinched back. "Mr. Stray is telling you the truth. The . . . person . . . who created the wraiths is gone. I'm terribly sorry, but there's no way to undo what he did. Think of it like an accident . . ."

"But it wasn't an accident." Leah couldn't help that her voice was rising, a little shrill. Okay, maybe she was losing it. So what? These people had no right to suggest it was random. "It was *Shadow*."

The man had pulled out his wallet and extracted a business card. "If you contact the Segue Institute . . ."

Leah sneered at him. She'd heard about that Segue place; they *killed* wraiths there. She wanted to save her sister, not put her family through more hell. How dare they stand there and lie to her and then try to give her the shove off. "I want an answer now, or I'll . . ." She didn't know what she'd do, but something. Ms. Dolan would listen. Leah had been quiet about this too long.

"The Segue Institute is your best resource. Tell them Mason Stray referred you." The man put his wallet away. "Cari, are we done here or do you have work?"

"I have to pick up a few things," she answered.

The man moved in to Ms. Dolan. He had his hand around her upper arm, keeping her close to his body, while blocking Leah as they walked past. Leah watched them walk away from her, leaving the heartache and nightmare of her sister behind them.

"Witch!" Leah yelled after Ms. Dolan. Desperation overcame her. She drew an even deeper breath to shriek it so everyone would hear. *"Witch!"*

Chapter Four

Cari was relieved when the door closed behind her and shut the woman's cries outside. Cari was breathless with shock. Less than a week ago, she'd been ready for the future. To take over the future. She'd felt strong and secure. Dolan was rising.

And now? "I'm going to need to increase security."

"Yes, and fast." Mason walked at her side toward the elevator. "I've seen some disturbing things in my work, but the implications of that woman screaming *witch* has to top the list."

Pitchforks and torches came to Cari's mind. The last female Dolan to inherit the House had been hanged as a witch in the seventeenth century.

"The world is changing." Every day seemed more wild and unstable. Magic was covering the Earth and it could not be undone.

"The world is going backward," Mason said. "Information would help."

The elevator closed, so Cari could speak freely. "That her sister had to *choose* to become a wraith?" Because the woman was right: it wasn't an accident. Her sister had to have wanted immortality, and wanted it desperately, and that's exactly what she'd gotten. Wraiths couldn't die, couldn't be killed by any mortal means, but gradually devolved into monsters unless kept on a steady diet of human souls. But how to explain that, especially to a sister? Cari had two of her own.

"I'd rather know," Mason said darkly.

"You grew up with magic. I don't think humans can cope."

Which just made Mason give her a long, dry look. Maybe he didn't know his mage history. She'd been tutored at length since she was five. Case in point: it started with one woman screaming witch. She wished she could talk to her father about it; he would've understood. He would've known what to do.

But now *she* was in charge. And that look from Mason made her think that her tutors hadn't quite covered everything. It occurred to her that a stray might know things she hadn't learned or couldn't learn from the safety of her House.

Frustration made her stand up straighter. Why had Kaye Brand wanted Mason here? All he did was make Cari feel seventeen and unsure again, when she really needed to be the Dolan now. She had work to do.

Cari went to her office first, called security to alert them to the problem outside, then began gathering her papers. She touched base with Special Projects on DolanCo's big advancement in Shadow. The idea was simple: A container with magic held inside. A little vial of concentrated Shadow. Mages were all able to direct Shadow in some way, but none could actually hold and transport it. Shadow was chaos; it smoked through all barriers. But a little more work, and Dolan might just have the solution—a new kind of synthetic membrane.

Mason waited in the doorways of the various offices she stopped in. She could feel him looking at her, though when she glanced his way, he was always examining her father's personal art collection, exhibited throughout DolanCo offices.

"One last stop, and I'll be done," she said to Mason.

She picked up the membrane prototype and put it in her purse for safe-keeping. Then she had to make it clear to staff that Erom Vauclain would no longer be working on the project.

Today of all days she didn't miss the irony that her company's big advancement was mentioned in the faelore of the Old Ones. Mason was right in that respect: the world *was* going, or at least reaching, backward. Or maybe time moved in circles. And if *that* were true, then magekind had no hope at all.

Gary Skinner, a human who'd worked for Dolan security for many years, found her just as she was ready to leave. He'd been aging into his pot belly since she'd started at DolanCo six years ago, but he was loyal and had good timing. She'd wanted to have a word with him anyway about keeping things calm now that it was public knowledge that DolanCo was a mage-owned company. He'd known for some time now.

"It's too late to try to calm them down," Gary said. A crowd—including a local news van—had gathered at the courtyard exit to the parking lot.

She and Mason looked out of an upper story window to assess the situation. The overcast sky put a gray ceiling above. Below at least thirty people had congregated to blame her for the darkness now shrouding the world, when she'd been born with it in her blood. If she listened closely, she could almost hear them chanting: "No more Sha-dow. No more Sha-dow."

What did they think she could do about it? It was like protesting oxygen. Magic had always been a part of the world, to one degree or another.

"And so it begins," Mason observed.

"Police are on the way," Gary said.

A second news van turned into the lot. They'd only been there a half an hour. How could one woman screaming "witch" grow to this?

"Why here? Why now?" Cari wondered aloud. She left

off *Why me?* But it didn't seem fair that she should be singled out when there were so many other Houses that used humans for terrible purposes. Feeding their wraiths being one. Dolan had never used wraiths. And her father had always paid the humans that worked for them over the national average.

"They finally have a target," Mason answered. "Someone local and accessible to blame. We need to get out of here while we can."

Each chant struck her mind. *No more Sha-dow. No more Sha-dow.*

Several years of fear growing in the world—monsters in alleys, talk of black magic, the fae closing in—and now people knew her for what she was.

The exposure felt like a hot sun blazing down upon her, *just* her, while everyone else was safe in the shadows of the gray day. Panic, her constant companion these last few days, flared in her chest and battered her ribs with the beat of her heart.

"Let me get some more men." Gary lifted a walkie.

It had been an egregious oversight not to have hired more security following her father's death. But then she'd been ill, and was just now getting back up to speed.

No more Sha-dow!

She should have insisted on her House guards accompanying her today. That would be two more men, Shadow-born, to see to her safety. But it was too late now for recriminations and I-told-you-so's to Mason Stray. She was in charge; he was only the stray Brand had forced upon her. Why had she listened to him?

"You might not be coming back here for a little while." Mason didn't seem all that concerned, but then this wasn't his business, his family's livelihood at stake.

She'd thought she wouldn't be back because she'd be elsewhere looking for the source of the mage plague. Now this. "I've got everything I need."

Three other security staff members joined them on the ground floor main exit. They were all DolanCo had on site, and they were humans, too.

The chanting was louder down here. The plan was to exit in force and quickly get to Mason's car before a real mob could form. When she was back at Dolan House, she could figure out what to do. At least there the wards would keep everything and anything out.

Five minutes of shock had reaffirmed what she'd been taught as a schoolgirl: humans weren't going to accept Shadow. They hadn't in ages past, and they wouldn't today either. It was a bloodstained fact of mage life. When the Council spoke of war, this was what they meant. *Witch!*

"We'll be fine." Mason concentrated on the crowd outside the glass doors. "We just need to leave. Are you ready?"

She took a breath, as if she were going to dive into deep waters, and nodded.

He pushed open the door, and Cari could hear a siren from far away, wailing over the chants.

No more Sha-dow!

Gary and his men got them across the courtyard, pushing people back like she'd seen on TV. It was all confusing and fast and loud, too many questioning, angry faces suddenly around her. The humans seemed to rush them, slowing forward progress. Not all of them were DolanCo employees. They must have been waiting for her to show.

To hell with you mages!

"This is Dolan property!" Cari's composure was cracking. "You will all leave now!" But her voice didn't carry past the *Sha-dow* chants. And those nearest didn't listen. Wouldn't hear.

Mason's arm went around her shoulders, his hard chest close, heartbeat steady in her ear. His back was a safe traveling wall of strength. His scent wrapped around her senses, intimate in a moment of extreme publicity. She was ashamed of herself for needing him, but couldn't help holding on—two mages in a suddenly angry world.

She'd be ready next time, she promised herself.

A man with a large professional video camera closed in, the round, giant black eye recording and transmitting her face to the whole world. *Mage. Shadow-born. Living among us. Exposed.* A couple of policemen were attempting to hold people back; one wrestled a red-faced man to the ground, cuffing him.

Another man—older, taller, straight-backed—rang a bell and hollered about Dolan being a blight on the face of the world. The prophet's eyes had a fervent glow. "Soulless offspring of the dark!" All of which was true.

A rock hit her cheek. Hurt.

"Chin up, princess," Mason growled in her ear.

She raised it like the Dolan she was, gritting her teeth to stop their chattering.

Mason reached, fast, and grabbed the video camera off the guy's shoulder. The humans around them recoiled in fear that one of the mages was becoming violent. Cari's heart rate tripled and she tried not to cringe. The panic within was almost unbearable; it darkened her sight.

Mason murmured something to the camera under his breath—*You are a hammer*—but it didn't make any sense to her. The veins in his muscle-corded forearm suddenly ran gray-black with Shadow. The bulk of the camera hissed and smoked with magic.

Cari stopped breathing. *Sweet Shadow forever.*

He was going to do something. In public. Against mage law.

He brought up his arm, fist still clenching the camera, and drove the thing into the pavement. Shadow rose from the point of impact like a sea of dust. A crack like black lightning parted the way before them, like Moses and the Red Sea, waves of Shadow harrying the humans back so that they fell on each other.

He'd always been a show-off. Nine years later, and he was no different.

Cari opened her mouth to say something to him, but nothing came out.

He shrugged, and gave her half of a cowboy smile. "I'm good with my hands."

The feeling in her chest cartwheeled. She was no longer afraid. Almost laughing. Borderline hysterical.

He didn't even seem concerned.

His arm went around her, tighter this time, and they rushed down the walkway. Before they reached his car, he said, "Kitt?" and the engine rumbled to life. She remembered he'd said that the car ran on Shadow. He shut her in the passenger's side, then darted around to the driver's.

People, recovering, were moving for the car.

"This is horrible," she said, as Mason climbed in.

"I've seen worse." He accelerated forward, up onto the grass, sending the humans screaming back again. It was a clear shot from there across the field to the main road. They were out.

She had no idea what to say, so between pants, she opted for, "Why Kitt?"

Was it a magical word? Some kind of incantation? Shadow didn't work that way.

"Fletcher's name for the car."

They took the curb with a thump that had her bouncing in the seat. She held on for her life and attempted a lame joke. "My car has a remote start, too."

Mason grinned over at her. "Mine will come when called."

Cari couldn't help but laugh, and when she got started, found she couldn't easily stop. Too much had happened. She'd kept a lid on herself long enough. Too long. And she didn't care anymore. Tears ran down her face—but she couldn't have named which of the many recent horrors in her life had caused them.

"You do this for a living?" she finally managed as Mason outstripped pursuit. She understood now why Kaye Brand had wanted him on the job. Cari was officially in full agreement. He'd been impressive before, in so many ways, and nothing had changed. Not really.

"A man's got to put food on the table somehow."

Mason expected Dolan House would be like its name, a dark place. But the house was high and bright, full of women talking over each other, and more people looking on from the back of the house. Or at least that's how it seemed since he and Cari couldn't even get in the door.

"Really, I was fine," Cari assured them.

"It's all over the news." It would be.

"You've been crying." More tears to come.

"The phone won't stop ringing." Every House thinking the same thing: danger now everywhere. Keep quiet. Keep secret. Watch and wait. Retreat. No, too late.

Mason's phone had been buzzing in his pocket for the past twenty minutes. But he'd ignored it. He wanted to get his own mind straight on what had happened before discussing it with anyone else, especially Brand.

What would Cari's life be like now? His, of course, was less impacted; he had no roots, no business to protect, no dependents anymore.

When they finally got to the entrance foyer—the *third* House into which he'd ever been invited—Cari made the introductions. He'd have preferred she didn't. He just wanted a back room with a bed until they got a call that someone else had fallen to the mage plague. Hopefully only one victim, with no danger of contagion. No families. If there was any mercy in this world, no children.

"Mason, this is my stepmother Scarlet." Cari had left off the Stray.

The woman had silver hair wrapped up on her head and a long, thin nose to look down; she did not extend her hand, so he figured she didn't need the "Stray" to know what he was. He got a pinched mouth and a sharp look from her black eyeballs.

"And my stepsisters Zella and Stacia."

He didn't remember them. They were younger than Cari, so hadn't run with the same group of friends. Both women had a feral kind of appreciation on their pretty faces. The younger had red and black jagged hair—her keen assessment kind of scared him—and the other had gone long and platinum with her hairdo. She was smiling at him way too much. He hoped they weren't bold enough to try anything. House women, even too-young ones, were dangerous. A stray ought to know.

"Nice to meet you all." He tried to keep clear of the crush. "If someone could just point the way to where I'll be staying, I'll give you your privacy."

Cari had a quizzical expression on her face, a twist to those lips. She was amused at his discomfort. Well, she should get her laughs in where she could. The woman had more than enough to worry about.

Was that the *wump-wump* of a helicopter overhead? The news crew had followed.

Dolan House would soon be under a modern siege. And then the whole damn world would know the value of wards.

She turned to a staff member waiting inconspicuously nearby.

"Allison?"

Mason almost smiled, even today with the world ending. Princess Cari. All grown up and mistress of her own little castle. He'd only known her while he'd been with Liv, who'd been dedicated to pissing off her family by keeping company with a stray. To the others Liv hung out with, he'd been a novelty they indulged. But sometimes Cari, pretty Cari, would shoot him a look or say something under her breath, and for a second, he'd feel like one of them instead of dirt on a shoe. Back then he'd been ignorant enough to delude himself.

Allison headed for the stairs to show him his room. Up, where family would sleep, not back, where the staff rooms probably were.

He followed.

A sense of air and light dominated within the house, but yes, there was also the silky cling of magic, like a fuzz on the edge of awareness. The broad architecture seemed designed to hold stillness, which made his tension even keener by comparison. At the top of the main stairs, a large marble statue of a languorous woman reclined. The piece was in the Greco-Roman style, and probably had a story behind it. The marble made her skin pure milk, caressed her naked breasts and left her eyes vacant.

With a snap of understanding, Mason perceived that Dolan House was dominated by women. Even the air seemed female, the energy feminine. Shadow seemed more seductive here. Caspar Dolan would've been incongruous in this place. Which made no sense at all. Caspar Dolan had been an extremely powerful man. Wouldn't his House reflect his character? He'd only been gone a week.

Allison showed him to a guest suite—high ceilings, simple elegant furniture in fair hues. He dropped his duffle on the glass top of a low table with fancy legs. The decorator had managed to girl-ify the color blue.

When the door closed behind him, he put his hands on his hips and hung his head. Well, here he was. Invited to stay inside a House. And not some servant's room either, which would have suited him just fine.

Comfort and safety. Everything he'd wanted so long ago, and yet it meant nothing today. It was, in fact, a bad and bitter joke.

How many times when he was younger had he looked at

every mage man and wondered if he could be his father. Then there'd be the shock of discovery. Pride. The mage would claim him—*my son*—and Mason would be shown into a room like this (or a masculine version). And suddenly the orphan stray would have a massive family around him.

The fantasy had been impossible. His father, it turned out, was human. There had never been a room like this set aside for him. And now, he didn't want it. Not even this one, the best of them.

The Houses could have their large, fine estates. He just wanted his little house on the island in Alexandria Bay, or even the cabin . . . and Fletcher.

His dream was Fletcher. A family of two.

This great House made Mason hurt. The room was too big. Too rich. He didn't like the quiet, because then he had to think.

What was Fletcher doing now? Was it too soon to hope for an e-mail or video message?

Mason pulled out his laptop. There was an e-mail from Webb. It was explicit, though miserly with detail, and yet what lay under the message brought Fletcher's and his situation into crystal clear focus. Not that he was surprised, though his heart still squeezed and squeezed until the room seemed to tilt.

```
Mason:

Fletcher is settling in well. He and
Bran have constructed a rather
impressive fort in my son's room.
Their tutor was taken captive for a
time, but managed to survive the day.
I anticipate Latin will be
particularly arduous tomorrow.

It has come to my attention that
DolanCo has made a breakthrough that
```

would enhance the interests of Webb
House and our allies. They have
managed to contain Shadow within some
kind of a membrane. I'd like to know
how. While you are so fortuitously
placed, please look into it.

                                      R.W.

Mason had worked for many a House doing unpleasant
jobs in return for favors, or for money to live. It was the only
work open to him. Steal, cheat, kill—a mage did not collect a
human paycheck. Doing so meant utter isolation, and possibly death, especially under the previous Council.

Was discovering information on this membrane the job that
Webb had wanted to hire him for back at the Stanton May
Fair? Didn't matter.

Of course, there was no offer of payment here, and that's
because Webb knew that Mason didn't need to be paid. Not
anymore. Webb had Fletcher, which was more than enough
motivation. The fosterage arrangement made Mason a very
passionate supporter of Webb's interests. The contract was a
two-fer. That's simply how fosterage worked.

Didn't matter that Mason liked Cari, didn't want to investigate her business. He was first and foremost Webb's man.

Fletcher noshed on a cookie as he lay back and considered the blanket they'd used for a fort ceiling. It was droop-
ing again. He and Bran were going to get the most out of
"just tonight" if it killed them. Tomorrow they had to clean
up and Fletcher had to sleep in his own room. Welcome celebration over.

Fletcher was a pro at forts. His dad had taught him everything he needed to know.

He and Bran had found flashlights in the kitchens, grub
and soda too, and stashed it in a corner of the fort that he

called the canteen. They had an ammo cache of rolled socks
to beam at anyone who came to check on them—his dad had
always said to make sure he could defend himself. A piss pot
and source of fresh water would've made the fort complete,
but Mr. Webb might have gotten mad about that.

They loaded the floor with bed stuff from Fletcher's room
and ate until the sheets itched. And Bran made monsters out
of the shadows of their hands on the standing mattress they'd
turned into a barricade.

When Bran finally fell asleep, which took forever,
Fletcher's boredom disappeared.

Time to become Stealth. It was his secret name, what his
dad had called him after the silent stink bombs he'd dropped
as a baby. Changed to codename Deadly Vapor for a while,
then Miasma, when he got that stomach flu, but anything that
ended in an "a" was a girl name. Stealth stuck, and now he
kind of liked it. And only his dad knew about the baby thing.

His sleeping spot was next to a dark gap under Bran's bed.
Lots of Shadow there. He scooted under the bed and kept
scooting until he reached the wall.

Bran's bedroom wall was shared by Mr. Webb's bedroom
wall, which was why Stealth had suggested using this room
instead of his.

Stealth told the Shadow what to do. If he made no sound,
he could hear the low grumble of Mr. Webb's voice. If he
looked hard enough, made his eyes look through the wall,
then he could watch Mr. Webb's mouth move, and he could
figure out the words.

The wall dissolved and only black spots coasted in Stealth's
vision. He knew to ignore the whispers that hissed in his
ears—those were just the fae, coming closer. His dad said not
to acknowledge them, so he didn't.

Mr. Webb was in a brown robe and slippers. Veiny ankles.
He'd put his glasses down on his night table, but was speaking

on a smart phone. "No, he won't report my request to the Council. I have his son."

. . . hissss sssson . . .

Stealth peered harder to catch everything. Mr. Webb could only be talking about one "son"—him.

Mr. Webb grunted with frustration. "The stray will do as I tell him. He's gotten his hands dirty before."

Stealth went hot. Mr. Webb was scheming against his dad.

A long bit of quiet.

"Yes, I am prepared to do just that." Mr. Webb looked over at the wall, almost as if he could see him. But Stealth had been doing this bit of magic for too long to be scared. "I'm sure he'll be very cooperative."

Stealth glared right back.

Cooperative? An archnemesis? Never.

"What do you mean he's staying here?" Scarlet demanded of Cari. "Did he seduce you so easily?"

Cari paced around the far end of the formal dining table, Umbra research in hand. She'd wanted a large surface to lay everything out and her father's desk was already covered. Unfortunately, her family saw no reason not to bother her here, even though she was trying to work. Actually, they'd bother her anywhere if they wanted.

Zel, who was sitting on the table swinging her legs, rather than occupying a chair like an adult, laughed out loud. "Mother!"

Cari didn't need this. She laid out the membrane integrity graphs to see if she could find any regularity in the findings. "You want me to throw him out to them?" The protesters from DolanCo now camped just outside the Dolan House wards.

Scarlet didn't flinch. "He's a stray."

Stray meant his blood wasn't good, wasn't pure. That he

had no true loyalties. That he couldn't be trusted. That he would seize an opportunity.

Well, there had been that one time . . . Mason leaning in, his warm breath on her cheek, her heart pounding so loud she was sure he could hear it . . . but Cari wasn't going to mention that, nor think about it too much herself. It still made her heart pound, and it had been years ago.

"Mason is my partner, and it would do no House, including ours, any good for him to be in danger, at the mercy of the hysterical masses, when wards could protect him."

Besides the fact that he'd gotten her out of a very tight situation. Maybe her stepmother needed to see that news clip again. The stations were playing it over and over. Boom went Mason's great big hammer. That helicopter might even still be circling the house.

At least the house was well stocked for everything they might need, should they be stuck inside the wards for a while. Her father had always thought ahead and had prepared for this very situation. Food stuffs. Supplies. Generators. In-ground well. For now, they were fine.

"I'll keep an eye on him," Zel offered suggestively. Her fingers undid the braid in her long hair and she shook it free into streams of silvery sunshine. She let the mass fall around her face and made bedroom eyes at Cari.

Scarlet rounded on her. "You will not. Need I remind you that you are betrothed to marry?"

Zel, age twenty-four, did kissy fish lips at her mother.

Cari was definitely not going to bring up the fact that Stacia wasn't going back to school.

Scarlet, like a variety performer spinning plates, turned back to Cari. "Is this the way you honor your father?"

Which just pissed her off. "I don't deserve that. And I don't want to hear one more word about Mason staying here. He is. Period." And to Zel, just in case, "You leave him alone."

Zel pushed off the table. "That's okay. Stacia's called dibs anyway."

Scarlet went white. "That's not funny."

Cari kinda thought it was, but she kept her expression straight as she looked at her pages. The jagged red line on the graph in question went up and down, no rhyme, no reason.

"Well, *someone* should bang him," Zel said.

Silence.

Cari did a double take, surprised that Zel evidently meant her. Heat flashed over her skin, but she managed to be blithe. "I have other work to do."

"Delegate," Zel said.

Scarlet sputtered. "What will the Walkers think?"

Cari pointed to the door. "Out."

Zel actually did as she was told. Shocker. Scarlet would be more difficult. Cari wasn't going to get any work done until Scarlet had said her piece.

"Did you know he has allied with Webb?" Scarlet's tone was smug.

Cari paused. She'd just found out about the fosterage agreement; Kaye Brand had failed to mention it when she was here. A convenient omission. But Cari wasn't all that surprised: Brand and Webb were allied; it made sense that Mason was, too.

"I ask you, how does a *stray* make that kind of arrangement? Webb is an old, prestigious House."

Cari repeated what she'd been told. "Brand says it was the bargain struck for him to investigate the mage plague."

"A stray doesn't have that kind of pull."

"Brand was a stray herself once."

Scarlet scoffed. "Not really."

"Her House burned to the ground."

"Word is Brand lit the match herself."

Cari put her arm around Scarlet's shoulders and led her to the door. "Please, Scarlet. This investigation is on behalf of all our Houses, so of course he is going to have allies we don't share. And if those allies are powerful, then he must have earned them, which means the likelihood of our finding the source of the plague is greater." And, to cover all of her stepmother's objections. "I promise to guard against his formidable powers of seduction."

He did have a cool car and had claimed to be—Cari would never forget—good with his hands.

Cari eased Scarlet out the door. Then shut it on her protest.

For the love of Shadow, her stepmother was going to drive her insane. Cari was the Dolan now, responsible for all of them, the house, the company, but she didn't think the rest of her family recognized the distinction. She didn't know whether to hug them or demand a little respect.

She went back to the table to concentrate on the membrane tissue again. A prototype was nested in a box. She lifted out the vial, formed out of the thinnest, most delicate of lab-grown membrane. It was shaped like a palm-sized teardrop, black with magic. DolanCo was going to call their new product Umbra. The logo was a stylized U representing the unusual vial.

It would be her father's legacy. Her throat tightened just thinking of him.

Perhaps if she could see the Shadow and the containment more clearly, she could figure out what was wrong.

Maybe . . . ?

Why not.

Cari drew from her Shadow within, just a little, but once again, she received too much. The power submerged her in waters of possibility and promise, making her feel strong, when she knew she should be tired, and it made her feel invincible, when she'd had very recent proof that even the mightiest mage could fall.

* * *

Maeve giggled as Cari reached for power like a newborn kissing the sea for a drink of water. Maeve paced along the bank, restless and wanting.

Child, yes, take it. Draw deep. This is your inheritance.

Cari could open her lips wide and fill her belly.

Want more? Why resist? Indulge.

Dolan. Dark House. Revel House.

Royal House.

Cari Dolan, daughter of Shadow, be not afraid.

Welcome me and we will rule together.

Cari turned abruptly. "Who's there?"

Her Shadow-logged vision swam with murky fronds of magic, a ready, ecstatic kind of feeling, like the build-up to a climax. But the alarm that zapped her system stung, and she concentrated on that.

Someone was definitely in the room. She'd just *heard* them. She turned again.

Nothing. Just drifting Shadow, warping her senses.

Cari felt like she was swimming in circles. Whoever was with her remained hidden behind her. She wanted a mirror to see what or who was in back of her, playing a game.

The feeling made her skin tingle, her neck tense. She'd felt this before, in the courtyard at DolanCo. This sense that someone was with her, watching her. There had been rumors about the fae crossing into the mortal realm. And since this had happened only when Cari attempted to use Shadow, then yes, her stalker had to be fae.

Her panic swelled: first there was fighting among magekind, then the angry attention of humanity, and now something altogether different . . . within Dolan House?

"Who are you?" she demanded aloud.

I've been with Dolan since the beginning. And will be to the end.

The answer came from within Cari, in her own voice. She had to grip the back of a chair to keep herself upright.

"Are you fae?" Cari already knew the answer. Dolan House, like any other mage House, was on the brink of the Twilight wilds. Curious fae were going to come; they were to be treated like dangerous guests and directed elsewhere for their diversions.

I am a god, the voice answered. *And I am your mother.*

No. "My mother is dead." And a mage, once dead, is always dead. Mages did not possess everlasting souls as humans did. They had one life of magic and then oblivion. So live large.

I was mother to Dolan eons before the woman that birthed you.

"Interesting. My father never spoke of you." It was well-known that fae lied when it suited them. Or rather, that the fae didn't know truth from lie.

Caspar loved me. He gave you to me, and he gave me to you. My darkness feeds your umbra.

Father had never mentioned any such thing. He rarely brought up the fae at all. He was practical, not passionate, in nature.

Use me and see. I will give you everything you want.

The fae laughed, the trilling feeling dancing up Cari's throat. The sensation of the fae—a wild, giddy leap of energy—was located within. Cari finally understood that the fae was the source of the panic that had seized her since her father had died. The fae was the pushing, no-breath feeling. The fae was inside her.

Passed down each generation, lord to heir. Son to son. But this *time, this once in so very long, father to daughter.*

At the recitation Cari went rigid, a sudden hot sweat chilling on her skin. The room began to spin, her palms going damp.

No fear. It does not suit my line.

Think. She needed a specific detail about this fae so she could find information later. "Who are you?"

Laughter. *I am Maeve. I am yours. And you are mine. What do you want most? I'll give it to you.*

Okay, Cari thought bitterly. "I want my father back."

Maeve wailed and it was the sound of Cari's own grief wracking her heart and closing her throat with sobs. Cari guessed that meant, no can do.

"Then if you're so powerful, why didn't you save him?"

I saved you. I saved you. Pleading now. And who knew if it were true? If Maeve had saved her from the plague, then who had saved Mason?

"Okay, then I want to know who killed my father." Who brought this plague down on all the mage Houses?

Anguish again: *I cannot see! I cannot see!*

Cari wasn't surprised. "Then what use are you?" Faery. God? Mother. Please.

First, she'd search her father's things for a mention of Maeve. She had to go through them anyway and had clearly put it off too long. Then, she'd widen her scope to the faelore. And she would find time to do this when? Her panic rose; Maeve again.

You need me. Use me.

"No." Cari wasn't a fool. Dolans weren't fools.

Not yet?

Cari considered what she'd been taught about dealing with the fae: Don't make her angry. Placate. "Not now," Cari clarified through gritted teeth. How could she push the fae out of her mind? Out of her guts? Out of her Shadow soul? She let go of her pull on magic, released, and felt the fae go distant, like a leash pulling quickly through her hand. It begged the question: who was bound to whom? Was Cari the pet or was the fae?

Maeve crooned, a sound that Cari had never made in her life, *We belong to each other.*

Chapter Five

Mason was on the inside of a mage House, and like never before, he could sense the flows of magic and almost hear the hiss of the fae as they looked in from their world. It was an uncanny, skull-crawling awareness, one that reaffirmed that he, Fletcher, and even Cari were sliding down the knife's edge of danger toward certain doom—plague, mob, magic—and there was nothing he could do to stop it.

Cari's company was trying to contain Shadow in some sort of membrane (as far as he knew, an impossible feat); Mason needed to know how. He couldn't deny Webb's assertion that he was "fortuitously placed." He was. Ridiculously so.

The new Dolan was about to get a very good lesson on why strays weren't permitted inside warded Houses. Maybe she *needed* to learn, so that in the future she wouldn't lose just her company's most exciting product, and at the worst time possible. The best thing that Cari could hope for was the misfortune of some other mage House to contract the plague so that he and Cari would have to leave Dolan property. In that case, they could finish their investigation and part ways.

He hoped for it too because he still liked her, the sweet girl turned mistress of a small empire. Made him grin, what she'd become. She'd always been capable, if a little soft-spoken.

And damn smart. Scary smart, which he'd admired. And scarier still was the way she looked at him, like she was thinking complicated things, maybe guessing the worst. And yet, they'd been friends once, briefly. At least he'd thought so. And there'd been that one day when he'd gotten up the courage to make a move . . . Her tricksy, telling mouth had obsessed him. He'd wanted to kiss her so bad he still felt the disappointment nine years later.

He'd been such an idiot. Cari Dolan, of all people. Her father would've killed him, after torture and dismemberment.

And now this Webb business with the membrane. He wanted to watch her rise, not be the instrument of her downfall. Or one of them, at least. There were so many ways she could crash.

He regarded the flat screen in his room, tuned to a cable news program that specialized in hyperbole. The celebrity newscaster spoke in exclamation marks and agitation. *Shadow! On the ground! What's anyone doing about it!?*

Humanity had caught a mage fever to go with magekind's plague.

The main road that led to Dolan House's extended drive had a small encampment of humans, barely visible through Cari's security cameras, but clear on the webcast streaming video that someone had set up to watch the house. Signs that read, *No More Shadow!* were stuck into the ground. The area surrounding the house was protected by wards—which had made headlines as well—so that any who tried to approach were blocked. One brilliant soul had tried to shoot in the direction of the house, but had ended up with a bullet in his elbow.

Shadow's first casualty! Who will be next? Are your children safe?

It was making everyone within the wards a little crazy, too.

He was almost certain that the stepmother was plotting to kill him. Shrewd lady. And the weird sisters had made a game of catching him alone and dropping increasingly lewd suggestions. One of them, the blonde, he thought, had stood outside his bedroom door singing, "Cupcake delivery." He was pretty sure that the "cupcake" was her. He'd bolted the door, then switched the lock so that no one could get in.

House women.

Cari, at least, was like him and had locked herself in her office. He hadn't seen her in two days, though he'd tried to catch her more than once. Thoughts of Fletcher were consuming him, making Webb's request more pressing. He was going to have to create an opportunity for himself. It was all Cari's fault; she shouldn't be this trusting. Her father should've taught her better.

So be it. He'd put it off long enough.

He didn't trust the empty hallway. The naked lady statue followed him with her empty eyes. He went down the stairs, softly, as only a parent can. Across the main foyer. He knocked when he got to Cari's office, identified himself through the wood—it had been embued with magic, a good precaution, though that wouldn't keep him out—and then entered when the lock released.

The change in her was startling.

She looked exhausted, gray, the antithesis of the flighty birds that were her sisters, and yet still more deeply beautiful than either. There was something substantive about Cari, but he was still trying to figure out what she was made of that was so compelling—maybe her sense of duty, or maybe her absolute loyalty to her House. And she was powerful, maybe too much so.

Although this morning he couldn't feel the churn of Shadow that Cari kept bottled up inside. Not good. Mages needed Shadow; where was hers? She looked thinner, too, which was strange after so short a time. The lack of Shadow was costing her body.

Huge house, full of people . . . Who was supposed to be

taking care of her? She couldn't do everything on her own, although the Cari he remembered would try.

Mason noted that Cari covered the book she was reading with her hand. A loop of script was visible though—a journal?—so the contents had to be personal.

A soft shuffle behind him brought his attention quickly around. A stray always knew who was at his back, though he could have guessed: either the stepmother, with a knife rushing toward his spine, or one of the sisters, to torture him with innuendo.

The sisters. Perfect.

Mason turned to the head of Dolan House. "I want it known that I have made no advances and refused all of theirs."

Cari smiled, humor sparking in her wide eyes, still so lovely, even when tired. "They're just messing with you."

". . . haven't even begun to mess with him . . ." The one with the red-black hair sighed under her breath.

Mason raised his eyebrows at Cari. *See?* Liv's family had tried to kill him. He wasn't risking a repeat without at least committing the crime first. And these girls didn't tempt him.

"They're scared and bored and don't mean anything by it," Cari explained. "Do I really have to defend your virtue?"

"I don't have any virtue," he told her. "Never did." Virtue was too much like good-breeding; it was hoarded and parceled out to the deserving. He had nothing to hoard, and had never been deserving, least of all now, when he planned to steal from her. "I just don't want any misunderstanding."

Cari glanced back and forth between her sisters. "Cut it out."

Stacia pouted. Zel made a *pft* sound.

They didn't seem to be taking Cari's request seriously.

Mason sensed magic gathering fast within Cari, too fast, frightening, like storm clouds rolling into sudden potent and electric density.

"You will leave him alone." Her voice was filled with command, underscored by an implicit threat disproportionate to the issue. It was disproportionate if the sisters were, in fact, just messing with him. Appropriate, however, if they really wanted to tangle with the stray who'd already ruined one mage woman.

Her sisters sobered, their postures changing instantly. Who knew they could be normal?

"Sorry, Cari," Stacia said. "I didn't mean to stress you out."

Zel had gone tentative too. "Can I help with anything? Get you something to eat?"

So they were at least *trying* to take care of her. They needed to try harder.

The concentration of magic slowly disassembled, as if Cari were swallowing it. She looked down at the books and papers on her desk. "I just need peace and quiet."

"But if you'd let someone help . . ." Zel argued.

Maybe they *were* trying harder.

Cari's face was still angled down, but the black of her irises shifted up to look at Zel. Cari was the picture of mage menace: isolated, besieged, not able to trust anyone who didn't share her blood. And her stepsisters did not.

Mason's instincts said, *Danger*. This was why she'd been left alone.

"You can't help me." Cari's body had a feminine frame, but somehow she dominated her father's big chair. But Mason didn't trust it. He knew Cari, and she'd seemed off from the first moment he'd arrived.

Zel's face reddened. She nodded, her mouth going into a white line. "I'd do anything for you, ya know."

Stacia put her hand on Zel's arm to pull her back. "Just give her some space. She'll figure whatever it is out. Cari can do anything."

No answer from Cari. Just that dark glare.

Mason found himself unwillingly liking her sisters. But

they were idle, and that was a mistake on Cari's part. He'd
learned that lesson every single time Fletcher got bored.

Stacia and Zel retreated from the office, but Mason was
staying. He shut the door, then met Cari's blackened gaze with
his own. Dead-on. "What's wrong with you?"

He couldn't help the way the air snapped between them,
nor could he quell the impulse that he'd find out more if he
were touching her. If there was any Dolan woman he was
interested in, she sat before him. And she was utterly untouchable.

"I have work to do." She didn't look at her spread of papers
and books, and she didn't have to in order to make her point.

"I can sense concentrations of Shadow." Mason cast his
eyes over her messy desk. "You feel different than you did
yesterday. You feel weak."

She flinched as if stung. No mage liked to be called weak,
but her instinctive reaction confirmed that she was beyond
her strength. It was strange to speak to her like this—he'd
have kept his distance with someone who was merely a business associate, but Cari was more than that. There'd been
something between them once, and damn if it still wasn't
there, tugging at his gut.

"Are you ill? What's going on with your Shadow?"

She smiled, mean. "I could ask you the same question."

Mason frowned. "Nothing's wrong with me." Nothing that
distance from here, from her, returning to his home, and playing with his kid couldn't cure.

"Your Shadow isn't right either. I can't find your umbra
when I look." She pulled back to turn a page, scanning down
the text. "So you're hiding something, yourself really, from
me. You must be very strong to hide like you do, when it is my
House's purview to see."

His umbra, or lack thereof, was none of her business, so he
didn't answer her observation, and went back to his own.

"You're in trouble. You should let your sisters help you with your work." It was honest advice, intended to help.

Wasn't she supposed to be involved with Erom Vauclain? Where the hell was he? Must have just been gossip, or the relationship was over. What kind of a man would leave her to deal with her nightmare alone? What kind of a man would leave Cari at all? But then, thinking of Erom, she was probably better off.

"My stepsisters' talents skew toward beauty and attraction. I'm surprised that you haven't enjoyed their attention." She gripped the book, pulled it close to her.

"I'm not interested." Among her skewed papers he spotted the word *membrane*. Cool logo. "They could clean up your desk, for one."

"Then I wouldn't be able to find anything."

But neatness would help him find what *he* needed. "They could take care of basic corresp—"

Cari interrupted with a strained smile. "I can't trust them with this." Her long, heavy, black lashes swooped up. Her gaze hit him. Hard. "Can I trust *you*?"

She was on to him. He must have given himself away. He stepped back.

Damn, she was smart. It had always turned him on. The rush of his blood sharpened his mind. She was the real thing. The epitome of mage royalty—too powerful for comfort, Twilight beautiful, ruthless. Cunning.

And that was just skimming the surface. He wished the man who did marry her luck. He'd need it. Cari was just getting started. Give her ten more years and she'd surpass her father.

"No," Mason answered. "You can't trust me." He wished she could, but that's not what life had in store. Fair warning.

An eyebrow arched upward. Aloof. But her mouth twisted, sardonic—revealing how she really felt. She was mocking him. "Thank you for the truth."

"I lie when it suits me." She had to know. He was even now trying to compartmentalize the morass on her desk to identify the information he sought.

Those lashes went up again, fringing the heart of her face. Deadly. "Noted. Again, thank you. I appreciate your candor, so I'd like to hire you."

He took another step back. Distance to gauge her. She'd been so quick with the offer, she must have been considering it before he'd come down.

"You just suggested I get help," she pointed out. An advance. "And I happen to have someone with an impressive reputation right here."

Caspar would be proud. The way she maneuvered, even when exhausted. Keep your enemies close, and all that.

Mason preferred her relaxed and laughing, like the old days. But maybe that would be more dangerous. It was better for them both to be on their guard.

She sized him up with a scrape of her eyes. "I witnessed a brilliant performance just two days ago at DolanCo."

He didn't take jobs that conflicted with each other. And Webb had him already. "What's the nature of the work?" He didn't know why he asked. He knew his answer.

"I'm looking for information." The book she was holding went down on her lap, a crooked finger marking her page. "On the fae. Crossing over into this world. How they do it."

But he was not helping Webb with the fae.

"Has a fae crossed?" It was happening more and more, the most worrisome of this era's dangers in his opinion.

"Not that I'm aware of, no."

A dodge. Cari could lie like the best of them. She had a fae problem to go with the rest of her troubles. Plague, business, mob, her father's death, the impending theft of her company's membrane project. He wanted to tell her it would be okay.

But nothing was going to be okay.

He shook his head. "I can't work for a House opposite my

allies." There. Was honor satisfied yet? He was no good at being a gentleman.

"Okay." She took it with grace. Kept that Dolan chin up. Her eyes were hard, with sketchy Shadow in their depths.

He was actually afraid for her.

"My father built this house anticipating a siege or two." The tone of her voice told him she was disengaging. "So there are entertainments—a media room, a gym. You're free to use anything. My sisters won't bug you, or not much. The rest of the family will keep their distance. You might keep an eye out for my stepmother, though."

Mason made to draw a breath, but found he'd been holding it already.

It was only information. Lore, even. Not work. A way to pass the time.

He wouldn't delude himself. It was a way to spend more time with *her*. Pretty Cari, who'd looked so hard to really see him. And him, looking back.

What was he doing?

"I'm not interested in being hired, but I do. . . ." His neck was tightening. This was a bad, bad idea. "But I need something to keep busy." In addition to stealing her membrane concept. "I have an interest in faelore myself."

She'd followed. He could see it in her eyes. "You'll help. But I can't trust you."

He liked her so much. He nodded.

She laughed, and he actually thought her tension eased. "And I thought *I* had to walk a fine line. I don't know how you do it."

He didn't know how either. But he knew why. Fletcher.

For Fletcher he leaned over and touched the back of the screen of Cari's laptop. For Fletcher, he reached inside and left a stitch of his Shadow behind, so that he might access her computer from his later.

Cari didn't seem to expect an answer. And he wasn't about

to detail how everything about his life was gray and growing darker by the day.

"Okay—" She seemed to be organizing his task in her thoughts. "I'm interested in any faelore that refers to the creation of the mage Houses, mine in particular. Specifically a fae named Maeve. You have contacts, access to resources that I don't."

You ask him for aid, a human, but not me?

The rabble of lesser fae behind Maeve screamed and quailed.

Daughter mine, you are a fool.

Ask me, need me, call upon me.

A chill rippled over Cari's body, raising the hair on her arms. She'd fought the push and presence of Maeve for two days, each hour more difficult than the last, and was more tired than she had ever been in her life—but she was too stunned to smother the voice within her now.

Human?

Yesssss.

She closed her father's journal, losing her spot—she'd find it again, the day he'd inherited Dolan House from his father— and smiled up at Mason. The expression felt too sunny, too fake, so it withered on her face.

You lie, Maeve.

Not to you.

How, then? Mason had access to so much Shadow. A reputation that had earned him connections to great Houses. She'd witnessed his magic for herself. His hammer, how it had parted the way for them to escape.

And his soul is so very pretty. Can you feel it? I want to feel it. There is nothing in any realm like a fierce soul. Burns a

*little at first, going down, but even that is ecstatic in its own
way—human emotion, memory stirring the belly. Yessss. . . .*

"You don't mind if I go through your library?" Mason
asked. "See what you have?"

Cari drew a deep breath to concentrate on him. Mason. The
man that had set the bar for all others. Human. And yet, Erom
had never had a chance.

He'd mentioned the library.

There was nothing there that Cari didn't already know—
her father had insisted on a thorough education and she'd
been up all last night re-checking. "Please, go ahead. But I
was hoping for more first-hand knowledge."

Mason's eyebrows went up. "You mean Khan, at Segue."

Thanatos. Cari stifled Maeve's groan. *He's tedious and
cold. Choose heat, dove. Choose Mason. He is right here and
he's playing with you.*

Cari couldn't have Mason. She'd learned that a long
time ago.

But yes, Khan. That's exactly who she thought might have
her answers. Mason had a connection to Segue; he'd even
mentioned it the other day to that girl at DolanCo. And Khan
was associated with that place. Khan, Shadowman, the Grim
Reaper—whatever he was called—was as old as the world.
He'd know who Maeve was.

Did Khan know that Mason was human? That he had a
soul? Cari couldn't see his umbra because, according to
Maeve, he didn't have one.

*Like a displaced star, a rich jewel, drenched in Shadow. I
could wear him.*

Mason. Human.

Cari's father had always said that time was the most powerful of the Order's weapons against magic. Forget. Disperse.
Intermingle. Houses, weaker ones mostly, forgot who they
were and had intermingled with humans. Magic belonged in
fairy tales with fairy godmothers and princesses.

And some Houses did mate with humans. Though, not Dolan.

Then magic stirred again within mage blood—her father said he could name the day, the very moment, when it quickened inside him. A thousand years, and finally the Houses remembered who they were, *what* they were. Under Ferrol Grey, Brand's predecessor on the Council, the humans within each great House were rooted out, killed, the bloodlines purified for the coming Dark Age. There would be no intermingling of the races.

Seems he missed one: a mage with a soul.

Funny thing was, if Mason had actually been claimed at his birth, had been brought into his mother's House, for example, he wouldn't have survived long. Being a stray had saved him.

No need to kill them. Maeve pouted, childlike. *Such a waste to douse the light right away. Just look at him.*

Cari did; she couldn't help looking at Mason. She'd always liked looking at him. Strong. Dark. Late at night, it was Mason's image that came to her sleepless mind.

He said he'd lie if it suited him, and his being in her House was a lie. Did Brand know? With that angel for a lover, she had to. Typical.

Let's take him together.

Stop that.

I know you like him. Let me give him to you. He already needs punishing. If you only knew . . . Just ask. Let me tell you what he's done.

Cari ignored the fae and focused back on Mason. "Do you know Khan?"

"We don't go out drinking together or anything, but I think he'll talk to me. His grandkids and Fletcher have played together."

"His grandkids and your son . . . played together." Mason never ceased to amaze her. How *had* he risen so high? "Well, then."

"Might take a day or two to actually reach him and set something up for you. He refuses to carry a phone and comes and goes from Segue without warning."

So tedious, dove. No need to seek out Shadowman. He can't change anything. Never could. Death is, as ever, himself.

"We have other work to do with the plague, so a couple of days is fine." Cari gripped her father's journal.

Her father would tell her many things. But she did have to concede, once again, that Mason, even as a human, had his uses. At worst, the knowledge that he had a soul would be the way she could control him.

Such a pretty *soul.*

And, okay, maybe Maeve might just have her uses, too.

Erom Vauclain sat on a hard, low stool across from his father's wheelchair. The old man had tubes up his nose and curd on his eyeballs and the corners of his slack mouth, but he was still technically alive. The wheeze of his breath made Erom feel oxygen-deprived.

Erom's brother Francis came into the room adjusting his shirt sleeves so the cufflinks twinkled. He stood behind their father, a hand on his shoulder, the heir to Vauclain prematurely playing lord.

"This really isn't necessary," Erom said to Francis. His brother made Erom itch inside, annoyed. Made him hot enough to want to punch him in the face. Wouldn't that feel good?

Francis tightened his hand on their father's shoulder. "Father thinks it is."

Francis had always been a dick, but never more so than when he'd started pretending to read their father's mind.

Erom knew better than to roll his eyes. To irritate his brother, he dropped his gaze and spoke to his father directly. Even decrepit, their father was still the head of Vauclain House. Francis technically had nothing to do until the old man died, and he'd already made it to a hundred and eight. Francis would be very old himself before their father bit the big one. Rumor among the staff was that Francis had stopped feeding him. Old man must be living on Shadow alone. Shadow and spite.

"I'm sorry to have disturbed your rest," Erom said. His father used to scare him shitless. Now look at him.

"We want to understand what happened with Dolan." Francis's voice.

"She's grieving." Erom shrugged, as much for air as to dismiss the question. His brother made him so fighting hot. "Needs some time to get over her loss."

The old man blinked. Goop migrated across his irises.

Francis's voice came from above again. "Are you or are you not in a relationship with Cari Dolan?"

"We have a long history, she and I." Erom wanted to pull at the collar of his shirt, but recalled it was already open. Still couldn't breathe with the old man sucking in and out like that.

"Are you still a couple?"

"I think so." His father's gimlet eyes forced him to add, "But we're taking a break."

"You knew it was essential to secure that alliance. It was the one thing you were good for."

"Cari approves of the alliance as well," Erom defended. She'd said she had. They'd started planning their future.

"Did you take care of her in bed?"

"I did the best with what she had to offer." His shirt itched. "Believe me."

"You, of all people, should know how to satisfy—"

Here he goes. The tirade about another delay with Cari, this time mixed in with the number of other women he slept with and the danger of Cari finding out.

But Francis didn't finish.

Erom forced himself to look up to see why Francis had

broken off. He'd be enjoying himself about now, his big brother, some twenty years senior, who'd never said a word to him that didn't mean, *One day I get to boss you around.*

Francis had withdrawn his hand from their father's shoulder. "Where did you go after Dolan House?"

Erom sneered. None of his business. A man had to get some relief; Cari sure wasn't providing it.

"Where did you go?" Francis demanded again.

Erom felt a drop of sweat slide down his face. Made to swipe at it. Came back with Shadow-tinged blood. *Wha . . . ?* His heart boomed as he felt for the itchy spot on his face. Found a mound that ached when his fingers probed it. The skin broke. More slimy blood. *Oh, please Shadow.* He couldn't breathe.

Francis reeled back. "Where did you go, you stupid son of a bitch!"

He never should have lingered outside the wards. Never. A quick lay wasn't worth this, no matter how many weeks he'd been cooped up.

The plague. Erom tried to stand, but his legs wouldn't hold him, so he went down on one knee with a crack. His back, his spine, hurt. The base of his skull was splitting.

"Help me," he begged Francis. "Please, you're my brother . . ."

Francis wavered for a moment and then did step forward. Lunged even.

Thank you, Erom thought. He'd love Francis. He would.

Francis kicked the brake on their father's wheelchair and pushed the handles, so that the chair rolled straight toward Erom.

Erom grabbed at the chair's armrests, only to collapse into his father's lap. The old man smelled sour, like dry urine.

The heat. The itch. They were coming together for a burn,

but Erom didn't have enough air anymore to scream. Terror wouldn't let him pull a breath.

He looked up one more time to beseech his brother. *Please . . .*

And caught the flash of movement as Francis exited and shut the door behind him.

Chapter Six

Cari paced the kitchen in the small hours of the night, sleep no longer just distant . . . it had become almost an enemy, refusing to have anything to do with her, no matter how tired she was.

She'd held out as long as she could. She couldn't stop the constant flush of magic that roared through her. Every minute since her father's death it was stronger.

At least no one was near to see her struggle. She had to be strong—the new, mighty Dolan. But she wasn't so mighty, not like her father. She was just herself, cracking under the pressure.

A wave of heat rolled over her body, her skin flushing with prickles and tingles and deep, good aches. Her plague welts itched, but that's because she was healing more quickly now, faster than she should. Air in her lungs felt potent, more invigorating, while her brain begged to shut down, just for a little while. But her senses were aroused by the mere thought of a stimulus. Chocolate—she could taste the dark, velvety sweetness. Silk—she could feel the cool slide on her skin. A man—she could scent Mason and feel the vibration of his voice within her. Her body didn't care that he was human. Not in the slightest. She was drawn up tight inside, fisted. And eating a plate full of brownies did nothing to satisfy her.

She threw her head back to endure a roll of rough sensation.

She was changing somehow, and she knew it. And she couldn't trust anyone enough to try to explain it to them. No, that wasn't right. She could only trust certain people with certain parts of her situation. Her sisters were loyal, her stepmother concerned—but if they thought the House was compromised, they might "help" Cari by bringing in other members of the family to take over. And she didn't want to disappoint her father that way. She, and she alone, had to be enough. She had to be enough.

If anyone could understand, it would be Mason, and without even being told. He spoke in parts himself: I'll help you, but don't trust me. It seemed like an impasse, but at least their positions were clear. Somehow he could sense what was going on, which made him dangerous enough to kill. Why then was it a relief that he was just upstairs?

Again. Just the thought. Heat crackled through her.

Was the fae Maeve manipulating her body? Was she responsible for this?

Or was this a side effect of being inundated by Shadow? Of becoming the Dolan?

And if it was just herself, losing control, wasn't that more frightening?

Mason sat on a chair, his elbows braced on his knees, head low. Wan starlight filtered through the sheers on the windows and made the blue room glow. His head ached with exhaustion, but there was no way he could sleep with magic riding so high so close to him. It was potent, ominous, and worse . . . inescapably female.

His stray-honed senses told him it wasn't safe to rest. His heart rate was up. Blood rushing. Skin prickling with sweat.

Danger. Watch your back.

What in Shadow's pitch was Cari doing now? Did the woman never sleep?

Rocking with sensations, Cari gripped her father's journal for dear life. Had he gone through this? Had he known the fae named Maeve?

The journal volume was dated thirty years ago, during the period of time immediately following her grandfather's death, before Cari was born. Her grandfather had died of a heart attack at fifty-five, survived by a large extended family, but only one son, Caspar Dolan.

Cari almost didn't recognize her father's scrawl. As a younger man, his writing was wilder than the precise script she'd come to know. The person on the page also seemed foreign to her. The journal was written by a man who was fraught with insecurity and pride. It took a while, but she found what she sought.

My aunt says she knows nothing of the fae, that she has never heard a voice in her head. That my father never heard a voice either. She suggested a doctor. I think she envies how Shadow gathers to me. I think she is bitter because magic is neglecting her.

The fae voice had to be Maeve. Focusing on the text was difficult, with this restlessness under her skin. Cari paced from the kitchens to the large, formal sitting room, starlight lighting the pages.

She's going to fight me for control of the property. She said I'm too young for the responsibility. She showed the family my mistakes at Dolan and Company as proof that I'm at best not ready, at worst, inept.

"She" had to be her great aunt Florence Dolan, now dead. Her son, Cari's uncle, was staying in one of the cottages at Dolan House now. He always had something to complain about, from how long it took for the water to heat his shower to his allowance from the Dolan trust. His attitude had to be rooted in the rift between her great aunt and her father, an old argument about inheritance that had never been settled. But that her father, the great Caspar Dolan, had ever been inept? Impossible.

The room was too still, so Cari moved again. She wished she'd changed out of her slacks and blouse and into something more comfortable, but she didn't trust herself to go upstairs feeling this way.

Control. Her father had always advocated control.

Where in Shadow was hers?

But the voice in my head says there is no question. She promises me power, saying that I'm the true heir. I asked her how to prove it to everyone and she told me where to find the ward stones.

Grey, Verity, Brand and Vauclain have already found theirs. Nothing can touch their Houses.

I'll bring back Dolan's. And I'll put them on the table right under Aunt Florence's nose. If she can command them, then she will be the Dolan. And

if I can, I will. I feel like Arthur,
about to pull the sword from the
stone. I am stronger every day,
soon invincible. I want to see that
patronizing expression of hers wiped
off her face.

Maeve had come to him, too. Had made promises. How had he handled her? Cari flipped through the pages more quickly. There was no mention of the fae for weeks. Then this:

Aunt Florence is dead. She tried to
take the stones, but they wouldn't
obey her. Everyone said she had a
heart attack like my father, but I
saw. I saw it all. Through me, the fae
sucked the life out of my aunt until
her heart just couldn't beat anymore.
She was a cruel woman, but was this
justice? I don't know.

I don't like being used.

I have made a decision. Names have
power. To use hers is to summon her
voice into my mind. To draw Shadow
from Twilight is to bid her near. I will
shut the fae out and never speak her
name again. Dolan is closed to her.

Cari made a face. Shutting out the fae was hard to do, and near impossible while using magic. But yes, she could push Maeve away. Exhaustion did it too, which was why Cari thought her mind had been blissfully silent these past hours.

Cari paged through the journal, reading about the first allies her father had made—Vauclain House, Grey House—and the subtleties of the negotiations at Dolan and Company. But there was no further mention of the fae that they shared. It seemed her father had got rid of Maeve.

A few words scratched across the page made the act seem easy.

Cari arched her back, as heat stroked her skin again. She craved—tastes, touch, and more.

Had he really shut Maeve out? Could she drive this possession from her life, too?

For the first time ever, Cari didn't believe her father, the man who'd always told her the truth and had taught her to do the same.

And here he was, the great Caspar, the paragon . . . lying to himself.

The Twilight trees drooped, their leaves becoming jewel-toned tears, as Maeve wandered the unending forest, dragging her soul-heavy cloak behind her.

She was giving the Dolan girl's body forever. Cari's neck would not break at the gallows drop. This skin would not be broken by a blade. Her bones would not crumble with time.

Why then wouldn't the girl welcome Maeve when she'd come bearing gifts? Did this age have no hospitality?

The creatures behind Maeve wailed a grievous sound.

How was she to cross, if the Dolan did not bid her come?

Maeve put a finger to her lips and wondered . . .

All her Dolan get were stubborn. They'd been born to rule, and their first subject was always themselves. Cari Dolan was no different.

What did the girl want?

Maeve smiled and the lesser fae laughed once again. Yes. Him.

* * *

Enough. He was tired.

Mason knew that Cari's business was none of his, but if there was a fae bothering her, prowling around Dolan House, then he should check it out. Not knowing was dangerous, plus, he wanted his sleep.

Shadow hummed in his blood almost immediately upon leaving his room. The hum grew electric when he put his hand to the top of the stair's banister. When he hit the main floor, his nerves were screaming Shadow in a mix of pain-pleasure, which wasn't his thing at all. He'd had enough of pain. Now he was a pleasure man all the way.

Damn it, Cari.

Down a wide and high main hallway, a light gleamed from the bottom of a closed double doorway. It was queer, like silver, and dense like water.

He approached, then opened one side. "Cari?"

She turned to face him. Her face was streaked with mascara tears, but her eyes were clouded with Shadow. She pulsed with dark light, her skin glowing with the anti-luminescence of earlier that afternoon. She looked almost fae, though he'd never seen a creature of Twilight. But this Cari was not of this world. A leather-bound journal was clutched in her hands.

"I was just thinking about you." She wavered on her feet, as if drugged. She bit her lip to ruby red, her wide eyes asking for help.

"*I* think it's time to go to bed." What had she been playing at, he wondered?

"I can't sleep." She was standing at a slant, holding on to a table to keep herself from falling. She'd found a new enemy—gravity.

He hadn't thought she could get any worse, but then Cari had always surprised him.

"That makes two of us," he answered, surly.

Since she was obviously high on Shadow, he had to be the reasonable one. He picked her up, and ignored how her soft, sweet body curled into his. It had been a really long time since he'd held a woman. The fact that he was holding this particular woman didn't help matters. He powered up the stairs, grateful that the chugging of his heart fought the direction of his blood.

"Where's your room?" he said low in her ear.

Her mouth moved to his jaw. "Any room."

"I want *your* room." She was not sleeping in his.

She straightened a leg, pointing with her toe. "That way."

Good. He took her down the hall to that door. He tried to turn the knob with his arms full of Cari. Took three tries, increasingly loud in the echoing space. The statue behind him watched. Didn't help his coordination that Cari was doing something to his shirt. "Stop it, Cari." She found his skin—her touch sizzled, sending a current of magic across his chest.

He finally got the door open. Kicked it wide, he was so fed up. As he turned her body so she wouldn't bang her head on the jam, he caught sight of her stepmother. Mage black eyes, like glossy coal. She looked like she wanted to spit. At him.

This was not what it seemed.

"Faster, Mason," Cari whispered.

Apparently it was.

He swept Cari inside, his irritation making him stronger, and slammed the door shut behind him. Cari could correct mistaken assumptions tomorrow. If the stepmother was going to kill him in the meantime, he hoped she'd make it quick and clean.

Tucking Cari in bed was like peeling off a kitten. She was going to have a blister of a headache tomorrow. He covered her with the blankets, warning "stay." But her gaze burned so hot that he didn't trust she would.

And if she got up? Would a male member of her staff say no?

He wasn't going to defend her virtue, regardless of how she'd mocked his—Cari could sleep with whomever she wanted—but he would see to her dignity. The new, mighty Dolan, undone by magic. Careful, controlled Cari would be mortified.

She was sitting up, pulling at the neck of her blouse. She couldn't seem to understand how buttons worked.

Another man might tempt fate and try to "make her more comfortable." He wasn't stupid. He didn't need to see her glowing skin to challenge his willpower. His mind was already stuttering with his response. He'd slept in his clothes many times. So could she.

His attention caught on a side table cluttered with small decorative bottles meant to hold scent. They gleamed in the late night like fat, gaudy jewels, and were stoppered by slivers of moonlight.

They would do just fine.

Mason handled each one, working Shadow with each discovery, his rough fingertips on the crystal planes. He knew Cari watched from the bed. He felt the weight of her interest in the beat of his blood. And when she was just about to sit up again—she'd remembered how to push buttons out of the little holes made for them—he tossed the bottles in the air above her.

She leaned back on her elbows. "Oh!"

He spun the bottles on invisible strings of magic. He'd crafted similar mobiles for Fletcher so many times—with action figures zipping around above his bed. It'd been the only thing that would get Fletcher to actually lie down and stay put long enough to let his body rest. How on Earth did humans manage bedtime for their kids?

Cari settled back, dazzled, watching the jewels spark and spin. "Father gave me those."

Mason felt the loss in her voice; it echoed his own. What a lonely pair they were.

He sat heavily in a chair near the window and watched her from there. The minutes ticked by and the queer light seemed to leave her skin. Her eyelids fluttered, lush curling fans, then dropped.

He watched her for a while after she slept, the shallow rise and fall of her chest, and smiled at his younger self, who would have been on fire to set foot in Cari's room. *No, boy,* he wanted to tell himself. *Not in a million years.*

When he replaced the bottles on her table, he thought that they did suit her. A small, private extravagance, yet deeply personal. He liked how she wasted nothing on herself, not really.

The glow in the room went pink, the sun finally cresting the horizon. So much for sleep. Of course, with the way the stepmother had looked at him, it was probably for the best anyway.

Cari finally found her spine, forced her gaze away from the bright midmorning light coming from the windows in Mason's suite, and looked the man in the eyes. "Thank you for helping me out last night."

She'd waited downstairs for him, but he'd been working in his room all morning. The short table he was using for a desk held an open laptop. A notepad was sketched over with notes in a rough hand. A coffee cup was making a ring on the pages.

"Don't mention it." He'd shaven, his hair still wet and a little wavy from a shower. The man had no finish, no affectation of status; he was unrefined and growing more so with clear signs of wear.

He could've taken advantage. Why hadn't he? The thought was tinged with disappointment.

She shrugged. Stupid vanity. "I haven't had Shadow poisoning since I was fourteen and huffed Shadow to try to spot a fae." That's what it had to be. An extreme version of it, this time brought on by her unexpected inheritance.

His brows drew together quizzically. "Huffed Shadow?"

He didn't know what she was talking about. Why would he? He hadn't grown up in a House and tried all the off-limits stuff with magic. "It's a thing kids do. Huffing Shadow. No? Well, you go down near the wards of a House. The foundation, where Shadow is at its thickest." She'd actually been at the Walkers' with Liv when she'd attempted it. "And then you try to take in as much Shadow as you can, cross over—which, yes, I know is impossible—and thereby attempt to spot a fae."

He looked horrified. "Too much Shadow can kill you."

"Yes, it can. What's the old saying? *Too much Shadow and the flesh weeps.*"

"And this is common?"

She nodded. "I'm pretty sure every kid tries it, sooner or later. I've never *seen* my father so angry. But I was so sick, bleeding, that I was actually relieved to be punished."

Before her eyes, Mason's rough edges frayed just a little more. He had a son in a mage House, and she'd just given him one more cause to worry.

"I've never actually heard of a fatality though."

His jaw flexed.

She wanted to say something that would ease his mind, but couldn't think what. Talking to him was like walking through a mine field. She backed up instead, collected herself.

"About last night. Like I said, I was pretty worn out. But I've slept now"—a whole five hours—"and it won't happen again."

He looked at her a long moment, then said, "Pity," and lifted a comic rakish brow to smolder her way for a second.

Cari smiled, suddenly feeling warm. "The magic with

my bottles—it was charming." Human or not, Mason was constantly surprised.

He shrugged. "A simple trick."

For his help last night—no, for the *way* he'd helped her last night, she made an uncomfortable admission. "I don't think there's anything simple about you."

Mason had worked through the early hours of the morning. He'd called Segue and left a message with Adam for Khan. Adam invited them to stop by and catch Shadowman personally, and Mason had to concede that in-person was the best way to speak to Khan, who did not favor technology.

He'd also spent an hour in the Dolan library. Access was an unexpected treasure. Cari had a true mage library, with the oldest tomes properly cared for in their own cases, and cotton gloves nearby for handling. He was tempted to pore over those first, but he'd gone instead for the contemporary limited edition Shadow Press titles, published about twenty years ago. The indexes of each mentioned progenitor fae, so the books were a good place to get a base knowledge. Plus, they were portable.

Years ago, when he was with Livia, he'd sought out all the resources available to a stray to piece together what he could about magekind. He'd traded favors for information so that he wouldn't be ignorant next to Liv. And when she was in the mood, she'd occasionally throw out a tidbit—a prize to him, nothing to her. In those moments, he felt the difference between them. He, begging for scraps. She, uncomfortable giving them. She'd never liked the difference between them either. But she hadn't been keen on correcting it.

Cari, in comparison, had been generous in the extreme. And here he was, repaying the favor by stealing information from her company.

He hit the program shortcut to the directory he'd set up for

DolanCo's files. Last night, it had filled up nicely with all the files from Cari's laptop. Some had been encrypted but his program had taken care of that already. He'd filtered the directory based on the "membrane" term and had a list of twelve files, all contained in a folder called "Umbra."

He glanced down at his laptop screen to the Discovery Report he was writing for Webb.

People would line up for a vial of pure magic, humans and mages alike, and how fitting that she'd named it Umbra—referring to the particular aptitude of her House. But the membrane they were using was only a partial, and unpredictable, success. So no breakthrough as Webb had hoped, just lots of possibility.

Mason tore a page from the middle of his yellow notepad—where coffee drips had not yet reached. He began to fold, origami-style, a small cup like a scalloped pinecone, open at the top. While he fashioned the shape, he threaded each crease with Shadow, which was left smoking inside the little paper vial when he finished. It was diluted magic, not near the potency of what Dolan was after, but the vial held.

That is, until he set it down, balancing it against the side of his coffee cup, and let go of the paper. Then the Shadow smoked in all directions, unimpeded, through the paper into the air.

Hmmm . . . He wanted his tools. Different materials.

Mason lifted the paper vial again, and Shadow once again swirled into its cup. He was waiting to see how much he could gather, how dark it could get, when his phone rocked a superhero theme.

He knocked over the books in his grab to answer, then forced himself to say calmly, "Hey, my man."

It'd been five days, but it had felt like forever.

"Hi, Dad." Fletcher sounded good. Excited. Didn't miss his dad yet, though Mason was bruised inside. There'd been times when they'd had to be separated for weeks, so a few days' absence shouldn't have hurt, but it did. Badly. Fletcher seemed a world away, starting a new life.

"How's . . . Bran?" Not the question Mason wanted to ask.

Call waiting beeped in, but he ignored it.

He wanted to know how Fletcher had slept, what he'd eaten, if the big house scared him, if Riordan Webb was good to him.

"Bran's good. Tutor says I'm behind for my age, though. Wants me to do catch-up work."

Behind? The kid was brilliant. Fletcher was easily beyond grade level. Mason had made damn sure every year. What had they missed?

"So I asked him if I could have fries with that."

The ache in Mason's chest exploded in a surprised laugh. His eyes watered. The kid was brutal.

"Get it?" Fletcher sounded proud of himself. "CATCH-UP and FRIES."

"Yeah, got it. Smartass." Mason rocked forward, braced elbows on his knees to contain the warmth and hurt that was Fletcher. "You're okay, then." He was okay.

"Yeah. I'm okay. I just don't know like . . . a hundred languages."

So that's what it was. "Two's a good start." English and, thanks to the part-time nanny, Spanish. "Work hard on the other ninety-eight."

Call waiting again. Not now.

A snort. Fletcher sounded so good. "Did you get the bad guys yet?"

"Doing my best. It's a tricky one."

"You need a secret lair. An epic lair."

Still with the "epic" it seemed. Bran's influence.

"I thought we were getting our own plane." It was a long-standing debate. The kid and him, looking up at the stars, discussing the merits of this or that hero paraphernalia.

"Eh. Changed my mind. Lair."

Another *beep beep beep.* Call waiting could just. Damn.
Wait.

Mason figured the switch to lair was a hold-over from the
fun of the fort. "I'll build it in my spare time." Best lair ever.
It'd be ready when Fletcher was all grown up.

"With a built-in secret escape."

"Of course. Who'd make a lair without a secret escape?"

"Because you always need a way out."

Mason's attention caught. Hovered. His heart trembled,
mid-beat. "Do *you* need a way out?"

"Nah. Just saying."

"Fletcher."

"Shit," his son said. "Tutor's back."

"Don't swear." Mason could feel himself aging. What
had Fletcher meant, *a way out*? Had something happened
after all?

"Shoot, I mean. Sorry."

"I'll spank you later." He was a crappy father. The kid talking like that. And what did he mean?

Fletcher laughed, and Mason thought he might finally be
able to locate his soul without any angelic help. Maybe
humans felt it all the time. His was in agony. All he wanted
was Fletcher. In fact, all he'd ever really wanted was Fletcher,
even before the kid existed.

A man's voice in the background. The tutor, Mason
guessed.

"Love you, Dad. Mañana."

"Love you, too, kid."

Mason held the silent phone for a while, his senses numb.
His heart was blasted to pieces.

He encrypted Cari's Umbra file and his Discovery Report
with his own personal key, and prepped a quick e-mail to
Webb. Attached the file. Hit SEND.

Chapter Seven

Cari looked out a front parlor window, across the rolling lawn, and into the sycamore trees that blocked a direct view of the house from the road and its encampment of the magic-obsessed. But she saw nothing. Shock had wiped her senses, even locked out the fae, and all that was left was the *oh, please, no* that had been her first words when she'd taken the call from Kaye Brand. Mason, who was just upstairs, had been unreachable.

Erom Vauclain and his father, Salem Vauclain, were dead.

It would be Erom.

He'd come to see her because she'd let him. He had come to make their union official, as they'd discussed many a time over the past few months. Dolan and Vauclain *Sitting in a tree. K-i-s-s-i-n-g.* Then she'd refused him, surprising even herself.

Scarlet and her stepsisters hadn't said a word when they'd heard. They'd been careful with her, too careful, gazes askance.

And they didn't have to say anything. Cari knew already. This was her fault. She never should've invited him to come. Or should've kept him here after. She was so glad, glad to almost weeping, that she'd slept and was strong enough to keep the rush of Shadow at bay, to push Maeve away, because she had to have herself together to face Francis Vauclain, Erom's brother.

Erom had died because of her. His father, too, the great, near-immortal Salem, whom Erom had joked would never die and give Francis the satisfaction of Vauclain House. Francis must be mad with grief to lose so much so fast. He'd hate Dolan now, and her in particular. And she didn't blame him. Erom had had so much life before him. He'd been so smart, so sharp, so ready to take his own piece of the world, independent from House expectations.

She heard the footsteps of a heavy, long stride. Masculine. And turned to the door.

Mason leaned in, his leather duffle bag in hand. "You ready?"

He didn't look away from her. Didn't let his eyes slide, though he must have known she and Erom had been a couple. All magekind had been expecting an announcement from their Houses.

She nodded, a slight upward jerk of her chin. "I am."

They'd decided not to take his car this time, which had streaked across television screens everywhere and was now very recognizable. He'd drive her Audi, which Mason would have to admit was an acceptable form of transportation. Plus, it had dark glass, so that no one could see inside.

But all he said when he saw the luxury vehicle was, "You depend on the car to do too much."

They'd have to get past the small encampment of humans outside her wards. She was sure news and websites would report that a car had left Dolan House. There was no helping that. Mason would have to lose any daring followers on their way. He'd already assured her that he could.

"I depend on the car to drive," she answered.

"No. You depend on the GPS for directions, instead of reading a map and knowing where you're going. You depend on buttons to roll down the windows and to adjust the mirrors. A button moves the seat. A computer controls the temperature. You have to *ask* the car to do stuff for you instead of telling it what to do."

"And in winter the seats warm up, all by themselves." Cari found herself relaxing. Sparring with Mason made her feel better. Who woulda thought?

He gave her a deadpan look to show her how unimpressed he was—discussion over—and opened the door for her to get in.

When he got in the driver's side, she looked over to see how he fared. She was pleased to see him suited to the silvers of her luxury vehicle. He'd inadvertently dressed for the role— black jeans, black collared shirt, one button undone, his shirt- sleeves rolled up to midarm. He sat as if he owned the car. Or maybe he mastered every vehicle.

When she lifted the wards for them to move out onto the main road, he kept a steady forward creep. The humans banged in rhythm on the hood, roof, trunk, and windows of the car—*No more Sha-dow! No more Sha-dow!*—so loud that Cari winced. Cameras were lifted to show the viewing public they were leaving the property. And sure enough, there was that straight-backed older man, the one who had looked like a prophet, ringing his bell like a preacher calling for an an- gelic intervention. He had a poster this time: *To save the world, you must die!*

Regardless of what the Council wanted, Cari was going to have to make a decision about how to handle the mob. She was gripping her seat long after they left the last human run- ning after them. "You think they'll ever get tired and go away?"

"Will Shadow go away?" Mason shook his head. "I think the crowd will grow in proportion to the fear that people feel for their families and for the future. There will come a time when you won't be able to get out the front gate."

"The Dolan property has another exit." She had staff making sure it was clear.

"They'll find that one too, if they haven't already."

Panic rose, but Cari pushed Maeve down again.

Cari wanted just one voice in her head—her own. She could still hear the chants striking her brain. *No more Shadow!* Her father had warned her that this time was rapidly coming. She had just thought it was the type of "coming" that stayed on the horizon, a threat used to scare kids, never taken seriously.

Mason turned onto Concord Avenue.

As they left the mob behind, Cari forced her thoughts away from home and down the road. One thing at a time. The plague now. She'd been too late for her father, but Erom and Salem had died just yesterday. Francis should've called the Council immediately, but considering all he'd lost, Cari could understand the delay.

She knew the way to Vauclain House by memory, no GPS necessary, thank you. Twenty minutes into Boston, where Vauclain had a gorgeous Victorian brownstone, a turreted four stories of meticulous brick set back from Beacon.

Cari directed Mason to the arched portico at Vauclain House and told him to park there, as Erom had always done when they'd come down to his family's seat. Staff usually took the car on to the garage.

She was tense, anticipating the recriminations she was about to receive. It couldn't be helped now. She'd made a terrible mistake. The best thing that she could do was find the perpetrator of this sickness quickly. The Council would bring him or her to justice.

Cari knew that the Vauclain wards protected the building itself, rather than the property as a whole—such was city life. When staff didn't immediately open the door, she pressed the intercom button to speak. "Cari Dolan and Mason Stray here on Council business."

A moment's silence, then, "The stray stays outside." Francis himself.

Cari looked over at Mason, who was less than stray; he was human.

She pressed the button again. "The Council has designated us as a team, Francis." What was she doing keeping Mason's secret from one of her allies?

"He's Brand's insult in our time of sorrow," Francis answered. "I won't take it."

Cari had felt exactly the same way when Kaye Brand had shown up, uninvited, in her father's office. An unforgivable insult.

Cari turned to Mason. "It might be better if you wait outside."

"I'm going where you do."

Surely he could understand. "The man just lost his father and his brother . . ."

"You're projecting your own grief." His voice was clipped and low. Angry. "Francis Vauclain is the Lord High King of Bastards and his brother Erom was the same. Believe me when I say that when the lovely Cari Dolan comes to call, he will not turn her away. Even if you're with me."

"I'm the reason Erom and his father died." Not so lovely.

"No. The House who poisoned Shadow with this plague is the reason. This time they did magekind a favor."

She scowled, frustrated. Wasn't this hard enough? "Stop. Salem Vauclain was a great man. And Erom and Francis were brothers, highly respected." She wasn't going to add that Erom had always hated Francis.

"Erom and Francis once left me bound to a tree, naked, in the middle of nowhere."

Her stomach turned, suddenly remembering that summer so long ago. It had been a joke, but a mean one. And back then, Mason had been someone to be jealous of. He might not have had a House, but he'd seemed to have everything else.

She could somewhat understand why Erom acted stupid—
he was a teenager—but not Francis, who'd been twenty years
older. She was ashamed herself by association, and wouldn't
compound the insult now.

"Point taken." She turned back to the intercom. "You will
open your wards, or I am leaving you to the Council's dis-
cretion."

A moment passed while she waited for an answer. Then she
stepped back, turned toward the car. She'd make sure the
Council knew of his lack of cooperation. There were too
many dead to use a stray as an excuse to impede catching the
killer. Francis Vauclain would feel the recriminations of
magekind.

Mason stopped her with a hand to her arm. He cocked his
head, as if listening. "There."

He must have seen the question on her face, because he
nodded toward the door. She looked back at Mason, amazed
again. How could a human know such things about Shadow?
The moment a House's wards were lifted?

And just then, the front door opened. Oliver, Vauclain
House butler, stood waiting to escort them inside.

Detective Brian Anderson pretended to select something on
his iPod, but his attention was on the residence of Salem Vauclain, a known mage. And if Brian wasn't mistaken, Cari
Dolan and her male companion from the DolanCo incident,
identity still unknown, had just exited the vehicle in Vauclain's driveway.

Brian noted the time. 11:23 a.m. He radioed in, requesting backup. "Unit Bravo-12 requesting backup at the corner
of Beacon and Dartmouth." These two had a high potential
for trouble.

Pretty day though. Blue sky. Smell of cut grass in the air.
The small park across from the Vauclain property wasn't

good for much. Some elderly folks were sitting on the benches—they looked like long-time sweethearts—feeding the birds. A lady with a young child and a high-end stroller. No joggers or walkers; the park was too small.

But Brian had that restless feeling something bad was going to happen.

It was why he'd become a cop in the first place. His instincts were right way too often, and at least this way he could do something about it. He'd ignored the feeling once, and after that, never again. All the condolences in the world—*but how could you have known?*—didn't count for jack. He *had* known.

Which was why he took a sip of his coffee, long gone cold, and stood to throw the cup away. Glanced down Dartmouth Street. Everything normal. Then glanced the other way. Same.

No one wanted trouble, and mages seemed capable of causing quite a lot, if Cari Dolan's male companion were any measure. That was some crazy shit he'd pulled to get out of the DolanCo compound. Though for what it was worth, Brian thought the use of force was warranted.

Ms. Dolan and her friend had gotten out of harm's way before the mob had had a chance to really grow, get really angry, and her house had been quiet—boring—for days now. They'd done nothing to make the situation any worse, but the hysteria everywhere was heightening. Even his girlfriend jumped at shadows and blamed magic for everything scary.

A lot *had* been scary lately.

He'd seen a bona fide ghost for one. About shit himself. And he'd spent one day on the wraith task force—and had gotten two cracked ribs and three weeks sick leave. But he was still undecided if magic or these mage people—who did skulk around as if they had something to hide—were necessarily to blame for it all. Cari Dolan didn't have so much as a speeding ticket on her record. Her father had been a generous philanthropist. Okay, maybe he gave too much, if that was a crime. And the Vauclain property over there had stayed in the Vauclain family for going on two hundred years. There were no records of their ever disturbing the peace.

Something was happening though. Every nerve in his body was screaming danger. Felt like invisible ants crawling on his skin.

For the first time in a long, long while, he was afraid.

Movement brought his gaze over.

Pedestrian coming into the park. Interesting-looking character—gray, unkempt hair, fair eyes, dirty neck. Six foot. His pants were loose at the knees and his old plaid shirt was dark with sweat stains. He carried a large cardboard sign that read, *The End of the World.*

Brian hoped to hell it wasn't true.

Mason was rarely awed by magic, he couldn't afford to be, but the stained-glass ceiling in the massive foyer of Vauclain House was, in a word, awesome. Or maybe audacious. Figures stretched and arched, some anthropomorphic, some animal, trapped in the vivid glass. They lived, even seemed to move, in a two-dimensional plane of light-imbued color. There was no doubt: Fae existed within the glass.

Cari allowed Francis to kiss her cheek, though Mason could see that she didn't like it. And she did not press her pretty mouth to his face, which Mason found strangely satisfying. Her lips didn't belong anywhere near that SOB.

Francis didn't acknowledge him at all, and that was just fine. Being beneath notice endowed him with a certain kind of freedom and protection. If people couldn't see him or were even more foolish and *chose* not to see him, it was they who were vulnerable. Not him. *By all means, Francis Vauclain, look the other way.*

He followed the two while Cari uttered earnest condolences about Erom.

Seemed the two *had* broken up. Trust Cari to have seen the fool for what he was. She had to have been dating the House before, not the man, and probably out of some sort of misplaced sense of duty. An arranged marriage? Had Caspar put them together? The idea of Erom's hands on Cari . . . Mason shook the thought off; it did cold things to his blood. The material point was that the man was dead. Happily ever after. The end.

"I had the bodies burned immediately," Francis was saying as he led them through the massive entry to a large set of wood-worked doors. "I couldn't risk further contagion. Like you, I am the last of my line. Everywhere either Erom or my father touched has been purified. I'm afraid there's nothing left to examine."

A dog-whistle high vibration came from the glass above. The fae, straining in their glass prison. Made the fine hairs on the back of Mason's neck stand up. Hell of a place to live.

"I'm not actually looking for clues in the here and now," Cari explained.

Francis opened one of the doors and they all entered. The space had been emptied. A beautiful wood floor gleamed golden. Fat moldings lined the pale blue walls, with lighter patches where paintings had hung.

Cari walked to the center of the room. "I'm looking for the antumbra of the mage who created the plague. I waited too long to look at my father's death. The trail was too far gone for me to sense who killed him."

Mason kept back, his stray instincts zinging. He folded his arms across his chest. Concentrated on Francis. Something not right about him.

"And will you tell me what you find?" Francis kept back as well, perhaps still concerned about contagion. He seemed resistant to move further into the room. "My House deserves satisfaction."

"We all do," Cari told him. "But yes, I will tell you who I

find. In a way, our murderer is still here. I just have to look back in time to discover him."

Mason could already feel the Shadow rising within her. Awareness of it rushed him, heat and blood, a dense roil of power. The intensity this time had him clenching his jaw. Cari's draw on darkness was unlimited. He knew that now. She might seem composed and quietly beautiful, but she was undoubtedly raging inside with magic. It drew him, though he fixed every muscle to keep himself from moving toward her.

"What do you mean look back in time?" Francis started forward.

But Mason grabbed hold of him by the arm. He would not approach Cari either.

Francis resisted, yanking forward, but he'd gone soft in his middle age. Mason only released Francis when he stopped fighting.

Cari was all Shadow, her skin gleaming, eyes darkening to black milk—not unlike the all-seeing sightlessness of the voluptuous statue at the heart of her home.

The fae trapped in the glass keened. Mason wanted out of there. Wanted *her* out of there. Something wasn't safe.

Cari's mouth curled downward, so he knew she'd found something.

Her expression flexed in shock, eyes watering, head tipping away as if she didn't want to see, as if something smelled bad, but she had to experience it anyway. When she covered her mouth with her hand, her fingertips were trembling.

Mason wanted to go to her. Stop this. Break her trance.

But he had to watch Francis, whose breath had quickened and face had reddened.

Several long moments passed while she observed what had to be the death throes of Salem and Erom Vauclain, and then she finally lifted her Shadow black gaze and fixed it upon Francis.

"Patricide."

* * *

"But he'd already *been* in the room with Erom for a while before I got there," Francis protested. He took a step back from her, guilty. "He was *already* going to die."

"You don't know if your father was infected or not." Cari strode forward, obliterating the scene that had just sprung to life in her vision. "And I know what I saw."

Children will play, Maeve said in her mind. Indulgent.

The fae had surged within Cari the moment she had reached for Shadow, and now Cari was fighting again to push her back down.

This wasn't a game, Cari told her. *It was murder.*

Cari felt Mason put a hand to her waist, to keep her away from Francis. She had no doubt Mason was ready to step in should the new Vauclain so much as twitch. But she was in no danger.

You're invincible, Maeve whispered.

Quiet, Maeve.

"My father was past his time," Francis argued.

"But not dead yet," Cari shot back.

"Listen." Francis's face hardened. He leaned his forehead into his argument. "They were nothing. Nothing. *I* am the master here. Dolan and Vauclain can *still* unite. Erom was a fool, and I'm too old to care that you're frigid. We are both the heads of our Houses and we both need heirs immediately. You were going to marry a second son; surely you'll take the first."

"You silver-tongued devil," Mason drawled.

Cari would've cracked a smile at Mason, but she was too shocked and revolted by Francis.

A little squeeze and I could burst his heart, Maeve offered.

No, thank you, Cari returned.

Francis must have mistaken her silence as an indication

that she was actually considering his proposal and was about to decline.

"You *owe* me," Francis said.

For Erom's death. Because he'd come to see her when she'd asked. That had to be Vauclain's reasoning. Her fault. Cari braced for the recriminations. *Here they come.*

"You just can't cut Vauclain out of the Umbra project now." He nodded as if he agreed with himself. "You owe me for Erom's work. Umbra is Vauclain's future just as much as it is Dolan's. That's our stake, too."

"The romance of it all," Mason muttered.

Cari did smile this time.

So Francis didn't blame her for Erom's death.

Dark House owes nothing to anyone, Maeve hissed. *This world is yours to begin with. Let me give it to you.*

Francis didn't care about losing Erom. Only Umbra, her father's legacy at DolanCo. Francis had nothing whatsoever to do with it. Erom hadn't been working on behalf of Vauclain House; he'd wanted to split from his family, and work together with her. And now Cari understood why: Francis had waited so long for his father to die, he'd gone crazy.

Time does have a maddening effect, Maeve observed.

"You owe me," Francis said. "And I'll take it before the Council."

Power leapt within Cari. "What do you think I owe?"

Francis licked his lips. "Umbra is worth a fortune, and you know it."

Maeve? Cari called. The fae had been helpful before and had promised so much more.

Yesss?

I need a fortune. Now.

Because there was no way in Shadow's pitch that Francis Vauclain was going to have anything to do with Umbra. She would not condescend to fight his lies before the Council. Maeve had said Cari could have anything she wanted, and so

far the fae had failed miserably at providing. Cari set aside all
her reservations about her fae stalker, the implicit warnings
in her father's journals, the sleepless nights of heat and restlessness. It was about time for Maeve to prove her worth.

Dark girl, my darling, my one and only, a fortune is yours.

Cari could feel the roll of Maeve's pleasure. It rippled
through Cari's blood in an ecstatic shiver so that she squirmed
in her skin at the rush of magic. A gush of darkness coaxed
Cari's empty hands to open and come together, and as soon as
she did, rough, egg-sized stones filled her joined palms. Her
arms shook with the weight of them, fingers splayed to hold
them all.

Mason's expression went from irritated to serious and
wary. He looked at her as if she were a wild tiger.

Okay, so he was concerned, and Cari knew that maybe she
should be too. But this felt too good. Too rich. Sensual
beyond anything she'd ever experienced. Frigid? She wasn't
frigid now.

Large, raw jewels, dusty and crusted with time, were in her
grasp.

Francis's eyes grew huge.

This ought to do it. Payment in full.

"Your fortune." Cari dropped the lot at his feet. They
knocked and rolled on the wood floor. A diamond glimmer of
wealth winked up at him.

Then she stalked past both men like an ancient queen who
owned the world. She strode into the large main entrance,
drawing a potent wake of Shadow behind her like a royal
robe. Faery brothers and sisters cried out above her where
they were trapped in Shadow-leaded glass.

How dare that Francis, that small, fat bug, entrap gods?

"Cari!" a low, male voice shouted.

The human.

She turned, Shadow sweeping behind her, to relish the brilliant blue light of his soul. She heard his heartbeat in her

mind. *Ba-boom, Ba-boom.* Smelled the earthy funk of sweat, iron, and semen. Could almost taste the sweet salt of him.

She'd been wanting him. It'd been so long since she'd had a man and now was as good a time as any. Blood beat between her legs in anticipation. She was alive!

The human grabbed her arm and pulled her toward the door. The fae trapped above screamed with her passage.

Not now, pets.

"What the pitch was that?" he demanded.

Such passion. She laughed and twined an arm around his fine shoulders. Put her mouth to his neck.

"Francis!" the human yelled. "The wards. Now!" Then lower. "Got to get you out of here."

The bug appeared holding a stone. Or maybe the stone was holding him. She couldn't be sure. It could go both ways with greed.

The human dragged her toward the foyer, wrapped his arm around her waist, and pulled her close to his hard body as he opened the door. "Your nose is bleeding," he growled.

She licked her lip. Sweet. Delicious.

The thin veil of Shadow cloaking the place disappeared. What a curious thing.

"Now," the human said and pulled her across the threshold.

Outside, the sky was blue blue blue—a *day* sky—not Twilight black. She tilted her face upward and opened her heart to take the sun inside her, while her entourage screamed at the searing heat.

"What did Francis do to you?" the human demanded when the door slammed shut.

Francis? Oh, the bug. Yes. She sent a flick of Shadow back, heard the crisp shatter of glass, the cry of the fae . . . the scream of the bug as the dark ones took him.

The human looked at her in horror, which was not quite the same as passion—she was about to instruct him thus—but a searing light across the way had her earthly eyes squinting.

Her mood soured as she recognized what had disturbed her. "Angel," she spat.

Patience. Watchfulness. Preparedness. These are required when hunting a cunning rat.

Xavier kept his distance from the Vauclain wards, but took his adversary's measure.

Cari Dolan.

The father, Caspar, had been scorched from the Earth, but the plague had passed over the heir. And of all magekind, she was the *first* that needed to die.

Cari Dolan's death was imperative.

Ignorance is not the same as innocence. Youth is not the same as purity. Blood will out. Dolan House required destruction, or every other effort was lost.

Thus far, she'd been protected by exposure—television crews at her place of business and cameras held by the rabble of humans at her home. This age was too filled with technology to hope for secrecy. He'd had to let her pass by him too many times.

But the time had come. His enduring patience had indeed provided.

Divine light filled Xavier with scorching purpose. The world could not suffer her to live. Not again. Never again. He dropped his sign, proclaiming *The End of the World*, to reach for his spear. He lifted the heavenly weapon, primed his arm, his aim sure, and hurled it toward the witch.

Detective Anderson flew at the vagrant. Where had the fucking yellow spear come from? He hit a wall of strength, as if the old man's body were made of solid rock. Brian's 200 lbs didn't even shift the vagrant's balance; Brian bounced back, hit a park bench cock-eyed—his still-healing ribs screamed.

Wheeling toward the Vauclain property, he watched the spear cut through the air to where Cari Dolan and her companion stood.

And he groaned with relief when the aim faltered.

Mason shoved Cari behind him, heard the dull cough of her body hitting the wards. The dense concentration of Shadow went out of her as a steel-bright spear whizzed by them. It hit the Vauclain wards with a warped tang that all but shattered his teeth.

Cari whimpered at the sound. Her hands gripped him at his sides.

Mason drew his gun and fired, the report barely kicking back to his wrist. His weapon, treated with Shadow, never missed.

But the old man snatched the bullet out of the air with his bare hand and dropped it on the ground beside him.

What had Cari said? *Angel?*

Kaye Brand and Jack Bastian had stopped the hostilities between Shadow and Order. Had something happened? Was this war?

Mason locked eyes with the angel across the street in the small park. He was old and dirty—looked homeless—and yet absolute in his perfection. The way he stared at—or through—him was uncanny.

Mason drew himself up. His gun was a joke, so his best defense—for Cari and himself—was his soul. An angel wouldn't hurt a human. They were bound to *protect* souls, and if Jack Bastian told the truth—though Mason wouldn't put it past him to lie—then this angel wouldn't go through him to get to a mage.

"Your life will be a noble sacrifice. Cari Dolan needs to die." His voice carried effortlessly across the street between them as the angel started forward to finish what he'd started.

Shit. Mason glanced at Cari. Her nose was bleeding. She was half-collapsed against the Vauclain Wards.

He needed a different kind of weapon. Less predictable.

Mason lunged for a man-hole cover on the sidewalk. As soon as he touched it, Shadow pushed through the metal, overcoming and replacing the bonds of the atoms with Mason's will. The bolts holding the cover in place spun at his command, and Mason lifted and flung it in a desperate wind and release.

The thick, metal disk cut through the air, propelled by magic. It hit the side of a speeding car—a red M5—which fishtailed. And hit the back of a Prius, accelerating the vehicle to strike the angel at his hip. He went down. Score.

Mason, chest heaving, backed again to Cari, who'd smeared the blood from her nose across her cheek. Her eyes were still glazed.

And the motherfucker angel was getting up again. The zigzag wreck of the cars slowed him slightly, as did the drivers now opening their car doors.

Mason looked around for more ammo—he hated clean and tidy streets. Saw the spear stuck like a sliver of sun in a bush. Grabbed for it.

He'd held all sorts of things with sharp ends, but never a spear. He made to clutch it with both hands, but the weapon was already morphing in his grip to a slender sword, lighter, easier to wield. Yes, much better for hacking up angels.

The angel in question smiled as he gained the sidewalk. "You must be an emissary of Order for the weapon to change into the required blade of the moment."

Mason raised the sword. "Believe me. I'm not." He didn't like any of the angels he'd met.

"The weapon reveals it to be a foregone conclusion," the angel said. "You will be angelic. Perhaps momentarily."

The angel's arm licked out, but Mason's stray instincts had him already dropping to evade. He swiped simultaneously.

The angel dodged, but not before being slashed along his side. Scarlet bled into his rent shirt. Mason rolled back up, but the angel's reflexes were superhuman. He got there first, jabbing Mason in the back so that he went down again, vulnerable, on all fours.

Then the angel lunged toward Cari.

But not before someone else got in the way.

"On the ground!" a man shouted, gun drawn and pointed at the angel.

Mason grabbed a breath and spun to his feet. He hadn't even noticed the other man's approach. Seemed like a plainclothes cop.

Another cop, backup, appeared and braced himself opposite. "Let me see your hands!"

A third joined them, gun ready. But this one looked over at Mason, his eyes blazing with terrible white light, so Mason knew him for an angel, too.

Brand and Bastian's peace must have failed.

"The peace holds," the angel police officer said. "He must be rogue. I do not know him."

The other cops looked confused. Well, so was Mason.

"I'm no rogue," the old angel replied. "I am What Must Be."

"He's mad," the angel police officer said. "Run, Mason Stray. Get the Dolan warded. Run while you can."

Chapter Eight

Specifics were foggy, but Cari was almost positive she'd been collected again in the strong arms of Mason Stray. *Up to the bedroom, please,* she thought. *Let's try this again.* His steps jarred this time, but his pulse seemed just as fast. The blue sky—weirdly out of place—bumped overhead. Her muzzy head was on his shoulder—he smelled good, and she liked being close enough to know it.

"Can you stand, Cari?"

Maybe. But she didn't want to. In his arms was a good place to be. He was solid and made her forget all the scary stuff that she had to deal with as the Dolan . . . A flicker of a vision recalled the bolt of lightning that had just skimmed by her shoulder. Her ears were still ringing from it. Hallucination. Had to be.

But they *had* been at Vauclain House.

"Cari Dolan, I need you to stand so I can break into this car."

Ugh. Okay. She lifted her head. Dizzy. She swallowed to wet her dry throat. Maybe she'd caught the mage plague again. Was she going to die this time?

Mason was already putting her on her feet. When she listed immediately to the side, she grabbed the trunk of a car for support. Held herself upright. Glanced around and took a full breath.

He sure loved piece of shit cars. This one was even older than his other, and an eyesore to boot. It was painted orange and had garish hippie stickers all over the back. The yellow smiley face blaring at her was particularly annoying.

"What's wrong with my car?" She touched her nose, which felt slightly crusty. Came back with a congealing dab of blood.

Oh . . . Vauclain House . . . Maeve . . . all that Shadow. *Too much and the flesh will weep.*

That time as a kid when she'd huffed Shadow—her nose had bled until her father had stopped yelling and had gone down on his knees to apply pressure himself.

Pitch. She was going to have to be more careful. There was a reason her father had refused the fae.

Mason put his fingers through the space above the car's driver-side window to force it down. The owner must have left it cracked so the car wouldn't get too hot. "Your car? Not enough time to retrieve it, princess. We need to get you home now."

She liked it when he called her princess, even though he didn't mean it as a compliment. The gruff roll of his voice felt good. She wanted to crawl up in that sound and sleep for a hundred years.

"And this is easy to steal." He had the door open, threw the sword inside, and leaned over to unlock the passenger side.

Her mind cleared enough to remember the source of the ongoing *twang* in her head. Why had an angel attacked her? She was too dizzy to recall the provocation. Or what had happened right before . . .

Maeve?

Silence.

Mason moved to support her once again.

"I'm fine." She waved him away, but he followed her

around the car anyway. He shut her inside. The vehicle smelled like dusty, dank carpet; the owner should have left the windows down all the way. Mason ran around the front. He put a hand to the hood. The engine turned, then rumbled to life.

Mason and his cars. He liked machines he could boss around. He mastered things to use them; they did not master him. It was a compelling idea—mastery. Her father would've approved, both intellectually and in practice. Her father might've actually liked Mason.

"What happened at Vauclain House?" he demanded. He was out of breath. Checking the mirrors as if someone were following.

This was easy to answer, and a little satisfying considering Mason's connections. Cari decided she'd be angry just as soon as she had the energy to be. "I believe an angel threw a spear at me." Not a hallucination, but her memory did get foggy after that. Nevertheless, she was going to report what had happened to Kaye Brand at the first opportunity. Her angel lover wasn't keeping up his part of the truce between Order and Shadow.

"Yeah, I think I got that much." The car turned onto Mass Ave. "I meant, what happened inside Vauclain House? You went batshit crazy on me."

Oh. "I used too much Shadow again." She'd simply had to ask, and the fae had given her great big jewels. A fortune that easily—not that jewels would matter in the time to come. Who cared about diamonds when they needed bread? But maybe Maeve could give that, too. Cari had been trying to push Maeve away, but maybe that was the wrong thing to do. It wasn't working anyway.

Wait. Had Mason just *brawled* with someone out in front of Vauclain House?

"That's not all." He was angry. "You were totally out of it. You *came on* to me."

Yes. He'd brawled with someone—that angel . . . the street prophet?—to protect her.

"I don't know what happened," she said. A lie, because she was starting to remember.

His scowl deepened, as if he were mad at the road in front of him. He shot her a look. "Cari, I *know* you. I've studied you. Your umbra has always been steady and true. But you are different now. Tell me why."

Why? "My father died."

"And?"

And she missed him. She missed him so bad. Felt like he'd abandoned her.

"Cari, answer me."

Fine. She sat up a little straighter. Chose her words. Tried to avoid the emotional landmines. "All this extra Shadow"— she would not name Maeve—"is part of my inheritance. I just have to figure out how to manage it." How to manage the fae, in particular. It was the mastery question again.

"Is that why you wanted me to look into the faelore about Dolan House?"

"Yes. I want to understand the nature of this power."

"Shadow's pitch, Cari—you went *way* overboard with those rocks. Since when are *you* manipulated into doing something out of anger? You always had a cool head."

"Not always." Take their history, for example. She'd been furious and crushed when she'd found out that Liv was pregnant with Mason's child, though it had been weeks after they'd broken up. But after he'd done that lean-in thing, so close she could feel his body heat, the way he'd contemplated her mouth, and then had never followed through . . .

"Was it worth it?" he demanded. "What did you see at Vauclain House?"

He meant the source of the plague. "Nothing." Failure again.

"You said Francis killed his father."

"Yes, absolutely. He left his father with Erom, who was dying. His father caught the plague and died as well, which made Francis head of his household."

"And his glass ceiling. The fae trapped in it? You did something . . . ?" Mason was looking at her as if she should know what he was talking about.

The bug . . . Francis had seemed like a blood-fat tick . . . a lash of Shadow to break the glass.

Had *she* done that?

Cold frosted up her spine.

No. She had not. Maeve again. "That wasn't me."

"It came from you."

She didn't answer. How could she? She remembered her father's journal entry; the situation was similar: *Was this justice? I don't like being used.*

She agreed with him.

Mason exited on to I-90. "You got no sense of the person behind the mage plague?"

She laid her head back, disappointed herself. "No. Just raw Shadow, the same as with my father's death."

"Raw Shadow how?"

She tried to think about how or what it felt like, and came back to Mason in her mind. Mason, always him, mage, stray, or human. He'd fought for her today. "Raw Shadow like yours."

Xavier held open the palms of his hands, red with blood, stained with soul. These human lives—police officers, peacekeepers—were on the Dolan's head, not his. That the Mad Queen would hide behind souls revealed her to be the blight on the world that he'd always known. He remembered what she was capable of. This was just the beginning. The world would run red.

He wailed to the sky, begging for grace. But the sky was silent, as it had been for so long.

He knew what that meant: he must persevere.

Maeve shivered with joy. Her daughter was perfection, a monarch emerging from a chrysalis. The girl took her own time, but Maeve would grant her that. Another gift. Time was so difficult to manage anyway; *then* and *now* such prickly flowers. Cari's flesh needed to be still stronger to bear the power, as a ruler does her mantle.

The immortal do not wither, do not die.

The world would be theirs.

"That's right, an angel," Mason told Webb over the phone as he paced a small lane between some two-story brick cottages on the Dolan property.

There was no reason to hide the call—after all, his son now lived with Webb—but Mason still found himself looking left-right to see if anyone might overhear. The Dolan clan had stayed out of Cari's general domain, but everywhere else, family was stashed pending the resolution of the plague investigation. He hadn't seen many children though, or maybe their parents kept them away from the dangerous stray.

Cari was inside the main house sleeping. He'd gotten them past the entrenched humans outside the compound, though they'd again shouted at the windows and pounded on the hood until Cari lifted the wards for the car. Since this car didn't have tinted windows, Mason made certain that all of the photos and film taken would come out Shadow black. There were enough images of them circulating already.

Her stepsisters and mother had looked at him with acute loathing to see the smear of blood on Cari's face and the waxy gray of her pallor. No sparkle from the sisters *this* time, unless the daggers in their eyes caught the light. If Cari hadn't been lucid enough to say "not his fault" he'd be under lock and key. But he wouldn't put it past them to have him watched.

Behind the main house, he paced back the other direction, facing rolling lawn.

"And this angel came after the Dolan?" Webb asked. "Her specifically?"

With one hell of a weapon, now Mason's.

He drew breath to answer, but Webb beat him. "Of course he would. Why bother with a stray?"

That wasn't exactly it, but Mason wasn't about to say that the angel wouldn't hurt a *human*. Who knew if the angel would go after a stray? That was the reason Mason had called Webb in the first place: so that Webb would not be complacent about Fletcher's safety, not around the Order. The kid might not be born to a House, but he was a full mage.

"The truce is ended," Webb concluded.

Mason bowed his head, kicking a stone across the pavement. "Not necessarily. Brand says that the angel was rogue and that the Order is hunting him as we speak."

"Rogue. An unlikely excuse." Webb dismissed it out of hand. "Has the Dolan made any progress toward finding the House that caused the plague?"

"Nothing certain." Mason didn't mention Cari's "inheritance." Webb already had enough information to potentially screw her with the DolanCo Umbra project. "But I'll contact you immediately when we have something."

She'd said that the Shadow was raw.

Mason shook his head. No, she'd said the Shadow was raw . . . like *his* Shadow.

Because he didn't have an umbra?

Maybe the source of the plague didn't have an umbra either. Maybe the source had a soul. What if they were really hunting someone like himself? And if that were the case, how would he go about it?

Set a trap. Lie in wait. Make the perpetrator come to him.

"I'd like to talk to Fletcher." The one he really wanted to warn, though he had no words for what to say to a kid. Don't trust anyone? He couldn't teach him that.

He just wanted to hear Fletcher's voice; he'd know everything he needed to by the "Hi, Dad."

"The boys are out back playing soccer."

"Out back" at Mason's properties would've only required a yell.

Disappointment knifed him. "Tell him I called." Earlier Fletcher had seemed okay. Except for that moment when he'd said that their lair needed a secret way out. *You always need a way out.*

"I'll do that." Webb summarily cut the line.

There was nothing worse than uncertainty.

And Webb, a father himself, would know this, too.

Mastery. Cari needed it *now*. Word was that the angel was rogue and that he would be apprehended by the Order soon. Not good enough. Without Mason, she would've been vulnerable, made so by the fae within her.

She sat on the end of her bed, post shower, wrapped in a robe and grappling with life. She'd recovered much more quickly than she'd expected. One deep sleep, a good meal, and she could take on Francis Vauclain again. That is, if he still lived. Take on that angel, too.

Fact of life: everything was different. Her father had told her that becoming head of the household would set her apart. She'd anticipated friction over authority with some of her family members. Relationships might grow thin, but they would be made new eventually.

And there was the endless work of her House, the responsibility of turning over the Dolan legacy to the next generation.

But "set apart" had a whole new meaning now.

Her skin felt golden, as if the precious metal had mixed with her blood, turning Shadow into a rare alloy. It was armor and beauty, a kind of forever feeling. She was becoming something, but what that was, she had no idea. "Stronger" barely scratched the surface of what she felt.

She had to figure out what was to be done next.

She'd tried to *deny* Maeve, with mixed, ultimately unacceptable results. Exhaustion and weakness, leading to a lack of control. That state wasn't going to work, unless Mason was there every night to put her to bed. She suppressed a smile at the thought.

And she'd *used* Maeve, with mixed results as well, also unacceptable. Great power, but with yet another loss of control—the jewels, breaking that glass ceiling, putting her mouth on Mason, the common denominator.

She shook him out of her head to concentrate on what mattered.

Survival meant mastering the fae. And with this gold pumping through her body, she thought she might just make some headway.

She needed to find her limits, so that magic didn't cost her body strength. *Too much Shadow and the flesh will weep.* The maxim was short one word: *Too much Shadow and the flesh will weep* blood.

She didn't attempt to draw on Shadow, as she'd had to do most of her life. She didn't employ any effort, as she'd had to in the past.

She relaxed into herself and inhaled the perfumed, humid air that had trailed her from her bathroom. The muted tones of her bedroom shifted through the visual spectrum to a palette of ultra-color. In her mind's eye, the walls became immaterial and she could sense and identify each of her family members scattered as they were throughout the house and grounds. Scarlet, Zel, and Stacia were in her stepmother's bedroom.

She sought out the staff and other members of her family, constellations of starry magic in the varied field of Shadow.

But where was Mason? Could she *see* him, too? The human who wielded magic?

She sought him throughout her property. She knew he had a soul, but figured that she'd be able to pinpoint his concentration of Shadow. She searched for him, but discovered that her House had many random concentrations of Shadow—the stuff pooled in corners and sucked into closets. And within the wooded area along the boundary of her wards? Magic black as pitch.

But no Mason.

She pulled gently for more power—not so much that she might hurt herself again or that Maeve might stir—but just enough to discover whether or not her sight could perceive a soul. It was an interesting question. She turned her sight to her property again.

Nothing. She released the Shadow, irritated.

Someone knocked at her door. *Ugh.* She became more so to be interrupted right now.

Then she stood, abruptly. And smiled triumph.

Someone was at her door, and she couldn't see who it was. But she knew anyway. "Yes?"

The door opened. Mason stepped over the threshold. "What the hell are you doing now?"

Funny he should ask. "I was looking for you."

As soon as she'd answered, he wanted to step right back outside Cari's bedroom and close the door. He should respect her privacy and ignore his awareness of magic condensing into frightening potency.

He wanted to step back out, but he'd frozen, dumbfounded.

It was pure idiocy for him to come here. A stray had to be smarter, more mindful of self preservation.

Cari Dolan, pretty Cari Dolan, stood before him like a goddess. There was none of the girl he remembered, only woman. In the mid-morning of her room, she gleamed with a heart-breaking radiance. She wore a silver silk robe, which plunged into a long skinny vee, stopped at the loose tie of her belt. Obviously naked underneath, her skin was dewy from a recent shower—the fragrant humidity still hung in the air— and her hair was slicked back. Her huge black eyes were smug and smiling.

He shook his head. Dropped his gaze to the wood floor. Climbed his thoughts over his suddenly raging reaction. "What did you want?"

What *he* wanted went against the most bitter lesson he'd ever learned in his life. And he'd learned more than a few. He wanted Cari. He wanted to touch her, to breathe her in, to fill her up with himself. When had the house gotten so damn hot?

"Mason?"

Why couldn't he move? Was she working her magic on him?

Stupid question from a stupid man. Cari didn't need magic to work him over.

"Mason."

He dragged his gaze back up to answer whatever question she had. And then he'd get out of here. Fast and far. House women, and she was the worst.

He'd sworn to himself never again.

But she saw what she wanted in his expression. Her eyes widened, just a little bit. Her head tilted slightly, so that a wet curl slipped down to her forehead. Her smile morphed from smug to . . . shy? happy? sweet? and sexy all at once.

He might as well be nineteen again.

If she'd realized her power over him, acted the seductress, he could've easily left her alone. He'd had enough of that. But she was *Cari*. It took every iota of will to back the hell out the way he'd come, into the hallway. He sent Shadow reaching through her doorknob to turn the bolt mechanism. Not that he

couldn't open it again, but at least it was one more deterrent
in his way. When the lock snicked into place, he stepped back.
But not before he heard her low, throaty laugh. It was her
secret laugh, the same she'd had years ago when she used to
make wry observations under her breath to him about this or
that mage. But he didn't think she was making fun of him
right now. More like sharing the joke, which made his arousal
worse, but he couldn't help joining her with a smile at the
closed door.

"Did you need something?"

He startled and turned to find the redhead, Stacia, arms
crossed and hating him. Her flirtatious simper from yesterday
was so far gone, he couldn't even believe it'd ever happened.

He lifted his hands in surrender. "Nope. Just checking
on her."

"FYI, she's fine."

FYI, she's more than fine. Dangerously, so. But Mason just
nodded and walked away.

Takum Blake walked out into the dusty farm fields of his
property. He crushed crickets with every step. Drying husks
let up gasps of dust as they crackled under his boots. The
dust had gotten into his lungs and left him with a hacking
cough. The farmhouse behind him screeched with its imped-
ing fall. He held it upright with the Shadow in the ward
stones.

Lorelei, his firstborn, turned her head toward him at his
approach, but she didn't turn around. She'd been almost completely silent in the year since Ferrol Grey's defeat by Kaye
Brand and the subsequent shift of the Council. Lori had been
bold and brave, which had gone against her usually quiet
nature. The failure to capture Brand wasn't hers. Grey had
made mistakes, in spite of his careful planning, and Brand
had had secret, powerful friends. Angels.

But for Lori's part in the debacle, she'd been shunned by magekind. Even her husband had left her, left the children behind. No one liked a Lure, and the Blakes understood why. With a touch, they could override any mage's will and supplant it with their own. Lori had touched Brand, had forced the fire mage back into Ferrol Grey's grasp. Few Houses had called them friend, until Grey. And now, only the one . . . A single friendly House remained.

Who had called with this terrible idea. A last chance.

Farm life suited the Blakes, suited Takum anyway. He found the land's restless quiet a reprieve from the suspicious looks other mages sent toward his family. But his home wouldn't last. It was dying with him, and he knew it. His heart had slowly turned to stone. It was used up.

"Comandra is driving me crazy." Lori put her hand to her skull as if to dispel the effects.

He remembered when he was a parent of teenagers. "Sixteen is a difficult age."

Lori swatted at a bug near her ear. "She says she has no life."

"I heard." The whole house had rattled with the girl's shouts and slams.

"She's right, though. There's no life for her. No life for her brother either, when he gets old enough to think about it."

Takum closed his eyes. His daughter was unknowingly arguing in favor of the plan, though she didn't know it would cost her life.

Lori was as good as dead to Kaye Brand, and therefore the Council. No, Lori was as good as dead to magekind. She'd done the worst: she'd betrayed one of her own kind. If the Blakes had had any honor, she'd spent it.

Takum put his hands in his pockets to stop himself from reaching out and stroking her hair, his errant girl. "I've had word about the plague."

Her shoulders turned, eyes wide for news.

"The Council has asked Cari Dolan and Mason Stray to discover the House that initiated the sickness."

"They don't think it was us!"

"That would be convenient for them, but no. Salem and Erom Vauclain died and they went to Vauclain House to investigate."

Lori's gaze didn't waver. "Did they find out who?"

Takum reported what he'd been told. "Apparently Francis had cleaned up the bodies, fearing further contagion for his household."

"Oh." She waited again. It seemed like she'd been waiting all this last year. He'd been waiting with her, patient.

And here they were at the end. It had come with an opportunity, which had not been expected.

"Dolan and Stray will investigate the next death," he said. "The body is to be left in place. The House affected is to let them through their wards so that they can search for the culprit's antumbra."

Something moved in Lori's eyes. She was his daughter, after all. She would come to his conclusions.

Her head tilted with the weight of his plan. "Cari Dolan will enter the wards of *any* House affected by the plague?"

Dolan House was wealthy, respected, solidly built. A touch on *Cari's* will might be just the thing to restore the Blake Farm, with Dolan as its (unwilling) patron. Plus, magekind would owe Blake their thanks and condolences for helping identify the plague dealer. And the blot on their House that was Lori's interference would be removed, perhaps in time forgotten.

"As always, you and I think alike. You know how this might be our House's last chance to recover. You know why we need to recover in the first place. And you know who should take responsibility."

Lori's mouth opened, but she didn't speak. She'd just been

dealt a killing blow. She'd expected a violent, fiery reprisal from Brand, not a strike from her father.

"I will hire a human driver to take you away from here and see that you get back home in time to die here. And I'll help Comandra take your place as heir. It might make her a little less . . . crazy."

Lori straightened, giving him her back once again. "And if I refuse?" Breathless.

The house was falling down, the fields barren. This was a last-ditch effort.

"Then this chance falls to Comandra, by force, if need be."

Chapter Nine

Riordan Webb returned to his office after taking a call. Bran and Fletcher scurried like small animals away from their play at his desk. Seemed they had been using his chair to spin as fast as they could without throwing up. As his papers and computer seemed untouched, he was not going to begin by getting them in trouble. They had each taken their seats—stationary ones, thank Shadow—within an impressive three seconds.

Riordan first assessed the attention of the stray boy, Fletcher. The child managed to sit perfectly still, his gaze fixed on Riordan's face, as if prepared to listen to every word. In many ways, the stray was a good example for Bran. Mason had done well to teach Fletcher his place, and with it, some self-control. Bran was swinging his feet and had wiped his nose on his sleeve.

"A House is more than your name," Riordan began. "It's who you are."

Fletcher had to learn this to, as Webb was now his House. He was a clever boy, given to mischief, but respectful. He didn't collapse on furniture saying how bored he was. Bran was already leaning sideways.

Yes, the pair would do very nicely, would become almost

brothers. Which was fine, even if Fletcher was a stray. Bran
would need someone loyal to do unpleasant business, and he
would reciprocate with acceptance and love and welcome.
There was no risk here of jealousy over birthright, as was
often the case with brothers. Fletcher was now positioned
better than any stray had a right to hope. If he needed occa-
sional reminding later, so be it.

"The House is our mage immortality. Its strength is our
legacy to future generations."

Bran had made a mustache out of Shadow. He lolled his
head over at Fletcher, who shook his head at him. No.

Good boy. Riordan tried not to smile at the child and anger
Bran. He wanted the boys to continue as friends, not rivals.
They would share everything. Riordan already liked Fletcher
and could see himself becoming quite affectionate toward the
boy. Really, Brand's fosterage idea was excellent.

And the association with Mason was proving very beneficial—
just as Riordan had expected. Dolan's Umbra project was
compelling, to say the least. Now, if it would just work.

Yes, Riordan would do right by Mason's son. He'd raise
him strong and give him a place. Bran had been lonely too
long. This business would be good for all.

"Each House has its aptitude with Shadow. The Webbs
have long been storytellers." This was the simplistic version
of what they could do, meant for Fletcher. The Webbs could
tell stories. Bran did so all the time with his shadow play. And
when he was older, he'd be taught to tell stories about real
people and real events, and in so doing, influence how those
people acted and how the events played out. It was a subtle
art, but a persuasive one.

Bran sat up. "What's Fletcher's aptitude?"

Fletcher colored.

The poor boy was embarrassed.

Riordan was certain the stray had magic. But what form his
practice would take was yet to be determined. They would try

some things and see. Mason was supposed to be a superior craftsman. It made sense that his son would follow suit.

Riordan leaned down to Fletcher. "What can you do?"

Fletcher's breathing quickened. No need to be anxious.

"I can sense Shadow," he offered.

Webb smiled to help him along. "What do you mean?"

"I can tell when a mage is near. Without looking. I can feel magic."

Interesting. Might explain Mason's stealth. "And your father can do this too?"

A sense of misery from the child, even though they were all allies. But he finally nodded. Good kid. Really. And his aptitude could be useful, especially to Bran in the dark times ahead. Riordan could instantly imagine situations when Bran might need to know that there was another mage near. Fletcher could watch his back.

Riordan stood upright again. A rush of warmth in his chest made him pat Fletcher's head.

Yes, this was going to work very nicely.

Stealth went for his mobile phone right away. He'd hidden it underneath his bathroom sink, inside a toilet paper roll, every day a different place. He was on a mission, and communication was critical. Mr. Webb's desk had been very interesting, and the old man hadn't suspected a thing. Stealth couldn't make a call because he was supposed to be peeing, but he typed a quick text to his dad: *The Lures are on the move.*

He felt bad that he'd had to tell one of his dad's secrets—about sensing Shadow—but he hadn't been able to think of a way out. At least he had one of Webb's secrets in return.

He deleted the sent text from the phone's memory, just in case, and replaced it back under the sink. He needed a cool theme song, not a lecture on what a House was, how a House was strength, how a House was who you are.

A House was family, and that meant his dad. No one else.

Mason stared down at the text from his son. A Lure? As in from Blake House?

What had a Lure to do with anything? Except maybe that they were as friendless as strays. Did Fletcher think to befriend a Lure? Because the Blakes were outcast for good reason. A simple touch and their will would override any other mage's. It had almost cost Kaye Brand her life.

Would the Blakes stoop to using a child? Mason's heart *boom-boomed* at the thought.

Not his child. Not Fletcher. Where the fuck was Webb? Wasn't the fosterage agreement supposed to protect Fletcher?

Mason called Fletcher, but his son didn't pick up—a bad sign—so he debated who to call next: Webb himself, and let him have it. Or Brand, to have her remove Fletcher at once and to dissolve the fosterage agreement. She, of all people, wouldn't let anyone else, especially a child, be lost to the influence of a Lure.

Mason braced a hand on the wall to think it out. Webb or Brand? Fletcher might need help now, so Webb. But Mason had been having a bad feeling—*everyone needs a way out*, echoed in his mind—about Webb since almost the beginning. Build a case against him? Or trust Webb as a father to keep Fletcher safe?

Mason lowered himself to rest his forehead on the wall. Why had he agreed to the fosterage in the first place?

No, he knew the answer, and it was a good one. Fletcher needed wards. Riordan had them. And he had a kid Fletcher's age.

Mason couldn't trust his *own* motives here. He missed the kid so badly that he'd do anything to get him back.

Anything . . . but endanger him. Mason breathed in. Let it out slowly.

He should take this up with Riordan first. If Fletcher could be safe at Webb House, could have a good life, then he should stay there, or all of this was for nothing.

Mason queued up his contact list on his phone to search for Riordan, but a call came up first on the screen. Jack Bastian.

He almost didn't take it for fear that a Lure was right then, at that moment, about to touch Fletcher. But he picked up the angel's call anyway.

"Yeah?" As in, cut to the chase.

Jack obliged. "There's been another death. Plague. And it's a tricky one. Blake House."

"I'm sorry, what?" He didn't catch the name.

"Blake," the angel said.

"The Lures?" Mason's brain wasn't working. Fletcher had just texted him about the Lures. It had been Fletcher, hadn't it?

Mason checked his text log while Jack kept talking.

Yes. The text had come from Special Agent Taco Sauce, aka Fletcher. *The Lures are on the move.*

What the fuck did that mean? And would it have killed Fletcher to do without the spy crap for one minute? Did he know what he was doing to his father?

Jack kept talking, but Mason sent a text back to the kid. *Explain, please. Right now.*

He lifted the phone back to his ear. Interrupted. "I didn't catch any of that. I was distracted."

A pause from Jack. "Is something wrong?"

"I hope not." Mason squeezed the back of his neck to stop the tension from pounding in his head. "I might have to go in a sec. Can you bullet-point it for me?"

"Okay. Lorelei Blake has died of the mage plague. Takum Blake is demanding that the Council treat his loss the same as they are treating every other House's."

Mason checked for a text. Nothing. Fletcher was a handful, but he usually minded him. A week in another household did not undo eight years of semi-good behavior.

His jaw was tensing up. How did Fletcher even know about the Lures? Mason had never discussed them. What was he learning over there?

"Kaye is right now asking if Cari will go to Blake House as she did Vauclain and investigate the death on behalf of the Council. Regardless of Kaye's history with Lorelei, as High Seat, Kaye can't pick and choose which Houses she will serve and which she won't."

Mason already knew Cari's answer. "Cari will say yes so that she can find out who killed her father."

The Lures are on the move.

This wasn't a coincidence. This was a warning. From his eight-year-old son, who was most likely, almost certainly, still safe inside Webb's wards. He'd just heard or seen something to do with plague, their investigation of it, and the Blakes.

His kid was on to something.

"What's the matter, Mason?" Jack had his tired angel on, and he was too far away to read Mason's mind.

"I think the Blakes will try to overcome Cari."

Otherwise, how could Fletcher possibly know that a Blake had fallen victim to the mage plague, and that it would have anything to do with his father? That he would need a warning?

"And you know this how?"

Mason wasn't quite ready to condemn Webb without thinking about the repercussions for Fletcher's safety. "Instinct."

"Well, have your instincts keep Kaye informed. Call me back when you work out the details with Cari."

The line went dead, but Mason was still working. The only explanation he could figure was that Webb and Blake were somehow connected, and Fletcher had found out about it. And Webb had already demonstrated an interest in DolanCo's work. Which Fletcher would only be able to discover if he were snooping where he shouldn't.

Webb and Blake were colluding.

This was a trap for Cari. A wild gamble for Webb via Blake to control the great Dolan House.

Mason texted the kid back: *Nevermind. I get it.*

He wasn't going to discourage future behavior via text. Their next call, however, would be very serious. The whole point of Fletcher being at Webb's was that his son would be safe. And meddling in Riordan's business would do the opposite.

The Lures are on the move.

Fletcher sure knew how to age his father. The kid meant it as a warning, and Mason would take it as such. The Lures were going to use their grief to their advantage and touch Cari. Webb had at the very least encouraged them to try.

But none of them knew what they were up against. Cari Dolan was suddenly capable of some very unexpected things. Even with that deranged angel on the loose, Mason's money was on the princess.

Xavier had walked the earth for thousands of years. He'd encountered other angels thousands of times. If he didn't want to be seen, didn't want to be found, he could remove himself from their minds.

Except perhaps from the rare angels who were as old as he.

"I know you're here, friend." Laurence didn't bother to stalk. He stood in the middle of the road, basked in streetlight. A dare.

Xavier wasn't young or foolish enough to take it.

Discovery outside of Vauclain House meant that he'd had to flee rather than pursue and kill Cari Dolan. This wasted time could cost the war. Was this the moment that Shadow overtook Order?

"You've lost your way," Xavier said. He didn't have time to be educating someone who should know better; they both should be hunting the Dolan. What was she doing? Where was she? "Order and Shadow do not belong together."

He'd have to find Mason Stray. Trace him and he'd find the woman, though it would be more difficult now that Mason had learned, probably had been instructed, to conceal his soul.

"The Earth is dying." Laurence faced into the darkness. "She needs Shadow again."

"Shadow *is* death! You've forgotten."

Laurence smiled to the night. "I haven't forgotten *you.*"

Cari watched Mason check his phone for a text for the tenth time in the last half hour. "It's not safe to text and drive."

A helicopter had taken them from the Dolan property—first time she'd released the wards upward, to the sky—to New Haven, where a car had been waiting. An old Camaro, typical of Mason, but she understood his reasoning a little better now. Apparently there had been three other landing sites and cars waiting, the choice made only after they were in the air. These were the precautions to avoid the notice of the rogue angel.

Mason put his phone back on his lap, looking grim. "Sorry. I'm waiting for a message from Fletcher."

So that's what it was, or who. His son was on his mind. The worry was evident in the set of Mason's jaw and the long silences during their journey.

"Was he exposed?" The immediate concern of every mage these days.

Mason looked over, surprised. "No. Not since the May Fair, anyway. It's just the transition has been a little hard on him. He should be fine."

Cari didn't like the phrasing "should be," but it wasn't her place to ask more. She wanted to though—Mason as a father captured her attention in strange ways. She wondered what he was like with Fletcher—she had felt echoes of it in how he'd treated her and wanted to see the real thing with her own eyes. Giving up his son had to have been difficult. Something about Mason was stricken, and it made her hurt, too.

He drove within a few miles per hour of the speed limit, so as not to draw attention. From I-71 to Route 146. And off an exit into what seemed like an oblivion of flat countryside. The summer wind gusted, and a massive cloud of thin, parched dust rolled across the used-up land. Any car out on these farm roads would attract attention. The farmhouses seemed like deserted, hollow shacks. The Blake property was by far the largest, yet still . . . dead.

Mason came to a stop in front of a long drive with a mailbox built into a crumbling brick gateway, though the gate itself was missing.

Cari had heard that Blake House was basically falling down, but that wasn't true. Not yet, at least. To her the place resembled a house of cards. The structure of the farm house itself was all right angles and gabled roof, a rectangular porch jutting out from the front door. But the consistency of the paint-peeling wood and other materials seemed somehow flimsy, disintegrating, unsafe. She couldn't be sure, but she thought that the place was still standing by the power of the Blake ward stones alone. Without magic, the house would fall.

She reached for her bag to get out her phone to alert the House they'd arrived and to release their wards. But Mason— who must've sensed something—was already accelerating down a cracked concrete road toward the House. They both got out of the car. Mason came around in time to shut her door, but his attention was on the building.

That house, she knew, was packed with Lures, and she wanted to get out of it, preferably with him, of her own free will.

He grunted with dislike. "You will stay close to me."

Cari looked over at him, the human daring to boss the Dolan around.

A hint of a smile crinkled the outside corners of his eyes, the fine lines crisscrossing into a strange form of hieroglyphics. They weren't smile lines exactly, or not only. What other powerful expressions had created them? She knew if she studied him, as he'd said he'd studied her, she might read the story of his life. She didn't know if she could bear what she'd learn, though.

The thought was more dangerous than any Lure. So she regarded the house again.

"If you feel uncomfortable," he said, "no one would blame you for backing out. You have a House to think of."

"I'm not worried."

His cowboy smile flashed in her peripheral vision. "Well, *I'm* worried."

She laughed. "I won't let the Blakes get you."

"I'm not afraid of the Blakes." He put a hand to her lower back to start them forward, a casual touch. But the Lures knew how potent a casual touch could be. From the point of contact, warm glitter diffused throughout her system.

She wanted him. Fine. She admitted it. She was tight with wanting inside of her—a rare feeling in her experience. She'd wanted him for almost a decade.

Then take him.

Cari nodded to Maeve, though the fae couldn't see her. *I think I will.* She would not live with this wanting-and-not-knowing any longer. Eventually she would have to marry, and she did not want Mason in her fantasies when she did.

They approached the pathway to the house together. When they came to the front porch's steps, Cari looked down with a pang of alarm. The boards were in all the right places, some of them split and crumbling, but it appeared that nothing was actually holding them together. Fun.

The front door opened as she tried her weight on one. Mason moved more quickly, stepping up and putting himself in front of her.

She couldn't see which member of Blake House had come to welcome them, because she was staring at Mason's back. But she could sense the umbras of seven people beyond him, grouped on the main level, on the other side of the house. Two were nearer, one just behind the door.

"You will not approach us," Mason said.

"We only want vengeance for our dead," rasped an elderly voice. "Same as any other House. We want the source of this plague found."

Cari gave Mason a little push to get him to step aside. A Dolan didn't hide.

Mason moved, but just enough for her to follow him up to the porch proper. It had to be Takum Blake before them. He was built squarely, with no excess on him. His eyes had begun to yellow around the black irises. His white hair was sparse, and his umbra was weak. She didn't know yet the limits of her new access to Shadow, but she felt she could predict that this one was going to die soon.

"I'm here to gather what information about the death I can," Cari told him. "Mason Stray is going to assist me."

Takum glanced at Mason with loathing, but managed to twitch a sort of invite.

Good enough. Cari started forward.

But Mason put a backward-facing hand out—touched her belly this time—to hold her back. Every touch seemed to warm her.

"You will go back into the house," he said to Takum, "and we will follow."

Cari found she was a little uneasy about entering, too. Her heart was skipping beats.

The Blake sneered at them and entered his house, leaving the door wide open.

Mason turned back to her and murmured. "I feel Shadow just beyond the threshold, to the left."

"I see it," Cari answered. Then one-upped him. "I think it's a woman."

"All right, then." He let out a dry cough. "I don't feel superfluous."

His wisecrack helped her find a few of her misplaced heartbeats. He could never be superfluous. She knew that now. If something needed to be done, she'd want Mason to do it. Kaye Brand had simply figured that out first.

"It's a good thing you're pretty to look at." She flushed. She obviously didn't know how to flirt. Never had.

He led the way across the porch, glancing back once with a cockeyed smile. "You think I'm pretty?"

Her heartbeat went perfectly even. Mason's secret magic was to make her feel up to any challenge. When they got back to Dolan House she was absolutely going to proposition him. She'd have to think of a better line.

Dingy stairs clambered upward to the far right. An open room was on the left, smallish, which led to another room beyond. The ceilings were lower than she was used to, making the place feel close, and Mason seem extra tall, extra broad of shoulder. The walls had once been a pale, sunshine yellow— happy for a farmland—but had since gone dingy.

What kind of life was it to be born a Lure with an aptitude only to entrap those of their own kind? No one welcomed them. No one wanted them for friends. Could a Blake turn his back on his own House and choose a human life instead? Maybe as a teacher, a lawyer, an artist?

Could she ever turn her back on Dolan House?

Could she deny who or what she was?

No.

So she'd give them as much respect as she had the Vauclains. "Where did Lorelei die?"

Upstairs. Narrow hallway to a bedroom with a sloping

ceiling. None of the Blakes followed, which was simple self-preservation against possible contagion. Cari and Mason were immune. The Blakes would need to find a way to burn the body afterward, hopefully without burning down the rest of the house.

Mason opened the door first, looked inside the bedroom, and sighed. The strain across his forehead told her to prepare herself.

Cari followed him to where the Lure who'd once captured Kaye Brand waited.

Lorelei Blake lay on her bed, her head on her pillow. Her skin was gray with death, not Shadow. Deflated blood blisters were scattered across her visible cheek; an egg-sized mound festered below her ear on her neck. Her eyes were open and dewy with slime. She still wore a shoe, so it appeared that she'd collapsed in bed almost immediately upon arriving in the room. And the smell . . .

Takum had preserved everything for them, but then he wasn't covering up a murder like Francis Vauclain had been.

"Carefully, now," Mason said.

As she had practiced in her bedroom, she did not draw on magic, did not call upon Maeve. She used only what came to her naturally to see. This had to have been how her father had worked: use only what was in the world already.

Shadow cloaked her sight, and the past lurched into the present.

Lorelei's antumbra staggered from behind them this time. Cari whipped around to see the Lure clutch the doorframe to keep herself upright, then trip on the bed where she trembled in pain and fear until she was dead. The Shadow evaporated, but the body lay in the same position.

Cari sought the umbra of the House that had killed Lorelei, and this time, at long last, she perceived something different in the Shadow of its latest victim: Blood.

Magic had been infused with the organic matter of life.

The Shadow itself still had the raw quality she'd sensed both at her father's death and at Vauclain House. No umbra, no identity. This Shadow had been blooded.

"It's not mage-made, is it?" Mason scrubbed his mouth and chin with his hand, as if to control his reaction.

She glanced over at him. His skin had turned dusky, every line and plane a monochrome of untamed magic. He was potent, there was no denying. Someone like Mason, with great ability, but no thumbprint, could have done this. Mason, who was a wild card of loyalties. *You can't trust me.*

Had she, as her stepmother had suggested, been unknowingly seduced by him?

She was in fact seduced. Every part of her wanted him. Had he . . . encouraged that in her?

Cari reached out gently for magic from Maeve, because she had to see Mason. She had to know him so that she wouldn't be tormented by doubts of what he was capable of unleashing on magekind, the race of people who'd shut him out all of his life. He had reason to be angry and bitter—his life, his son's, all the insults to his blood. Had he created the mage plague?

Cari asked, and Maeve gave: the Shadow within Mason eddied, then convulsed. His eyes narrowed at her, so he knew she was using her power on him. That she suspected him of something, one more insult to his stray pride.

For so many reasons, this couldn't be helped.

Mason's Shadow was like stormy clouds over a bitter sea, but she was the mistress of Shadow, the queen of the night, and if she willed it, the Shadow clouds would part.

Yesss, dove . . .

At her command, they did part.

Maeve had mentioned that Mason had a beautiful blue star of a soul within him—a pretty thing that she had wanted to toy with. But Cari had no words for the light that pervaded Mason's person. A star? Only if she were standing this close, three feet, from the star itself, its heat and radiance challenging the constitution of her flesh and bones, her umbra. She wanted to hide her sight from his brilliance.

Tantalizing, is he not? Maeve sighed.

Cari's eyes burned and she filled with longing. She wanted one of those, to be like him, and burn forever so brightly. But the mighty Dolan was like Lorelei, who had been left with nothing at death. A generation, and she would be forgotten.

No wonder there were wars between Order and Shadow. No wonder Light always won. Mason Stray, outcast and human, the *least* of the Shadow born, was astounding.

Mason endured the brush and soul stroke of Cari's power. She'd suspected, or had known outright—there was no hiding. She shredded the hold he had on his Shadow to look inside him.

He was human.

Had she suspected he was worse than that? A killer? Yes, he'd killed before. Or did she think he was even more evil? The source of the plague?

Look hard then.

"You finished?"

Cari let go of the Shadow and cleared her sight. He was innocent; she knew it with absolute certainty by the magic of her House. "You're right. I think that whoever is doing this isn't a mage. There's blood mixed in with the Shadow, and I think it's the blood that is killing the mages. Poisoned. Burning us from the inside out."

"Angelic?" He was referring to the angel who'd thrown a spear at her.

"Or human," she said. She would not force an admission of humanity from Mason. But someone like him—if there was another—needed to be considered.

Mason's jaw twitched at that, but he didn't defend himself. Cari suspected his pride wouldn't let him, and she didn't want to push him any farther just then.

Maeve, am I right? Cari didn't like addressing the fae, but she didn't want to lose this opportunity. She had her father to think of.

I cannot see who brought death upon that child. The child being Lorelei, though she must've been in her forties.

Then could it have been made by someone with a soul?

Yesss.

Mason's jaw flexed. "We need to warn Kaye Brand, though Jack Bastian will know more about what to do."

Maeve rose inside her, causing a panicked feeling in Cari's chest. *I don't. Like. Angels.*

"At least we have a theory to report." Cari could barely look at Mason, with his bright soul. She'd had a crush on him once, and even then her fantasies had seemed ludicrous.

"We'll need more than that." He looked around the room.

She tried to follow his gaze, careful of his anger. "What are you looking for?"

"We need proof." He took an empty plastic water bottle that had been left to the side of the bed. Opened the lid. Let the water inside glug to the floor. "We need a sample."

She almost laughed—bitterly. "We can't hold and transport Shadow." That's exactly what her Umbra project was supposed to do. She'd scream if Mason managed it with a plastic bottle.

"The Shadow won't keep, but the blood will." He went over to the body and scraped an open wound with the funnel of the plastic top. A little bit of Lorelei Blake glopped to the bottom of the bottle. Gray, bloody pus lay in a smoking, noxious little lump.

Cari was going to be sick. It was the most disgusting thing she'd ever seen.

Mason screwed the cap on. How he could get his skin remotely close to any smear of the stuff was beyond her.

Shadow wisped inside the bottle. Grasped in his hand, he raised it. "Hold," he said. The plastic of the bottle crackled with lines of black magic, like shattered glass.

Shadow filtered out through the sides, like mist. "How did you do that?"

He didn't seem in the mood to answer. "Open your purse."

She almost complained about putting the unclean thing in her very nice bag. But it was the logical place to transport it. She fished out her phone and gave it to Mason to hold in his pants' pocket. He rolled his eyes when she handed over her driver's license and credit cards, too.

Then she opened the bag wide and let him drop the awful thing inside.

"Let's get out of here." He had good reason to be angry. She'd invaded his most intimate space, sought his soul. After seeing its light, she understood what an insult, what a terrible breach that had been. There was no way that Mason could've ever set the plague on magekind. She *knew* him.

"Mason—"

"Not now." He gripped the open door.

Cari let the matter go. She wasn't going to apologize later either. She'd had to know, and now she did. She shouldered her bag.

"They're all below, at the base of the stairs."

Yes, a gathering of Lures, standing in a semi-circle like a smoky net to catch them. "Maybe they're just waiting for word of what we found."

"They're not. They want you, the new Dolan, at their beck and call, and this is probably their only chance."

It was simply what their House did for power, and she had to concede that Dolan was a tempting target.

"I'm not afraid." She'd been practicing. "Let me go first."

He started out into the hallway without looking back. "I'm here for a reason, princess."

He'd failed, a gut-punched feeling. He'd been discovered. There was no good reason for her to keep his secret. She didn't owe him a damn thing.

How was he—or anyone—to have known how much she was capable of?

Didn't matter. She knew. He had to think. Now. Of what he could offer to compel her silence.

Problem was, as always, he had nothing but his life and the labor of his hands to his name. And neither was worth this secret when it would give her a chance to strike at Kaye Brand. Never mind that it would also impact Webb . . . and therefore Fletcher.

Cari followed, but she wasn't about to play the weak woman just because she felt bad about insulting Mason. She was the Dolan, and these Blakes would understand what that meant if they tried anything.

Mason drew a gun from the holster on his right kidney underneath his shirt. The weapon smoked, so she knew he'd tricked it with Shadow, too.

"You can't get all of them one bullet at a time," she said.

Maeve, I can't let any of them touch him.

Is he ours, then? Maeve sounded thrilled.

He's mine. Cari didn't trust what Maeve intended to do with or to Mason's star soul. *Mason Stray is mine alone. I want him.*

At the top of the stairs, Mason paused. "You'd be surprised how fast things go when you hit the target every time."

Cari hadn't the experience with shooting people to argue, so she started down after him. She put a hand on Mason's

shoulder to keep their progress synchronized. Below, the
Blake family waited, including what looked like two teenage
children. It didn't take long before the Lures noticed Mason's
weapon.

Takum flicked a hand toward it. "What are you doing?"

Mason descended a few more slow steps. "I'm being
careful."

A Blake woman leaned toward them. "Did you find anything? Could you tell who did this?"

"No," Cari said. "The investigation is still inconclusive." She
wasn't going to inform them that she didn't think a mage was
responsible. "But it was very helpful that you kept Lorelei's
body the way it was when she died."

One of the children, a girl about sixteen, gave a gasp of
outrage. Her eyes were red-rimmed and bloodshot, her voice
thick. "Aren't you supposed to be able to, like, *see* everything?"

Cari stepped down when Mason did. Soon the Blakes
would have to back out of the way, or declare other intentions.

The old man, Takum, growled at the teen. "Shut your
mouth, girl."

The teen rounded on him. "You said the Dolan bitch would
know who killed my mom."

Takum's eyeballs did a quick swivel to see if the word
"bitch" had done any damage. "I said they were trying to
find out."

"You're a liar!" the girl screamed.

This was familiar to Cari. Stacia and Zel had screamed a
lot, too, when they were her age. And this girl had good
reason to be upset—Lorelei was her mother. Cari knew exactly how it felt to lose a parent—cold, desolate, isolated.

Mason had halted four steps up from the bottom, probably
waiting for them to comfort the girl or take her away to explain that there wouldn't be any immediate gratification.
Some things took time.

But Takum was more direct with his communications. He back-handed the girl with a slap that had the teen whiplashing around, her body flying limply, painfully, to collapse . . . at Mason's feet.

Cari felt him shudder under her hand.

Could a Lure ensnare a human soul?

Mason answered her question. "If this child does not remove her hand from me, I will damage her."

The teen immediately cringed. "It didn't work!"

Takum grabbed one of her legs, which was sprawled near him, and dragged her off the stair. Her head bumped and she screamed again, then scrambled back behind the others, who closed in on Cari and Mason's progress.

"The Council will never recognize Blake House again," Cari said. It was a safe bet, though Dolan House was positioned opposite Brand and she had no authority to speak for the High Seat.

The old man gave a yellow smile. "I think our standing with the Council is about to rise."

A bright crack to Cari's right signaled gunfire from a Blake, and her sight blackened with Shadow.

Oh, no you don't. *Give me power, Maeve.*

Mason turned to fire back, but it seemed he moved in achingly slow motion. Both shots hovered in Shadow air, sparks glinting from their sources. The moment had no beginning or end; it stretched and twisted and Cari understood that time wasn't as Ordered as she'd thought it was. Time was nothing.

Magic filled her and filled her until there was no room for air in her lungs. Maybe she didn't need to breathe.

All Shadow is yours. Draw magic into the world as only you can. Darken the sun. Burn the land. Bring the stars blazing down to earth.

Cari snorted. *I just want to get out of here.*

The Blakes' house began to rattle. Its loose boards clamored against each other, dark faelight gleaming through the cracks. The place trembled like chattering teeth. A strange sensation of airiness filled the stair area and the rooms within her sight, as if she were freshening it up. The teen was screaming again; if Cari tilted her head this or that way, the sound could be laughter. The other child, the boy, had backed toward the front door to escape. Cari wanted him to run, because then she could pursue.

Mason's voice cut through her delight. "Back it down, Cari."

She smiled, feeling glorious. "No. I got this." It was strange how good it felt. The Blake wards were as weak as old Takum, but being able to overcome them filled her with a snap of pleasure. She could do anything. The world would be hers again.

The Blakes cringed and brought their arms up to shield their heads.

She'd worked for mastery, and all in all, thought she was doing pretty well. Would it kill Mason to acknowledge it?

"Enough," Mason said.

Seemed it would. Fine. She didn't want to be here any longer either. Her father had told her only to use what force was actually necessary. Nothing more.

She reached with magic and lifted the Lures off the floor so that their legs dangled in the air. Then shunted them over to the right, against the wall, so that the way to the front door was clear. "After you."

But Mason foiled her again. He stepped aside so that she could pass and he could bring up the rear—though she'd demonstrated pretty spectacularly that she could take care of herself. She walked down the rattling steps—they didn't challenge her balance at all—across the main room and out the door. The porch was even more unstable, and she had the odd awareness that in the crawl space beneath, dark things dwelled.

Well, they couldn't hurt *her*. And she wouldn't let them hurt Mason.

Her face warmed in the sun. Really, it was a gorgeous day. The sun had never been so gorgeous. So vivid, a burnished yellow. The great life-giver. Masculine to her ready soil. She wanted to bake under it, naked, let the gold in her blood run hot through her veins.

Take it then, Maeve said. *This is ours, too.*

Ours. The sun even?

A beat of want sent a tremor through her.

Inside, Mason was instructing the Blakes to release the wards so that they could leave the property. Then he came up behind her and took her arm. "Let's go." He led her forcefully to the car. "You can let go of the house now."

Oh. She looked back as they rounded the car. The house had seemed rotten and unstable before, but now the slats were worn and broken. The paint had flaked off completely, so that the structure was naked. Naked was the official state of the day.

She'd come here to find a house of cards. If she let go, would it collapse?

Mason reached across Cari to rifle through the glove compartment. Not his car, so he didn't know what he'd find. Happened on a pack of tissues. He handed the lot to Cari. "Here."

Her nose was bleeding again, and the princess hadn't even noticed.

She took the tissues and dabbed. "I did better that time."

"Better than what?" Every time she tried something, the sense of heavy, absolute night overcame him. Shaking Blake House—spectacular, but completely unnecessary. And he was not even going to bring up what had happened in that bedroom of death, with Lorelei rotting on the bed, how Cari had . . . reached inside him somehow.

He needed to find out what this new power was, and she did too. No one should have that much magic. No one. Once, even a week ago, he might have said that he trusted her with it, but now that he'd witnessed its hold again, he knew that not even Cari Dolan could manage it. This was danger the likes of which he'd never experienced before, and he'd seen some damn scary things.

"I did better than last time, at Vauclain House."

Mason glared at her incredulously, then shifted gear. Cari had been just as overtaken as she had before. That she could be articulate now was a miracle—her eyes were full black, drugged with magic. Her skin gleamed fae. Her beauty had become fierce, harsh . . . frightening. She couldn't afford to be oblivious. It was against her true nature, and she had a House to sustain.

"You're getting worse." He gripped the steering wheel. He wasn't going to soft-pedal this. She needed to know. "You're out of control."

"I beg to differ." The princess Dolan thing. "I'm exactly as I should be."

"In fact," Mason added, "I don't think control is even possible. If it were, you'd be the one to manage it. And you can't."

"Well, we'll just have to wait and see, won't we?" A sharp smile, from a sharp woman.

But because he'd been her friend once, he was not going to leave it at that. "We're going to Segue now. Get you some answers. They can't wait any longer." He redlined the car in each gear until the speedometer needle shook.

"Segue has no wards."

"Doesn't sound like you think you need them anymore." She'd been the one who'd wanted to speak to Khan. Where was *that* Cari?

"I'm not stupid. There's a crazed angel out there." She looked out the passenger window. Cold and stony. The bloody tissue was clutched in her hand.

"Segue has an angel or two if you are concerned," Mason said. "And everyone there is fucking crazy, too."

Chapter Ten

The princess had iced him out for most of the drive to West Virginia and had dozed, slack-jawed, the rest of the time. He liked her that way, vulnerable. Human, almost. But as the miles peeled away, he became more and more certain that this was the best thing to do.

Cari needed help, and she needed it badly if she could no longer recognize the fact for herself.

A couple hours into the trip and a new worry gnawed at him. Cari might just—no, he wouldn't fool himself either—Cari could *easily* challenge Kaye Brand. And while Mason had always liked Cari—more than liked her—he couldn't dismiss what Brand and her angel had accomplished between them: peace. However tenuous, there were too many other concerns—the fae came to mind—to allow anything to break the truce between Order and Shadow.

Cari could not take control of the Council.

It was close to midnight before Mason began the twisting climb that led to Segue's compound. Adam Thorne, its founder, had the full support of the US government, so soldiers stood at the ready before the massive gated entrance.

Mason braked the car to roll down the window to speak to a soldier at the main gate. The sweet smell of the surrounding forest and mountain air filled his lungs. He'd always liked it here. "Mason Stray. They're expecting me."

He recognized the guard on duty, and the guard recognized him, too. "And the lady?"

"Cari Dolan, also expected."

Cari had sat up and was blinking the sleep from her eyes. "Where are we?"

"Segue," Mason answered.

The guard must have received some sort of confirmation in his ear piece because he held up a hand and made a whipping, circular signal. The gate began retracting.

"What is this place?" Cari was getting that black-black glaze to her eyes. Her shoulders were migrating upward, tense. She must be scared.

"Stop it." Mason touched her chin to get her to look at him. "These soldiers and this gate are as close as Segue can get to wards. They won't hurt you."

She seemed to wake more fully, tucking one side of her hair behind her ear, straightening her blouse. She was always better after sleeping. He wished she'd been able to sleep longer.

He accelerated through the gate and drove toward the main building. The Segue Institute was run out of a retro-fitted turn-of-the-century hotel. The place was haunted, and its chief function was to dispose of wraiths, but all in all, it wasn't such a bad spot to pass time.

"They are very nice people." Mason wanted to put her at ease. "Fletcher loves Thorne's boys."

"Thorne."

"Adam Thorne. Runs the place. He's Khan's son-in-law, married to Talia."

He drove around the building to the back lot where Segue's staff parked. He embraced the dart of jealousy he got every time he faced the massive garage that housed Adam's very nice collection of cars. The '65 Shelby Cobra was definitely one to pine over. He'd spent a very happy afternoon poking around under its hood.

The combination of night and altitude had chilled the July air, so that it tingled against his skin and made Cari cross her arms. "This way."

The back door was already opening, silhouetting Adam against the light from inside. "Must you always come at awful hours?"

Mason laughed as he and Cari approached. "What's the matter, old man? Kids stealing your youth?"

"You would know."

Mason's hand was out for a shake, but the reaching motion became a kind of brotherly hug. Mason had been negotiating this strange kind of acceptance for the past year. He wasn't one of them, but the people at Segue didn't seem to know that. They all ignored his handshakes. Talia had once kissed him on the cheek. He'd brought something for her boys, a little gadget that Fletcher had liked when he'd been their age, but the kiss was still strange. He'd expected Adam to slug him.

Mason gestured to Cari. "This is the great Cari Dolan. Old family. Pure blood going way, way back. You're in the presence of mage royalty."

Cari put out her hand. "It's nice to meet you."

Adam shook hers. "I hear you've had some trouble at your place of business. DolanCo, yes? I saw the clip of the mob— very nice work, by the way, Mason."

"Not my first time."

Cari gave a diplomatic answer. "Magekind couldn't stay secret forever."

"I met your father once, a few years ago." Adam drew them inside the building where the sweet night air was replaced with the processed cool of air conditioning. "It was at a charity function for inner city youth sponsored by many companies. I had to go back and look it up, but I even have a photo of myself standing next to Caspar. I wonder if we would've come to know each other, become friends, if I had brought my wife that night. She's half fae. As it was, neither your father nor I had any idea that we both had Shadow in common."

They passed through the lab level, all white, sterile. Low ceilings. Some of the doorways were open a crack—the researchers kept all hours here. Others were shut and darkened for the night.

"I'm sure he would've liked that." Cari's polite voice, which Mason knew was meant to keep everyone at a distance.

So he made a sound of disagreement. "I don't know, Adam. The Houses usually tread very carefully where outsiders are concerned. Magekind, even now, keeps to its own."

Adam looked back at Cari as he led them to an elevator. "That's too bad. Maybe we can get beyond that with your visit."

"An optimist for the Dark Age." Mason laughed. But it wasn't going to happen, not with Dolan's allies at least. They drew strict lines.

Cari glanced his way. "I'm an optimist myself."

Mason sighed heavily. She was going to cause trouble among her faction if she mixed with outsiders. Humans, angels—they were barely tolerated.

The elevator took them up to the main level, which was illuminated with ambient light coming from the back of the building, where Mason knew the kitchens were. Too bad about Segue's cook, who'd been murdered by someone from Martin House not too long ago. Maybe that's why Adam was trying so hard to make nice with Cari. Maybe Adam was looking for allies. Martin and Segue had bad blood between them.

The ground floor rooms here were open, restored to the hotel's previous glory, though Shadow webbed the darkest corners. Magic was thick, but as there were no wardstones, there was no sense of movement, no prickly-neck feeling of being watched, as there was at Dolan House. Adam's attention to period detail was lost at night, but a feeling of open-spaced timelessness still prevailed.

Indistinct voices murmured ahead, so it seemed that others had waited up to meet them, too. Or rather, waited to meet Cari. If he'd come alone, he would've been let in by whoever was awake and would've had to fend for himself from there.

Through a pantry, Adam pushed a swinging door that led to the kitchen. The heady scent of coffee smacked Mason in the gut, made his mouth water. Segue was very much like that—a cup of good coffee waiting in the middle of a long night.

Introductions first.

Talia, Adam's wife, started forward when they entered. Pixie blond, her Shadow-black eyes looked tired, but her smile was fresh. She held out her hand to Cari. "I'm so pleased—"

But Khan was suddenly there, blocking his daughter with an outstretched arm and pushing her back. His severe face was drawn into acute wariness as he examined Cari. His height made him impressive; the blackness of his slick, long hair and the shape of his eyes said he had once been fae.

Talia was cut-off, midsentence.

Mason too had halted, mid-smile, caught by surprise. Well, this was the person that Cari had wanted most to meet.

Khan welcomed Cari, saying, "Your father was a weak, sentimental fool."

The gathering in the kitchen strangled into silence.

"Whoa." Mason put a shoulder in front of her and held up a hand to keep Khan back. As if the mage who'd once been the Grim Reaper could possibly be stopped by flesh and bone.

"I don't under—" Cari's smile flickered on her face like a lightbulb about to burn out.

Mason's smile had been snuffed already.

Khan didn't move forward, but was still undeterred.

"There's a very old saying among the magicked of the world: Never suffer a Dolan female to live."

Mason didn't dare break his concentration from Khan to find out who else had gathered in the kitchen to meet Cari. Adrenaline, however, had done the coffee's job. He was alert now, blood pumping fast and free. What had crawled up Khan's ass?

"Your father should have left you in the wild as a babe, exposed for the beasts of the world to prey upon."

"Mother of God, Khan!" Adam stepped back to protect Cari as well. "What's your problem?"

Khan lifted his chin to indicate Cari. "The Dark Age begins with her."

"You just met her," Adam said to Khan.

"I've known her for ages."

"I've known her since she was a teenager," Mason said. "She's a nice girl." Er, woman. But it was too late to correct.

Khan craned his neck down to look into Cari's eyes. "Mad Mab was never a nice girl."

Adam leaned his head toward Mason to mumble, "Reincarnation?"

Mason shrugged. He didn't know, but a hot and grim confirmation of his worst fears burned in his chest. He'd been worried something was wrong with Cari, and now he knew he was right. Mad Mab? Cari used to be the epitome of control and poise . . . until lately. Khan's reaction reaffirmed everything Mason feared. Cari's power *was* dangerous.

"Dolan Girl," Khan said, "would you lay down your life to save humankind?"

Damn, but she was making no friends today.

"I serve my House—" Her voice quavered. Few, okay, none, were prepared to meet Khan in person the first time. And it went beyond his physical stature and unusual looks. His power was life and death, and every living thing in his presence knew it.

Mason had had enough of this. Khan would step the hell back. The Dolan Girl had had a rough week. Besides, Cari had already given her life . . . to her House. It was her duty, her honor, to do right by her people. The future of Dolan rested on her leadership and her womb. It was House 101. Khan had best sign up for the course.

"Retreat, Maeve," Khan said into Cari's face. "Or I swear I will bend my power to smothering the Dolan line."

Mason put a hand on Khan's chest to move him back. The badass mage didn't budge a millimeter. "Enough. You need to explain yourself."

Khan transferred his attention to him, eyes lit with predatory humor. The stray . . . no, a *human* . . . tangling with Death?

So squash me then, Mason thought. *But lay off.*

"You cannot think to shelter her here," Khan said to Adam. "The fae queen abides in her umbra, and one day this poor girl will give birth to her, and madness will reign on Earth."

Mason hadn't thought Cari's condition was *that* bad.

"Cari Dolan"—Khan straightened, as if making a pronouncement to all of Segue—"you need to die. And I am more than happy to dispatch you."

Cari had steeled herself, but she couldn't stop a slight tremor on the inside. It would help if Maeve would shut up for a minute. Queen of the fae? Mad Mab?

Don't listen to him. Insufferable man. He always envied me.

Mason was arguing, and Adam Thorne arguing on top of him. Talia had rounded on her father, her pale fairness clashing with the jet black of his long tresses. And another woman stepped up, with reddish hair, and actually had the nerve to grab the arm of Death and make him turn to face her.

Cari's heart beat against her ribs. So much yelling, and her life seemed held in the balance.

Show them. Show them our power.

"No," Cari answered. She wouldn't argue or beg for her life. It was hers and she was keeping it. These people, even the scary ones, could argue all they liked.

Someone nudged her elbow and she flinched. A very strange man held out a coffee cup. He had the look of Kaye Brand's angel—perfection, though he was olive-skinned with dark blond hair—but Cari was certain that Shadow ran in his veins. The very darkest of Shadow.

Bah, and they have an angel. Death treating with Order? And he calls me mad?

The dark angel spoke: "They may be at this a while, so relax and take a load off." For some reason Cari could hear him over—or under—the clamor. "I'm Custo Santovari, and I have a fae trapped inside me, too. We should start a club for the possessed. I'll order jackets."

He couldn't be serious. Strait-jackets maybe.

I. Hate. Angels.

He held out the cup again. "It's good stuff. Adam always gets the best for his people."

She let go of Mason, utterly bewildered, and took the cup. The warmth in her hands did feel good. Steadying.

"They'll argue, but anyone who's spent any time at Segue could tell you the decision they'll come to. Each and every one of them would die *for* you before killing you. Including me, by the way."

She couldn't find a response to that.

Custo waited a beat, then said, "I understand you have something for me? A sample to analyze?"

He had to mean that bit of Lorelei Blake that Mason had scooped up. Cari hugged her purse closer. "I was going to turn it over to the mage Council."

"The Order can identify any soul by the person's DNA, and I hear both you and Mason think the plague came from someone with one. I swear, you'll be the first to know our findings."

He made sense. She handed him her purse, relieved to be rid of it. Everyone would want answers sooner than later anyway. Based on the raised voices in the kitchen, peace was deteriorating pretty quickly. Well . . . kinda.

Over by the sink, some other woman watched the argument with avid, almost happy interest while she dipped her finger into what looked like hot bun frosting and licked. She noticed Cari watching her and held out the platter of sweet rolls.

Cari shook her head to decline, then paused . . . This was familiar to her. Everyone arguing, but no real danger. In a weird way, this could be Dolan House.

"This is more like a rite of passage," Custo was saying. "A welcome-to-the-family, as it were."

"I have a family." She wanted to get back to them. Immediately.

I can take you back. Ask me to take you back.

Cari was tempted to do just that. But she didn't want to acquiesce to Maeve either. Mad Mab?

"Mason likes you," Custo continued. "Which means everyone else here does too, including Shadowman. It's a foregone conclusion. Tomorrow they'll probably ask you to babysit."

Shadow roiled around Khan. "You cannot mean to house her here!"

"Okay, maybe tomorrow *afternoon*," Custo corrected.

Cari hugged her cup. "I don't think so."

Custo sighed heavily and murmured, "I'll help them along; the buns are getting cold." Then to the room, "If Khan would kindly remember that his Layla opened a gate to Hell . . ." It was strange how the angel's voice carried.

The yelling dropped off for a second before Mason jabbed a finger at Death again. "Excellent point. The story *I* heard was that you and Layla were keen on filling the world up with devils. Didn't the Order demand *her* death?"

And the commotion began again.

Custo chuckled and leaned in to Cari. "Might as well enjoy it. Good times come farther and farther apart these days."

"*This* is a good time?" Cari wasn't in the mood for laughing.

Cari would *be the queen of the fae*. Or related to her.

Mason dropped an assortment of loaned clothing on the sitting room table, and he took some for Cari into the bedroom and tossed the stuff on the bed. "You sleep in here; I'm used to the couch. I'd have taken a separate room for myself, but I don't trust any of them anymore."

Adam's eyes had sparkled when Mason had declined.

Yeah, yeah. Funny man. Nothing happening here. She knew he was human.

But there was no way he was going to let Cari sleep alone. She or Khan would find a way to bring down Segue. Mason's bet was on Cari—she'd just rattled a warded House.

"It's fine." Cari stood out of the way, by the fireplace. Her face looked drawn. Arms folded. Tough. Alone. Dolan proud.

Maybe they never should've come here. Queen Maeve? Mad Mab? The Shadow he'd sensed in Cari was in fact wild.

He turned slightly to ask her directly, "Did you know already?" Because that would've been just peachy. Not that it was any of his business. He was just the stray assigned to protect her during this plague business. What reason had he to demand answers or any kind of disclosure?

"Yes and no." Her chin was stubbornly up. "She talks to me sometimes."

"Is she as insane as Khan says she is?"

"She's fae."

"She's hurting you."

"I'm getting stronger, more able, every day. And besides, it's not as if I can evict her."

"What does she say is her relationship to you? Does she

want you to somehow . . . birth her?" Khan had said that Mad Mab would want to come back into the world through Cari.

"She says she's my mother."

"That's it?"

Cari looked away, toward the wall, toward nothing. "She might've also said she's a god."

Mason lifted his hands up in a sour hooray. "You've got yourself a faery godmother? Well, now we know this will end happily ever after."

She dropped her arms and stalked toward the only bedroom. "I'm going to bed."

He was being an ass, and he knew it.

He'd always called her princess. Had always thought of her as one. And here it was, in a twisted way, true. Descended from the faery queen herself. All magekind would look to Dolan.

"What did your father tell you?" Mason asked her back.

She cocked her head, but didn't face him. "Nothing. He told me nothing. I discovered all this the day you and I went to re-examine his death."

"What does your stepmother say? She has to know something."

Cari shook her head. "She's said nothing. And I haven't told her. She's not a Dolan."

"I'm not a Dolan, and I know."

"I don't know *what* you are."

"I'm pretty sure you do," he shot back, "after that stunt you pulled at Blake House."

She turned and looked at him a long minute. Mason waited while she was deciding his fate, and in so doing, Fletcher's. *Well, let's have it then.*

"You're just Mason, same as ever." She actually seemed a little sad, though he had no idea why she would be.

The answer was too ambiguous, and he could not tolerate

any gray where his son was concerned. "Please don't hurt Fletcher." He'd beg if he had to.

She gave a short laugh. "Do you really think I could?"

"You come from a purist family."

"I'm expanding Dolan horizons."

That made no sense. "Why would you protect us? You could screw Brand with this information." Brand had sent a human into their Houses while they grieved.

"Yeah, well, I'm your friend. There will be other opportunities to screw Brand."

She couldn't possibly be giving up this chance. "You're my friend?" he repeated dumbly. What was her game? What new maneuver was this?

"Aren't I?" She was so powerful, but now, strangely, vulnerable.

No game. She'd never been one to manipulate. He knew that.

He was a total shit. He'd stolen from her. And he knew that Webb was trying to undermine her in terrible ways—including the Lures. "I specifically told you not to trust me."

"You're probably the only person I can trust."

He shook his head. He missed his kid, and he cared about this girl. When he looked at Cari, the woman she'd become, he saw flashes of her at seventeen, smiling up at him, waiting for that kiss. Back then he'd had to resist the urge to grab hold of her. Right now he wanted to grab hold of her just as badly. But to shake some sense into her. She had to know her enemies—this Queen Maeve and . . . him. Him especially.

"What about a truce?" Cari's expression was calm, but her mouth was pressed together in a line, nervous or stressed. Her tattle-tale mouth told him she was barely hanging on.

"You need to go to bed," he told her. Sleep had helped her every time she'd been overcome with Shadow. Maybe it would help her think.

"A truce," she repeated. "Segue is Switzerland."

"We'll talk in the morning."

She sighed, irritated. "I'm *trying* to work our argument around to getting you to come to bed with me."

His heart chugged, then stopped, but it was enough circulation for his brain to last a few seconds longer.

"I'll try one more time." Her eyes shined, unblinking, while she flashed a falsely bright smile. "I propose a truce between Dolan House and Mason Stray."

The implications of "truce" were beyond him just then. "I'm sorry, I'm still on 'come to bed with me.'" He'd been working with her for seven days. Albeit, seven days backed by an obsession with her when they were younger. Did that count?

"I don't want to be alone with Mad Mab, and I'm having a hard time pushing her out of my mind since Blake House. I'm hoping you'll take me up on the friend thing."

Mason was speechless. What was she saying? Friend thing. In bed? He began to shake his head no. Bad idea. No matter how pretty or wonderful or sexy he thought she was. He started forward to tell her as nicely as he could that there was no Switzerland in magic. See what a good friend he was? Only a friend would refuse her.

She understood though. She backed away a step, stopping his trajectory.

A small adjustment and she was all poise again. She'd done that before with him. "You're right. I'd better get to sleep. Big day tomorrow. I'm supposed to attend the inaugural meeting of the Possessed by the Fae Club. Apparently, I'm going to be secretary, as I declined running for any of the official offices Custo suggested. Anyway . . ."

She went into the room, leaving the door open. Was the offer still open, too? He saw her rifle through the loaned clothing, and then a flash of her profile as she went into the bathroom and closed the door.

He couldn't . . .

He had Fletcher to think of. Who was right now asleep elsewhere.

And he'd stolen from her, and he didn't know if he'd do it again if pressed.

And he'd sworn never to touch a House woman again. Never a House woman.

Cari came to the door again. She was in soft blue sweats, which made her look younger than yesterday's silk.

"Night," she said, and closed the door.

He was still stuck in the same spot, mouth dry, heartbeat sub-standard.

Her stepmother would kill him for sure if he touched her. Somehow he knew she'd find out.

And those loyal stepsisters would carve him up in pieces for the vultures.

But if he didn't go in there, he'd curse himself every day for the rest of his life. Who knew how long he and Cari would be here? Who knew if he'd die at Khan's hands tomorrow defending her life?

Cari Dolan. Who hadn't ever cared that he was stray, and didn't seem to care that he was human. *Mason, same as ever.*

She really wasn't thinking straight. She was the Dolan. Someone should remind her.

He brushed his teeth in the sink of the small kitchenette. Checked to see if he smelled bad, then washed just in case. Would she prefer he shaved? He didn't want to scratch her perfect skin, so made quick work of his face. He nicked himself on his jaw and had to use a bit of paper towel to stop the bleeding. And then he debated what to wear—something he'd never done before in his life. But he wasn't striding in there naked, all jacked up and rearing to poke her. Not Cari. He'd been a dad way too long to have an answer.

He was in his boxers only, a T-shirt in his hand, when the bedroom door opened again. She stood on the threshold worrying that bottom lip with her upper teeth. "You make up your mind yet? I'm getting nervous."

"Not more nervous than I am."

She smiled sweet relief, then her attention caught on one false plague wound after another. Her mouth twisted. "Did you even ever have the mage plague?"

He shook his head. "These"—he gestured to the itchy one at his rib—"come courtesy of the Order."

She looked at the mean wounds again, wincing on his behalf. "You're an idiot."

"Human," he corrected. There. He'd said it out loud. It was real now. Could he even still call himself Stray?

A sneaky smile. "I plan to use your humanity against you somehow."

He loved her mouth. All he wanted to do was kiss her. He'd been waiting years to do so. "I thought you might."

"Could I leverage it into some kind of action tonight? I'd like to see the master at work."

"Master?" It'd been a while since he'd slept with anyone.

"You're Mr. Experience."

"Very funny." An experienced guy wouldn't have to causally cover up the evidence of his arousal. And she was just standing there, fully clothed, doing nothing anyone else would think was enticing.

"Well, from what Liv used to say . . ."

"I was nineteen. Teenagers exaggerate." Or in his case, outright lie about the number of his conquests. "And I've been a single father since then." Not celibate, but he never brought women home with him. Was he actually trying to convince her that he didn't know what he was doing? He should throw himself off the roof.

"That's okay. I'm not any good either. I have it on excellent authority. I don't expect fireworks."

Now he was mad. Erom Vauclain needed to be killed again. Cari? Not any good?

Mason dropped his shirt and strode toward her. "What kind of man do you think I am?"

She backed up, stammering. "No, I just meant that . . ."

"Because I'll take care of the fireworks, thank you very much." That *he* would see them was a foregone conclusion. He was a beggar at a feast.

"Mason." She looked away, her face coloring. Miserable.

He kicked backward to slam the door shut and get her attention.

Her gaze snapped to him; her mouth went in that line again. Angry, maybe stubborn. He wondered what other shapes he could make her lips take. He was going to have the best time finding out. This was an inspired idea, the truce. Brilliant. Like a time-out for grown-ups.

"Should I get a condom?" Because he learned from mistakes. He hoped to hell he still had one in his wallet.

"I'm on the pill," she snapped back. "And by the way, it's a bad idea to use Shadow for any kind of seduction," referring to Maeve.

"I might have already figured that out." He hadn't, but he wasn't going to admit it. His pride had suffered enough tonight. "I'm going to kiss you now."

She made a *pfft* sound. "I wish you'd just get on with it. I'm starting to regret—"

He was well out of practice, but he knew enough to make sure she didn't finish that sentence.

Heat enveloped her as his mouth came down. His arms, all that muscle, took her weight in a backward lean. And she was glad she could close her eyes because it had gotten very hard to keep from staring at his well-defined shoulders and pecs, that cut six pack with the happy diagonal obliques that gestured to the dizzying protrusion behind his shorts. Even with the curtains closed on her sight, she could still picture him perfectly.

She wished she had something sexier to wear to make her seem more like a woman of the world and not some House-bred girl who didn't get out much.

"Stop thinking," Mason said against her lips.

She drew a breath to laugh, but inhaled sweet shaving cream underscored by pure masculinity. Mason didn't use cologne. Didn't go for fancy or expensive. Just him. Anything more would be overkill. But she doubted he knew that.

He deepened the kiss again, and she focused on the sensation of his mouth against hers—the firm rasp and seal and broken gasp of his touch. The past few days had tormented her with sensations; now she wanted fulfillment. She wanted *this,* wanted to be able to lose herself, just once as she'd never allowed herself before, and this was the man with whom she could.

"Cari," he murmured against her.

She nodded, breath broken, in answer. Just Mason.

He initiated a conversation in an old language she didn't know, but in spite of the thumping of her heart, found she could understand perfectly. His mouth said, *I want you. I need you. I'm hungry for you.* And she responded by wrapping an arm around his neck and repeating the words back in her own feminine dialect.

This was just the beginning. She knew it. Every nerve was sparkling, her blood going golden again in anticipation.

And with the currents of energy came a dark stirring, like a panic. Cari lifted herself above it. Denied the surge of Shadow. Closed herself viciously to any unwanted company. No magic tonight. Not that kind, at least.

She gave him her body with an upward arch, and took his, an arm around to his back, nails scoring for purchase, a hand fisted in his hair. She wanted one night away from her constant companion. A night with someone she knew she shouldn't trust, but did anyway.

And he lifted her, his mouth sliding to her neck. His teeth snagged her ear and she cringed and giggled.

"Ticklish, eh?" He said it as if storing up weaknesses to exploit.

"Don't you dare," she warned.

He laid her across the bed the wrong way, and she wondered how he thought this was going to work with half his big, long body hanging off the side of the bed. But he was cleverer than she, because with one push of his arm the blanket and sheet fell off the foot of the bed.

"I'm always cold," she told him. A girl sometimes needed an artfully-placed sheet.

"I'll cover you."

Oh.

Thwarted. Now there was no way to hide the worst of her healing scars. On a man they looked like heroic bullet wounds, and his were even faked. Hers were just ugly.

He must have noticed her nerves. In one fluid gesture, he stripped off her sweatshirt. The sudden change in temperature made her nipples harden. Of course he noticed that, too. Mason noticed everything.

He stroked the underside of one of her breasts with the back of his fingertips. She tensed. Exposed. She was used to hiding in so many ways. Shadow was her refuge. But then he bowed his head and blew warm air across that same bit of sensitive skin, and her tightened muscles quivered. Her core fluttered, an ache beating between her legs.

He looked up again, black gaze sharp, assessing. One side of his mouth curled in satisfaction. "Interesting."

His mouth moved down to her hip. The heat from his breath warmed her, but when he raked his teeth down a dip beneath her belly button, she surprised herself by whimpering aloud.

His gaze flicked up to assess her again, lingering on her lips before his own stretched into a wide grin. "Excellent."

And then she knew what he was after, and it was too late to back out, to get him to stop, to throw up walls between them. What had she been thinking? This was Mason. He was going to unlock her body's every secret, find her out, and then there'd be nowhere she could hide. He was after mastery.

He slid a little lower and blew heat onto her bare abdomen. She clutched inside, wet and hot already, effortlessly, and barely noticed that her sweatpants and underwear were gone. He was moving again. With one arm under her shoulders, he maneuvered her onto the pillows, semi correcting their position. But she understood now—the bed no longer had an up/down orientation. The covers were gone, the pillows soon to be askew. This place was merely a soft tableau upon which Mason would know her. And by now she'd fully realized he planned to investigate her thoroughly.

And if she had an iota of sense or courage left, she'd learn him too. Mason Stray, hers for the night. She couldn't believe it. This kind of thing didn't happen to her, and yet, she was pretty sure it had been her idea. She'd lost a chance once, she wasn't about to lose it again. He'd get as good as he gave.

She went for the base of his neck, where flexed muscles met and crossed, and she stroked with her mouth. Kissed him there, more tentatively than she'd have liked. Made herself tremble, but his breathing cut off, mid-inhalation. A small victory, but hers nonetheless.

He lifted her arm and heated the tender skin on the inside of her elbow, just above one of her recent scars. The touch made her ache differently, to feel so beautiful, when she was obviously flawed in that spot. He was smiling as he dragged his mouth up her arm and began a dual exploration—breath at her nape, which she knew was a tactical diversion, a hand skimming down low across her belly, to the curve of her hip to coax her closer.

She found herself straddling one of his legs, her hot core flush against his thigh. Shocked, she rocked her hips in protest and collusion, perilous beats of pleasure traveling to her toes and collecting deep.

He remained braced above her, discovering with heat first, then a rough hand on willing skin. She didn't tense when he tried the underside of her breast again. She inhaled and lifted into his palm, which earned her a groan from him. He was careful with her hurts and possessive of her secret places, priming with soft strokes that incited recklessness.

She grabbed hold of his hair and possessed him, too, by kissing him deep and hard, with the pent-up yearning of years. His weight came down and his torso went flush with her bare breasts, sizzling with impossible heat. She might not have the bedroom skills others did, but when he finally drew back, his eyes were dark and hungry, as if he'd gone without for too long himself, maybe his whole life. He looked at her with the longing of a hundred years.

It was his fault—she fought angry tears—because he'd stayed with Liv. He'd chosen Liv, when Cari had wanted him more than anything. *She* would've run away with him. She would've left House and family behind just to feel like this. How could he know just how to touch her now and not know that she'd been crazy about him?

He adjusted his position and she was sorry to lose his thigh pressing at her most intimate place, but then his body centered, and a scorching hot weight dropped between her legs. But it was the expression on Mason's face, the thoughts behind his eyes that told her he was no stranger to regrets, and he was bent on settling some old scores right now.

She was shaking, slick with want, and perspiring with the fight against it. Her breath was ragged, her body willingly opening up to him. She licked her lips to tell him, *wait,* but his mouth came down and spoke against hers again, so fluently she couldn't mistake his meaning. His kiss said, *You're mine. And I'll have all of you. We've been waiting too long.*

She agreed, and told him so by lifting a knee to bring him even closer. Shockingly close, because this was Mason, who knew her darkest secret and still touched her like that.

His hand worked her hip to a tilt. In one deep stroke, he assumed the weight of her frustrations and worries, the many cares that burdened her life, so that all that remained was startling brightness and pleasure. She clasped him tightly to her, fisting her hand in his hair, and rode him right back. His flushed, primal expression told her that he was just as affected. Higher and higher he drove them until they were well past any firework atmosphere. He took her to the brink of the world, the elemental fire of beginnings and endings. He rocked with her, strained with her, groaned as her leg curled around him to take him even deeper. She'd never felt more powerful. The bliss was sweet and dizzy, her flesh simmering on the brink.

A soft brush of his mouth on her temple, a harsh breath, as it occurred to her that he was waiting for her. That he'd wait forever for her, like this, until she fractured. The night would turn into an eternity, and she would spend the rest of her existence speared by him, by hope, by ecstasy. He would be right there, inside her, surrounding her, surging without end.

"Come, Cari," he said.

And a white starburst of sensation lit her from the inside. It wiped her mind clean of anything but the fullness within her, the heat and heartbeat of the man above. She buried her face in the crook of his neck and quaked against him, holding on for dear life. With a final groan, he poured himself into her, and she wrapped both legs around him to take it all.

Mason was trying not to crush her, so he heroically hefted himself onto his forearms and considered summoning the will to move away from her to let her breathe. He glanced down to see if she was still alive. Her eyes were closed, but she wore a drugged, lopsided smile.

He absolutely, unequivocally loved her mouth.

After the birth of Fletcher, this was the best day of his life. He'd thoroughly satisfied Cari Dolan. He was the king of the world. There was nothing he couldn't do.

He grinned down at her. "How about a shower?"

She didn't bother to crack a lid. "I don't think my legs can hold me just yet."

"I meant a shower together. I won't let you fall." He nuzzled her and nipped at an earlobe.

She stretched under him, just a little, as if considering. "It's warm here."

It was; he was still inside her, but he wasn't near finished. He kissed her pretty neck. She tasted salty. He used his tongue to make her shiver. "The shower will be hot. I promise."

Her hips moved, testing, and he could feel the results in a tightening within her. She brought his head down and kissed him, slow, languorous, tasting him and sucking on his tongue. And his hips moved involuntarily, too. A seeking movement.

She made a sound, which—Shadow save him—he took for agreement. They weren't done. Not nearly. Not until he had her in every way and tasted every hollow. One night was all he had to discover her.

The kiss went dark as he shifted, collected her in his arms, made for the bathroom. He blindly found the shower lever and set it full blast on hot, though Cari's skin was already misting with heat, her legs wrapped around his waist. He caught sight of their shapes in the mirror—a primal clutch of his-and-hers shadows—and realized that whatever the circumstances of their births, tonight they were the same.

Chapter Eleven

Cari woke, naked, but cocooned in covers and instantly missed Mason's thermal spooning. Then she just missed Mason. She tested her body, flexed her feet, and stretched her legs. She wanted a massage. Somehow she was sure his hands could ease her sore spots, though the rest of her felt lighter than ever. There was nothing to do but find him.

She sat up and instead found a note on the bedside table.

> *Princess—*
> *Had to speak with Adam. Back soon.*
> *M*

The clock said 10 a.m.; it was way past time for her to get up. There was so much she needed to do—call home, check her e-mail, touch base with Brand—but she figured she'd get a better gauge on the day if she located Mason and put that strange man Custo's theory to the test regarding Segue's change of heart about her.

She dressed and wandered downstairs in search of the kitchen, but was waylaid by the light streaming through the windows on the main floor, the way they warmed and stirred the errant dust curls of Shadow.

With little warning, a pack of small boys came racing through the wide, connected rooms, laughing and disappearing at the end of the stretch. She figured she couldn't be in too much trouble if children were free to encounter her. Pushing the still-swinging door from the pantry, she let herself into the kitchen. Again, several people—Adam, whom she'd met last night; his wife, so fair compared to her father; a couple others whose names she couldn't remember; some dark-haired girl was prepping to make an omelet; Mason, who made her blood rush—were standing about. The heady scent of coffee was in the air, the plate of sweet buns empty.

Mason was speaking with Adam. They both looked very serious, and Mason gestured for her to come over, without breaking their conversation. She'd hoped for more of a welcome from him, so she gathered her hopes up, just in case she needed to stow them away. The night was well over.

But Mason took her hand and pulled her close to his side. Felt surreal to have his fingers lacing through hers. Erom had never held her hand like that.

She went serious too when she heard Adam mention "feeding tube." Then she followed Mason's gaze over to where a boy sat. The child had to be very young—five maybe. He was beyond cute, beautiful, with Adam's coloring. He had big blue eyes fringed by extraordinary lashes, but his gaze was lost—not vacant—rather looking somewhere at something that she couldn't see unless she drew from her umbra, and she wasn't ready to stir Maeve yet.

"We just don't know what to do anymore," Adam said. "He hasn't responded for a few days now. It's happening more and more often."

They were speaking as parents, which instantly caught her attention. In the next few years, she'd have to face this prospect on behalf of her House. And she really wanted to know this side of Mason.

He studied the boy. "What does Khan say?"

"That he's a child of two worlds, and he's not interested in this one."

"He's not interested," Mason repeated.

This world could not compete with what Cari knew of the Other—Twilight was dreams and fantasy, or else abject nightmare and madness. If this child could really perceive what existed beyond Shadow, he'd be lost to this world. No contest.

She pulled herself closer to Mason to ease the tightening around her heart.

Adam scrubbed his worn face with his hands. "Ever feel like your kid can't grow up fast enough—so that they can be safer, better able to cope, to fight—and yet you still try to hold on and protect their innocence—keep them little—at the same time?"

"I know the feeling well." Mason sighed vocally, and Cari could feel the roll of it in his chest.

He brought her hand up for a kiss, then let her go to reach for an already-read newspaper on the kitchen's island. He walked over to the table where the boy sat and took a chair opposite him.

"Hey, Michael." Mason opened the newspaper and tore a page out from the rest.

The boy didn't react. Cari darted a look at Adam, and was surprised to see wary hope in his expression, the concentrated slant of his eyes. What did he think Mason could do?

Talia had halted in her conversation with another woman. She watched Mason and seemed to be holding her breath.

Mason began folding the strip of paper, the smoke of Shadow looping and trailing from his fingertips, as if stitching together whatever he was creating with magic. His hands did a graceful, practiced dance as they worked the paper. A twist here, a crumple there.

The boy's head cocked slightly, as if interested, though his gaze was still distant. It was something, at least. A response.

Mason's clever hands pinched and ripped the paper in his hand. The kitchen grew quiet as everyone watched. Cari found she was holding her breath, too.

And then with a little push, Mason set his creation—a man made out of newspaper—walking across the table. The little man strode over to Michael and tapped the child's hand with its own paper one, a blunt fold with a triangle for a thumb.

The boy looked down, and the paper man affected a deep bow from its waist, its arm sweeping low to its waist.

Michael looked up at Mason, now with bright, clear eyes, and laughed out loud. "Is Fletcher here?" The paper man climbed onto Michael's hand and began a trek up the mountain of his arm to the summit of his shoulder.

"Fletcher couldn't come this time." A tone of heartache, if one knew to listen.

Cari had wanted to see Mason-the-father, and now she almost regretted it. Felt like a knife got stuck up under her ribs, making breathing excruciating. And this kid wasn't even his.

She never should've slept with him. And yet, night couldn't come fast enough for her to do it again. Could they stay here longer?

Talia dove to kneel at her son's feet so that she was eye level with him. She brushed the hair from his forehead. "Hey, buddy. Where have you been?" There was no mistaking the relief in her tone.

Mason slid out of the seat and backed to the counter next to Cari.

Talia snapped her fingers behind her, and Adam had a carton of ice cream and a spoon ready. "How about some of your favorite?"

Ice cream in the morning? Cari guessed they were willing to do anything to keep the child in this room with them.

The little paper man leaned in to Michael's ear and whispered a secret.

Michael laughed out loud. "He wants some, too."

Cari leaned over to Mason. "How'd you do that?"

The little man sat down on Michael's shoulder and crossed his legs.

"Used to do it all the time with Fletcher."

That's not what she meant. "How did you *know* to do that?"

He shrugged and grabbed a mug from a tray. "Just thought it might interest him, too. Want something to eat? You slept in."

Heat rushed her face, recalling last night. "I was pretty tired." She looked back at the little boy, wanting to watch him play with the newspaper man.

But Mason's strong arm went around her waist, and he kissed her, right there in front of everyone, who yes, seemed to accept her solely on the basis of his companionship, regardless of the fact that she harbored a mad fae queen inside her.

When she drew back, her heart was locked up with feeling. She'd been asking herself for days how Mason could've possibly earned the notice of the Council or someone like Khan, but she understood it now. And the knowledge came painfully, because deep-down, she'd already known. Protector and father—that's what his horrible life had taught him. He'd become everything he hadn't had himself. That's how he could come here, and on the strength of his word, she would be welcomed. And she actually liked these people, with the exception of Khan. They seemed dependable, in a completely erratic way. They seemed true.

Mason was the kind of ally her House needed.

Which meant—this realization was a hot, sick rush—that Dolan House was on the wrong side. Brand was supposed to be an enemy, the mage that the Dolan was supposed to topple from the Council Seat, and Cari had shrugged off an opportunity just last night. Further, angels were to be reviled—one had thrown a spear at her—but she kind of liked that Custo.

Dolan had kept its bloodline pure, but it seemed that for the modern age, strength was in a different kind of unity.

Oh, sweet Shadow, she was in trouble. This was probably the most dangerous of all—she was shifting her loyalties.

Centuries worth of the careful cultivation of allies, and she had to undo it. The Dolan's duty was to see to the strength of her House . . . and it wasn't with Vauclain or Martin or Walker. The Walkers were stupid not to have snatched up Mason when they could, but Webb had been smart. He'd even taken in Mason's son to raise with his own. Very clever.

She'd have to think which to approach first. She was suddenly feeling a little dizzy at the prospect.

"You'll want something to eat before our chat with Khan." Mason put a mug of coffee in her hand. The omelet the brown-haired woman had been making materialized in front of her, too. "Eat up. The Dark Lord is waiting."

Maeve crouched, her fingernails lengthening to scratch out the crow's eyes.

Shadowman.

How she hated him. He'd gone into the service of Order ages ago, ferrying souls from this world to the great gate of the next. Of course he would take up with angels at the first opportunity. Fool. No matter how he groveled at their feet, he would never be one of them. No light for him, unless he stole it and ate it.

Mid-day on Segue's mountaintop was prickly and sweet with pine scent, but the chirping bugs stayed away from the main buildings. Mason sat across from Khan on the terrace, keeping Cari at his side. He didn't want her in the direct path of Death's fury again.

Khan was looking out into the trees, his dark, almost alien eyes peering into the greenery.

Cari took an audible deep breath to get his attention. "I want to thank you for meeting with me."

Mason bowed his head to hide his smile. Trust Caspar's daughter to take control of the meeting at the outset, even against the likes of Khan.

Khan's attention didn't waver. "The wild creatures are moving, drawing nearer, attracted to still greater wildness."

Mason turned in his seat to look too, but couldn't see anything. There were bears up here. Wolves and coyotes, too. Maybe even mountain lions. "Dangerous?"

Khan regarded Cari, his keen eyes slanting to assess her. "Certainly not more dangerous than she."

Cari sat up a little straighter, to go head-to-head with Shadowman. Mason didn't want her to wear herself out already, so he flung an arm on the back of her chair and tugged her shoulder back. Nothing to worry about.

"I am dangerous." She stated it like a fact, with a little whatcha-gonna-do-about-it? thrown in for flavor.

Mason liked her so much. He played with the ends of her hair with his fingers, relishing the wide silky loop of a natural curl. Wanted to brush her hair off the back of her neck and kiss her there. Again.

Khan didn't seem amused. "I have been chastised at length throughout the night. I see no hope for you, regardless of whether the Maker is at your side or not, but I will acknowledge the possibility, however slight, that the world might survive you."

Mason felt an inner tug at hearing the word "Maker." Khan had taken to referring to him that way over the past year, and yeah, Making was the kind of magic Mason specialized in. It must have been the aptitude of whatever House had given him a drop of their blood. He liked to work with his hands.

Trust Cari to pick up on it. "Maker?"

"Bah," Khan growled. "If you don't even know what Mason is, the world is indeed doomed."

Cari's shoulders went back, offended.

"Khan!" Layla's voice came from behind them, on the other side of the patio doors.

Mason smiled. Khan's wife was just as bullheaded as Cari. Khan must face his own doom every other day.

The Grim Reaper regrouped. His eyes twitched. "The world might survive you, Cari Dolan, though the possibility grows ever slimmer."

"Bra-vo," Mason said.

Khan's black eyes burned. "My woman is due to have our child soon and I have upset her."

Cari looked stunned. "I'm a little lost. Maker?"

Mason craned his head back over his shoulder. "Take a load off, Layla. We'll be all right." Then to Cari, "It's just what I do—make things. Like the little newspaper guy for Michael."

"Makers are rare." Khan gave him a vindictive smile. It seemed if he was going to be uncomfortable, forced into making uncomfortable admissions, then Mason was, too. "They are born only at the rise of Shadow, and sit on the right hand of kings."

"I'm a friend to mage royalty," Mason said. At least as long as that "friendship" lasted.

Khan's lip curled. "You do not take Mab seriously enough."

"Who's not serious?" The voice came from behind. Custo prowled out, uninvited, to join them. He leaned on the stone banister near the table. The angel looked like one dangerous motherfucker, especially when he had that wolf grin stretching across his face.

Cari didn't seem to object to his presence however— Mason recalled they'd formed a club last night while everyone else was fighting. She leaned toward Death. "And Makers are mages?"

Mason closed his eyes. He knew what she was asking. The human thing again. She wanted to know if Khan knew, and what he thought about it. But this wasn't supposed to be about him. Makers make. Done.

Khan sat back, crossed a leg, enjoying himself at Mason's expense. "Makers are Shadow and Light. Such is the requirement to create anything that lasts, that can hold. Michael is still playing with that puppet."

"By the way, the other kids are getting jealous," Custo put in.

"I'll make more. I used to make a whole collection for Fletcher." Just thinking of his son made him worry. There'd been no contact since yesterday's text about the Lure. If not for a phone appointment with Webb in an hour, Mason would be going out of his mind.

Fletcher's fine. A human made a delivery to Webb House early this morning. He was soaked by two rotten kids with water guns.

And you know this how? Mason pinned Custo with a glare.

He shrugged. *The angel watching over Webb House picked it out of the delivery man's head.*

The Order is watching Webb House? Mason didn't know how he felt about that. If Webb discovered it, there could be trouble, in spite of his connection to Brand and Bastian. Jack Bastian was tolerated, which wasn't the same thing as accepted, and a far cry from embraced.

Jack Bastian said it was part of your agreement.

Mason's heart beat harder, sweat breaking out on his neck. Took him a sec to realize that Cari and Khan were watching him in silence. "What?"

Then understanding dawned on Cari's face. "Angels are telepathic. They can speak right to a soul."

Damn it. She knew he was human, but he didn't want to be obvious about it.

"Why is this about me, anyway?" So he made things, so

what? "Weren't we supposed to be talking about Maeve, or Mad Mab, or whatever the crazy fae queen is called?"

Khan lost his good humor, too. "What's to talk about? Dolan is the mage offspring of the mad queen. The Dolan line has *always* known to kill any females born to them, to stop Mab from entering the world again. Cari's father was either ignorant, or was too weak to do it."

Cari shook her head. "Not weak. He loved me."

"And Caspar was not ignorant either," Mason told him. "His library alone contains more knowledge than all the other Houses combined."

"Bah," Khan said. "He knew better. By the time you were born, he had to know that Maeve was mad."

"He controlled her. And I can control her, too," Cari said. "I'm getting better and better at it."

Mason kept his mouth shut. She already knew what he thought about her ability to manage that limitless Shadow. No one could control it.

Khan tilted his head as if he were talking to a child. "How long has Maeve been with you?"

Cari exhaled audibly. "About two weeks."

"Bear Mad Mab for a year, and you will welcome her into your mind, into your body."

"Cari's father lived with Maeve for decades."

"He was a man. Dolan is a *female* line. Maeve would have been but a whisper to him." Khan looked at Cari. "Is she a whisper to you?"

Her eyes got that full look, as if her mind was filling with awful conclusions. She shook her head. No.

Mason bore down on Khan's point. "If Maeve is so evil . . ."

Khan shook his head. "Not evil. If she were evil, then good in equal force could be marshaled against her. The fae don't recognize good or evil; they live on whim. They are elemental, essential, like death and dreams. You can't fight an elemental. You can only keep it in its place. The sun must stay in the sky. The seas must not ravage the land. Dreams must stay within Twilight, lest they become nightmares on Earth."

"That would be Order," Custo said under his breath.

Khan glowered at the Shadow-darkened angel. "Wolf, you asked me to kill you once. I'll oblige you now."

Cari's gaze went distant, internal. "The angel that threw the spear at me. He knows about Maeve?"

Custo answered. "Yes. He's on a personal quest, though. Not Order sanctioned. He is being tracked by a team, led by the best." He looked over at Mason. "You met him, I think. Laurence?"

Mason bobbed a nod to say, yes, they'd met. The mention made him restless and uncomfortable. Laurence had looked inside him. He'd seen all the horrible things that Mason had never wanted brought to light again.

Khan gazed off into the trees, his alien eyes squinting. Wild animals. "Tell Adam that the children should not play on the grounds today." He looked at Cari. "Maybe for a few days."

"Will do," Custo said.

Cari put a hand to Mason's knee. "I should go."

She meant she didn't want to be the reason anyone here got hurt. If her thoughts kept going down that road, she was going to make a terrible decision about herself.

She's a keeper, Custo said.

Didn't work that way among magekind, so Mason didn't answer him. He took Cari's hand, and she stood when he did. "We'll head out right away."

Her lips pressed together, as if she were going to suggest something. Mason knew what was on her mind—her "*I should go*" had given her away.

Mason shook his head before she could put her thought into words. For reasons he wouldn't bother to enumerate to the very smart Cari Dolan, he said simply, "Together."

* * *

Xavier strode into the crowd that moved in constantly morphing packs through Harvard Square. He attached himself to the back of a family. Camouflage. The Order was pursuing him. He wiped the mind of a father mid-conversation with his adult children, and supplanted his face in their memories. The true father wandered dumbly on with the wave of people. A baseball cap and an animated discussion about the children's university coursework were his disguise as angels filtered through the throng in search.

"—so then Dr. Schmidt, the program chair, said I could look at witchcraft in *The Scarlet Letter* in terms of the modern mage movement. I mean, the concept of 'the woods' alone will be an entire section of the paper."

Xavier had to resist the impulse to look around and gauge how close the angels were. He felt their eyes on the back of his neck. He hid under the voice and mind chatter all around him. Music up ahead sent punctuated ripples of sound all around. As he hadn't been in ages, he was self-conscious of his rank smell. Would one of these young angels think to use his nose?

"Dad, are you listening?" The young woman grabbed his arm, and Xavier was forced to look down at her. "So I submitted a proposal to the department's top scholar's program, and in light of current events, they awarded the grant to *me*."

Adversity had never deterred him before. But now that he'd been identified, and at least part of his mission revealed, success was not assured. His heart ached with disappointment he could not afford. All this time. All this waiting. The excruciating silence of the days. The loneliness.

No. He could not afford self-pity.

Victory must be assured. In the darkest moments, he must

still hold fast. It didn't matter what it cost him. He'd pledged his soul to combating Shadow, and he still had that soul to give.

"Dad!" The young woman sounded hurt.

Her mother looked around, forehead wrinkling. "What's the matter?"

Xavier's skin flashed cold with the threat of exposure.

He waved the mother away with a smile and feigned interest in the girl's topic. She was interested in mages?

Soul light burned his back behind him, but he forced his head to bend down to the girl's ear. "Witchcraft."

She nodded, an adult begging for attention like a dog.

He should take precautions. People needed to know.

Xavier moved into her mind as he whispered. "If you're going to be passionate about witchcraft, what about the one in your midst? Cari Dolan."

Her eyes were blank for a moment, then sparked. "Might be an interesting angle if I could get an interview."

Xavier pushed harder at her mind, directing her interests.

The paper receded to the back recesses of her brain. The light burned brighter. "Cari Dolan," she said, voice full of fear.

Xavier leaned toward another person in the crowd, and whispered the same thing. "Spread the word."

If he were to be caught now, or tomorrow, or the next day, he needed to make sure others would finish his mission. That there was hope.

Xavier whispered to another and another, planting seeds where he could, like a gardener sowing thought. "Cari Dolan is the end of the world. She must be stopped."

Cari folded the last of the loaned clothing. The bed was still in shambles, covers and sheets spilled to the floor. One pillow had fallen off the side of the mattress, while the other was a cloud in the center of the bed. She put the clothing to the side and reached to grab the sheet. It was way too obvious what had happened here.

"Princess Dolan, making a bed."

She didn't look at Mason. "My father always had us keep our own rooms tidy." She folded and tucked an expert hospital corner to prove it.

"You okay?"

She straightened. "Well, let's see—both a rogue angel and Khan seem to think that the world would be better off if I were dead. There's even, supposedly, a mage saying about it. 'Never suffer a Dolan female to live,' is how I think it went."

"Your father made a different call. And he was a very smart man."

"Doesn't matter. I'm here now. I'm certainly not going to roll over and die." That's not how her father had raised her. He'd raised her to be the next Dolan, with all the fun and games that entailed.

"Never thought you would," Mason said from the doorway.

In spite of it all, the news hadn't changed anything, not really. She'd received her answers from Khan, but Maeve's answers had actually been similar, minus the part where Cari needed to die—so everyone was in agreement there. Dolan was a great House, an old House, with a faery queen for a patron.

"Good." Cari snapped the blanket to whip it flat across the bed.

If not for Maeve's protection, she would have succumbed to the mage plague, which was systematically decimating the Houses. When she'd needed power, Maeve had given it to her. And even if Mad Mab did speak in a grandiose, megalomaniacal way—she was fae. They had no sense of proportion. Khan was not so different. She thought of his grumbly voice: *I would be happy to dispatch you. Blah blah blah.*

"Adam is loaning us the use of his helicopter to get back to

Dolan House." Mason came up behind her and put his hands on her shoulders.

The muscles underneath quivered in exquisite relief. He had great hands.

She sighed hugely. All she could really do was continue to be cautious where Maeve was concerned. She could work for mastery. Her body was getting stronger, better able to bear the massive amount of magic. And if she benefited from the faery's gifts, then good for Dolan.

This place—Segue—mixed her up. Everything here was worse . . . and better. So much better.

"Custo said he would contact us when the Order had identified who the blood from the tainted Shadow had come from. Should be soon." With Mason behind her, she felt so good. Why had she resisted during this past week? Maeve had told her to take him from the beginning.

Wait until you taste his soul.

Cari shoved Maeve out of her mind and turned to face Mason.

He'd had a look of concern in his eyes at first, but it was darkening now to match her mood. All her life, Cari had tried not to abuse her privilege by being greedy. And it hadn't been too hard, because she'd pretty much had everything she wanted.

Except for that once, when Liv had stolen Mason back after breaking up with him. Cari had been left wanting then, and had been utterly unable to do anything about it. And now that she understood exactly how much had slipped from her grasp, she was wanting again.

"Cari?"

The periphery of her vision was occluded by a growing haze. *No reason you should go without.*

She wasn't going to just give up and die. She was going to live life to the fullest. She was going to crush the person who'd killed her father. She was going to summon enough

Shadow to raise Dolan to new heights. Magic swelled within her. After everything, maybe Maeve was right: Maybe she could have it all. No, she *would* have it all. The alternatives— failure, death, obscurity—did not interest her. And anyone who got in her way—

"Pitch," Mason said.

Maeve hissed frustration.

He crushed Cari to him, his mouth taking hers, robbing her of breath. The kiss devoured, and whether from oxygen deprivation or the shock of the pleasure of his tongue rubbing on hers, she melted against him, body and heart. This close, she could feel the blue bright of his soul burning away the Other night that had permeated her umbra. Mason's soul could defeat anything.

And his hands—*please Shadow*—his hands. Where he stroked—waist, breast, collar bone—he remade her. He'd learned her last night, and now he applied his knowledge. His hands remembered how she used to be—years ago, what seemed like forever—without this harshness in her mind.

Only when she tasted salt did she realize that she'd been crying. Who was she fooling? She was so afraid.

He must have tasted her tears, too, but he didn't relent. He drew patterns on her skin like a mystic tracing symbols of power. The presence in her mind was banished by his touch. The clothes fell like leaves from their bodies. The tidy bed was destroyed.

He bowed over her—sorcerer, lover, friend—filling her up so that there was no room for anything else. And she held onto him with all her strength.

She didn't know how—her brain was too loose to make a plan—but she wasn't going to let him go.

Chapter Twelve

"See?" Kaye Brand dropped her purse on the bare floor of what would be her sitting room—when they had time to shop for furniture—and turned to face Bastian, her eyes flashing. She was ready for his bad mood, but she headed him off with, "Home safe and sound."

Her confidence felt a little thin, beaten as it was by the hammering of her pulse these past two hours that she'd been meeting with the senator and the Special Committee on Shadow. The rising furor against magic had to be stopped or someone was going to get hurt. The crowd around Dolan House was swelling, not settling down. She had to make it clear that the Houses would reciprocate against violence if the law wouldn't or couldn't protect them.

"The Order could have handled it," Bastian cut back and slammed the door behind him.

"The Order cannot be the executor of mage Council business." The tolerance of the Houses where angels were concerned was already strained, especially with the rogue on the loose. She was barely holding on to the Houses as it was.

His hands to her shoulders, he restrained her now as he couldn't before. She actually kind of liked it, so she leaned forward to brush her mouth across his, adding a little sex to his fury. Her angry man. *Just try to boss me.*

The ice in his eyes belied the heat underneath. "It is too dangerous for you," he said, "for the Council, for peace, for you to leave your wards. I won't let you do it again, not for anything."

"I'll do what I must." She loved to bait him. It was one of her favorite things, ever. Better than shopping. A close second to sex.

"You don't think I can stop you?" A threat.

She smiled darkly. "I think you've met your match, or do you need me to demonstrate?"

The light in his eyes shifted. A shadow of pain. "Kaye—"

That tone in his voice, her Bastian wounded, did more than his arguments could have.

So she softened, too. Where he led, she couldn't help but follow. "It'll never be completely safe, Bastian."

"You don't have to keep proving how brave you are."

"Yes, actually I do." And all the Houses had to see it, or else they'd forget. Kaye Brand, firemage, did and would continue to burn every day, every night, under any circumstance. "It's what holds their respect, that I will do what needs be done. And you were there to protect me, as always."

Tensions had escalated perilously high, rivaling the time of Ferrol Grey's tenure in the High Seat of the Council. The threats came from all sides now and whispers had begun that perhaps Grey's plan had been the better one after all. What would Grey have done about the plague? Something definitive and foul. Would he have tolerated the mob growing around Dolan House? Not for a minute.

"Stop it," Bastian said. "Do not begin to doubt yourself."

Kaye smiled. "At least now you're arguing my side."

"I'm always on your side."

Her thoughts had shaken her, and she could think of one

easy way to feel good again. She'd bet her considerable shoe collection that Bastian would cooperate.

She stepped back out of his reach, and with a smile that promised utter sin and ruination, started down the buttons of her blouse. Soul-hungry desire filled Bastian's eyes. The silk fell to the floor. The pencil skirt next, with a zip to the side. She wiggled her hips to help it fall. The slip floated down a second later. She stood in her underwear and heels, and stretched her arms overhead, both to lift her breasts to show them to their best advantage and to ease the tension ache at the small of her back.

Bastian did come to her, as she knew he would. She didn't understand the pull between them, but couldn't ever deny it either. She was his; he was hers. The universe had decreed it so. Didn't matter that she was born to Shadow, and he to Light.

He grabbed her raised arm, so gently, stroking the hollow of her armpit with his fingertips.

"This is new," she observed. "I'm not saying I'm not into it, but—"

Actually, he was making her hot. He always made her hot.

"Burn, Kaye," he commanded. His voice had gone harsh, so she knew he was worried.

She craned her head to look, too, and found blackening fine lines converging into an abscess under her arm. Even Bastian's softest caress ached.

Her mouth went dry. Tremors began to shake her, when she'd made sure that she never showed fear. Her legs buckled, but as always, Bastian was there to catch her. He lowered her to the floor. "You need to burn. Burn this sickness out of you. Come back new."

He was so calm. Her soldier, battling himself.

Plague. Few survived this. She could name three mages, not including Mason. The poison had taken the strong and weak alike. It could take her.

"Burn." Bastian held her.

And that's how she knew he was scared, too, in spite of how composed he seemed. He wasn't thinking. Faefire burns on angelic skin never healed. He had a trophy on his arm from last year, and it would sear his skin for the rest of his life.

She could feel the sickness now, poisoning her Shadow within. She was used to heat, but this didn't come from her. It lacked the erotic pulse and shimmer of Twilight. This heat scorched in a way that fire never had before. It crackled and ached as it raced through her body. A terrible pressure pained her chest. She had to do this now.

She pushed Bastian away. He fought for a moment, and then let her go so that she could have her chance. She would never forget the unblinking agony on his face as he crouched nearby.

Kaye had never been so happy, so relieved, he wasn't Shadow born so that he would not be taken up.

She reached for the drumbeat of her umbra, the bit of her that was elemental, which was power. She stoked it upward, carelessly, accelerant to flame, and gave herself to the eruption.

Bastian rocked in a near-fetal position. His head was roaring, senses rough as he watched.

Kaye was burning again, a second fiery molt, this time silently. Every time she came back—her power resurrection—the plague ate at her again. Sooner or later she wouldn't want to return; she would linger in Twilight rather than face the pain and horror another time.

He was tempted to grab hold and burn with her. Remind her to come back or follow her into darkness. Anything was better than this.

* * *

"We have confirmation."

Mason opened the door wider to let Custo inside the small suite. That the angel had come up here to speak to them privately meant he was respecting the deals made by Brand and Bastian. The results of the blood test were back.

Cari came out of the bedroom, dressed just in time, a questioning look on her face. "What's going on?"

Mason directed Custo to a chair with a quick nod. "Have a seat."

Cari came to the correct conclusion. "Who is it?"

Mason took her hand and tugged her toward the couch opposite the chair. She was better now. There had been a moment before when he'd been worried for her. Strong, dutiful Cari grappling with bad news after more bad news. But her gaze was as direct as ever. Her composure set. Maybe the Dolan aptitude for Shadow was really courage.

"The blood belongs to the rogue angel, Xavier, the same one who attacked you outside Vauclain House."

Mason groaned. The angel. So much for Brand and Bastian's peace. Maybe Cari would have to take Kaye's place after all. Magekind would not stand for Order in their presence when they learned this.

"*Rogue* angel? Don't make me laugh," Cari said in the voice of all magekind. "I don't believe you. He alone is well on the way to accomplishing what the Order has done time and time again—crush Shadow."

And here Mason had thought she'd liked Custo. Not anymore.

"Angels have the same capacity for evil that any other soul has," Custo told her. "He is very, very old. Found a way to sustain himself, probably with Shadow. I'm told that as a human he had the same aptitude for making that Mason here has."

Mason caught Cari glaring at him. "I'm not like Xavier."

Custo leaned forward. "He created a pathogen that his

angelic blood could carry and that could be disseminated via Shadow."

Shadow, the bread and breath of magekind, contaminated.

"The Order is tracking him. Xavier can't run forever. We will not tire, not after what he's done. He will be apprehended and escorted to Hell."

Cari was about to come off her seat. "Not good enough. The Houses protect and defend their own. He has injured my people. *We* discovered his identity and *I* will make him pay for what he did to my father. The rest of magekind can stomp on the leftover pieces. The Order may clean up the resulting smear."

Mason had closed his eyes during this recitation. Spoken like the head of a mighty House.

She wanted Xavier's absolute death. Mason expected nothing less from her. Angels were embodied souls. If they died on Earth, they died forever. Such was their sacrifice for dedicating themselves to the service of humankind.

Custo looked every bit the wolf when he responded. "You can't track him. Not even Mad Mab can find him, or so Khan tells me."

"I don't need to track him." Cari was too smart for her own good.

Custo knew what she was thinking, too. "He won't go for you as bait. He's old enough to know a trap."

"If he wants me bad enough, he will."

Custo shook his head. "You can't defeat him alone. He'll wait you out. He has patience to spare."

"I have a fae queen."

So she'd decided to embrace Maeve after all. Not that she had much choice, but still. "I've seen you in the thrall of power, Cari," Mason said, "and you weren't fighting an ancient angel. You'll lose yourself and therefore your House, everything your father worked for. You know this."

"I don't, actually," she returned. "Every time I've partnered with Maeve, I've been successful."

Partnered? Sweet Shadow, Cari was already mad. He'd hoped for a minute there . . .

"It's a viable solution," she said. "A calculated risk."

Mason could feel Custo's interest shift to him. "You have another idea."

Not really. He was looking for ways to mitigate the risks that Cari intended to take. She'd do something regardless of any warnings. She'd loved her father and she had to prove herself as his successor. Allowing the Order to go after Xavier and bring him to justice was not an option for the new Dolan. "Refinements to Cari's plan, actually." Besides, it was part of his agreement with the Council that *he* end the threat of the mage plague.

"Well, let's have it," she challenged, as if bracing against him, too.

Mason didn't feel good about this. "You as bait, somewhere far away from other people, should things get out of hand."

"I'm stronger by my wards."

"Hundreds of people now surround your House, Cari," Custo said. "Please don't put them in the middle of everything."

She smiled. "They are welcome to leave any time."

"I'm thinking of *my* house," Mason said. "Such as it is."

He got a lifted eyebrow from Cari.

Custo looked like he was considering it, as if he had any say in the decision. He didn't.

"It's on a little island. I have water for my wards." Mason smiled a little, remembering how he'd worked to make water obey him. "He'll track my soul there, just as Jack Bastian tracked me to my cabin in New Mexico." He glanced at Cari. "Since you and I have been inseparable, and my thoughts . . . occupied by you, he might guess that we've gone there for a retreat of sorts while the Order hunts him and your House is under siege."

"We go to *your* house," Cari mused.

"It's not much." Once, it had been everything. But it was the people inside the house that mattered, not the structure.

Custo was shaking his head. "He'll know that angels are waiting. He'll see their souls."

"No angels will be waiting," Cari said, but she was looking at Mason. He could feel her mind moving in concert with his.

Custo groaned with frustration. "You can't mean to use Mab. You don't know the danger of giving her any purchase in this world."

"I was thinking meaner, hungrier," Mason said to Cari. She was looking into his eyes now, deeper and deeper. They were connected by a strand of understanding cast years ago. Now it carried the weight of this terrible business. Blood and violence between them.

Custo suddenly frowned, disgusted.

Cari gave a magey smile, all edges. Would her father recognize her? He'd be proud.

"That's vicious," said the angel with a wild wolf trapped within him. "The Order would never even think to do something so bloody. Would never condone it. It is evil."

Mason didn't care. "That's why it will work." How many deaths had Xavier delivered to the Shadowed? Fletcher almost among them. In this, Mason felt completely the mage—vengeful. "He won't know they're there. He won't expect us to use this means. Wraiths don't have souls." And they were super strong, healed quickly, and were driven by a hunger for one thing.

"They'll go after you first," Custo argued.

Mason shook his head no. "The wraiths will be contained by their traps. And when Xavier arrives, I'll conceal my soul before releasing them."

"What if he can conceal his, just like you?"

Mason slid his gaze over to Cari.

Cari dipped her head into a deep, satisfied nod. "I can part Xavier's Shadow. I've done it to Mason. The angel will have nowhere to hide."

Mason hadn't even had to explain it to her. She'd come to all his conclusions, seen all the steps he'd take. A couple words and she could follow his thoughts step by step to their conclusion, no matter how ugly.

Custo stood and walked to the window. "It's a risk."

"Ours to take," Mason answered. "Do you think Adam would loan me the use of a bunch of his monsters?"

"I want to watch the monsters feed on that SOB," Cari gloated. "Gobble him down just like his plague took my father."

"They'd be trapped on the island anyway," Mason pointed out to Custo. "Easy to recapture. Not a great problem to the human population nearby."

Custo swallowed the terribleness of the idea. "How fast do you think you can get this together?"

Was it decided so quickly then? No conference with the Order?

Mason's attention narrowed. Custo wasn't telling them something. "Depends on Adam."

"Travel time," Cari added. "Besides the obvious, why the rush?"

"Kaye Brand fell to the plague this morning," Custo said. "She's cycled through fire and resurrection twice already. Jack doesn't know how long she can hold out. He's past his breaking point himself, especially because Xavier must have been picking details from *his* mind to target the Houses he attacked. Bastian was the Council's weakness."

Mason's heart knocked hard as the implications snapped into focus. The peace between Order and Shadow would break if the Houses knew. Would Cari tell them?

Further, Fletcher's fosterage agreement had been made

with Kaye Brand. She couldn't die. There was no Brand heir as yet to succeed her and fulfill her part of the contract.

Mason thought of the way his Making magic worked—things remained animated or held their function until he lost his interest and released the Shadow from his control. He imagined death would accomplish the same thing—everything Xavier had made would become inert.

Mason looked to Custo for confirmation. "Kill the angel, end the cycle?" End Xavier's control of the plagued Shadow?

Custo nodded. "That's the hope, if there's any left to be had."

Xavier strode down an alley behind a pizza joint, the smell of tomato sauce heavy with garlic overriding the funk of the garbage bins. The smell intoxicated him, reminding him that his neglected body needed sustenance. But he didn't have time to stop. He could feel the net closing around him.

He had to get free of the city. Get out of this warren of closely packed shops and restaurants teeming with people. He had to find the Dolan. It was Imperative.

The brick buildings to each side pointed upward to the sky, a symbol of where his mind should be. His purpose. The laughter of people inside burst into the alley as a boy popped out of a kitchen to throw away a bag of trash.

The boy spotted him and went rigid with alarm.

Hold! commanded a figure at the end of the alley. A female angel.

Xavier took the bag of trash from the boy's grasp and with a hand to the kid's chest, pushed him back inside the restaurant. Xavier threw the trash into the bin. "I have work to do," he told the angel ahead. It was a young one, earnest and resolute in her stance.

Such sadness had the fae queen wrought, and she was not yet even born to this world. More death, more grief. Darkness everywhere.

Xavier approached, palms open. "Peace, sister."

"Come home," the angel said.

Xavier filtered through her memory so that something would be remembered . . . after. Diana was her name. Her human life had been a good one, and she'd dedicated her angelic one to giving back. But she had to die. Would she have chosen to give *this* much, had she known? His quest was more important.

"Xav!" Laurence shouted from behind him. Too far to help her.

Xavier broke Diana's neck, fast, clean, so that he could get by. One more soul destroyed by Mab.

Cari walked up the pier. The roof of a house ahead cut angles out of the tops of trees. There was a hollow knocking, wood on wood, blustered by an incoming storm. Mist whipped off the water of the bay. The leaves shushed the wind, but it gusted on to rattle something metal, like chains. A beaten path fixed with uneven stones dug into the ground led the way around to the house. High grasses bristled near the water.

She cast her eye as far as she could see along the shore—water did have magical properties. Mason's "wards." The man had done the best he could with what was available.

Mason caught up behind her, supplies in hand. "Adam called. Wraiths are a half hour out."

There'd been a furor at Segue when Mason had requested the use of a bunch of wraiths to combat the angel. At first there'd been outright refusal. Adam wouldn't stand for any soul to be devoured by one of those monsters. But Kaye was barely hanging on to life. And the angel Xavier was practicing genocide against magekind. Adam had finally conceded, saying his soul was damned anyway, and even Shadowman had agreed, saying that Xavier had forfeited his soul long ago.

Custo had been silent. Five portable wraith cells were being flown in from the satellite New York site.

The most recent sighting of the angel placed him in Boston, where he had killed another of his own. That was two angels dead because of him, and a couple of police officers outside Vauclain House.

But now that Cari was here, at Mason's home, she partly regretted the impending destruction. Her nod to Mason became another look around, a little wistful. "This is a lovely spot."

The little island wasn't grandiose, like the manses of the mage Houses. But a place this idyllic didn't come cheap—millions, Cari thought. He had to have some means.

"My first couple of jobs—bloody work—paid for it." He shrugged. "I also scared the shit out of the owner when a better offer came in."

Cari could imagine. "Good for you."

"I had a toddler keeping me up nights. I was in a bad mood. All my patience—and back then I didn't have very much—went to the kid."

The trees stepped out of the way as she turned a bend in the path. An overgrown lawn ran up to the back porch, which held some kind of awkward metal and netting apparatus. Trapped underneath was a soccer ball. The house itself was a white cottage. Very sweet. Well cared for. The hedges under the windows were a little wild, but Mason had been away.

Mason had to wrestle the soccer goal out of the way to get the back door open. He tried to hold it open, but the bags in his arms made his effort clumsy, so she held the door for him. It gave her the chance to look around without being observed.

Kitchen to the left. Out of date and cluttered with counter appliances. Silly flowery curtains with ruffles on the window above the sink. To the right what had to be the dining table, but it was scarred from use and held some kind of project. Screws. Bolts. Tools. Mason had been making something.

Curious, she wandered over while Mason made banging noises off somewhere. A large piece of paper was folded open, a drawing—plans—sketched in detail, but just lopsided enough that she knew it'd been created by the son, and not the father. A little bit of their arrested life together. She was greedy to absorb all the details she could.

Movement turned her head. Mason, in the living room. "They'll land on the front lawns, and we'll pull the cages into the trees to conceal them."

She walked forward into the living room. The threshold of the pass-through was marked up. Upon closer examination she realized the pencil marks had dates that grew progressively more recent as they inched up the doorway. The last was a couple months ago. Her heart ached as she realized she could guess how tall Fletcher was.

A beat up leather sofa set faced a smoke-scarred stone fireplace.

Cari let her gaze travel, taking in the minutiae of their life. His home made her feel strange, sad and angry, as if in another world at another time, she'd been the one to defy family and run away with Mason Stray. This was where she'd have ended up.

She couldn't understand how Liv—stupid, proud Liv—had abandoned this home. Cari looked at the curtains again—those flowery ruffles. Maybe Liv had tried.

"Not your style." She pointed to the window and hoped she wasn't being obvious.

Mason leaned a shotgun, smoking with Shadow, by the front door. "Maria. She gets fussy sometimes when I'm away. Said the place needed a woman's touch."

"Maria." Another woman, caring for him and his son. Adding touches. How nice.

Mine, Cari's heart rasped.

His eyes narrowed as he smiled. "The nanny. She just celebrated her sixtieth. Fletcher and I made her a pasta gizmo."

He shrugged. "Granted it was so she'd make us more ravioli, but she seemed to like it."

Nanny. Maria was practical, not personal. Well, not personal in the way that Cari had feared.

"Does she know about Shadow?" If Maria took care of Fletcher, she must.

"She said she raised seven of her own and that she could handle anything." He chuckled low, as if remembering something. "Fletcher put her to the test. I was so exhausted by then, there were a couple nights I wept for sleep. Maria took pity on me."

Cari walked through the room, her heels knocking on the wood floors. She came to stand by Mason to look out the front door. The wide and deep lawn needed to be cut, but the state of overgrowth made the spot storybook-magical, though big gray clouds rolled overhead. "I've been in a lot of Houses," she said. "Great Houses. And this one is among the best."

It was an effortless, feel-good place, exactly how everything about Mason seemed to go easy on her—always had. She could imagine curling up on his sofa, wrapped in a blanket, or wrapped in him, and feeling more herself than she ever had in her life.

He put an arm around her waist, and she let her head fall to his shoulder.

And in what—a day?—this perfect place would be decimated by Shadow and Order.

A dark swell of anger made her heart beat harder.

Mine.

If she survived this, and she intended to, she already knew what she was going to do first thing. She smiled, thinking to herself of the bomb it might set off among the Houses. She was going to enjoy every moment.

She was going to claim Mason Stray for Dolan House.

She was sure counter claims would be set. Brand was

expected—she'd valued Mason from the beginning. Webb was a lock for Mason as well—he'd already gone so far as to take on Fletcher. She'd have to fight the fosterage agreement. Were there other Houses interested? She should plan on it, and disappoint them all. Her first big coup. She'd have to offer him something big to lure him away from other offers—something more than the status of a vassal, which was what the other Houses would give him—and she had just the thing in mind.

Scarlet was going to pitch a fit, but Stacia and Zel would be okay. If they could just see her and Mason together, really together, then they'd approve.

Mason's shoulder rose under her cheek as he drew a big breath. "Webb is trying to take the Umbra project from you, and I've been helping him."

She stopped breathing. His shoulder didn't fall, so he was holding his breath, too.

Umbra.

So that's what it was.

She heaved her own sigh, but stayed put in the crook of his arm. She'd expected some terrible thing—he'd warned her not to trust him. His breath came out slower, waiting for her reaction.

Umbra, her father's legacy, a commodity that would be highly prized now, and even more so as the world fell to magic.

The world has already fallen . . . to you.

She swallowed the bitter taste in her mouth, and ignored Maeve.

Mason was allied with a different faction within magekind. It was expected that either he or she would attempt to seize an advantage. Plus, Webb had his son. Mason had warned her not to trust him, yet had just proved that she could. By revealing Webb's intentions, he'd just trusted *her* with his son's life.

So she laid it out for him, truth for truth. "My House needs Umbra."

All her father's hard work. All the resources they'd dedicated to its development. She had so many people to take care of. Every day the world was more perilous. If predictions were correct—and recent events revealed they were dead on—then industries, including DolanCo, would collapse. Currencies would lose their value. Dolan would be able to trade for goods, services, safety, and more with Umbra. Which was probably the same reason Webb wanted it.

"Your membrane is promising," Mason said. "Using a synthetic living tissue was brilliant, but I don't see how it can ever work the way you want it to."

He'd obviously been at her research as well.

"Our refinements have had very encouraging results."

"Shadow is just playing with you."

Ridiculous. "Shadow doesn't *think*." Results were results.

"Sure it does." He turned his head to look down at her. "Shadow is fully aware of what you want it to do, and it is ambivalent about your success. You have to be able to tell it what to do, what to become."

His mastery. She met his gaze. She loved his face. Those troubled eyes. Which made her glow with satisfaction. "Mason Maker," she named him to persuade him to voice the idea turning in his head. She could guess. She'd been thinking about it herself since that terrible conversation with Khan.

Humor glinted in the black of his irises. "Yeah. I think I could do it." He looked back out to the dense greenery of the trees. "I would do it for you."

She was so going to claim him. Mason was hers. Webb could have the ambivalent membrane. See how that worked for him.

Some things were just meant to be. It was a human thought, since only humankind was ruled by Fate. No mage had ever had a destiny—without a soul, their lives were completely their own. But Mason was human, so maybe *she* was caught up in his fate.

Which was fine by her.

Really, they'd hit it off the first time they met. She even thought her father would approve, regardless of Mason's status. Joining with Mason Stray was by far the smartest thing she could do, on every level.

She wasn't going to spill her plans just then. She needed to work out the details, particularly pertaining to his son. She adored the kid already—any son of Mason's would be amazing. There was some negotiating to do with Brand, if the firemage survived her bout with the plague, which Dolan would have a hand in assuring. And she'd have to address the Houses that were Dolan's current allies.

But one thing was for certain. She tightened her hold around Mason, breathed in his scent. "I'll make it very worth your while."

He chuckled. "I look forward to the negotiations."

It hadn't occurred to Mason until he set foot on his little island that he didn't want bloodshed here. This was supposed to be a safe place. He'd poured all he had—magic, money, sweat—into making it safe. He half expected to hear Fletcher bounding down the stairs two at a time, shouting, "Dad!"

But it was quiet. "There are some realities to face, Cari."

"There are a lot of things that I'm worried about, but Umbra isn't one of them. It's going to work out."

Not just Umbra.

The air above was suddenly bludgeoned by the sound of helicopter rotors. Monsters coming. Right on time, and still too soon. And yet even as the Sikorsky helicopter pivoted in the air to land, the trees screaming as they bent, the grasses dancing, the dark future seemed to gleam with pinpricks of possibility.

If Cari, aka the *Dolan*, accepted him—a House opposed to the Council and not affiliated with the Order—then maybe Webb and the other Houses would also cope with his humanity. The "Maker" angle, which before this he'd ignored, might keep magekind's interest. And Umbra would be the perfect project to demonstrate his worth beyond taking on random and questionable work. But it wasn't going to be easy.

Five individual, remotely controlled cages, each filled with a shrieking wraith hungry for a soul, were unloaded and camouflaged around the property. The wraiths rattled and stank with their deterioration; if not fed, they devolved further into wights, utterly mindless and unsubstantial corporeal beings, shivering in disgusting flesh.

The soldiers at Segue's disposal did their work with swift efficiency and within an hour seemed ready to depart again and leave Mason and Cari to their trap. When the rotors started to once again beat the air, a last soldier approached Mason. He had a small brown case in his hand. "Sir. I was told to deliver this to you."

Mason took the case from him, and the soldier ran back, crouching before the gusts of wind. Mason squinted against flecks of dirt and unlocked the case as the helicopter rose. Nestled inside the foam was a dagger with a magic black blade.

"That's a Martin House dagger," Cari said.

Mason nodded. He recognized the craftsmanship of the blade—it was a perfect weapon, steel infused with Shadow. The wicked edge narrowed to a deadly lick. One strike of the knife backed with the intent to kill, and Shadow took its victim, even if the blade only managed a scratch. A weapon of darkness like this was made to kill angels. And Martin House was the machinery of war that led the battle.

"How'd Adam get hold of one of these?" Segue and Martin were at war.

"No idea," Cari said. "Martin is one of Dolan's allies."

"Ever been in a knife fight?"

"No. You?" She looked at him warily.

"Several." But he flipped the blade over in his hand and offered her the hilt. She should have it. "Basically, stick them before they stick you."

The hilt wasn't a natural fit for her small palm. Mason covered the back of her hand with his and sent Shadow coursing through the blade. The metal moved like moonlit water and the knife reformed, longer, thinner, into a malevolent dart. Her grasp became more certain.

"Better." She breathed deep, as if to fill herself up with courage. "I like it. I want it."

He smiled at her possessiveness. It wasn't in her nature to acquire or want, except if something had real value. This knife was of the best quality. "You'll have to take the matter up with Adam." After. Mason would make sure there'd be an after.

She sighed. "Are we ready then?"

His smile faded. It was time for the beacon to draw the angel here. He parted the dark mist that covered his soul. Bastian had said any angel could find him. *Well, here I am.*

Cari looked forlorn.

"I'd give it up if I could," he said of his soul. Be like Fletcher. Like her.

Her eyes gleamed and she shook her head, pain twisting her mouth. "Please don't. You make me want one of those, actually."

He couldn't help but love her. He'd always loved her. What she did to him. He cupped her head and drew her forward to kiss her. She rose on tiptoe to make the press fiercer. More desperate. His mage princess, Martin dagger in hand, rocking his soul.

"How much time do we have?" she murmured against his mouth.

He shifted his grasp to lift her without breaking the kiss. "Could be hours, could be days."

Her legs came around his waist, and he supported her . . .
forearms to her hips, hands to her ass. "Did I ever give you a
tour of the house?"

She brushed her lips across his, a slide of her satin. "Nope."

"My apologies. Let's start upstairs." His feet knew the
count of every step. The choreography of dodging a mess in
the upstairs hallway was ingrained in his muscle memory,
past Fletcher's room and the bathroom, to the third door,
where in the seven-plus years he and Fletcher had lived here,
Mason had never brought a woman. The bedroom was tiny
compared to his suite at Dolan House. No more than a closet
with a double bed.

"I love it," she breathed, but she hadn't even looked at the
room. She'd been looking at him, her mouth full and soft—
truth-telling.

He loved her back. "You're welcome any time."

Chapter Thirteen

"What are you doing?"

Fletcher whipped his attention around. His heart whammied. But it was still kinda fun.

Mr. Webb, his archnemesis. The skinny old man's bushy eyebrows drew together. His cheeks went hollow.

Now we meet.

The flash drive was still in the laptop. Getting the passwords had only been a matter of watching Mr. Webb at work through the walls. The screen restored after the files finished copying. Stealth didn't know what bad stuff would be in them, but he was sure it'd be something his dad would want to know, especially since Webb thought he could boss the Strays around. Webb couldn't tell his dad what to do.

Bran peeked into the office behind his father. Traitor.

"How did you get in here?"

Answer nothing. Stealth doesn't speak. Stealth is a ghost.

Stealth gave Webb his best, hard glare.

Turned out Stealth could not only see through walls, he could move through walls, too. It'd been so easy—all he'd had to do was try. Now he was a master spy who could creep undetected in and out of anywhere. He reached up and pulled the drive out of the side of the computer. Maybe they'd make a movie about him.

"What is that?"

Stealth backed to the side wall.

Mr. Webb held out his hand. "Come on, boy. Give it up."

Ha. The fate of magekind rested on the information on the drive. Probably. He didn't know what some of the words meant.

"Stop this foolishness."

This was not foolishness. This was life and death.

He gripped the drive in his hand and worked his magic. He didn't know if the wall itself changed, or if he did. Fireworks burst in his sight. The fae whispered strange words—could Mr. Webb hear them, too?

. . . run run run run run . . .

"What are you doing!"

Stealth grinned. *Now you see me, now you don't.*

He dodged into the next room. A woman—Bran's aunt—stood up abruptly. So he kept running. Through the kitchen—smelled like roasting meat and potatoes—where someone was shouting. Too many people. *Keep running.* Pantry. Butler's office.

"Sir, he just went through the wall!"

Stealth crawled into a space underneath the stairs. It was dirty and webby, but no one could get him if there was no door. The hiding place smelled cold, felt cold, too.

He pumped his fist in a yes of victory.

His breath slowed. Heart cooled off.

Uh . . .

Now what was he supposed to do?

Shouts moved far away.

Time passed.

He got colder.

And it came into his brain that he was trapped.

Somehow Mr. Webb had got him anyway; he just didn't know where Stealth was in his web.

Fletcher's stomach hurt, but he could only keep hiding.

Mr. Webb would be so mad at him. What if there was really bad stuff on the flash drive?

"Fletcher!" an angry voice said, suddenly close.

Everyone was mad.

If they caught him, he didn't know what they'd do. Torture? Death?

He had to find a way to call his dad. Wait until he came and got him.

Then they'd finish Webb together.

Xavier looked out upon the silver of the bay where a blue lantern had been lit, calling to him. He knew the blue light better than the face of the man himself, Mason Stray. More distinctive than a fingerprint, the light was the real person, and couldn't be faked. The air smelled like rain mixed with the scent of spruce trees. The wind lifted his stale hair and the collar of his shirt, felt like a caress, a promise of relief that the end was close. He was so weary of this. So tired of blood.

But he had to be sure. Xavier moved into Mason's mind, and intruded on one of the most common of human activities.

Caught a vantage of rising breasts, and the long, lovely column of a woman's neck. A stray thought . . . *So beautiful . . . Cari . . .*

Cari Dolan. Whoever was with Mason had no soul, which meant mage, so it was probable that it was the Dolan with him. Mason had, after all, been steadily falling in love with her. The rapture of Shadow. The beguilement of the witch. Mason, human and Maker, should have learned this one thing by now: All magic is black.

Was this a last chance? Had the lovers come here, now that Dolan House was nearly unapproachable?

The angels' pursuit had broken off miles ago, leaving him to the boundary of the shore. A trap? A new tactic? Or did they at last believe in his glorious purpose?

All he'd been able to glean from the Order was that the High Seat of the Council was battling his blood. Was it actually possible that he would prevail after all? The Council broken. Cari Dolan within his grasp?

He didn't trust this sudden good fortune, it was too fae.

. . . sweet Shadow, so good . . . think of something else . . . baseball . . . goddamn, Cari . . .

Xavier peered down the shore on both sides of him. If there was a boat, it was pulled up into the grasses, but the distance was an easy swim.

This would be the end, one way or another.

Mason was leaning forward on his kitchen counter, a cold beer in his hand, when he felt Shadow moving behind him. Cari. "You should be sleeping."

Her hands brushed the bare skin on his back, which made his blood move faster, and he couldn't help but want her again. And the fact that it was her? Made him feel like anything was possible. He was old enough to know better—experience had been his teacher—but he was starting to think that maybe something unexpected would happen—like when Fletcher was born.

Her arms came around in a hug, her fingertips playing lightly on the ridges of his stomach. He'd only put on his jeans, couldn't find his T-shirt in the dark and hadn't wanted to wake her.

"I couldn't stay asleep."

He turned to hold her and was disappointed to find that

she'd dressed completely, all the way down to shoes. Some kind of stylish sweat suit in gray, borrowed from Layla. He knew nothing about women's clothes, but she seemed ready to kick angel ass and show all magekind how to conduct House business.

Just in case she was thinking of taking unnecessary risks, he reminded her, "The wraiths will handle him, or at the very least distract him while you or I do the rest." His life as a stray had taught him to wait until the right moment, no matter how hungry, tired, or in pain he might be. It was how he'd kept himself and Fletcher alive.

Her eyes went hard. "You mean kill him."

"Yep, that's what I meant." But it wasn't as easy as she thought it was. The actual strike was quick, like the pull of a trigger. What was unexpected was the phantom pain that echoed from victim to killer. Mason could still feel the punch of bullet holes in his own torso, though he himself had never been shot.

He kissed her head and reached for a plaid button-down hanging on a peg by the kitchen door. He shrugged it on. Had grease on the sleeve from the boat's motor.

A shriek of rage and hunger split the air, a primordial bird sound—one of the wraiths.

Cari's eyes went big. The monsters had been quiet in the hours since their cages had been situated and the night matured to deepest black.

"Water's still calm," Mason said. But he took the Glock from the counter and put it in the back of his pants. Shoes would be good, too. "You need to rest while you can." He stuffed his feet into his running shoes, no socks. Who knew how long it might take for Xavier to come here? He might not come ever.

Cari looked at Mason as if he was insane. "You try to rest." The black of her eyes had turned inky. Her Shadow was stirring—she was reaching for power.

"Too soon, Cari."

Another wraith shrieked and banged against its bars.

Cari drew out the Martin knife. "Maybe they sense something. Like, I don't know, dinner?"

"They could just want me." His soul was still exposed. They could be sensing him.

She shook her head. "It's happening."

"Cari." The water wards—a mist of Shadow and atmosphere—hadn't been disturbed.

"He's here." She said it definitively.

Cari was rock-solid. She always had been. If Cari Dolan said an angel was here, then damn it . . .

Okay.

Mason concealed his soul with Shadow, hiding himself from the wraiths' hunger. He reached and hit the remote release on their cages. Xavier would be able to take one or two on his own, but five?

"Yes." Cari nodded. The motion had an under-tremor that she tried to flatline with a clenched jaw.

He turned off the kitchen lights and motioned Cari away from the window. The quiet closed in as they stood in the dark together, he maneuvering to put her back to a wall. Her breath brushed his neck.

Of course, if this was a false alarm, wrestling inhumanly strong creatures gone insane with hunger back into their cages was going to be a lot of fun. But he trusted her instincts. This was not a panicky woman.

A shadow moved outside the window. Had a human profile—a hunter.

Coming.

Cari clutched the Martin knife in front of her. Every muscle in her body was strained.

"Blink," Mason murmured. "And breathe." He used his rushing blood to loosen his limbs, making them ready and fast.

242 *Erin Kellison*

At last: a vibration on the fine hairs of his nerves told him the water wards had been disturbed.

Another shriek, this time from the direction of the water near the back of the house. In the water?

He looked to Cari and gave a single nod to indicate that the angel was indeed here. He knew it now, too. Maybe the angel had been swimming around, looking for the best place to come to shore. The wraiths had sensed him, had cried out in hunger.

A scream this time, human, adult, but so high with fear that Mason couldn't tell if it was a man or a woman.

"Got him," Cari said, nodding as if all was as it should be.

Yet another shriek, all converging on the same place.

"That's what it sounds like to me." Mason straightened. It did something cold to his stomach to know a living, breathing person was being consumed not far from their location. He didn't like death—it was an unmaking.

"I have to see it. I have to see him die." Cari's eyes had gone demon black to challenge the bright of the angel. Again, Mason had the eerie certainty that of all the terrible beings gathered here, Cari was by far the most dangerous.

"Can we go out?" she asked.

His stray instincts said no, but this was a different kind of job, one that required her doing part of this herself, not just making sure it got done. The Dolan had to strike a blow.

"Stay behind me." He wanted this over.

They exited his House through the back door. The cries, human and wraith, had come from over there, by the rocks. He crossed the lawn, wishing for his shotgun, which slowed wraiths better than the single shots from a handgun. He hated the soul suckers—dirty, stinking bags of flesh. Their distended jaws.

"I hope they chew on his guts," Cari said.

Mason *shhhhhed* the fae, because that's who was talking

now. Cari would want an efficient death. She wasn't one for excess, even in revenge.

Through the trees, following the smell of decay, used-to-be-humans gathered around a fallen body. Their jaws were slung low, unlocked to consume. They were vultures at their prey, the angel gutted, ravaged, his lower face and jaw hanging loose. The infamous wraith kiss done a little too exuberantly.

Disgusting. "He's gone."

Mason felt Cari push him out of the way. He reached after her, but then remembered, she had no soul, and so had nothing to fear from the wraiths unless she purposely antagonized them. He figured she needed to see the death of the angel who'd killed her father and so many more.

Mason followed behind, the smell and sight ahead pissing him off. He didn't like the ugliness, not here in his safe place. But the wraiths had been useful after all, in the most abhorrent way ever.

Knife in hand, Cari leaned over the wraiths, who didn't even seem to notice her. Her silhouette was very much like a witch bent over some dark magick, these monsters her minions. She flipped the knife in her hand—a gesture too practiced for the Cari he knew—and stabbed downward where the heart of the angel would be.

Made Mason think that maybe he and Cari were the bad guys.

Or maybe there were no good guys anymore. Maybe that's why the Dark Age was here.

A slight shift in his senses and he turned—

—but not in time to escape the narrow burn of a knife slicing across his neck.

Xavier.

Mason's hand came up to his throat as he dropped to the ground. Warmth spurted through his fingers, the tips of which were already sizzling with magic. A press at the wound compelled Shadow to staunch the flow at his jugular. He willed his heart not to pump quite so hard and then worked his Shadow to knit the flesh back together.

This wasn't the first time someone had tried to slit his throat. Not the first that he'd used Shadow to heal his body. The trick was to accomplish the feat before losing too much blood.

There were many ways he could die, but this wasn't one of them. The few times before, the attacker had left him for dead, just as Xavier did now. A quick, quiet attack so he could move on to his other quarry.

But damn Mason was cold. The ground moved in a slow career. And the iron smell of his blood nauseated him. He couldn't stand yet, but he managed to turn his head in the grass to watch Xavier silently approach the site of the carnage.

The poor dead bastard being fed on by the wraiths had to have been a decoy. Smart of Xavier, but then he'd been around a long, long time.

Cari's attention came up. Mason saw her gaze flick from the angel to him on the ground. Her eyes widened at the shock of seeing so much blood.

Still alive, sweetheart.

She didn't have the presence of mind to note that he still breathed and was looking right at her.

Her expression shifted through hurt and heartbreak—*Cari, see me*—then blackened into raw, Otherworldly rage. A tsunami swell of Shadow rose within her. The earth shuddered with the impending rush. A choral keening filled the air— multilayered, eerie voices from Twilight shattering the night. The air smelled like tears and blood.

Cari had used a lot of Shadow during the plague investigation, but not nearly as much as this.

Didn't matter that he'd lost a lot of blood fast.

It was time to get up.

* * *

What was left of Cari's thready control broke.

Mason, glassy-eyed. Pallor gray. His throat slit, blood dripping into a macabre collar. Breathing his last.

The angel was going to die. By her hand. Now. He'd taken too much from her already. But no longer.

Angels are the scourge of the world.

Yes. She reached for the Martin dagger, buried in the heart of a dead man.

The Order needs breaking.

Yes. She lifted the blade and drops of warm blood skated onto her clenched hand.

There is only Shadow.

Yes! She held the knife up, ready for its true victim.

Magic burst from Cari in a cataclysm of night. Shadow roiled out from her body until the black, star-studded sky above became a cloak, the silver on the water glittered for her adornment. The consciousness inside her merged with her mind so that she and the fae were one in sight and power and purpose. The fit was perfect, as if Cari were a vessel born to hold such power. She was the ultimate Umbra. Dolan. Dark House. The world, hers to rule.

The angel raised golden weapons to combat her. He had age and glory on his side, but she was as old as the Earth.

"You killed my Mason." Her voice echoed in many tones, all of them anguished.

"He was already dead," the angel yelled back at her.

No. Not an hour ago Mason had moved inside her. She had been going to claim him for her House and offer him her hand. Mason Maker. And this island would be the place they came to escape the politics of the Council, the pressures of all her duties. This would've been their happy place. But now, the whole wide world would be.

"He was dead the moment you were born."

"And yet *you* are the one who has taken lives." House after House. Her father. "I've only saved them!"

She swiped at her bloody nose, felt a warm gush between her legs, tasted iron—the magic was challenging her flesh. And at the same time, she was changing to accommodate it. She could feel the golden turn of each cell and nerve, a gorgeous ache in her womb. She was becoming immortal and shedding weakness.

"I remember the last time Queen Mab gained a foothold in the mortal world and plunged humanity into darkness and despair."

Cari stalked toward him. All the living things in her wake screamed, just as she was screaming inside. "I've done nothing to harm any human. They surround my property, pound on my car, shoot at my wards, yell foul things, and I do nothing." While this angel-fiend in his pretty, glowing skin had bled her Mason. "I *loved* a human." Now she'd kill for him.

The angel lifted his spear. "Do you even remember what you do with your human lovers?"

Eat them. Nothing felt so good as a bright soul within her. She'd always wanted one—so pretty, prettier than any jewel, any golden bauble—a soul. She'd seduced men and women alike to give up theirs. And for a little while she could have one burn inside her breast, too. It hurt a little, but then, pain and pleasure were sides of the same coin. Sometimes it was difficult to distinguish between the two.

Mason had belonged to her.

Movement. She looked over as Mason lurched to his feet. Mason. Alive? He stumbled once to the side, pale and sick to death.

Joy made her eyes wet.

But he was alive. Soaked in his own blood, but alive. And now that she was really looking at him, she could see the Shadow that had sealed his wound.

Clever Maker. He'd be at her side forever.

Mason drew out his gun, his eyes going cold black to match hers. He aimed with both hands at the angel—still steady, even after Xavier's attack. He fired three shots in rapid succession.

Xavier didn't even look over as he swatted the projectiles out of the air like summer bugs. "You have to die, Cari Dolan." He surged forward, light bursting from his being, his spear aimed for her chest.

And her limitless Shadow countered in a rush of her own.

Lightning snapped between the two forces as each strained forward, the spear piercing the monstrous wind of Shadow. Cari bared her teeth in a primal snarl. She was going to tear the weapon from the angel's arm. She'd take his arm, too. Rip him apart, like he'd tried to rip her life apart and had almost succeeded.

Her vision fell to utter blackness. A storm blew the grass and trees and water into nothingness. She stood on a ruined plain of scorched earth. The desolation was beautiful and serene.

This is mine. This is all mine. It has always been mine. And why shouldn't it be?

"Cari!" a voice called.

Mason. Shining bright. Wading into the fray after her. He'd picked up a shovel, now smoking with magic. Mason was so beautiful, the hue of his intensity shifting to white. White hot. She wanted him inside her. Deep, deep inside her. Wanted that shattering feeling every moment of every day.

Xavier must have seen the rapture on her face. "You will snuff out that light. You won't be able to help yourself. Give him up."

"He's mine."

"Save his life. Give *Mason* the world."

Mason's head was down to angle into the storm. His shirt was blown back by the gale, the open sides flapping. His chest and belly were flexed with his effort. He'd grabbed the shaft of the shovel, lifted it, twisting his body for additional force.

And it occurred to her that Mason and Xavier were two of a kind. Her fae-turned mind couldn't discern which of the advancing lightning souls belonged to the man she loved and which to the one obsessed with killing her. The glare of Shadow and Light washed out their features. Both strove with equal intensity.

Had to be the one with the spear. But he was pretty, too. And the earthy scent wafting from his body—it had a pull that she could only describe as intriguing.

Maybe she would take him, too. She tightened her grip on the Martin blade.

Part of her mind rebelled. No. She didn't want either of them. She had a duty to her House. She was the Dolan. These creatures of Light were not her business.

Except she wanted Mason Stray.

She would have just that one.

No.

She didn't trust *how* she would take him inside her or *which* ecstasy her body desired.

Her nerves recoiled, drawing her tight with fear. She was frightened of what she could do. Of losing enough of her mind that she wouldn't know the difference.

"You can't kill me," she sneered in the face of a lesser adversary, but part of her meant it.

The world required magic to thrive, which was why Shadow was necessary. It was time for an age of beauty and innovation, when dreams could be rich with ideas. Heroes could rise, inspired by truth.

But she would take the world farther, into a time when magic dominated. Whim could be reality. Dreams and nightmares would be reified on the land, not just trapped in a slumbering mind. Made real. And humankind could conceive some terrible things. But nothing quite as terrible as she, queen of it all. Her great beauty would be barbed with thorns of fear plucked from the hearts of children. Where she stepped, flowers would bloom. Where she wept, they would die. And her House would grow to such proportions that it would blot out the sun.

No.

Cari dropped the Martin knife. Shadow still fought the angel—she couldn't help her nature to strive against Order— but if the angel could reach her with that spear, he could end her brief reign.

The moment was not unlike waiting for the nod of the gallows man. The last Dolan woman had chosen to hang.

"Fight!" Mason shouted.

She was fighting, but on the side of the angels. She'd already come to this conclusion at Segue: she needed to change her House's loyalties. Well, she was giving it her best shot.

She used Shadow to yank the shovel from Mason's grip. It whistled off into the wind and disappeared over the flatlands that had been the lake before she and Maeve had emptied it.

Xavier primed his arm, the gold spear aiming for her chest.

She wasn't afraid. And she wouldn't, couldn't die. She might not have a soul, but she was immortal just the same. She just belonged in the *Other* world. The stars would keep turning in the sky. The waters in the sea. Everything in its place. How this little island would bloom where her blood had been spilled.

"Take me back," Cari said. The angel needed to strike while the madness was controlled by the reason her father had taught her. She raised her Dolan chin to take the blow. The storm could rage and rage, but she was a queen and could face anything.

But I want this world, Maeve roared in her mind.

Xavier had the moment—she'd given it to him like a gift—but he hesitated, surprised, seeming confounded by her cooperation.

Cari braced—hurry! Maeve was writhing within her, a ghost trapped in a bottle. Cari tried to hold her back, but the fae climbed over her resolve, into her skin and bones . . . through her like a doorway . . . ripped through her flesh in a bloody advent . . . and escaped into the world with Cari's gasp of dismay. Shadow convulsed around her, accepting the queen into the world. Formless she rose into the air, free.

Maeve was free.

Xavier's expression flexed with an indrawn breath, ready to strike.

But he was too late, in more than one way.

Mason came up behind him, a hand to the angel's chin, the other curving around his forehead. Black spider lines etched through the angel's skin. With a hard yank, Mason broke his neck.

Chapter Fourteen

Even as the angel's neck snapped at Mason's hard yank, the wraiths let up shrieks of hunger.

Soul. Xavier's faded in his arms. Which left Mason with the only soul on the island. He tried to cover it again, but was too damn weak and too shocked by the blood gushing from Cari's nose to look beyond her. He tried to step over the angel's fallen body, but his own knees buckled. He was so cold. "Move!" he warned her. The wraiths would trample her in their rush to be the first to suck his face.

She whirled around as he dropped to his knees. He ended up propped on Xavier's back, where he would have collapsed if not for the alarm stringing him upright.

Cari's arms had lifted to the sides, outstretched as if to hold the monsters back. Wraiths had superhuman strength; she was no match for even one. She had to move out of the way.

Their jaws were low, razor teeth ready to clamp like a bear trap to hold their prey in place for their kiss. Their fetid stink preceded their rush, carried by a gust of air. Their sallow skin and eyes of terror suggested this was a horror to them, too.

Shadow convulsed—Mason felt it like a sonic punch.

And before his eyes the wraiths were mowed down by a scissor shear of lashing magic. It took them from behind so that they went down in pieces—living, immortal chunks of gore that putrefied his lawn. A disembodied arm, still twitching, landed at Cari's feet.

"Very thorough," Mason said.

She stumbled back as he pitched forward, so they caught each other. One arm held on to her waist, another around her upper thigh. Which was warm and wet. He brought his fingers back, to find more blood. It was a red night. The iron stink was everywhere.

"It wasn't me." Cari's teeth chattered audibly.

The wraith bits would eventually reassemble—probably as wights. The monsters were trapped in the world, no matter their state.

He pulled on Shadow to cover his soul, though he didn't know how long he could keep it up. Cari was trying to say something, but he was more concerned with how much she was bleeding. And from where. What the fight with Xavier and this wraith mincing had cost her. She had to stop. "No more. Not safe."

She turned, swiping at her nose, and smeared blood across her cheek. "Crossed, Mason. Maeve crossed."

Sweet Shadow, her eyes were scary blood-shot, too.

"Stop using Shadow. You're done." She was done, or she was dead.

"That's what I'm trying to tell you. I didn't do it."

He made himself stand. They'd lived. Now they just had to survive. First thing—he had to check Cari out. And he was dying of thirst.

"Mason, listen to me." Cari's irises had grown. The circumference had enlarged slightly. More black. More fae. "Maeve. She isn't in me anymore. She got out. I couldn't hold her back. She got out. I tried to hold on, but—"

Relief almost dropped him.

Had they won their happily ever after?

"Maeve got out. Good," he said. Cari needed to be free of her.

Cari shook her head in denial. "No, not good. Not *good!* She's insane. I saw *everything!*"

"As long as she's not in you."

"Not in me, but still here." Cari pointed to her chest. "Connected."

Movement on the water. Mason squinted to see. No more. Not now. Three boats skimmed forward. Mason grabbed hold of Cari to try to put her behind him, but the move was clumsy with the angel's body in the way.

Light and Shadow flickered, and the face of Laurence was revealed at the helm of the first vessel. He and several other angels were quickly approaching.

Mason surveyed the carnage. He put his mouth to Cari's ear. "Do not tell them about Maeve." Lest they take up Xavier's cause now that the worst had indeed come true. Mad Mab had crossed into the world.

Cari shook her head. "I have to warn them."

He grasped the sides of her face. He would not let them hurt her, but he wasn't worth much now. "Please trust me. My friend. My sweetheart. My love."

Her chin quivered.

"Do not tell them. They will have to try to cut the threat out of the world. And what will Maeve do to *them?*" She'd diced the wraiths into pieces.

"She hates angels."

Yes. Perfect. "So don't pit them against her. We'll find a way. Just promise me . . ."

"Ho, Mason!" Laurence called.

"No more blood tonight," Mason whispered. "Please no more blood." Not Cari's.

He would not break eye contact with her until she nodded. Not even as the angels came ashore and approached the battle site.

"Cari." He needed her assurance. "Do you trust me?" That devilish trust again.

Finally, she nodded.

Angels were here. They were beautiful people in a clean, bright way, with eyes so clear that Cari thought they must see everything. A group went to deal with the shuddering, scattered messes that were the wraith leftovers. She couldn't bring herself to look over to see how they handled the muck.

A trio came to collect Xavier's body from where she and Mason stood. Two lifted him and carried the dead angel away, his arms slung over their shoulders like a wayward friend who'd passed out from drinking too much.

A white-haired angel remained behind to speak to them. His eyes were sharp blue, like chips of ice.

"Do not go into my mind," Mason said between clenched teeth.

Cari knew he was covering for her. He didn't want them to know about Maeve, when they *should* know. It was the end of the world.

"I always ask," the angel said.

Mason shook his head, disagreeing.

The angel gave him a beatific smile. "The day we scarred you?"

Mason jerked.

So this was the one who'd put the plague sores all over Mason. And here the angel looked like distilled peace.

"Mason Stray, you *showed* me everything you are, of your own free will. But then, you were in so much pain after leaving your son that I don't think you realized it. Your mind is your own. I will not invade it without permission."

"He's going to fall over," Cari said. And so was she. Mason was so heavy.

"Will you let us care for you?"

She didn't know what that entailed.

"After all, you took care of our problem. Let us do what we can to finish this business."

Please let's. "I don't think either of us can walk."

The angel raised a hand and a female approached. She was slender, almost androgynous in her body's angles, but utterly lovely. Cari reached out to her, as the white-haired angel caught Mason's inevitable collapse.

"Xavier cut his throat," Cari said so they'd be extra careful.

But it just made the white-haired angel look very sad as he one-shouldered Mason's weight.

They were gentle, quiet, and organized.

She was taken to the kitchen, where she was stripped. She was washed, the blood cleaned from her body. The angel had the efficiency and detachment of a nurse. A needle found its way painlessly into a vein in her arm, and with a tingling rush, Cari didn't feel so bad at all.

In her drugged vision, she imagined a being of great golden beauty looking on curiously. Her proportions were strange: Very tall. Taller than any person she'd ever seen. Her skin was burnished to a brilliant shine. Her lips were full and shimmered with metallic sheen. Her eyes tipped up like a cat's, and while the concentric circles of her irises were rings of varying black, her lashes were indigo, exaggerated into a thick curl. Her black hair waved away from her forehead and licked and twisted in tendrils and spits of silky magic.

The Lovely Being sneered at the angel before she squinted her eyes to examine Cari, peering into her face. Cari squinted back into hers. It was a strange face. One Cari thought she should know, but her brain was too slippery to find and attach the name. Father would know her name. She'd ask him just as soon as she saw him.

The angel nurse didn't seem to notice the third person in the room while she helped Cari. She was trying to dress her in big, ugly gray sweats. Cari pushed the heavy cotton away.

"They're Mason's," the nurse said. "We couldn't find anything else that would be comfortable. Your other clothes are too fitted for you to rest."

Oh. Mason's. That was okay. She stopped fighting. "Where is he?"

"He refused to sleep, so Laurence set him up on the sofa."

"So-fa. That's where I want to go, too." Wherever he was, she wanted to be.

The Lovely Being reached out to put a finger to Cari's lips. The touch sent a shiver over Cari's whole body. *Don't tell them I'm here.*

The white-haired angel came into the kitchen. "How is she?"

The Lovely Being hissed.

"No injuries that I can see. I think her blood loss was due to Shadow poisoning. But she's shivering again, so I'm watching for fever."

"'Too much Shadow and the body weeps,'" the white-haired angel said. "There's so much of it here."

The Lovely Being turned toward him. She bent her beautiful neck and licked him on his jaw.

He startled and stepped back. His gaze skated around the kitchen, seeking with those keen eyes.

The nurse paused in her fiddling with the IV line. "What?"

"Fae. They're everywhere."

The Lovely Being poked him in the chest with a long black claw of a fingernail. She needed a mani. The white-haired angel frowned.

"Crossed. End of the world." Wait. Cari wasn't supposed to say anything. She covered her mouth with her hand. She'd been taught to keep secrets.

The sharp blue eyes turned to her. "The fae have been crossing for almost a decade."

"Not like this," Cari said. Her hand wasn't doing a very good job. Father was going to have another long talk with her.

"No," the angel said. "Not like this."

* * *

Cari Dolan was beautiful. Maeve couldn't stop admiring her. The delicate sweep of her eyelids. The gentle dimple in her upper lip. The small knob and arch of her collar bone. She was perfection. Dark royal blood seeped through her veins.

What an exquisite child.

If ever there was a vessel to hold umbra, Cari Dolan was its model. And at just the right moment, she'd tipped the pot and poured out upon the world a faery queen.

The act had harmed her though, which was the only reason to tolerate the presence of the angels. Cari needed to be well and strong, in this her final change. Without the flesh, there was no anchor to keep Dolan Shadow in the world. And Maeve wanted to stay. Now that she was back, she intended to stay forever. She and Cari would live together and celebrate this world.

Night still cloaked the sky, but Maeve could hear the growing hum that would be dawn. Sensation was at its most exquisite when it hurt just a little. She would go out onto the water—wet, limpid, cool—and wait for the cruel master that was the sun. And she would quiver under his unforgiving rays, this once again, since time forgotten.

And she would laugh in the old bastard's face.

Late morning was moving into the glare of noon, and still the Order was crawling all over his place. Mason sat on the sofa with his arms around Cari as the angels conducted their final assessment and clean-up of his little island. She couldn't stop shaking. She'd said she was cold though the day was coming on humid and hot. She'd dozed a bit, and he'd wanted to, but he didn't trust the Order. Didn't trust anyone where Cari was concerned.

She'd said that Maeve had crossed. The fae queen was in the world.

Cari had been so beautiful in her fight against Xavier, with golden light shining through her skin, eyes an unfathomable black of magic. Shadow had whipped all around her. Until that moment, he'd never considered that Night had its own brilliant illumination.

The ordeal with Xavier was almost over. How ironic that the angel himself had brought about what he'd most feared. Xavier had all but invited Maeve into the world.

The skin at Mason's neck itched. Laurence had put something on the wound. Shadow had sealed him back together, but maybe the Order's stuff would hurry the healing process along. He wanted the Order gone, but would endure their clean-up. He hated disposing of bodies.

There was some hammer banging, so someone was repairing something. Very considerate of them. The house itself had not taken any obvious damage, but he could sense that the structure and foundation had been infused with Shadow—the fae whispers found in the great Houses now hissed within his own.

Laurence finally sat down opposite them, heaving an exaggerated sigh. It was the most human Mason had yet seen him. "Your land has been restored, though it will take a few weeks for the grass to grow back in places. The wraiths have been collected. The dead are now being taken elsewhere for burial. The other body was that of Stanley Piernik, whose home is on the Canadian side of the bay. Xavier used him to test for a trap."

Mason had guessed as much.

"And Jack Bastian has sent a message that Kaye Brand has survived her bout of mage plague and is recovering. The mage Council has been notified as well. Word has begun to spread that you were successful, though thus far, all the mage Houses remain closed. I imagine over the next days some will begin to venture out."

Mason knew there had to be more. "The punch line, please."

Laurence smiled patiently. "Our information suggests a growing consensus among magekind to replace Brand with Dolan, re-aligning with Dolan's purist allies. This would be the end of cooperation between the Council and Order. It may be inevitable—few thought that Brand and Bastian's peace would last. But if Brand is to be supplanted, we have high hopes that *your* partnership—human and mage—will continue and that peace is still possible."

Mason felt Shadow rise in Cari. "It's possible," she said. "It's what I want."

Mason's sluggish heart thumped. It was one thing for them to privately discuss continuing their "partnership." But telling the Order as much meant that Cari had decided absolutely.

It wasn't that easy—the Houses might not accept him, even as a Maker—but he'd steal any moment he could with her for as long as possible.

"I'm very glad to hear it." Laurence dropped his gaze for a moment. "One last thing. Mason, I know that you are more than capable of handling yourself in a fight. And you have enough blood on your soul to do what you must efficiently. But I cannot quite understand how you could best Xavier. I don't know if I could have beaten him, hand to hand, and I know I can beat you."

At the moment, anyone could beat him. "I came up behind Xavier while he was concentrating on Cari."

"A hundred of you could have come up behind him, and all perish."

"He hesitated," Cari said.

Laurence shifted his attention to her. "What do you mean?"

"He could have killed me, but he hesitated."

"Xavier hesitated," Laurence repeated, taken aback. "Why, when he'd waited so long already?"

Cari looked away. "I don't know. He could've had me."

Laurence's eyebrows went up, his eyes going bright with feeling. "Perhaps he reconsidered his purpose." He braced his weight with a hand to his knee as if his heart were too heavy to carry without help. "He was once my friend, you know. I hope he reconsidered. I hope he did very much. Because if *he* thought there was a chance, even if it was in the last moment, then I can believe it, too."

The calls started coming shortly after the Order left. To the Houses, Cari was her father's daughter in every way. She'd survived the plague, whereas other infected mages had died. She'd hunted down and identified the perpetrator, who was none other than an emissary of Order. And she'd exacted revenge for the honor of her House and the strength of magekind.

The calls all had a similar underlying message: Dolan could have it all. Meaning the Council, which had been her father's ambition for her, too. The congratulations made her miss him. She would've liked to have seen the pride in his eyes. Would've liked to have had his advice on how to proceed. But she didn't have him.

"He did not say anything outright," Scarlet told Cari of Gunnar Martin, "but I think Martin House will back you if you decide to try for the High Seat."

Cari's hand shook as she put it to her forehead. She didn't want to think or be careful. It felt tedious to her. She just wanted to feel. To be. To take. Which was Maeve's residual influence. Where was the fae? But the old Cari had always done her homework, and would continue to do it. Family business was her duty, too.

"Did you make him any assurances?" she asked her stepmother. Would she have to do damage control for Scarlet's meddling?

"I only said that you would take swift action."

She shook her head. Definitely damage control. "Swift action to do what?"

"Why, to seize the future that your father always wanted for you."

Okay. This needed to stop. "Scarlet, you are not to speak on my behalf or on the behalf of Dolan House."

"This is the moment, Cari. You are too young to recognize it for what it is."

"I recognize the moment just fine. I lived it. And I, and I *alone*, am planning Dolan's next steps." She just had to think through how she was going to make new allies, while appeasing her current ones. She was going to rock the boat, big time. "Scarlet, you will only embarrass yourself if you say or promise one thing, and I choose to do another."

Silence. An old tactic to get Cari to back down, but she couldn't afford to. "Put Zella on, please."

Mason came into the kitchen from checking the property. He looked older, but his color was better. He kissed her on her head and got himself a glass of water.

Cari had asked for Zel, but got Stacia instead. "Oh-mighty-head-of-our—"

Which made Cari smile in spite of everything, remembering their conversation. "Stay out of my closet."

"But I have to have the perfect clothes if I'm going to be entertaining potential husbands." Stacia had sarcasm down pat—it was light and airy and full of bite.

Seemed like Scarlet had been very, *very* busy. She'd been running the whole Dolan show apparently. "Is she actually entertaining offers?"

"She's got a list, Cari. And you promised that I wouldn't have to get married."

"You don't. And you can tell Zel that she doesn't have to either."

"Mother will freak." Voices rose behind the call. Scarlet's was loudest. "Strike that. Mother's already freaking."

"I'll take care of—"

Mason took the phone out of her hand. He looked at her expectantly, and when she nodded, so very grateful, he ended the call.

"You're a busy girl." He set the phone down next to her.

"Your phone's been ringing, too."

He frowned deeply. "Neither Webb nor my son has returned my calls. And they are the only ones I want to hear from."

Cari had a call in to Webb as well. No message back.

She'd told Laurence that she intended to maintain a partnership with Mason, and Fletcher was the key to that.

"I imagine there are offers waiting for you," she said, hoping he'd drop a hint. Some smart, strong House would claim him soon. And she'd have to counter, just as fast.

"I'm waiting to speak to Kaye."

Brand. Her other competition.

"You haven't heard from her? What about Jack Bastian?"

"Nothing from them yet."

"And you're loyal to her?" The thought made the room darken slightly.

His hand went gently around the nape of her neck, mouth settling on hers. Felt good, but that wasn't the answer she wanted. She ignored the flutter in her belly.

"I need to find out what's going on with Fletcher, and Kaye can make Webb answer."

"You'll have options now." All those messages.

He skimmed his knuckles down her bare arm. "Princess, I always had options. I want you."

Her face warmed. Her chest filled with pressure. "I come with trouble. It might not be wise to stay too close." They hadn't discussed the fae problem. Cari didn't even want to mention Maeve's name.

Mason put a strong hand to the back of her neck and massaged. She loved his hands. She'd have claimed him for his hands alone. The fact that they were attached to the rest of him . . . easiest decision ever. She couldn't wait to make him hers. If Webb or Brand would just call her back so that she could claim Fletcher, too.

"This is not the first time a fae has crossed," Mason said. "Segue has had experience with several others. Now that the wraith threat is somewhat under control, their time is taken up more and more by the fae. There *are* resources. We have a base of knowledge to draw from. We need to assemble a team of people we trust. And we'll come up with a solution."

"There's an obvious solution."

"Even Xavier thought better of it. And you were pretty wicked looking."

She lifted an eyebrow. "Oh, yeah?"

Was wicked good?

His eyes lit as he bent his head to kiss her again. "Oh, yeah."

She guessed it was.

His mouth moved against hers in a caress. With his hand at the base of her skull and his lips pressing hers, her tension eased. Maybe it would all work out. They'd faced an ancient angel. What was an immortal insane fae, really?

"We should get you back to Dolan House," Mason said, pulling away.

Cari nodded, regretful. She had a lot of work to do, and it was best done from her father's office. "But I want you to know, I love it here."

"We'll come back." The lines around his eyes were smooth and easy. He meant it.

She went upstairs and he followed. She changed into her own clothes, though wrinkled. Ran a brush through her hair, and then tried for a smart ponytail for the boat. She put on mascara, but the blush in her compact had cracked and now was a crumbly mess. Well, only her stepmother would expect her to look polished after fighting an angel.

She was just lifting her bag, on loan from Layla, when

Mason leaned into the bedroom, gun in hand. "Someone just broke through the water line."

Groaning, she dropped the bag. "What now?"

"Maybe someone doesn't want you to try for the Council."

She screwed up her face. "Preemptive assassination?" This just got better and better.

They both froze when footsteps sounded on the back porch. Mason put his back to the wall and pushed her into the bedroom. Very gallant, but she wasn't hiding.

The back door downstairs opened, the screen banging shut. "Hello?" a female voice called out.

Maria? Cari mouthed to Mason. The nanny.

He shook his head no.

Didn't sound right anyway. The voice was too young. Too familiar, though she couldn't place it.

"Mason?" the voice called again.

Then Cari knew. Her stomach cramped. She'd utterly forgotten to consider one other House, one other woman, who might claim Mason and Fletcher.

"Son of a bitch," he said.

Bitch was an apt word to describe her.

"Mason?" Livia Walker called. "I'm home."

Stealth peed inside the wall between Mr. Webb's office and the little study where the old lady, Bran's aunt, liked to read. The yellow arced like a stripe of rainbow in the beam from his stolen flashlight and splashed on the wood.

The search dogs had led the house guards to the places where he'd gone to the bathroom. The first time had just been lucky, but after that he'd made sure to pee everywhere he could fit, except the hidey-hole where he slept and kept his stolen grub. Too bad he couldn't get at a phone. His had been found and the one on the kitchen wall had been dismantled. They were on to him.

"Well, we now know what the child can do," Mr. Webb said to one of his men. They were on the outside of the wall, in the hallway that led to the office. "And it makes sense, considering he has *Walker* blood. I should call them and find out what they do to keep hold of their children."

Fletcher frowned. He hadn't thought this superpower could come from his mom. The idea made him feel funny inside. She hadn't wanted him, but he was still connected to her. He was like her, even though she'd left him behind. He wanted to be like his dad. Would his dad be mad if he was like her? Was that why he'd been left behind again? Why hadn't his dad come yet?

"I've had enough of this," Mr. Webb said. "My office is beginning to smell. And now that Brand is recovered, she's going to press me about him. The stray has already left several messages."

Fletcher's chest went bright. His dad had been calling. He'd come and get him soon.

"Bring me Bran. It's time I ended this nonsense, and my heir should see how it's done."

Six years. She'd walked out six years ago. And now she thought she could just walk back in? "Stay here," Mason said to Cari. "I'll get rid of her." Took balls for Liv to call this house her home. He was going to throw her in the water and let her swim the half mile to shore. What if Fletcher had been here? What would this have done to him?

Mason put his gun in the back of his pants and started down the stairs. Cari, who always did as he said, followed at his heels.

They did not need *this* now.

Liv was just stepping around the sofa when he spotted her. Her blond hair was lighter, styled a little loose and curly. She'd gone with a red dress that showed a lot of cleavage and a lot of leg. She had gold around her neck, on her wrist, and her fingers. And a crocodile smile that turned into a grimace when she spotted Cari behind him. "Cari," she said by way of hello.

Mason braced himself with one hand on the wall. "What are you doing here, Liv?"

She rapid-blinked to brighten her smile again. "I have news."

"You have nothing to say that could interest me."

"Oh, I don't know about that." She was doing the posing thing she used to do, where she'd shift her weight to accentuate her curves. He used to like it, but now he wondered if she was going to eventually throw her back out.

"And this isn't your home," he added. It hadn't been for a long time.

The Shadow in the air grew more dense. Not a good sign.

"I believe my name's on the deed."

Okay, that had been stupid of him. He'd wanted so much to make his own House with her that he'd put the place in both their names. "I'll buy you out." He didn't have the money right now, but he would get it. The messages on his phone meant that he had job offers. He'd take the dirtiest and give Liv a pile of money she didn't need.

"I don't think so." Her scent hit him—a perfume toned low and sensual. It was the scent that chiseled through his anger to where the pain of her leaving was stored. For her he'd tried to build something solid. Something that he could depend on. She'd made promises.

"I'll give you double its worth," Cari said.

No, he'd own this for himself. The Alexandria Bay island was his and Fletcher's. Even though only one of them was left.

"I don't want to sell it." Liv looked around the room, as if remembering good times. "The house is beside the point anyway."

Not beside the point. Never beside the point, after what he'd done to get the place.

"Just say it," Cari said.

Mason glanced at Cari, whose jaw was twitching. How did she know what Liv was up to? Dolan and Walker were ally Houses, but still—Cari hadn't said a word about Liv to him. Until this moment, he'd thought they didn't interact much. But maybe they connected occasionally. Or maybe they were friends.

Liv smirked as if she'd won something. "It's what we always wanted, Mason. Walker House is claiming you and Fletcher as our own."

Bitch stole my line. Cari was going to kill her. She was going to wrap her hands around Liv's neck and squeeze until her eyeballs popped out of her skull.

Cari slid her gaze over to Mason. His face was flushed, veins standing out on his forehead. His hands had migrated up to his hips in a fake gesture of calm when every line of his body had gone taut. "I'm not interested."

"Oh, come on," Liv said. "Not a month ago you were begging Walker to take Fletcher."

Her words were like a blast of heat. Cari burned at the thought of Mason begging. Mages hiding behind their wards. A child exposed. Who could he have turned to? Walker. He'd appealed to the mother, no pride for himself. For his son, he'd do anything.

It was now official: Walker and Dolan were no longer friends. No great loss.

"Your House can take its claim and screw itself," Mason said. He blew out his breath and the tension in his neck and shoulders seemed to morph into a loose and ready strength.

"I'm Fletcher's mother."

"He has no mother."

"He doesn't miss me? He doesn't want to know me? He doesn't want to be with his true family? To know his *House*?"

Cari's throat locked. Walker was Fletcher's true family. Liv, his mother. Cari knew that under no circumstances would she be able to deny her family; she couldn't expect Fletcher not to want his or Mason to deny his son's place. And where Fletcher went . . .

"Fletcher has a House now," Mason said.

Webb. Cari almost groaned aloud. It wasn't the same thing. Not at all. Liv knew that, too, and the only reason Mason didn't was because he hadn't been raised in one. House was blood. House defined a mage on a visceral level—it was a mage's hope for immortality, grounded by the ward stones.

The confidence of her position showed in Liv's smile. "My father is petitioning the Council to dissolve the fosterage contract."

"It was endorsed by the High Seat herself," Mason said.

"But you have no standing in the Council," Liv said. "You are *stray*, so your name on the contract means nothing, and Brand had no grounds on her own to act on Fletcher's behalf."

"You abandoned him."

"I chose to live in the safety of my House. I begged my father for Fletcher to be able to come with me."

"Your father wouldn't even open your wards to him during the plague."

"He could've been a carrier. We'd already lost family."

"And you were a-okay with losing him, too."

The frustration in Mason's voice was making Cari shake with anger. How dare Liv come now? Nine years ago Liv had taken Mason away from her. And now she was trying to do the same again. This was not going to happen.

"I'll fight you," Mason said.

Cari flexed her hands in frustration. Then fisted them in a refusal of this new turn of events. This time—finally!—she didn't have to watch Mason walk out of her life for the sake of his child.

"There's no need to fight her, Mason." Cari was surprised at the calm in her own voice. But then she was all grown up now. "Livia Walker will be very cooperative; her father will see to it. Fletcher can know his House, even bear its name, but he doesn't have to live there. You'll have your pick of where you want to raise him."

Liv wouldn't step down. "Dolan, like that Brand bitch, has nothing to do with Fletcher."

Cari shrugged. "Well, either you'll be petitioning Brand, or you'll be petitioning *me* in that very same Seat."

Liv's stance changed. Her boobs weren't so far out anymore. She was leaning into the argument with her shoulders. "You can't take my son away from me."

"I'm not. I'm backing Mason. Whatever he chooses."

"You'd choose a stray over an ally? Walker will oppose Dolan House. We'll break Dolan."

"You think you can break my House?" Cari wanted to laugh, but saved Liv the humiliation. She was having a bad enough day.

"Cari." Mason pulled her close to his side. He was looking around the room, lines of tension coming back into his body.

"Dolan is a *royal* House," a new voice intoned. Sounded like her own.

Maeve. *Shit.* Liv must have ticked her off.

In the sunlight falling through the window, a gold profile appeared. Shadow swirled away from the fae face in cascades of magic. A hint of shimmer suggested her heavy gown. But it was her height that made Cari cringe inwardly. Mad Mab hulked in the space.

Liv had a clueless *what?* on her face.

"Livia Walker comes from a great House. She is allied with Dolan," Cari said to Maeve, trying to save Liv.

Alien eyes, full black, found Cari. "Does she know that?"

"I'm teaching her."

Liv scoffed. "Dolan will break—"

Dappled sunlight rushed across the room and whatever Liv had been going to say was cut off by Maeve's hand around her throat.

The girl's throat felt like satin under Maeve's hand. She stroked her thumb up and down to relish the texture. Underneath the skin were the flutter pulse of a heart and the hidden crimson of lifeblood.

"Let her go," Cari Dolan said across the room.

Maeve felt the command in a resonant echo from the Dolan stones that bound them.

"I want to see her smile first, and nicely, she who dared to mock my line."

The girl's face was turning purple. Weak thing. She had magic within her, but it was a middling power, a Walker's trait. The girl lifted her mouth, but the smile wasn't pleasing. It was ugly, and she smelled like stink flowers.

"I don't like it," Maeve said. The girl was grunting, swatting at Maeve's hand.

"She is from an *ally* House."

Maeve turned to Cari, holding out the girl by the neck. "You keep saying that. Ally."

The human man had a toy in his hand—what was called a gun; people used them to kill each other—but Cari pushed it away, not wanting him to play with them.

Later, Maeve hoped.

"Ally means they *serve* Dolan," Cari was saying.

Hmmm. That's not what it meant before, but words changed sometimes. And it had been quite a long time since she'd been in the world. The girl hadn't spoken to Cari like a servant. It didn't matter anyway—everyone would serve Dolan.

Maeve aimed the girl's dangling legs at the floor and set her down. Something cracked in the neck, and the head bobbled forward. The body went loose. A mistake. Oh dear.

The human male lifted the toy again. He had a fierce look on his face. She wanted to see that face, just as fierce, looking down at her, his body above hers. But no, Cari had already said she wanted him. And what Cari wanted, she would have. And one young human man was very much like another.

Maeve pushed the girl's chin up with her thumb. Her head still lolled a bit to the side. "She's broken." Ally. *Hmm.* "Do we shed tears of happiness, or do we weep?"

Chapter Fifteen

Liv was gone. Her body now dangled from the fae queen's large, clawed hand.

Mason squeezed the trigger. *Bang!-Bang!-Bang!*

It was the only thing to do. Not that he cared for Liv herself, not anymore, but she'd given him Fletcher, the meaning in his life, and he couldn't let Fletcher's mother go unavenged.

At the first bang, Cari tried to dive in front of him—"Mason, no!"—but his arm was already pushing her behind him. He'd die himself before that creature would hurt her.

Mad Mab gave him a smile that withered his guts. "I can't have you."

If the bullets had found their mark, the fae made no sign of it. The seething Shadow that came together in her form was like nothing he'd ever felt before. A sentient black hole was before him, drawing all Shadow to her, except this magic had no end and so she would only grow and grow until she swallowed everything and everyone in her wake.

How could she be destroyed?

Cari emerged quickly on his other side, a hand raised to keep the fae back. "You will not touch him."

Maeve dropped Liv's body. The skull hit the floor with a dull whump. "But he wants to play with me."

There had to be a way. Even Xavier had given them one moment of possibility. Maeve could be beaten. Somehow.

But those black eyes shifted to him again, effortlessly seeing straight to his soul. His heartbeat accelerated to a frantic tremor. She licked her lips. "And I'm hungry."

"He's *mine*," Cari said. There. She'd officially claimed him out loud.

Maeve's head inclined slightly. "Share?"

"I'm greedy." Out of the corner of her eye, she saw Mason reaching for something. She didn't know what it was, but his veins ran black, so she figured he was Making something.

"But he has such a pretty soul." Maeve's expression filled with longing. "And he wants me, too. Shall I not oblige him?"

"No." Cari put all her father's authority into her voice. And the sound that came out of her mouth echoed with his power, resonating from somewhere distinctly Dolan—the ward stones. Her father had always said that was where each House drew its strength.

Maeve's face went mean. "You're not Caspar."

Cari thought of her father's journal. He'd said he had to become a man all at once—that or die. "I'm his heir and you will obey me as you obeyed him."

Shadowman's counsel came back to her as well—how Dolan was a female line. Did that mean she had more or less power than her father over Maeve?

"Fine," Mab said. "Have him. I'll get my own."

In a blast of temper, Shadow jetted out from the fae's body. And when the darkness cleared, Maeve was gone.

"Nooo!" Cari screamed at the ceiling, the windows, the door. She put everything she was into the call, but the fae was gone. All that was left was Liv's corpse.

* * *

Rick Vincent stood from where he'd gone down on one knee. He tugged the ring out and dropped the box to slide the sparkler on Ysenia's finger. Her nails were done, though the black polish was a little more city than her usual style. She'd said she was surprised, but someone had to have tipped her off. His sister, probably, who'd approved the ring (after upgrading him from the seven-thousand-dollar princess-cut, to the twelve-thousand-dollar round-cut).

"It's perfect." She admired it on her hand for a second, then turned her gorgeous dark eyes on him. Her hair looked pretty tonight, too—she'd added deep red highlights to her natural black. Hair *and* nails? Yeah, she'd been tipped off for sure.

"You really like it?" Because those payments were going to go on forever.

"It's exactly what I wanted." Her hands went to his shoulders and slipped around his neck. The way her eyelids lowered made him think that stashing the blanket here earlier had been a brilliant idea. He might romance two yeses out of her tonight.

He kissed her again as he had a thousand times over the last three months. He'd known she was the one from their first date, though his sister was taking all the credit for setting them up. Which was okay as long as he had Ysenia in his life.

This time, though, her mouth moved harder against his, when she was usually so soft. Maybe she was trying something new here, too. One of her hands dropped to the center of his chest, and he covered it with his own. God, he loved her. Her fingers dug in—passion? It hurt and he tried to draw her hand away, but she was way too strong, and the bruisy feel turned sharp as her nails found his skin, even through his shirt.

He tilted his face down to break the kiss. "Honey—"

Her nails speared him, and he tried to push her away, but she kept him close. Except she wasn't Ysenia anymore. Her eyes.

"We were just getting to the good part," she said. "Hold still now."

Maeve shuddered with the bright light inside her. It burned with the boy's love—his hope, his terror. The best part was when his soul showed her life as only a human could perceive it. And for a flash in the stretch of long eternities, she was human, too.

She ached for the girl Ysenia, and the pain of it was a beautiful thing. And the fear that had propelled the two to accelerate their relationship? It was warm, with a fizz of hysteria that tickled. The broken love was so *wrong*. Murder and death. *Sin?* How wonderful. Not that it applied to her. There was no Hell for her. She'd had worse—everlasting darkness.

She wanted *this*—to feel *this*—devotion and passion, a willingness to tie one existence to another and make a shared life. To stand at each other's side. It's what the world was for.

Maeve went still. She was about to think.

The boy's soul was showing her a design, and she focused on it with all the acuity of one great eye, taking in the symmetry. An idea came into her old mind: Love wasn't just emotion—which came from Twilight. It was a Pattern, too—and that came from Order.

How could she have forgotten this bit of cunning?

She'd seen this pattern before.

And once again, she'd stamp it out. One soul at a time.

Next?

They'd had to leave Liv's body behind, though Cari made a call to Walker House to let them know that she was dead, killed by a fae. They refused Cari's offer to make arrangements, and were sending someone of their own to collect her. Mason admired the respectful detachment of Cari's voice. It differed so much from the stricken expression that etched her face.

Even in death, Liv inspired complicated emotion. But the one that laced them all together was anger. He'd pushed her death into the dark corner of his heart where he'd hidden all things Liv and had laid her body out on the sofa, wrapped in a sheet.

When Cari got off the phone, she said, "They've withdrawn their claim on you and Fletcher."

"I knew they would." He'd hoped so, too. He didn't want to fight them over Fletcher, with Walker House wielding Liv's death like a weapon.

"I'm sorry he won't know his House."

"Fletcher knows his House. This house." And it would have to be enough. "You ready to go?"

They took the boat to shore, where he had his garage. Kitt was still at Dolan House, but his GTO was ready. He'd rebuilt the engine and starter with Shadow, but it still wouldn't turn over without the key in the ignition. Cari, who'd recuperated much more quickly than he had, insisted she drive, at least for the first shift, but he woke as they were crossing the New York state line into Massachusetts on I-95.

Waking up to her driving his car was okay, though. "How long was I out?"

"About five hours. We'll be at Dolan House in another forty-five minutes. Kaye Brand is going to meet us there."

"You spoke to her?" He reached for the drive-thru soda she had clenched between her legs and took a long drag on the straw.

"Briefly. She is convening a special meeting of the Council Houses. She wanted the quick answer on whether or not I'm going to challenge her."

It had been a very important five hours. "And?"

"All things considered . . . I told her that she had Dolan's support and that I would not be seeking her Seat."

Mason tried to cover his relief. Cari was ambitious, but she could also see the bigger picture without imagining herself in the foreground. "This have anything to do with what happened to Liv?"

"Dolan is in no position to work for peace"—she cocked her head—"though I did tell Kaye that I had demands."

Cari using Brand's first name. Good sign. "And those are?"

She smiled. "You'll have to wait an hour and hear for yourself."

"Did you tell her about . . ." Names had power, and he didn't want to use Maeve's.

"No. Not yet. I don't know how without fae repercussions."

Cari was cautious of the same thing he was. She didn't want to summon the queen without a plan in place.

"Did Kaye happen to mention Fletcher?" He'd only left ten messages.

Cari smiled, nodding. "She said she'd spoken to Webb already. That Fletcher was fine, and that you will see him soon."

Relief did more than any amount of sleep could. "He's fine," Mason repeated.

"He's fine."

"Any other details?"

"Not that she said. It was a very quick call."

"Forty-five minutes." Then he could grill her himself. "Pull over and let me drive."

Cari sighed, but she humored him and exited the freeway. Not that he could accelerate time, but he could alleviate his anxiety with speed. Plus, when they arrived at Dolan House, he wouldn't mind hitting the Shadow protesters if they got in the way.

Stealth sneaked behind Bran and Mr. Webb down to the cellar, curious at how Mr. Webb thought he was going to catch him. Nobody could catch him if he didn't want them to. Uh, hello—he would walk through *walls*.

The whispers were louder down here—*follow follow follow us*—which had to be because of the ward stones. His dad had told him that all the great Houses put their ward stones in their foundations, and that's where they got their strength. It was like a little bit of Twilight, just for Webb. Stealth got the tingly feeling that the fae were watching him. He couldn't hide from *them*. No one could.

The cellar was a stone room full of darkness. Flashlights didn't work so good here. But Mr. Webb's candle did a lot better, throwing gold light all over the floor and walls. Which made Stealth remember another thing his dad said—that fire was better light than electricity. In the time to come, people would use candles again, or else they wouldn't see what was coming.

"Have a seat, Bran," Mr. Webb said. The candles made a campfire on the stones of the floor in the middle of the room.

Bran sat and crossed his legs. Mr. Webb, the spidery-man, sat and crossed his legs, too. Light filled their faces, but darkness leapt around them as if creatures danced around the circle. Smelled smoky, but good, too, like moss and woods and dirt.

"Remember the last time we did this?" the old man asked.

Bran nodded. "Someone was stealing things from you."

"And did we find her?"

"She came out of the Shadows and told us herself. She just liked shiny things."

"Some shiny things are worth more than others," Mr. Webb grumbled.

Well, Stealth wasn't coming out. He was going to keep peeing everywhere he could. In fact, he'd pee down here, too.

"And this is how we are going to find Fletcher Stray."

"We tell a story," Bran said.

Pshaw. A story couldn't make Stealth do anything. Stealth was an enigma.

"You begin," Mr. Webb said. The candle fire leapt and stretched, as if it liked him.

Bran's voice began uncertainly: "Once upon a time, there was a boy."

"That's fine. Keep it simple."

"He came from Shadow and Light," Bran continued.

"Did he?" wondered Mr. Webb aloud. "That means one of his parents was human. Very interesting. Do you see how the story can reveal him?"

Bran nodded, and Stealth frowned as meanly as he could. How did they know about his dad? No one knew about his dad. What kind of magic did Mr. Webb and Bran have?

He'd kill them, and then they'd be sorry.

"And the boy lived in darkness," Bran continued in a weird voice. Something reached up from the candleflame, but Stealth couldn't make out what it was. Probably just another one of Bran's Shadow puppets, that he used to tell stories with. "And he welcomed the darkness, growing in magic to become, like his father, an assassin with no equal. The one called Stealth will be tempered only and ultimately by the pale hand of a lady. This is his stor—"

"No," Mr. Webb said. "Do not let the story lead you. Do not be a mouthpiece. *You* tell the story."

Stealth backed up until he felt the burn of a ward stone behind him. They knew his secret name? And he wasn't an assassin . . . yet. But it was something he thought about. His dad had killed someone once, fast and gentle, but he didn't think Stealth had seen. Maybe the Webbs could see the past. Maybe they could tell the future.

"But the story is going a different way," Bran whined. "The words are easy. They feel right."

"No, Bran. Fletcher is a child and has no destiny. Rip him from that path and set him on yours."

He sighed. "But it's boring. Assassin is better."

"You can be more bored locked in your room after. Now tell Fletcher's story our way."

Stealth didn't want to hear Fletcher's story. Not anymore. There was too much tucked into the words.

"Fine. Umm . . . he thinks he can do anything," Bran said fast, like he was trying to hurry. "But he's really just a kid."

"Yes."

Traitor. Bran wasn't his friend anymore. Ever.

A coldness reached inside Stealth, like long fingers made out of magic. They scraped into his guts and made him shiver where he stood. Just a kid. He felt shorter. Not nearly as strong as his dad.

"And there's nowhere for him to go, since the wards won't let him out anyway."

"Correct."

And Stealth was stuck, no matter how many walls he could go through. Because the wall that mattered wouldn't let anything in or out unless Webb commanded it.

Bran blew his cheeks out while he thought. "And he should mind his own business and not be in your office."

"Neither of you should play in my office, but continue."

"And he should just come out of where he's hiding, because he's in really big trouble."

The long fingers grabbed Fletcher inside, as if someone had found him after all and was going to drag him out of his hiding place.

"Yes."

"And he's not so great after all."

He wasn't Stealth, not really. He was just Fletcher. The stray.

"You've established that, and threading jealousy into the story is dangerous."

Bran looked mad. "And his dad gave him to us, so he has to do what we tell him to."

Fletcher knew that was the truth, and so did the long hand

inside him. His dad had given him to Mr. Webb. Had left him behind, just like his mom had. He belonged to Mr. Webb.

"And Fletcher Stray must come when called."

Fletcher turned to run away. Maybe if he couldn't hear, he wouldn't have to obey.

"Fletcher Stray!" called Mr. Webb. "Come here at once."

The hand gripping inside of him yanked him toward the open part of the room. Fletcher tried to grab hold of something to keep himself in the dark, but his arms and legs were already taking him right into the circle of light. Never mind that the fae stood all around, looking at him with wonder on their strange faces.

Made him feel silly and small. Like he was going to cry.

"Protect the House," Webb told Bran.

Bran nodded. "And the boy would not speak of anything he discovered in Webb House."

Fletcher felt another magic hand come around his face to bind his mouth. He didn't need to try to speak to know that he couldn't. Bran's story had told him so.

Fletcher suddenly realized that *he* was now Bran's Shadow puppet. The thought made his heart shake.

"Very good, Bran," Mr. Webb said. "Your generation boggles the mind. What an age of power ahead of us. Well done, son."

Fletcher shook with sadness. He hurt inside. His eyes hurt. And his belly. Everything hurt. His dad had given him to this terrible man. *Dad, where are you?*

"Now—" Webb leaned down to him, his eyes staring into Fletcher's brain. "Tell me where you hid that thumbdrive with my computer files on it."

Fletcher felt the Shadow hand on his mouth tighten, so that no words could come out.

"Tell me," Webb insisted. He looked at Bran, who shrugged as if he didn't know what was wrong.

But Fletcher knew. He was inside the story, so he knew it

for sure. Bran had just told the Shadow that he couldn't speak of anything he'd discovered in Webb House, which, *duh,* included the thumbdrive. Bran's own story had messed him up.

"Fletcher, you will obey me," Mr. Webb said.

A Shadow hand still clamped Fletcher's mouth shut, but he had no trouble at all grinning meanly at Mr. Webb. *You can't make me.*

"Please move Mason's things to my room," Cari said to Allison. The roar from the mob outside the wards was now audible from the front door, a quarter mile from the street. It stole her breath, but there wasn't anything she could do about it. It had grown from fifteen loitering people to fifty angry ones in days. Police officers were on site, but this required a special intervention. Something needed to be done *now.* Or Maeve might become interested, thinking them postulants clamoring for her favor. Quite the opposite.

Scarlet's welcome looked a lot like anger, too. "The plague has run its course, so why is *he* here?"

"Lovely to see you again, Scarlet," Mason said, the stray turned gentleman. Cari was going to kiss him for enduring her stepmother's bite so kindly.

Here we go. "He's here because I won't give him up."

Which made Stacia snort to suppress her laughter.

Scarlet was going to have to be sedated when Cari told her she planned to claim him. The thought almost made Cari giggle hysterically, right there in front of everyone.

"Is Kaye Brand here?" Cari asked instead. Business, she reminded herself sternly. Dire, terrible business to do.

Scarlet was distracted from killing Mason with her glare. "Who? No. No one has crossed the wards since you left. How could they?"

Cari didn't tell her that Brand had a very useful vassal in Marcell Lakatos who helped her cross whatever wards she chose. "Stacia, can you check the office? And if she's there, offer her something to eat or drink. I'm going up to change and will be down in five minutes."

"I'll go with your sister," Mason said. "I want to hear about Fletcher."

Cari nodded. "In five, then." And she hurried up the stairs. The clothes she was wearing needed to be burned. She took a minute in a cold shower, found clean underwear, dressed in smart clothes. She glanced in the mirror to evaluate what could be done to her face in ten seconds, but the woman who looked back at her didn't need anything. She almost didn't recognize herself, except that, yes, those were technically her features. Just at their very best, with a little fae sheen mixed in. Even the plague scar at her neck was gone.

Maeve again.

Cari didn't know how she felt about that, and she didn't have time to think about it now.

She headed for the office, but Scarlet was lying in wait to intercept her at the top of the stairs.

"Darling, really," she said. "It's inappropriate that he's here."

Sigh. "I find him indispensible."

"But to what end? It's what your father would ask."

Cari grinned. "The end of time, if he'll have me."

"Oh, Cari. This has all been so difficult for you. You're not thinking. Do you really want him, a stray, to be the father of your children?" She was shaking her head no, just in case Cari was confused.

Cari's grin stretched wider. "I know with absolute certainty that there is no better father than Mason Stray. I've got to go. The High Seat waits."

Mason was leaning on her father's desk and Kaye was sitting in the chair before it, both deep in conversation, when Cari entered the office. "What'd I miss?"

Kaye sat back in the chair in a smooth shift. Cari wondered

how she achieved that easy sophistication. Her heels were drop-dead gorgeous. They'd be stolen in this house. Stacia was probably already plotting robbery. "I'm throwing a fancy party to celebrate your success," Kaye said.

"Oh, that's not necessary," Cari said. Not with the Maeve problem going on and the mob on her doorstep. DolanCo, House business. No, a party was the last thing she needed. "Thank you very much anyway."

Mason held out a large white envelope. "Our success is only what's going on the invitations. Which I've just learned have already been sent. And Webb has assured Kaye that Fletcher will be there."

Oh. Well that was good, at least. Cari took the envelope. Heavy linen paper. Gilt hand-lettering. Rushed, obviously. Kaye had spared no expense. And how funny—the party was tomorrow night.

"We must do this now, before my opposition has time to organize. The Council is broken," Kaye explained. "Martin House is arming for war against the Order and all of its supporters. The bad business with Segue earlier this year didn't help."

Mason grunted. "A couple of Adam's people killed Martin's heir, Mathilde."

Cari had heard. It had raised her father's eyebrows all the way up to his hairline. He'd told her that Dolan would stay well out of that dispute. Sorry, Father.

"That's the beginning," Kaye said. "Martin also cites the mob outside Dolan property as violence against magekind. I need a show of support from Dolan. Yours, like Martin's, is a dark, pureblood House."

Not for long, Cari hoped, thinking of Mason.

The room was quiet, and it occurred to Cari that they were waiting to see what she would say. Would she publicly support Brand House?

Kaye's face was a mask. Mason's eyes had gone dark. He

already knew that she wouldn't try for the High Seat, and he
knew why. Cari had assured Kaye that she wouldn't challenge
her either.

But a public show of support meant something different.

"I have three conditions," Cari said. This was the moment
she'd been waiting for since Segue, and now she had the am-
munition to make the demands. The first just made sense,
considering Kaye's request.

Kaye Brand, the High Seat, bowed her head. "And they
are . . . ?"

"If I'm going to realign Dolan's allegiances and effectively
defect from hundreds of years of connections with purist
Houses," which was what Cari had wanted to do anyway, but
Kaye didn't need to know that, "I would require the support
of all Houses that support Brand."

"You want to switch sides," Kaye said.

"Basically, yeah. I like yours better than I like mine." Cari
didn't like her allies at all.

"That will take time."

Cari didn't answer, because it *would* take time.

"Agreed. I'll do whatever I can to help you. Second?"

Cari faced Kaye, but her gaze slid over to Mason. She'd
meant to make a discreet inquiry, and then plot from there.
But, oh well. "You need to find a way to break or transfer to
Dolan the fosterage of Fletcher Stray."

Mason's face flushed. The vein in his forehead bulged. Cari
didn't know if his reaction was a good thing or not. Suddenly
she thought she should have checked with him first. But what
would've been the point if claiming Fletcher wasn't possible
in the first place?

Kaye's gaze flicked between them. "I know I'd have strong
resistance from Webb, who made the arrangement with me in
good faith. Would I also have resistance from Mason?"

Cari gulped under the weight of Mason's intensifying stare.
She gave him an uneasy smile. "Where Fletcher is, that's

where you are, too." In spirit, if not in body. Once she had
Fletcher, then she could discuss the rest of her intentions with
Mason. Privately.

More silence. He had to have guessed she'd go after
Fletcher after what she'd said to Laurence about an ongoing
partnership. Dolans were nothing if not thorough. She wanted
them both.

And to prove it, she added, "Webb is interested in a project
Mason and I are working on called Umbra."

Mason's brow creased. And Cari faced him fully, while still
speaking to Kaye.

"I'd be willing to share Umbra equally with Webb for
Fletcher."

His gaze burned, and she hoped it was with the promise
of an end to his separation from his son.

"No resistance from me." Mason's voice was ruined by
strong feeling.

Cari loved how his voice could stroke deep down inside
her. She wanted to throw her arms around him, even swayed
toward him, but barely managed to keep up her Dolan poise.
Negotiations now.

"I know fire in all its forms," Kaye mused. "I want credit
for putting the raw materials for this one together. And the
third?"

Yes. That. Cari shook her hair back from her face to give
her tears a second to dry. "I have a serious fae issue that
could very quickly become a large-scale, global, catastrophic
problem. I'm"—she looked at Mason—"*we're* going to need
some assistance."

Chapter Sixteen

Mason waited out the last flicker of Kaye's transport through Twilight to wherever she was going—Brand House, most likely—before turning to Cari. "I will make the Umbra project well worth taking Fletcher and me on. It'll be enough for two Houses." No matter what he had to do.

He was hopelessly in love with her. He was pretty sure she knew it. He'd thought (hoped) she might claim him, after what she'd said to Laurence and after telling Liv she'd double what his little island house was worth. Claiming was huge. But that Cari would leverage Umbra for Fletcher, a vassal? Of course the kid was worth that much, but he wasn't Dolan blood. This was generous—maybe foolish—beyond anything in Mason's experience, but he'd take it.

Cari's mouth screwed up a little, as if she wasn't entirely pleased by what he had to say.

So he hurried to add, "And absolutely whatever else Dolan House needs to have done. Starting with the fae." He'd never leave her alone to deal with Mad Mab. A plan was in the works already. Now that Cari was inside her wards, safe from any other angels who might seek her death, Kaye would inform Bastian, and he the Order. After the party tomorrow night, trusted parties would gather to make a plan.

Cari could not give her life to end this threat. Kaye even agreed that doing so would only make war with the Order certain. "I won't leave your side," he said. Not for a minute.

To her expression Cari added a line of concentration between her eyebrows. "Well, I'll need a ring, eventually."

A ring. Now he was sure he was missing something. Something Cari thought went without saying.

"And if it's okay with you and Fletcher," she added, "and assuming Brand satisfies Webb immediately, I'd like to formally claim you both at this party."

Women wore rings all the time—he glanced at her hands— all women, that is, except Cari, who kept things simple. A claim and a ring. The only ring he'd ever given a woman had gone to Liv, who'd clapped with delight, but had still never married him.

Now Cari wanted one.

The blood-beat in his head became a roar.

Mason looked down at the floor to breathe deeply through the full-body ache that had overcome him, then forced himself to look in her eyes. So damn pretty. "A friend would remind you that Dolan is a pure line."

He really didn't want to be her friend anymore. He wanted to grab her.

But she was the Dolan. Her heritage was the oldest, strongest, best there was. Ten years into the future, when everything had gone dark, she'd be one of the leaders of the new world.

She laughed. "No. A friend would tell me that the Dolan line could use some diluting. By half feels just about perfect for the next generation, don't you think?"

Next generation. Meant kids. Meant kids with Cari. He loved kids. And he wanted to be with her, wanted it so bad he'd kill any man who so much as glanced her way. Come to think of it, he was the only one she could marry. The world had enough violence as it was.

"You want a ring," he stated to make sure he'd gotten it right. Would he dare this again?

Her eyes sparkled. *"I do."*

Clever answer. "I'll make it myself."

Mason was so funny sometimes. What had he thought she'd meant? That they'd get it on until she married someone else? House women did sometimes take lovers. Emelda Walker had a longtime live-in. But that wasn't her. Wasn't him. Made the future seem knotted and hurtful.

But with Mason beside her, the vantage cleared. She didn't have to face that constantly gusting storm because the wind went gentle on her skin.

He was looking at her mouth, a slow smile growing on his. "I love you." Seemed like a weight off his shoulders.

She laughed again. "I know. Anyone else would be running far, far away."

He stepped forward, his arm going around her waist, breath on her cheek. "There'll be nobody else. No running."

He was speaking from experience. Liv, who'd left him.

Cari didn't want Liv in the room, so she turned her head to fit her lips to his mouth, spoke against them. "I've been counseled to put this desk to good use." She understood the advice better now.

He took over the kiss, making it deeper and darker. He would make all her kisses.

Warmth diffused from her heart to her fingertips, tingled down her thighs, quivered her belly, and went molten at her core. This was how she was supposed to feel. And everything about Mason was why.

"Oh? Counseled by whom?" His teeth caught her earlobe, where he knew she was ticklish. Devil.

But she bravely tilted her head to give him access. All of her was his, even the sensitive bits. "That would be Stacia."

He lifted her weight so that she sat on the edge, and she opened her legs to straddle him. His weight kept her on the desk, yet flush against him. "I like your sisters."

"They'll love you." A thumb stroke at her waist sent magic rippling over her skin, the sorcerer at his work. How his big hands were capable of such precision . . .

He laid her back, setting her laptop out of the way in the same motion. A book fell to the floor. The papers simply couldn't be helped. The glass within a falling picture shattered.

But she could barely care because his mouth was on her belly, smoking its way downward.

For the next hour, they owned that desk. He sat for a while in the big chair, working his magic until she cried out his name. She admired the creativity with which he utilized the massive wood piece of furniture.

The desk had been in the family for over a hundred years, but it now, indisputably, belonged to them.

Someone knocked at the office door.

"No damn peace around here," Mason said into Cari's hair. She always smelled good. He sat in the desk chair with her curled up in his lap. But upon turning his head, he found her breasts just below eye level. Perfect. He would investigate.

"Get used to it," she said, arching to lift up toward his mouth.

See how well they worked together?

One arm held her close around her shoulders, the other reached around her body so that his free hand held a soft cheek, which he lightly squeezed.

"Cari?" One of the sister's voices. He couldn't tell them apart yet.

Mason growled and held Cari tighter. He loved the taste of her skin. Just now she was slightly salty.

"She's not going to go away," Cari said.

"Eventually she'll have to."

"You don't know my sister." Cari's fingers feathered through his hair.

"She doesn't know me." Now was a good time to start.

"She has a house full of reinforcements. Zel, and my stepmother, and . . ."

The stepmother. Mason lifted his head. His mood would be shot, except for the fact that he held a naked Cari Dolan in his arms. And he was naked, too. "I was about to plunder you."

Which made Cari laugh out loud. "Are you a pirate? Plunder?"

"Definitely. Plunder." Somehow he'd captured her. How about that.

She leaned toward the door. "Go away!" She sounded happy. Made him even more so.

Silence from the hall outside. He narrowed his eyes at Cari in victory, then bent his head again. He was nowhere near ready to give her up.

"But Zel's upset and crying," came the voice at the door.

Pitch. Tears.

"Stacia's not leaving without me," Cari repeated. "Let me work out whatever drama is going on, and then you can plunder me."

Cari was missing the point. "You don't give permission to plunder." But he let her sit up and discovered a new angle from which to admire her lovely body.

She kissed him—a hearty smack on the mouth. "I'll be quick."

He sighed, resigned. He had to make some calls anyway. See if he could do the impossible and catch Khan on the phone. But he wouldn't have minded delaying reality a little longer. Watching Cari dress just made him hard all over again. He dressed, too, but he wasn't happy about it.

"How do I look?" She was tucking in her blouse, smoothing her hair.

The truth? "Satisfied."

She blushed, eyes wide. Then turned and made for the door, muttering, "I'm never going to get used to this."

"Good." He didn't want to get used to this either. Every moment got better than the last. He just needed Fletcher raising hell somewhere here in the house with them, and everything would be perfect.

He had his phone to his ear, was leaving a message at Segue, and patting the crumpled pile of Cari's papers he'd rescued from the floor. Organization was not one of his strengths. The broken glass on the other side of the desk had to be cleaned up soon. Aside from the immediate family, most of the Dolan people were moving back to their own homes now that the plague threat was gone. But just in case any of the kids were still around, he hunted for a spare piece of paper to scoop up the worst of the shards.

Someone cleared their voice, and he brought his attention up.

Scarlet. Just great.

She was a silver and black dart of a woman. He wondered if her sharp cheekbones hurt her face, or if her expression was always pained. Her hands were folded in front of her at her slim waist, the picture of composure, but recriminations jabbed from her gaze.

"There was some emergency with one of the sisters," Mason said, hoping to point her interest elsewhere. "Zella is crying."

Scarlet didn't go for it. "Why are you here? What do you want?"

Took all of one second for Mason to figure out what was going on.

Survival taught a stray to know when he'd been set up. Divide and conquer, Cari upstairs, him with Scarlet. He didn't blame them for trying to intervene, and this was probably just the beginning of their anti-Mason fight. He didn't deserve Cari, wasn't remotely born to her circle, had lived in dirt and blood most of his life—felt it on him now with Scarlet looking at him like that—but he still wasn't giving Cari up.

"I'm here for Cari," he said. "Whatever she needs." A vague enough answer to cover everything.

Scarlet's gaze rested coldly on the desk. His tidying effort was clearly beneath her expectations. Or maybe she thought the activity that messed it was crass—though she'd had two daughters, so had to have indulged in the same at some point. Or maybe she just didn't want him to get Cari dirty. Point of fact, they both could probably use a shower.

"Cari requires a mage of rank beside her," she said, approaching him. "It's what her father would've wanted."

"Well, she chose me." No disrespect.

"You're taking advantage of her grief. The plague. Of the stress of her transition to power."

"Maybe I am." He was sure Cari could deal with all that shit on her own. But the point was, she didn't have to.

"You admit it?"

"Yeah." Of course. "I would use any and every means to stay close to Cari. I want to make her work, her troubles, easier on her. I want to make her happy."

"By shaming her?"

That burned. But better Scarlet work out her prejudice on him before Fletcher got here and had to endure her small mind. Just thinking of Fletcher on the receiving end of this crap made Mason's mood narrow to a knife's edge. "Shame?" Screw that.

He managed a lazy grin to cut her back. "The most Cari's ever done is blush, and it looks good on her."

Scarlet's lips pulled back as she took the bait. She stepped up close, her face in his, for round two. "I love that girl. I've kept her in my heart with my own daughters. I swore to her father that I would protect her with my life. And that is exactly what I am doing."

For a second, Mason was going to observe aloud that all of Scarlet's points were his own, too. That they had Cari's best interests in common. But a searing punch at his gut told him that Scarlet was a woman of action.

She'd just stabbed him.

Cari stepped into the office and was immediately confused. Scarlet was close enough to kiss Mason, but Cari was pretty certain that the two weren't on the best of terms. Especially because her sisters had lied to get her out of the room so that Scarlet could say her piece to the stray. Or rather, against him.

Scarlet leaned her weight slightly further in, which was weird, and used Mason's belly to push her weight back. She took two steps away, her right hand shiny with red.

A hilt protruded from Mason's stomach. He wavered on his feet, then collapsed into the desk chair, a scowl struck across his graying face.

Shock made Cari go cold, a scream rising in her throat. But she'd seen him knife-wounded before, so she kept terror at bay. "Are you going to die?"

Mason brought his gaze over. "Nah." But he didn't look too happy about living either. His hands were on his stomach, and with a violent shiver, he pulled the blade from his abdomen and dropped it on the floor.

His shiver made her hands shake, but she took him at his word and approached her stepmother.

"It had to be done," Scarlet said tightly. "I'm not sorry. I promised your father."

Cari slapped her across her face. "My father is dead. *I* am the Dolan now."

Her palm burned as she turned to kneel and assess the damage herself. The wound was a wreck of blood, but it didn't seem to be actively bleeding. Her hands fluttered in the air above. She didn't want to hurt him. "What can I do?" Besides panic and summon Maeve to break her stepmother's neck, just like Liv's.

"I had to free you," Scarlet said in a strangle behind her.

"Really not necessary," Cari answered.

Though Mason's breathing was labored, fine jagged lines of Shadow crept over his skin like capillaries of magic. Good sign. She needed him in one piece. She couldn't afford for him to be wounded right now. Mage-kind couldn't afford for him to be wounded, not with Maeve loose, doing who knew what.

"I killed him for *you*, Cari," Scarlet said.

"Well, surprise!" Cari's cheer came out pissed. "You can't kill him this way."

Movement brought Cari's attention to the door, where Stacia and Zel peeked, their faces white. Accomplices.

Cari drew them inside the office with a glare. "Did you know she was going to do this?"

Stacia looked like she was going to bawl. *Grow up.* Zel looked back and forth from her mother to Mason and back to her mother's bloody hand—*yeah, that's blood all right*—while shaking her head no.

Seemed that they hadn't known. It was something, but not enough. They'd tricked her, the head of their House, on purpose.

"Dolan House cannot fall to Mason Stray," Scarlet said. "Not while I draw breath. I swore to your father—"

But her father was dead. It was time everyone accepted that fact.

"Mason—" Cari slid her gaze his way. "My stepmother and stepsisters have colluded to deceive me." Scarlet had been pushing the boundaries from the moment Cari's father was in ashes. But Cari wasn't six anymore. She was twenty-six, the head of the household by blood, the Dolan. This stopped now.

"As you're the injured party, you can say whether this House will continue to shelter them."

At least there wasn't a plague outside the wards anymore, thanks to Mason. Not that her family would ever thank him.

"You can't mean it." Scarlet's voice had dropped an octave.

"Cari!" Stacia gasped, as if she'd been hurt.

Cari stood and faced Scarlet again. "You've gone too far this time." They could've killed Mason. "And the world is just going to get worse. A mob on our freaking doorstep and you stab the man I love, the man I bring home to help me keep this House strong. No." Cari glanced back at Mason, who looked sad and in pain and miserable. Poor man, having to deal with this crap. He'd bolt if he were smart. Why would he ever bring his son here?

Too late. She was keeping him.

"Cari—" he began.

No. He had to understand, too. They could not doubt the people inside their House. "Do they stay or do they go?"

"You're not serious," Zel said. "The plague will—"

"Plague's been resolved." Just fear left over. "But who knows when the next one will hit?" If Maeve doesn't tear apart the world first.

"They stay." Mason tried to pull up a smile. "I'm fine. Scarlet missed all the important parts anyway."

Cari had known he'd say that. But they couldn't let Scarlet just go wash off her hands. She'd just. Stabbed. Mason.

"But they shouldn't go to Brand's party," he added.

Silence from her stepfamily. Parties were their playground, so their punishment would hurt. They would not see Dolan get its honors, and that was something, too. The celebration didn't belong to them after this.

Cari took a deep breath. "Look, you should know that Mason and I are a done deal. I'm going to claim him, and someday soon I hope he'll propose." He just had to make that ring first. "If you can't live in the same House, then you can pack up and go. But if you stay, you will not plot against him or me ever again."

"I won't abandon you," Scarlet said.

The aforementioned promises to Father.

"Easy. Then don't." Cari looked over at her sisters. "Think about it."

Then she turned her back on them and knelt again at Mason's knee. "Can you move yet? Can I help you upstairs?" Weak smile. "Can you wear a tuxedo tomorrow?"

Oh, how wonderful! Gifts, large ones, all lined up in a row.

Maeve commanded Shadow to raise her up. She peeled off the lid of the first offering and delighted in the screams that erupted from inside. Surprises always delighted her. Inside was a cluster of little souls, quivering together, candies all of similar flavor. She debated which to eat first and made up a song to help her decide:

Pebble, twig, dirt, and leaf . . .

This or that one? Which to eat?

With each soul, she would grow. Already her sight grew long, her strength deep.

A lash of Shadow flicked down out of the sky toward a morsel with purple streaks in her hair. Maeve wondered what the girl's soul would tell her about the world.

A hammering sound brought her attention down to the wide, gray path out in front of the house. The world of this time had so many toys. Shiny boxes rushed by; others with flashing lights circled as if to entrap. The houses nearby were emptying—her candies rushing to save themselves. But really, where could they go to hide from her?

Maeve raised the little human as she tilted her head back and opened wide. With a squish grip, the soul slipped out of its ruby-wet casing and fell down her gullet. As it began its burn in her breast, she tossed the empty shell aside, flicking bone salt from her fingertips.

This bite was just mature enough to have tasted her first passions.

Breathless anticipation with a slight scent of fear. The tremor of the first touch. A delicious invasion that ripped innocence away.

The girl still had the *before* and *after* in her mind. *Ah,* that's *how Time works,* Maeve remembered. She'd forgotten how it strung out in this world, because it didn't exist in the Other. Time. It was important, always changing, moving, and impossible to catch.

She peered back into her gift box, wanting to know more.

"You should have told us."

Alarm throbbed through Mason, slugging into the ache at his gut and rousing him from a slightly feverish doze. The Order knew about Maeve. It had only been a matter of time. Where was Cari? They couldn't have her.

"Mason," Jack said, starting toward where he sat. He had to have been let through the wards by Brand's Lakatos. "The fae queen has killed twenty-three people in the space of a day. You should've told Laurence immediately that she'd crossed."

A body count already?

"How many mage lives did Xavier take?" Mason returned as he struggled to stand. He was better than he'd been a couple of hours before, but still felt like shit. Cold, stinking shit.

"What's the matter?" Jack's attention dropped to the blood speckles bleeding through Mason's shirt.

"You can't have her." Mason tilted his head at a strange sound—oh, right—the mob had grown. Now their cries were a constant fuzz of TV static.

"I'm not after Cari," Jack said, swatting the idea out of the air. "I'm after information. Starting with what happened to you. I heard you'd had your throat cut. What is—?"

"Throat was yesterday. Scarlet tried to kill me today."

Jack was shocked silent for a moment. Good. Mason needed to catch his breath in case he had to punch the angel's face in.

A pathetic kind of pity washed across Jack's features. "Kaye told me you and Cari were something together. Good for you. But for the love of God, sit back down. You don't have to fight me."

Mason kept standing. "How many human lives are you willing to sacrifice for Cari's?"

They had to be thinking it: End Cari, end Maeve.

Jack shook his head. "A direct assault on Cari wouldn't work now that the queen has crossed. Laurence would've told you that if you'd been forthright with him."

"Cari says she's still connected."

"Yes, certainly. But if she's anything like the last Dolan who permitted the fae queen to pass over two thousand years ago, then Cari is near immortal right now. Nothing can kill her."

"You can't harm Cari?"

"No. It's too late for that. It's what Xavier had been trying to prevent. What else haven't you told us?"

Mason searched his mind, but as he was going lightheaded, he couldn't think of anything. Oh. "Liv Walker." How could he have forgotten?

"We heard about that, too. Walker House has petitioned the Council for your death and for Dolan to pay a settlement in lieu of talion for Livia's life." Talion, a death for a death.

"Groovy," was all Mason could muster. He blew out his breath and lowered himself back into the chair. Point was . . . Cari couldn't be hurt. Jack couldn't hurt her.

"Besides," Jack said. "Humanity stands to lose more lives if Cari doesn't speak on Kaye's behalf tomorrow. The other

Houses will come armed to depose Brand and kill me. You must be prepared for bloodshed."

"And here I thought it was a celebration in our honor." Bloodshed had to be averted; Fletcher would be there.

Relief washed over Mason at the thought. Fletcher would be there. The ache in Mason's belly eased.

"Is there anything else you haven't told us?"

Mason shook his head. "The fae crossed. Cari spoke to her, tried to command her—"

"And?" Angel bastard actually seemed hopeful.

Mason popped that bubble. "The fae couldn't be stopped."

Bran was playing combat games on the big TV in the entertainment room, but Fletcher wasn't going to play with him.

No way in Hell. Fletcher's guts were tied up because of Bran. They were supposed to have been friends, but not anymore. Never ever again. Death first.

Last night Bran had started his story by saying Fletcher was going to grow up to be an assassin, just like his dad. Well, Fletcher now knew the first person he wanted to kill: Bran, the person who'd reached inside him with a hand of Shadow. If all of Webb House's stories came true, then the assassin one would, too. Fletcher wished it with all his heart. The assassin story had been told over the same candlefire as the story that he belonged to Webb. There'd also been something about the pale hand of a lady, but that just sounded creepy, plus girls were gross.

"Fletcher."

He refused to look at Mr. Webb in the doorway. They could make him do *some* things, but for everything else, Fletcher would fight. He knew how to be mean.

Bran looked over at his dad though, and his character in the game was shot in the head with machine-gun fire. Blood and gray matter splattered. Good idea. Maybe that's how Fletcher would kill him.

"Fletcher, you've been traded," Mr. Webb said. "To Dolan House for business concessions. I have no idea what they'll do with you there. I can't have a traitor in my House, you see, though you will always and forever belong to Bran."

Bran creeped his eyes over.

But Fletcher wouldn't look at him either.

"Do you understand?"

Fletcher couldn't speak anything against Webb House. He understood that much. And he understood that no one wanted him anymore, too.

But that didn't mean he was going to answer Mr. Webb. Not a chance.

Mr. Webb clucked his tongue like a chicken. "I'll be turning you over to Dolan this evening," he said. "See that your things are packed."

Cari had three gowns to her name. She almost went with a deep purple, just shy of black—classic, elegant lines—but ultimately opted for a silvery blue corseted sheath. Something about the way the shimmery cloth was tooled on the bodice reminded her of armor. And after all, she was going to war.

"Diamonds," her stepmother said from the doorway. Her expression was as hard as the stones she spoke of.

Mason had opened the door and was standing two feet from his would-be mother-in-law. If he was worried about another surreptitious attack, his bland attitude didn't show it. He was letting them both know that he was here for good.

Cari hoped her stepmother was paying attention.

"Thank you," Scarlet said to Mason as she stepped inside,

each word a precious pearl from her lips, and then crossed the room.

It was a start, so Cari lifted a velvet box for Scarlet's inspection. The necklace within was a broad band of concentric white stones set in platinum. The earrings were short fat drops.

Appreciation bloomed over Scarlet's features. "Yes, these will do nicely. May I?"

Cari nodded and her stepmother fixed the jewels around her neck. They both looked in the mirror together to study the effect. Mother and daughter. Almost.

"I only want what's best for you," Scarlet said.

"He is best." Cari put the bobs in her ears.

A ripple of emotion crossed Scarlet's face, quickly concealed. "If you love him, he must be." She rounded on Mason, who stood ready in his tuxedo, off to the side, waiting for them to finish. "Home by midnight?"

His brow furrowed in consternation, lips parting to form what had to be a diplomatic reply.

But Scarlet stalked regally back to the door. "For pity's sake, it was a joke."

Mason's mild smile at Scarlet's turnabout faded as helicopter rotors chopped the air somewhere outside Dolan House, drowning out the cry of voices. "The mob is growing." Television cameras were pinned on the house all the time now. Law enforcement couldn't hold them all back, and Brand had argued against a military intervention. There was no way on or off the property anymore, except with Brand's help. Dolan House was officially under siege.

"Can't do anything about them now." Cari wrapped silver gauze around her shoulders. "We need to settle the conflict over the Order first, so that the fae can get her due attention."

"The fae queen isn't just your problem anymore." They were a couple.

"I brought her." Cari's guilt. She might be the only mage to have guilt. "The lives she's taken are my responsibility. Thank God mages don't go to Hell."

Mages rarely invoked God, so Cari had to mean it. Mason wanted to argue that this wasn't her fault. Blame belonged squarely to Xavier, who'd forced the issue when he'd tried to kill her. But then Cari would just argue back that Maeve would have found another way to get through her into the world. And that would start Cari contemplating her weaknesses, when she needed to be strong.

So Mason said simply, "One threat at a time. At least humanity has not yet found its power."

"Just like you, they will." The faint cries against Shadow filled the silence again. "Do you really want to bring Fletcher here?"

And have Cari for a wife and mother of his child? Yeah. He did. Besides, "No wards come stronger than Dolan's. All of humanity might be screaming at your gates, and this is still the safest place in the world."

The tone of the light in the room altered, magic flowering into a burst of Shadow that parted the veil between the mortal world and Twilight. Their ride to the ball. Marcell Lakatos must have been sick of his taxi service into and out of Twilight.

Cari wrung her hands, clearly nervous about her first transport.

But Mason was anxious to get going for another reason. His heart was bouncing with excitement. Fletcher was supposed to be waiting on the other side. "You'll love him," he said.

Cari knew exactly whom he was talking about and smiled. Something to look forward to. "Do you think he'll like me?"

Chapter Seventeen

Cari was shaking with power when she crossed back into the mortal world. It throbbed, alive within her. The Otherworld was her domain, just as it was Maeve's. The strangely toned music, the drugging scent of the air, the fluid brush of Shadow on her skin—it made her feel wild inside, so that when she emerged in Maya House, in a room with splendidly dressed people, she could only be disappointed by the dullness of the world.

"Shadow's pitch, look at her eyes," said Arman. His House was the only warded place with allies on both sides of the dispute against Order. And this room seemed to be located off the main ballroom, where the murmur of voices waited.

"It's a good look," Mason assured her.

Cari gave him an exasperated groan and turned in question to Kaye. At least she was a flash of vibrant color—fiery hair, porcelain skin, a sculpted red gown that screamed sex and power.

"Your eyes are all black, even the whites, like a fae's," Kaye answered. "It's frightening, which can only help us. You are still helping us, right?"

"My conditions?"

"Met," Kaye said.

Cari gave a Dolan smile. "Then you have my full support."

Kaye's gaze went wary. "Would you be willing to do it in the old way?" She was asking, not demanding. And the way she was worrying her manicure said she was nervous. Kaye Brand, firemage, nervous. Interesting.

"The old ways are all the fashion lately," Cari drawled.

"You mean fealty." Kaye wanted her to basically acknowledge Brand House as magekind's sovereign.

Kaye gave a short nod. Mason's brow tightened, disturbed. He was so handsome when he glowered. But the others in the room all seemed to have been prepped on this idea. Their eyes went shifty.

"Gutsy of you," Cari observed to Kaye. The last House that had asked for fealty was Grey House, and Ferrol was dead. Martin, for one, would never bend knee. This was inviting open hostilities against Brand.

"We've got a fae queen eating human souls," Kaye said. "This division among the Houses has to stop. Details will be worked out later, but I swear that for your cooperation, Dolan will be my First House."

So second in line for hostilities. An honor and a noose.

Cari glanced over at Mason. "What say you?" Dolan would be his House too if they both had their way. And with Kaye's help, they might just get it.

"I think you would be just as good as Kaye in the Seat," he said. A deep breath. "But her connection to the Order via Jack Bastian has broader repercussions."

"The Order is even now marshaling against the fae queen," Jack put in.

The heavy subtext was that they were already fighting Dolan's battles. Cari had no trouble admitting she'd need all the help she could get.

"I'd do this tonight, publicly?"

Kaye colored at the possibility of her acceptance. "It would have the most impact and at a very critical time."

Cari cast her gaze down to the floor, which she didn't see because her brain was working overtime. What would her father do? She shook her head no. She had to stop thinking of him. He was dead. This was her decision, and it would have far-reaching effects. If she did this, there'd be no ultimate glory for Dolan, but if Cari really wanted that, then she need only welcome Maeve. Maeve was all for Dolan glory.

She lifted her head again. Met Kaye Brand's black gaze. "Is there a title I should use? Formal language? Secret woo-woo symbol I draw in the air?"

Kaye broke into a brilliant smile. "Thank you."

Suddenly everyone was breathing deeply and looking at each other with tight smiles and jerked nods.

Kaye twisted a little toward Jack Bastian, but the angel was already there with a supportive hand to Kaye's elbow. "Jack remembers how the ceremony went from way back in the day. He's old."

Her last words made everyone chuckle, the tension completely broken.

"Ironic that an angel has to remind magekind about its own oaths," Mason said.

Surprised, Cari looked up over her shoulder. He'd somehow moved to her side in a blink. She liked that he was behind her. Liked the heat coming off him. Liked the stroke of his voice. Felt right.

"It appears I have something to memorize." Cari squeezed Mason's hand. He must be going out of his mind with this waiting. He had something better to do than listen to her recite lines over and over. "In the meantime, has Fletcher arrived yet?"

Mason let himself out of the side room where the others were settling in to an impromptu tutorial. The ballroom was full of mages in fancy clothes and cloying perfume. Gunnar

Martin had a severe frown of disgust across his face and had worn a sword that Mason didn't think was for ceremonial purposes. That was okay. Mason had come armed as well— he had the Martin House blade *and* Xavier's weapon of the moment. Both were concealed under his tux jacket, along with his holster.

But Mason wasn't looking for a fight. He was after a short stop, rib-high, whom he hoped was looking for him, too. Dad had saved the day. A grin from Fletcher was all he needed as reward.

Mason ducked around people, who felt the need to shove their palms into his for a shake, when they'd never deigned to recognize the stray in public before.

"Well done!"

"Congratulations!"

"An honor to meet you, Greatmage Stray." That "greatmage" and "stray" should be put together boggled Mason's mind. Like "esteemed" and "scum"—a laughable combination.

Alistair of Verity House actually bent his head to his ear and offered to claim him and Fletcher.

"Thank you, but I'm taken," Mason said, disengaging himself. How utterly surreal.

If he could just find Fletcher—

There. On the far wall, next to Webb. Mason should've been looking for the old man.

The kid was all choked up with a tie. And at second glance, he didn't look right in other ways either, though Mason couldn't quite tell how. An ice pick migraine jammed into Mason's brain. He'd thought it'd be pure joy to see Fletcher, but the intensity of the emotion remained as it morphed into acute alarm.

Fletcher's eyes grew big and unblinking when he spotted him coming through the crowd, but he didn't return Mason's smile.

"Riordan," Mason said, when he reached them. But he couldn't help lower himself to kid height. He looked into his son's black eyes, searching for the smartass inside. "You in there?"

Fletcher nodded.

But the drawn expression on his son's face made Mason burn. It'd only been two weeks. He'd left Fletcher with Maria for longer and had come back to elaborate, life-threatening pranks.

Mason wanted to grab Fletcher and hug him, to lay his hands on that head, stroke his hair, check his ears, feel the bones, smell him, anything to assure himself that his son was whole. That his kid lived was suddenly not enough. Not nearly enough. *Whole,* damn it.

But Fletcher had been sensitive lately to displays of affection in front of other people. So Mason had to satisfy himself by squeezing his shoulders with his hands and standing to address Webb.

"Does he know?" Mason asked.

Fletcher's face didn't light with the knowledge of good news. They needed a private reunion, so Mason could shake the kid back into himself. As it was, he could only snag his son by the collar in case he had to wrench him away from Webb.

"If you were looking for a House," Riordan said genially, "you should've mentioned it. I'd have been happy to claim you. Keep it all in the family, so to speak."

Bald-faced lie, but Mason wanted to stay nice. They'd have to work together in the future. "Cari made me an offer I couldn't refuse." Just wait until Fletcher heard.

"I'm very excited to begin planning the Umbra project with you," Webb said. "I have some ideas—"

"—which, I'm afraid, will have to wait until later tonight. I've got to introduce Fletcher to Cari." A lie of his own. Cari was busy. Mason wanted to grill Fletcher to get at what was wrong. The pressure of concern in his chest was getting unbearable.

"Certain—" Webb was saying.

But Mason was already pushing Fletcher ahead of him, while searching out a quiet corner. He resisted the instinct to pick the kid up and make a run for it. His instincts were screaming fire. Keeping his cool was an act of pure will, but the effort was making him sweat into his brand new custom tux.

Another door. Looked okay.

Unlocked. Even better.

Inside was a narrow room loaded with party miscellany. Perfect.

As soon as the door shut, Mason went down on his knees and grabbed his son into a tight hug. The small body went rigid in his arms, but the size, the contours, the density— tough and soft—were all unmistakably Fletcher. Mason's ear was at his chest. Fletcher's heartbeat was the sound of peace and rest and hope. But not cooperation. Mason sat back on his heels to beg. He'd rip out his own heart and hand it over, if only to get real answers. "What happened at Webb House?"

Took too long for Fletcher to answer. "Nothing."

The answer sounded truthful, but Mason didn't like it. He tried a different tactic. Ask around the issue. Come from a different side. "How did you find out about the Lures?" The first sign of trouble.

"I made it up."

Lorelei Blake's death and Fletcher's text message had not been a coincidence. "We promised we'd never lie to each other."

"But you left me anyway."

The first lie, and the root of whatever was bothering him. Mason did not mistake the recrimination in his son's voice. They were getting somewhere. Yes, he'd sworn that they'd stick together, forever. And then the plague had hit. Mason had thought his son had understood. Fletcher had even said it was okay. Mason was a fool for trusting an eight-year-old's understanding of adult nightmares.

"And Mr. Webb just traded me to some lady for his business. I'm going to her House tonight."

"What lady?" Was he talking about Cari?

"Like you care."

Two weeks had done this. Two fucking weeks. "I do care. I know the lady. Cari Dolan. I'm staying at her House. You'll be with *me*."

"I hate her. I'm going to kill her the first chance I get. She killed my mother."

"That's not true! I was there!" Mason took his son by the upper arms and shook. "A fae killed your mom. Cari tried to stop her."

But Fletcher's face closed. His mouth pressed tight. He was a small, but impregnable fortress of secrets. Something had been said. Some idea had taken root. His son had come to some awful conclusion and had built a wall between them when Mason wasn't looking. A sear of frustration ran along Mason's nerve fibers.

"Goddamn it," Mason said, standing, but keeping a tight hold on one of Fletcher's arms. He was never letting go of the kid again. Never. "We are resolving this now."

"Where are you taking me?" Kid's voice had turned mean.

"To meet her. To hear what she's done for us so that we can be together again," Mason said. *Together, like I promised.* "Then you tell me again how you want to kill her."

A bright spark burned in Maeve's eye, and she turned her countenance toward the Light. Another joined it, and another, until her vision danced with bothersome fireflies. Angels, here to fight the wrong.

But she was far more beautiful than they; she had the illumination of thousands within her. She was a torch, her mind heavy with their understanding.

She wasn't *wrong*. She was inevitable.

* * *

"And Shadowman, too? He'll help?" Cari was astonished at Jack Bastian's news. She'd learned her lines for the big announcement and the conversation had turned to the insane fae queen. Maeve was not Segue's problem—they didn't even have *wards*—but it seemed Adam and his people had agreed to throw down and fight against the fae queen, too. The Order was already actively engaged against her.

Cari put a hand to her chest to quell the rise of feeling, but couldn't express how deeply moved she was for the support. Any reservations she had about swearing fealty to Brand evaporated.

Bastian put a hand to her arm. "She won't be the only fae to cross. Darkness is rising. Dolan will have its work cut out for it in the years to come."

Cari clenched her teeth, steeling herself. Yes, she would do whatever she could. Her House, its long strength, was behind this effort. This was what she'd been born for. Plus, she'd have Mason beside her. It wasn't such a terrible future.

There was a sharp knock, then the door opened without their having had a chance to answer. A kid was propelled inside—Mason's eyes!—the father behind him.

Cari's stomach fell. Fletcher Stray. This was it. And Mason looked angry.

Jack Bastian disengaged and stepped back toward the door. "I'll let Kaye know you need a few minutes."

The mind reading thing. Cari now wished for that power herself. Her fantasy about Fletcher liking her was already crumbling. This was not how she'd imagined it going.

The door closed and Mason shoved his son toward her. "Fletcher, this is Cari Dolan. Cari, Fletcher."

Um . . . ?

Cari attempted to lower herself vertically as much as her dress would allow. "I've been looking forward to meeting you."

But the boy—beautiful kid, really—just looked sullen and angry. He wouldn't meet her eyes. He had killer lashes though. Was going to break hearts when he grew up, just like his daddy. Fletcher was already breaking hers.

"Apparently Webb told him that he'd traded Fletcher in a business deal," Mason said.

Cari looked up at Mason. "That's not how it was."

"And he thinks you killed Liv."

Cari opened her mouth to say no, but no sound came out. This was too horrible to contemplate.

"I told him already, but he doesn't buy it."

Cari looked Fletcher in the eyes as deep as he'd let her go. "I swear on my House, on my father's name, on my life . . . I did not kill your mother."

Fletcher just looked at her, unimpressed, though it was the only time in her life she'd ever made such an oath.

She straightened. "I don't know what else I can say."

Mason brought round a chair so that she could sit. "I thought we could explain our plans, let him weigh in. He might hear better after he gets the whole picture."

Cari settled back as Mason pulled up a chair for himself. She chewed her lip, trying to think where to start, then opted for the beginning to win him over. "The plague killed my father. Burned him up from the inside." Any sympathy? Nope. Moving on. "And I inherited my House. Dolan House. Have you heard of it?" Adult skepticism on the face of a child. That would be a no, too.

Mason jerked a nod for her to continue. What had happened? But his face was as stony as his son's.

"The mage Council asked me and your dad to find out who started the plague. And we did." No congratulations or way-to-go! "And at the same time we were investigating, we . . ." Cari looked up desperately. She didn't want her explanation to sound like Mason had been having fun while his kid was lonely.

"I got the girl, too," Mason finished. Blunt. Efficient.

Fletcher slid his gaze over to his dad, then back.

"But I knew that your dad could never be happy without you, so I offered to trade the only valuable thing my House has so that you two could be together again. Your dad was so worried."

Fletcher's hard expression didn't waver.

The issue of the moment. The impending claim. Even now Kaye was waiting for the announcements to begin. And this one was the first. "Fletcher, if it's okay with you—"

"No," Mason cut in. "It's happening whether it's okay with him or not."

Cari opened her hands, helpless. She was obviously terrible with kids. She'd cry about it later. "But maybe we should wait. Give him a little time to get to know me."

"Cari." Mason's voice had lowered. "There is no time. Martin came fucking armed to the teeth."

Um . . . *language?* She'd take that up later. A couple of wild wolves they were.

Cari looked back at Fletcher and sighed. She reached inside herself to find the right words to let him know that she only wanted to give his dad and him a home, and in return she'd get a family. The trade was pretty uneven, when she thought about it. She came out way ahead.

She was staring hard to figure out what to say when she caught sight of a wisp of his umbra. Little mage, so tough. Trying to be just as big and bad as his dad. They were twins, which meant Fletcher was going to be a handful. Already was. The more she looked at him, trying to see past the Mason in his DNA to the person he was on his own, her Sight revealed the shape of a child's hand, made of Shadow, clamped tightly on Fletcher's mouth.

She blinked. Looked harder. Yes. A child's hand covered Fletcher's mouth.

Cari dropped a hand to Mason's knee and gripped. "Fletcher's been bound."

The kid's hard eyes—not hard, no—*brave* . . . his brave eyes widened. Begged.

Mason slid off his chair, face reddening, to be closer to his son. He put his big hand over Fletcher's heart. "Wha—? How? *Fuck* Webb."

The vehemence in his voice was frightening. And it exactly matched her own. The language in this case was absolutely warranted.

"Oh, yes. Webb will pay." Cari clenched her hands together. "Let's see to Fletcher first though."

That hand across Fletcher's mouth was made of the umbra, the Shadow soul, of some other mage. A child, strangely. Cari reached forward and peeled it away from Fletcher's face. The hand smoked into obscurity.

Only a Dolan could've perceived it. Without her intervention, Fletcher would have lived his life with his mouth closed.

"Bran did it," Fletcher said, angrily. His face was pink, blotchy, and his eyes shined. And somehow Cari knew to look away, anywhere, so that he wouldn't be ashamed of himself. Stray pride.

"You will tell me everything," Mason said. He was shaking, so Cari put a hand on his shoulder.

"It's so I don't say anything about Webb House." His voice was off. Forced.

Cari looked at him again. Looked at him as a Dolan should look at everyone. There'd been a hand to his mouth. And pitch if there wasn't another holding on to his umbra soul.

To do this to a child. To have another child do this to a child. Riordan Webb would come before the Council and explain. Cari would see to it, if she didn't kill the bastard first. He was not getting any part of DolanCo's Umbra project, that's for sure.

"What about Webb House?" Mason asked.

Cari relaxed into her power. There was so much of it after her rush through Twilight to get here from Dolan House. Webb had a great aptitude for magic, but Dolan's was still stronger. She reached with her own hands of umbra—careful—and forced the child Bran's to release its grip on Fletcher.

And then the words just tumbled out of him, fast and free. "I don't know. That Webb's a dick, maybe. I got the files off Mr. Webb's computer, but I left it inside his wall. No way could he or his search dogs find me. I peed everywhere I could."

"You left his files—? Search dogs?" Mason seemed to be having trouble keeping up. Each thing worse than the last.

"They are files on a flash drive, duh. And I can walk through walls. It's how I got away."

A Walker trait, Cari thought, from Livia. Oh, this kid was going to be trouble. But he seemed okay now. Natural. A little cocky, which made her warm inside.

Cari flinched as Fletcher suddenly looked over at her. "You got *both* hands?"

Mason sat back, even more confused.

Fletcher had noticed. He must have felt the difference and had just connected it to her.

"Yeah, I got rid of the second one." To Mason, she said. "Bran had him by the umbra, too. Seemed like they weren't about to let Fletcher go."

"He had him by his umbra?" Mason growled.

"I guess you're okay," Fletcher said, examining Cari more carefully. "For a girl."

Considering her initial reception, Cari was more than happy to go with this. She had a feeling parenthood would be very humbling. "Thank you. Umbra is my thing, as Shadow walking is apparently one of yours."

"Huh . . ." Fletcher's expression soured.

Oh, no. She'd screwed up again somehow.

The sour turned into a full-fledged frown of disgust. "You and my dad don't hump, do you?"

"He's a thousand-year-old soldier," Mason said to introduce Jack Bastian.

"I'm older than that, actually," Jack said to Fletcher, holding out his hand. "Pleased to meet you."

Mason looked over at Kaye, who was waiting with Cari. Kaye raised her eyebrows as if to say, *Any time now would be good.*

Got to get the kid squared away first. Just wait until Kaye had children.

"You're the one who came to our cabin in New Mexico," Fletcher said.

"That would be me," Jack said. "But I didn't see *you* anywhere."

Fletcher smiled smugly. "I know."

Smartass. Kid needed a mother, Mason thought. Why hadn't he seen it before?

"That lady over there is Kaye Brand," Mason said, "and she's waiting to tell all these people how great I am."

Fletcher grinned.

"Try not to give Mr. Bastian too much trouble."

"I've got him," Jack said. Which meant that if Martin or anyone else should make a move, the thousand-year-old soldier would make sure his son was safe. It would have to be good enough.

Mason gripped the top of Fletcher's skull with one hand—an old joke they called "the claw of doom"—and turned to join Kaye and Cari in the empty space in the room. Mason found he didn't like being in the spotlight. But then, who'd be looking at him with the ladies in all their cleavage and jewels? He couldn't take his eyes off Cari.

A flute of Black Moll was handed to him as Kaye raised hers.

SOUL KISSED   317

The room fell silent.

"First, thank you to Greatmage Maya for opening his wards to the Houses tonight. We are gathered here this evening to celebrate the success of Cari Dolan and Mason Stray's investigation into the mage plague. Not only did they discover the source—an ancient rogue angel by the name of Xavier—but they killed him, too, thus ending the threat to our people. The Dark Age is upon us, and we have greatmages the likes of the Old Ones among us. I raise my glass."

The gathering sipped at their Moll. It burned down Mason's throat. He glanced over at Fletcher and Jack Bastian. Fletcher held a glass of the black stuff, too. Trust Jack to know all the mage ways.

Cari stepped forward before everyone's glasses came down. A low rumble of "Do-lan, Do-lan, Do-lan" swept the crowd. Mason knew it was support for what they hoped was her bid for Brand's seat. Kaye was a lit wick of poise behind Cari's armor. His princess, ready to do battle.

Mason blew out his breath. *Here goes* . . .

Cari swept her gaze across the room. "Dolan House has stood for time immemorial because we can sense the character of those around us, and so have gathered powerful allies to augment our own power. My father taught me to recognize value, and it is glaringly obvious in Mason Stray. Whatever his heritage, the man has proven his worth a thousand times over. He is the equal of anyone in this room. Dolan House claims Mason Stray and his son, Fletcher Stray, for our own. If any House challenges me in this, I'll scrape them off the earth."

Mason's soul was rocked by her proclamation. His blood boomed in his ears and bleached his vision. He was electrified all over. Cari awed him. And how amazing was it that he got to hump that woman whenever he wanted. It was a good day to be born stray.

Cari turned and looked at him with her fae-black eyes. He

glanced at her lips, his favorite feature, and read happiness in
their fullness. He gave her a smile of his own. He'd have to
get to work on that ring right away and claim her right back.
A little piece of jewelry, one of a kind, which would tell
everyone that she was his, too. He wished he had it now.

"Dolan for the High Seat!" someone cried from the crowd.

"Dolan!" another seconded.

Moment over. More fighting now.

A clamor rose among the throng, Shadow rising as they got
their blood up.

"The Dark Age needs no Order!"

"Give us pure blood!"

Mason refused the urge to grab Cari and put her behind
him. Besides the fact that the violent rabble here *wanted* her,
supported her, near-immortal Cari didn't need his protection.
Her blood was so pure, she was almost fae. It was Kaye,
who'd taken an angel for her consort, who was threatened.

And Kaye stared them all down, even as her skin leapt suddenly with faefire. The red of her dress made sense. She was
a living flame, untamable.

Jack Bastian must get burned every night.

Kaye raised her arms to heighten the stretch of the golden-
hot light. "Dolan House, do you challenge me?"

The unmistakable sigh of a blade unsheathing turned the
black gazes of magekind on each other. The crowd began to
move, the Houses taking sides, men edging forward. Jack had
a grip on Fletcher's shoulders, which meant that Mason would
do whatever he could for Kaye, if this came to violence.

Cari turned to Kaye, her profile to the gathering. "Greatmage Brand, I do not challenge you."

"Honor your father!" someone shouted.

Caspar's memory was probably her only weakness. Mason
knew her father had wanted the High Seat for her, and Cari
could do the job spectacularly. But . . .

In a voice that carried, Kaye said, "Prove it."

* * *

It was simple really. Not much to do.

Cari caught sight of Mason as she lowered to one knee. Magekind was chattering behind her, people shouting, people who'd respected her father and had his high hopes for her. But this was by far the better solution, even if they didn't understand why.

Already she could feel the hum of her House's ward stones as she prepared to speak, binding her Shadow to Brand's. "I, Cari Dolan, do promise and testify that my House will be faithful and bear true allegiance to—"

A tidal wave of Shadow rolled over the room, plunging it into darkness.

"Oh, I don't think so," said Maeve in her multi-toned voice. Fires sprang up to illuminate the space.

Cari quaked inside, but she stood and turned to face the fae. Back straight. Dolan chin high. *This* was what her father had taught her.

Maeve had taken on a solidity that made Cari's heart quail. And there was intelligence in her eyes that mixed with the madness, as if she'd learned some things. Terrible, powerful things. And to her omnipotence, she would turn her world-wise cunning. Behind her, magekind cringed. Only Gunnar Martin stood forward, gripping a black sword. Mason had pulled two knives—one gold, one black—from somewhere. And Jack Bastian, who stared in alarm at Kaye, had put Fletcher behind him.

"I choose Brand," Cari said to Maeve.

"How can a queen swear allegiance to a lesser House?" Maeve swatted toward Kaye, who burst into crimson feathers and flame and took flight. The phoenix circled the room with a primordial cry that together with abundant darkness and smoke, made the room seem as if it existed in a lost, ancient time.

"You, my dear"—Maeve stroked Cari's cheek—"you rule magekind."

"And what about you?" They weren't ready for her. They hadn't had a chance to plan with Shadowman and that angel Laurence. They were supposed to fight her together—that's what this allegiance was about—but it seemed like they'd have to stand here, now. And Cari was certain that all the power in this room was not enough to counter Maeve.

"I rule the world."

Maeve pushed Shadow at Cari, and Cari found herself buoyed up on magic to the pinnacle of a sudden high throne. Her silver gown disintegrated and gold filigree curled over her skin in an intricate lace that scrolled over her breasts, her thighs, her pubis—concealing nothing—and then rippled out into the flourishes of a decadent Otherworldly gown. The webbing pulled back her arms and hair and caught her in jewel-crusted splendor. The metal seeped into her every pore. She was an icon, rich in power, trapped in magic.

Magekind looked upon her in terrible awe. She was their queen. Not fire, not Brand.

Dark House, Revel House. Dolan House ruled.

Cari opened her mouth to speak to her people, and her first word was, "Run."

Chapter Eighteen

Cut Cari down, or go for the fae bitch first?

Mason didn't like how exposed Cari was, even if her skin was dressed in gold and wealth and beauty. She was trapped up there. In pain? Terrified, certainly. But Maeve was sentimental about her, so he concentrated on the fae. What would a Martin blade do to Maeve? Would the intent-to-kill work the same way? Or how about Xavier's weapon-of-the-moment? Did it know how to sever a fae from this world?

"The wards, Arman!" Jack Bastian shouted.

The wards had clearly not stopped Maeve from entering Maya House, so it was unlikely that other House wards would work either. Magekind was at Maeve's mercy. But none of the mages here could leave, nor any help get inside, if the Maya wards remained in place.

"You swore to me!" Mason yelled back at Jack, just in case he needed a reminder. Jack Bastian had promised that Light would protect Fletcher. Well, here was the moment. That thousand years of angelic experience now belonged to an eight-year-old mage boy.

Mason felt the burning attention of the fae queen before he had a chance to whip around.

"I remembered why I don't like love," she said to him.

She'd grown in size and density in the past two days. Or maybe she had no sense of proportion and thought bigger was better. "Passion, and desire, and all the agonies of the flesh I do like. But love is a trap set by Order, and you have ensnared my daughter inside it."

"You will not touch him!" screamed Cari. "He's mine!"

"Dove," Maeve said to her, "it will only hurt for a moment. I learned about time, too. And pain. Both are fleeting things. You'll see."

Maeve reached out with a jet of Shadow, and Mason ducked and lunged with his long knives. He drew an X on her belly to spill her guts.

Only the angel's blade had any effect. The slash went crimson, then healed itself and even the faery gown she wore was whole again. But it stung her enough that she backhanded him into the wall. The blades flew out of his grasp—his fault—he knew how to hold on to a weapon. The impact had dazed him.

People were screaming and looking over their shoulders in their haste to get out.

And Fletcher yelled, "Dad!" from Jack's struggling grasp.

Maeve struck down again.

Mason grabbed a drink tray—flutes of Black Moll crashed to the floor—and he held the platter overhead, while sending crackles of Shadow through the glass. His shoulders and back took the hot shock of the strike, but the tray itself held. A shield.

The phoenix dived from above. Maeve looked up, just in time for Kaye to take a faery eyeball from its socket. With a swat, Maeve sent Brand crashing to the floor.

Kaye's naked human body seemed crushed, collapsed into death. An audible gasp went round the room, the Brand fire snuffed, but then she burst into flames and ascended into the ceiling circle again.

Arman Maya cast an illusion of an angelic host coming to

the battle, but it was Gunnar Martin who lunged with the blade intended for Jack Bastian. Not the unity anyone expected, but Mason would take what he could get.

Maeve seemed beset by the little stings of inconsequential creatures.

"Get me down," Cari said, panting. "Get me down so I can help!"

Maybe Cari was the only one who could make a real difference. Mason dropped the tray and used a chair to climb up toward her. He gripped the gold lace that fastened her to the throne, but no matter how it tore his hands, the metallic stuff would not come loose. He needed one of his knives. Either would probably cut through the lace. He twisted from his climb to locate the nearest one.

And then his heart stopped.

Fletcher panted in the arms of the soldier guy. When the firebird crashed into the floor, the angel almost crushed him, but then the bird took off, and Fletcher was able to breathe again.

The fight was getting good. Made him bounce with excitement.

Crazy kong lady going down!

One of his dad's weapons was lost under the feet of the scared people. Stupid. The other knife, the gold one, lay waiting on the other side of the crowd. It glowed with light. So cool.

His dad was trying to get Cari down from the throne. She was going to need some real clothes, like right away, because he could totally see her boobs and belly button and *down there*, too. He'd have to tell his dad that with this and the humping thing, he was officially scarred for life.

The cool long knife first.

The soldier was watching the bird, so Fletcher knew how

to get free. The move didn't work on his dad anymore, but this guy? A thousand years of so-easy-sucker.

Stealth dropped his weight and spun to the side when the soldier grabbed forward. *I mean, really.* The angel got his balance back, but too late.

Stealth was already running. There were people in the way, but he was a Walker, so he threw his weight into a knee slide right past the crazy kong fae and into the crowd, smoking through the legs of one-two-three people who didn't even have time to scream.

"Fletcher!" his dad hollered. Okay, so maybe a grounding was in his future. Fletcher stood up and threw the gold knife in the air. Which his dad caught, no problemo.

And just in time for the angel soldier to catch up and yank him into a *serious* hold, the kind reserved for prisoners, bad guys, and assassins.

Hell yeah.

"He gets it from you," Cari said, as Mason began cutting her free. The stunt Fletcher had just pulled had turned her belly to water. "I swear you Strays are out of your minds."

The gown was exquisite chicken wire, made to fit her, but damn uncomfortable.

"He's punished for life." White lined Mason's mouth, a level of rage she'd not encountered thus far. Not even when she'd parted his Shadow to see his soul.

From her high vantage she could take in the action in the room. Most of the mages had cleared out—the wards must be open—only her closest allies and Martin remained. And he was slowly bloodying against Maeve's strikes. Kaye was relentlessly gauging at Maeve's eyes, to keep her sightless. And Arman Maya with his illusions had the fae twitching.

But every injury healed and the fae's energy didn't flag. The fae was immortal, elemental. There was no way to kill her. They had to find a way to drive her back into Twilight, and Cari didn't have the faintest idea how. Sooner or later, probably sooner, Maeve would get bored. And then what?

Bored meant death.

Just as Cari broke free, Shadow roiled like a dust storm into the ballroom. The air grew thicker, sweeter, more potent. And out of its abject depths, a new figure stalked onto the battlefield. Khan, aka Shadowman. At his side was Cari's favorite angel Custo, and he was snarling for a fight.

The cavalry.

"Insufferable," Maeve complained at Shadowman. "As Death, you must know that of the two of us, only one can die. And it isn't me."

"Hello, Mab," Khan returned. "Only one of us is suited for this world, and it's not you either."

Custo drew a golden blade, like Mason's. He shot a look to Jack Bastian, and Cari caught the flush of relief that crossed the other angel's features. Meant the Order was here now. Their rhythmic march was no Maya illusion this time.

The alliance was coming together after all, and with all the age and experience in this room, *someone* had to know how to send Maeve back.

Mason lifted Cari down from the throne, the gown dragging its elaborate train. She kicked off transparent crystal slippers the likes of which would make Stacia weep.

The knife in Mason's grip grew into a long, fat sword.

Khan threw a fistful of darkness at the fae queen and she aged before their eyes, crumpling in stature. Then inhaled and grew to even more staggering proportions. The menace in her eyes told Cari that playtime was well over.

Custo flung himself forward, then yelped as he was swatted to the side, unconscious.

Cari approached to face down her fairy godmother. She drew deep on Shadow to be able to fight, but the power that flooded her umbra came from Maeve via the Dolan ward stones. They were leashed together. There was no escape for her. Xavier had been right all along. And yet, the time was past to free herself from the fae.

"No escape," Maeve said, as if she knew Cari's heart.

Mason came up beside her, his arm around her waist. Sword ready.

"But you're trapped, just like I am," Cari said. "There's nowhere for you to go, but back."

An army of angels entered the room and settled into tight ranks for an assault. Their breastplates reflected the light of the faefires, and no Shadow touched them. They would come and come and beat back the queen for as long as it took.

"Retreat into Shadow, Maeve," Khan said. "This world does not want you."

"The world has no choice," the fae queen replied.

Her arm licked out.

Cari only had time to cringe as she was grabbed by her hair and wrenched from Mason's grasp. The force with which she was yanked toward the fae would've easily scalped her or broken her neck, but Maeve had made her immortal. She was a dolly, a plaything that had been lovingly dressed, but was now dragged around according to mood.

"Mine," Maeve said, petulantly.

Mason rushed them.

But darkness clouded Cari's vision, and she was jerked again, this time into oblivion.

The Order couldn't reach her here. Dolan House was impregnable; her line had seen to it. *Her* power sourced the wards. Humanity could clamor at her gates. The Order could marshal against her. But she was staying, forever. This was the Dark Age, and she was their queen.

And in the meantime?

Maeve cast Cari to the side and called upon black magic.

"What's going o—?" a fair-haired chit asked, coming into the great hall.

Maeve raised a finger at her. *Just a moment.*

Then she clenched her hand, and Shadow burst outward from her, like the dust from a crashing meteor. She writhed in pleasure as it exploded through the House, across the property, past the wards, and out upon the earth. It would cover the sky with darkness and everything thereunder would wither, unless it was her will that they should not. Their pitiful electricity could not pierce this gloom. Order would break if humanity, in despair, looked elsewhere for survival.

She smiled as the humans that mobbed the perimeter screamed their fear—so simple to control them—then she turned to the mage girl with the white hair. "You were saying?"

Cari had stood from her tumble. "Stacia, get away."

The girl Stacia cringed from Cari. *"Pitch!"*

Yes, Cari was the night—gold and black and stunning in her perfection.

A crone with glamour in her blood entered the room as well, and Maeve waited patiently while she took in a fae queen's grandeur. It would be overwhelming to one such as she to see true beauty.

"You," the crone finally said.

"Me," Maeve sighed. At last someone understood.

Laurence came forward. "We've already got a contingent near Dolan House."

Mason gripped his arm. "How do you know they went there?" Mad Mab and Cari had disappeared into a dark welling of magic, leaving gloom and fire behind them. He'd thought they'd both crossed into Twilight, and was prepared to go after Cari into the Otherworld, if necessary.

"Order, that's how," Laurence answered. "They report that

most of Middlesex County is blacked out. Dolan House is at the center."

Everywhere would be blacked out soon.

"Makes sense she'd go there if she felt threatened," Bastian said. "It's the Dolan seat of power." He had Fletcher grabbed by the collar; the boy's eyes were bright with excitement. "Maeve will be untouchable by Order unless Cari can get the wards down."

Cari. Alone. With that creature.

"The wards are made of Mab," Khan said. "There's no getting the wards down. Why would Maeve allow it?"

"Maybe not allow it," Mason said. "But she might be too distracted to do anything about it. A moment of weakness?"

"You mean to follow them, then?" Laurence said.

Mason nodded, though he was pretty sure the angel knew the answer already. "Any way I can." Where was that Lakatos?

And would Fletcher understand? He had to leave him behind again.

"I've got a good hold of him now," Bastian grumbled, lifting the kid from the back of his clothes.

"I can fight, too," Fletcher said fiercely.

Kid had a tenuous grip on reality. He didn't seem to connect the very real danger with the fantasy going on in his mind. Why hadn't Mason noticed before? Probably because *the father* was squarely to blame, nurturing those fantasies since he'd been born.

And what would Fletcher learn today, when that father took off to fight a creature that he couldn't possibly subdue?

Bastian answered. "That you fight anyway. I'll protect him until you come back."

Which could be never.

"Not for you," Bastian said. "Though you might come back as one of us."

A goddamn angel. The idea made him feel strange all over.

"The quicker you die, the quicker you can be back," Khan observed wryly. "I'll transport you."

A ride.

Mason shuddered out a breath. He grabbed Fletcher's face and kissed him hard on the forehead. "Love you, kid."

Fletcher wasn't embarrassed. He showed his big front teeth. "Kick some ass, Dad."

"Will do," Mason said. Kid needed a mother. Maybe an army of them to clean up his act.

"The Order will be waiting for the moment the wards come down," Laurence said.

"Ready?" Khan asked.

Mason dropped his chin into a one stroke nod. "Now."

Cari felt the punch of Shadow before she saw the bloom and smelled the trees of Twilight. She whipped around, her gown scraping heavily across the floor, to see Khan emerge from Twilight into Dolan House. She'd had no idea that Khan could cross wardlines too, but then, as Death, he must have been the master of all crossings.

And Mason was beside him. Sweet, stupid Mason. What about Fletcher?

"The wards, Cari," Mason said, even as Maeve flung him back at the wall. Cari heard the crack of his spine, felt it viscerally in a lightning strike down her own. But Shadow etched across his skin to hold him together.

Stacia screamed.

Mason's gaze bore into Cari's, as he gritted through pain while Khan and Maeve went hard at each other—black magic to death magic.

Right. *The wards.*

Meant they were bringing the fight here . . . all those innocent people outside . . . but then, compared to all the people there were in the world, it wasn't so many after all . . .

The wards had to be down for the angels to get inside.
Time and again across history, Dolan had held out against
an assault from Order. But this was the first that it was necessary to welcome them with open arms. Come on in. No,
really. Please.

She tried to lower the wards at will, as she'd done so easily
since she'd inherited. She forced all her strength and hope and
love into the effort. The blood pounding in her brain felt like
a stroke coming on. Bile raged up her throat. But her umbra
hit a wall made of faery, and the wards held.

"The cellar," Cari breathed to Scarlet. There was more
power to be had in the cellar, where the ward stones were
close, just buried in the foundation. "I need to get to the
cellar."

Mason pushed up from his fall, his face flexed into fury,
and he threw the fat gold blade at Maeve, where it *thunked*
through the fae's back and came out through her belly. "Go!"

Cari dragged her gown across the room, and the load got
lighter as Scarlet lifted it to hurry behind her. And almost
became weightless when Stacia picked up the other side.

Windows shattered behind them, but Cari didn't look back.
Help had to be able to get inside.

"You know Maeve?" Cari sobbed to Scarlet as they
rounded the hall to the double doors and gained the grand
stair that led down to the foundation of the House, where
magic was thickest, the fae's whispers loudest, the drugging
scent the strongest.

"I was married to your father for over twenty years."

"What the fuck—?" Stacia cried.

Cari almost tripped as she descended. "Did he say how to
beat her?" She should've asked Scarlet before. She should've
asked immediately.

"He said to triumph over her was to deny her existence." At
the base of the stair, Scarlet reached around to open another
door, older, made of thick oak and treated with centuries of

magic. "He said to allow her no purchase in this world, even in the mind."

Too late for that.

It seemed her father hadn't known that Maeve would be louder to a Dolan woman. That the fae would be more present, more insistent, more possessing to *her* than anything he'd experienced. A key component of the family lore had fallen away with time. He was right about one thing: time was magekind's most insidious enemy, even to a House as long-standing and prestigious as Dolan.

But still . . . "Why didn't he warn me?"

The cellar was roiling with Shadow, currents of magic pushing at her body and tugging her gown this way and that. For the first time in her life, Cari could clearly see the semi-androgynous shapes of fae prowling in the darkness. No huffing necessary.

"He left it to me," Scarlet said, "so that her name would never pass his lips. And until tonight, I had no idea she'd already touched you."

Maeve had touched her all right.

Cari gained the middle of the room, equidistant from all the stones. She reached for power over the stones to bring the wards down. Didn't matter that a mob was at the gate. Didn't matter that Order wanted to assail her home. She strove against the barrier until her nose bled, her hearing dimmed, her heart shuddered, and her lungs screamed for air.

Nothing. The kickback from the effort made her want to vomit.

Maeve was too strong. Forever too strong.

Cari brought her hands shaking to her head.

"What's going on?" Stacia cried. "What is that thing upstairs?"

"Faery queen," Cari murmured, a lump forming in her throat.

All Mason had asked her was to bring the wards down, and

she couldn't even do that. He might be dead already, and still the wards were up.

How to get more power? How to draw more than even a fae queen?

An eardrum-shattering crash came from above, and the house shook, dust falling on Cari's head. She needed to bring the wards down now.

The heavy door to the cellar opened, and Zel lurched inside. Half her face was purple-red and blistered, the eye bloodshot. A tooth missing from bloody gums. Scarlet reached her arms to catch her.

"No," Cari said. She needed Scarlet first. "The storage room on the other side. See what tools are there. Shovel. Or a pick. Anything. I'm going to dig up the stones."

Scarlet was shaking her head, her eyes full of rage and alarmed disagreement.

Cari shrieked at her to get her to move. "I'm going to fucking hold them in my hands and make the wards come down!"

Her stepmother wavered, white-faced, Zel heaving for breath in her arms. Was Scarlet going to follow direction and do what was asked, no matter how terrible?

Scarlet turned to Stacia. "Help me."

Okay. One impossible thing accomplished: her stepmother had cooperated.

Cari held out her trembling hands, palms down to the ground, to search for the warm hum of a buried stone. She found one in a dark corner, where the stony floor should have been cool, but was hot to the touch. Fae creatures looked on, omnipresent, but still on the other side of the Twilight veil. Cari knelt down and began prying at the cobbled floor with her bare hands. The ashy smell of old earth touched her nose.

Never before would her fingers and nails have been capable of tearing rock from concrete, but she was made out of stronger stuff now. Her nails raked across seams, fingertips finding only the slimmest edge by which to pry up a small boulder.

Scarlet and Stacia were chattering when they rushed back in, so her stepmother had to have filled in Stacia on what was happening. Zel got a shortened version, and concluded, "But there are people outside."

"Can't be helped." Cari reached out her hand for the shovel Scarlet held, then struck the floor with all her might to get at what she sought. The concrete cracked and the faeglow of a large, soft stone appeared, just small enough for her hand to grip, but too large for the hold to be comfortable. A Dolan ward stone. She pried it out with her fingers, which finally bled as she pulled the stone free.

The House shook again.

Oh, please Shadow. Mason.

Cari concentrated on the stone. Spoke to it with her blood, with the blood of her father, and his before him. All the generations of Dolan Dark House lined up to command one stone. But, as before, the wards wouldn't even weaken. Maeve was omnipotent.

In frustration, Cari rocked forward, and hit the stone against the floor of the cellar. Tears spilled from her eyes; helplessness weakened her resolve. The cold finally touched her bare flesh, even as the intricate lace pinched her skin.

Her stepsisters were weeping on the far side of the room.

She picked up the stone again and hit it harder against the floor, her sobs finding voice. Khan had said the Dark Age started with her. She'd done this. She smacked the stone down again, ill at the thought of Mason bleeding, dying for her upstairs. What good was she?

And then she went utterly frigid as she regarded the stone again.

"You'll destroy the House." Scarlet's voice was tight. She knew exactly what her stepdaughter had decided.

"That bitch is our House," Cari answered. But *she* was her

father's daughter, his heir, the Dolan. And if she wanted the wards of Dolan House to come down, then by pitch, they would come down.

Forgive me, Father.

She wiped at her snot with a dirty hand. Brought the ward stone up with real strength, fae-endowed strength, immortal strength, and crashed it down onto the ground.

The stone broke into two pieces of jagged mundane rock.

A sickening warp of energy rushed through Mason as he choked on his own blood. Khan wavered on his feet, arms raised to strike again. Maeve doubled over, keening. The mob outside the property roared.

"Whazzat?" Mason's jaw was swelling.

Khan drew his sharp face into a smile. "Did I ever mention how much I like your woman?"

The woman he'd thundered about killing not a week ago at Segue?

"Wha-she-do-now?" Mason panted.

Khan used magic to set Mason on his feet again and raise his sword arm, long gone numb. Fight not over yet. Mason was held together only by strings of Shadow.

"She's breaking her House."

Chapter Nineteen

What was this foolishness? A betrayal from blood? No. This would not do.

Maeve brought a hand up to count on her elegant fingers. How many stones remained? She reached with her senses to find and assign an earthly hum of stone to each digit. This one, and this one, and this . . .

"*Five* more," Shadowman said, throwing a blast of old age and decrepitude in her face.

The human followed with a long, hot stroke across her side from his sword. Did he wield his manhood as fiercely? Too bad he'd be dead soon, or else she might be inclined to find out. She tricked her body to again reform, beautiful as moonshine on a desolate earth.

"We'd best stop playing, then," Maeve answered. Cari had set a clock ticking down to a perilous moment. Six chimes, and the first had already sounded. Who would prevail?

Maeve's power had diminished but the cosmos had more than enough left for her. She drew from Shadow until the magic coursed like the sea. Creatures of faerie came with the surge. Humanity clamored at her gate. The statue of the white lady that had watched over Dolan House rose from her repose and stalked into the room like a sightless marble goddess.

"If Cari gets 'em all?" The human was a lickable wreck of blood and sweat. She even liked his earthy smell. Maybe she wouldn't kill him.

"Dolan House will be no more," Shadowman answered.

And Maeve's foothold lost.

A second warp of weakness shuddered her Shadow, but the excruciation was more intense, weakness doubly acute—two stones had been broken, each against the other. Maeve's power faltered for a moment. Those Glamour mages had to be helping Cari—they would pay in service and misery for eternity.

And yet . . . a vast source of power stood before Maeve, smoking with strength and purpose. Shadowman's magic was not his own—no, it was not—not since he fell out of Twilight and became mortal. His skin and bones and blood had cost him dearly—and for what? The silky cunt of a human woman? He could not get a soul for himself by fucking someone who had one. He had to *eat* a soul, or three or four, and thereby see and feel as a human could.

The fae queen reached out her hand for magic, and the Shadow within Death obeyed her summons. It came off his dusky skin like thick mist and twisted into a stream toward her. The one these humans called Khan gasped as his strength left him.

"No!" Mason sliced with his sword to cut the trail of magic, but Shadow has no substance. Magic hissed against the blade, but still flowed to its mistress. She grew and grew and grew until she was fully restored. Shadowman, however, crashed to his knees as if begging for mercy. Kill him now, or let him have the true human experience—utter weakness and dependence. And then death.

A fourth warped twang, followed by new weakness. Its shiver reminded her of the coldness of the Otherworld.

Enough. Cari's mischief was at an end.

Mason lunged to detain his queen, but she cast him back again. If nothing else, the man was relentless, yet another excellent trait in a lover. She *would* have him. Cari had sealed his fate.

The humans outside cheered their queen on.

Mason's vision blacked on impact with the doorway. Spots swam in his sight. Tangy blood coated his mouth. He tongued a loose tooth. His body pain was a muzzy hot blanket of stabs and bruises.

Khan was down on his knees, a palm planted on the floor. He'd said that Cari was breaking her House.

Breaking her House? Might as well be her heart. And Mason was helping her do this thing? Take apart her family? Her heritage? Her legacy to her children? The thought made his soul sick, worse than any of his other injuries.

No, Cari.

But she'd never been one to flinch. She was proud, but she would always do what she must. Must have gotten it from her father. And that was how her House had stayed strong. The people within it were Dolan's power, not the Shadow itself.

It's why he wanted Cari to be Fletcher's mother.

"If the House fails, so does Maeve." Khan's voice was only half its usual timbre.

But what would be left of *Cari* when she was finished crushing this part of herself?

Mason struggled up to face the faery queen again.

How many stones remained? A few or a million? Didn't matter. He would distract the witch and then spend the length of both this life and his next, his skill and magic, making Cari whole again.

Dragging the sword, he lurched forward, the last man standing.

"I want you, too, lover," Maeve said. "You will be the price for Cari's treachery."

And then the fae was gone.

It took a couple blinks for his eyes to pierce the dark murk of smoky magic enough to confirm that fact, as other things moved in the room, too.

Cari. The cellar. Ward Stones.

He dove past Khan, leaving Death on his knees. If Shadow-man could stand, he'd be doing so on his own. Down the hallway—thank pitch he knew the lay of the House—to the double doors, shut tight like a tomb. Shadow crackled through the wood where he clutched it.

As he hauled one door open, a woman's scream sliced through Shadow and up the stairs toward him.

He was too late already.

Cari scraped at the earth to release the fifth stone. Felt its smoothness, the heat of its magic soothing to her cold and bloody fingers. She wanted to hold it close to her to get warm. She felt like she'd never be warm again.

"You can't have her," Scarlet said to Maeve, her body interposed between the fae and Cari. Her hands were raised, as if she could possibly hold the queen back.

Cari lifted the stone.

"Caspar gave her to *me.*" Maeve thrust her stepmother roughly to the side.

Stacia cried, "Mother!"

The sound of pain put even more emotion behind Cari's downward strike. The force of the stone's destruction sent her flying back from Maeve, while the fae only wavered.

Scarlet was dead, her body a skinny long heap, too mis-shapen to ever draw breath again. Cari choked on sobs, her eyes burning with tears. Her head was so clogged with sad-ness she could only lever herself up to all fours. What had she done? Her father had entrusted her with Dolan House; it had taken her little more than two weeks to bring it down. And the only mother she'd ever known had just died for that decision.

Cari lifted her face as the door burst open across the room. Mason entered, his face so bloodied, she didn't know how he could stand. Zel held the last stone on the other side of the room, its light shining on her sister's face from below, her shock and loss amplified by the upward cast of the shadows. They were all stray now.

Maeve reset herself with beauty and wonder, as if she were illuminated from within, when there was only darkness inside.

The sixth and last stone was across the room. There was no way Cari could reach it in time. All this death and destruction, and still she'd failed.

And Maeve knew it. "Now, dove . . ."

Mason reached over and took the stone from Zel. His palm was easily big enough to clutch it. He used the sword as a cane to hold himself up with his other hand.

Did he think to throw the last Dolan ward stone across the room? It was absurd. Success was too far away, with too great an obstacle in between.

Maeve laughed, a trilling, layered sound of mirth.

"Just don't hurt them," Cari begged. She'd do whatever Maeve wanted, sit on that throne or whatever. "Please let them go. I'll belong to you." She couldn't face her sisters anyway, nor give Mason and his son the safe House she'd promised.

"No, Cari." Mason lifted the stone, concentration in the tilt of his head and strain of his body. The stone's glow flickered, making her feel strange inside, something weak tugging. "You belong to *me*." The gray stone riddled with jagged black lines, his Maker's power, and he crushed the last Dolan ward stone in his hand.

* * *

Dust and crumbled stone fell from Mason's hand, just as Cari dropped soundlessly forward from her knees, eyes wide open, insensible. He felt as if he'd crushed *her*.

And Shadow convulsed into a sudden hurricane of magic that moaned and howled, cyclonic in the deep earth. The scent of dreams and sex and seduction thickened in the storm, like the smell of rain in the desert. Maeve opened her mouth to speak or shriek, but her face and person warped in the gale and she was absorbed in the stewing torment. She had nothing to hold her here, no House, no kin to claim her.

A punch of noise, a million voices crying out, and the cellar became an antiquated basement. The silence was ominous.

But Mad Mab was gone.

And Dolan House with her. Cari was collapsed in tatters, her hands bloody before her.

A wail of anguish rattled up Mason's throat. The sword dropped. His weight pitched forward to lunge toward Cari. His transport from here to there was a blur, but then he was gathering her up into his arms.

"Cari!"

Her skin was cold. He pushed her hair out of her face, strands combed by her lashes. He put two fingers to her neck to search for a pulse. He'd have to get this awful gown off her so she could breathe.

The sisters had moved, too, and were sobbing quietly.

There. A flutter against his fingertips.

He pressed harder. Sought deeper. "Cari?"

Her heartbeat answered.

He put his cheek to her mouth and felt the warmth of breath. Still alive.

Relief burned through him, like lava in his veins. The pain of it was brutal, angry, and utterly welcome. Cari was still alive. "Sweetheart?"

No answer.

Alive, but her mind was very far away. Which was okay. He

could work with that. He'd find a way to coax her back to him. He'd been training for it all his life.

Pulling her up to him, he kissed her forehead, leaving a smear of his blood on her pale skin. Then he locked his arms around her, because he couldn't stand.

Help would come. The wards were down. An incredulous laugh shook him. Trust Cari to do what she had to do to get a job done. It was a good trait and a dangerous one. He was duly warned.

He looked over to Stacia and Zel. The elder had taken off her shirt to cover her mother's head. Next to the fallen body, the sisters held each other, faces into each other's necks.

One minute ran into another.

"Help is on the way," he said. The Order just might not know where they were. "Won't be long."

And they'd get to safety. He'd make Cari warm and comfortable. Make her sleep for a while. Get some food in her stomach. See if she'd come around on her own.

The sisters broke apart and Stacia turned to him. "Is she going to be alright?"

"She's alive," he answered. "It's a start."

Stacia nodded. "That's good at least." But she sounded empty. Shock.

To help her understand . . .

"Your mom," he began. "It was a good death." He'd already discarded any bad feeling over Scarlet stabbing him, had determined to win her trust. But he hadn't expected to love her. She'd bought Cari a minute more of life—a critical minute—with her own. It was an easy trade for a parent. It didn't require any thought, not even bravery, really. All personal considerations disappear when your child faces danger.

"I don't understand what happened," Zel said.

Mason inhaled to explain what he could, but the door flew open, cutting him off.

Armored angels filled the threshold, shining with purpose,

ready to do battle with darkness. A clamor of far-away voices was behind them.

Mason shook his head. "You're too late. Cari and Scarlet beat her."

Further explanations would have to wait.

"The fae queen is dead?" They'd be searching his mind about now.

"Gone," Mason corrected. "Back to Shadow."

A stunned pause, and then movement as Laurence pushed to the fore. "Let's get you out of here."

Mason wouldn't relinquish Cari, but was grateful for the assistance of two angels at his back, just in case. They were led up the stairs again and into noise and chaos and darkness. Shadowman was gone, and Mason hoped it was by his own power. Shattering glass had him bending over to shield Cari.

"No more Sha-dow! No more Sha-dow," voices chanted.

The angels urged his little group on, fast, to the front door.

Fire and smoke clogged the dark rooms and passageways. But he'd caught the gist: the mob was overrunning the house. They would not tolerate magic, especially after the unnatural darkness wrought by Maeve.

"We'll save what we can," Laurence said in his ear.

The way they were moved through the insanity without drawing attention made Mason think that the Order was buffering them from the interest of the mob, even though the witch everyone wanted was clutched in his embrace.

But the Order could not interfere with human free will— and it was the mob's will that Cari Dolan's house should be looted and destroyed. It was a scene out of place and time, but even as he was rushed outside, Cari in his arms, her sisters behind him, to escape and safety, Mason knew without a doubt—

The Dark Age was here.

Epilogue

Cari lived in a dream.

Each morning she woke in a spoon of warmth, Mason's strong arm around her. And as she turned into his heat, his calloused hands would begin to move over her, tracing lines of pleasure. He moved within her, whispering strange things, until she drew up tight inside and started her day shattered in bliss.

She learned to be calm when Fletcher made the most noise, and to seek him out when the kid went quiet for more than two minutes. She played in his tree house and always knew where to find him, even when his father could not. Fletcher's umbra was always in her mind, trouble in the making.

She couldn't worry about anything, though she tried. But the calculating parts of her mind, the Dolan parts, were sleeping. She knew that Zel had chosen to live with the family of her betrothed. And Stacia, who'd wanted a job, had found one working for Brand. The rest of the Dolan clan had their stipends and lived quietly. Humans did not like mages, though the greater danger was now coming from the fae. All that she put away. No more pain, please.

Sometimes the light was so bright and the wind so soft on Mason's island that she couldn't help crying, nor stop after beginning. And then she asked questions, among them, "If Dolan is gone, who am I?"

And Mason would surround her again until she didn't care and her mind was at peace. She was a Stray. Or would be when he finished his making.

"It's not going well," he said one day, dropping into a chair across from her at the dining table used for everything but dining. Between his thumb and first finger was a princess-cut diamond. Five carats, if she had to guess. Scarlet's had been about that size, but Cari's mind wouldn't go there either.

She had an idea what the stone was for, though she was living that fantasy already. "Not going well?"

He shrugged and sighed, obviously tired after hours in his shop, but there was a gleam behind his eyes. Trouble. Like father, like son. She smiled.

"I've been working on your ring and on the Umbra project."

Umbra. DolanCo. The asleep part of her got darker, more knotted.

Mason did that sometimes. Nudged her in uncomfortable places. And he watched her, as if he were studying her again.

"Umbra is coming along. I actually tried your father's membrane."

More uncomfortable words. She let them slide right through her. Held on to her peace. Because if she let go, she might crumble, just like—

"Then I tried to apply the technique to your diamond. I wanted a way to somehow bind us together"—his gaze sought a little more deeply into hers—"and I thought the diamond would be a good way to do it. You know, our future."

Why did he push her? He had to know that they were already bound. Couldn't he just let them go on like this? Happy?

"I'm pretty sure instead that I made a ward stone."

Ward stone. Blackness flashed in Cari's vision. Maeve

killing Scarlet. Mason's bloody face. The cries from her sisters. A scream rose in her own throat. "Is it—?"

He reached out and put his warm hand on hers. "No. You're not connected to her anymore. You're in that stone, but connected to me. Try though I might, Fletcher actually has eluded me. Probably because he's got Walker blood."

Mason's words were full of hurt, so Cari turned her hand over, palm up, to squeeze his back.

"So I have a Stray ward stone," he said. "It'll be pricey to get the five others I'll need to match it."

The darkness in her mind was loosening, her breath coming faster. "If you have a ward stone, you aren't a stray." But it was an afterthought, because something in her brain was turning.

Money wasn't an issue. She thought quickly of the DolanCo spreadsheets. The number at the bottom, in black. There was more than enough for ward stones. Safety. House. Ward stones were priceless.

A shiver ran over Cari as she touched the stone with her finger—how had she not noticed that part of her umbra had been captured inside, twined with Mason's?

She felt it now. Felt it now like a lifeline she could follow back to life.

"If not 'Stray,' then what will our House be called?" Those watchful eyes of Mason's were on her. Had been searching. Had found her. He'd never let her go. He was even now asking, "Are you still with me?"

Yes. Always. She'd just been sleeping for a while.

"Maker." Cari drew a deep breath. A waking breath. "We will be Maker House."